A TOM MA

COUNTER ATTACK

NEW YORK TIMES #1 BESTSELLER **TONY LEE** WRITING AS

JACK GATLAND

Hooded Man
MEDIA

Published by Hooded Man Media.

Cover design by L1graphics

First Edition: October 2023

PRAISE FOR JACK GATLAND

'This is one of those books that will keep you up past your bedtime, as each chapter lures you into reading just one more.'

'This book was excellent! A great plot which kept you guessing until the end.'

'Couldn't put it down, fast paced with twists and turns.'

'The story was captivating, good plot, twists you never saw and really likeable characters. Can't wait for the next one!'

'I got sucked into this book from the very first page, thoroughly enjoyed it, can't wait for the next one.'

'Totally addictive. Thoroughly recommend.'

'Moves at a fast pace and carries you along with it.'

'Just couldn't put this book down, from the first page to the last one it kept you wondering what would happen next.'

There's a new Detective Inspector in town...

Before Tom Marlowe had his own series, he was a recurring character in the DI Declan Walsh books!

An EXCLUSIVE PREQUEL, completely free to anyone who joins the Jack Gatland Reader's Club!

Join at www.subscribepage.com/jackgatland

Also by Jack Gatland

For Mum, who inspired me to write.

For Tracy, who inspires me to write.

For Alan, who encouraged me right up to the end.

CONTENTS

PROLOGUE

EVER SINCE HE WAS A KID, PETER LLOYD HAD WANTED TO BE James Bond.

If he was being analytical about this – as he'd been taught in training – he would answer that *many* kids wanted to be James Bond; the films were exciting, the stories filled full of action, adventure and pretty girls, at a time when Peter Lloyd had been *learning* about pretty girls. For Peter, it was more than a passing interest, though; he had an uncle who was a member of MI6 during the eighties and nineties, and he'd grown up on stories of the last days of the Cold War.

Well, the *first* Cold War, anyway.

He'd listened, enthralled, to stories of how MI6 spies would hang around St. James' Park, watching for their Russian counterparts, and either pickpocketing them to get what information they could find out, or even sitting down with their Russian opposites and working out what information they could pass to each other to keep their higher ups happy, and their lives intact.

Peter had spent his teenage years dreaming of facing off against Russian agents.

Then the Cold War had ended, and everything seemed to be falling apart a bit. People didn't need spies anymore. People didn't need agencies shadowing each other, and he didn't want to say it publicly, but thank God for 9-11. After the Twin Towers fell, intelligence agencies regained their impetus, and in the years following this, Peter Lloyd was reaching an age where joining the Security Service was a definite possibility.

He'd worked hard through his school years, preparing for this. He'd been mocked by his schoolmates, but didn't care. As far as Peter was concerned, they were going to be postal delivery officers or roofers or whatever they wanted to be, whereas he would save the country on a daily basis. His levels of reality to the situation weren't helped by James Bond or the *Mission Impossible* movies, fantastical stories of amazing spies, saving the world with two seconds to go.

Peter liked this. Peter *wanted* this.

So, when he'd got to Cambridge, he pretty much spent most of his years at university ignoring his art history degree, instead watching for the spook scouts, looking for people to invite him to cheese and wine parties, where they could scope him out.

His uncle had told him this was a way to be scouted into the service, and he hadn't been wrong. That said, Peter was very aware that if it hadn't happened, all he had to do was knock on the door of Vauxhall Cross, the green and cream block building on the banks of the Thames, mention his uncle was Davey Lloyd, and they'd probably let him in anyway.

Davey had a bit of a reputation, and it was always good to have a celebrity spy in the family.

His uncle hadn't, however, warned him on what to do when it was MI5, not MI6 that called.

Peter remembered the night he'd proudly told his uncle he'd been scouted by Thames House.

'Thames House?' Davey had asked incredulously, and then, after disconnecting the call, had changed his phone number.

So much for Uncle Davey.

When Peter had started, he hadn't been high up in the ranks. He knew he had to earn his stripes, but he didn't remember seeing stories about super spies sorting out filing systems and working as clerks. He wanted to start with gun training and look to rapidly move into a more physical, field-work area. But the more he looked, the more he realised that perhaps, rather than going to Cambridge, he should have joined the military. There were others who had gone that route and seemed to move upwards way faster than he was. A stint in the SAS seemed to knock you up at least two grades higher than Peter was at the same age.

But Peter kept his head down, did good work and, after a few years, finally went out into the field ... so now Peter was James Bond in all but name – and the fact he was MI5, and not MI6. But by then he was a team player and MI6 could go screw themselves. He had the weapons. He had the assignments. However, now he was in his early forties and he knew James Bond was nothing more than a fallacy, a "Boy's Own" story by a man who wasn't allowed to do anything more than information gathering during the war. Fleming knew how the system worked, but Fleming hadn't really done the things *he* wanted to do, either.

Even with all the toys, Peter still found himself mainly office based. There simply wasn't anything to do in his department right now; understaffing meant lower-grade jobs being the only game in town, which caused him to lose focus, constantly waiting for something more exciting.

It was why he joined—

Well, it was why he *joined*.

Today was no different. It was a quiet day. Nothing had turned up on the screens. The world wasn't in danger for a third or fourth time that week, and Peter wanted nothing more than to go home and lie in bed. He hadn't slept for several days now, working long shifts and then spending the nights on stakeouts and background checks on characters that didn't end up needing them in the first place. But he'd been called out to work on some bodyguarding duties; this was usually a job for Special Branch, but there was a situation here where MI5 wanted to gain some information on a particular visiting ambassador, and therefore a couple of agents were brought into the mix.

He didn't know if he needed to be armed, so he decided to go down to the gun room and draw a pistol, anyway.

He'd found he preferred the Glock 19 over the heavier Sig Sauer P228, a conversation he had had repeatedly with the guy behind the gun room counter. A spy who was apparently unaware that his time in the Service was over, stuck there because they had nothing more for him. Peter felt sorry for the poor bugger. There was talk that Tom Marlowe had once been one of the Security Service's brightest stars; his mother had been a hero and had the equivalent of a star on the wall in Langley when she lost her life trying to stop terrorists during the 7/7 attacks. But even so, Marlowe was the kind of spy that Peter didn't like; the ex-army reject who'd bypassed a chunk of grunt work to get to the goodie box. Although Peter respected Marlowe; he had gone rogue at one point, mainly due to some kind of unexplained PTSD, had pissed off into the US and almost got kicked out of the Service. But the lucky bastard had always seemed to be in the right place at the right time to fall upwards, and the higher ups had decided to give him one more chance.

It wasn't much of one, though, as now he was in a dead-end role, one that'd likely stay with him until he either quit or retired, stuck behind the counter of the gunroom, in a basement vault with no source of natural light, and no way to escape.

Tom Marlowe was basically screwed.

'Listen, you know if you want, I could help you out,' Marlowe smiled as he passed across the Glock. 'Get you a real gun better than this cheap plastic toy.'

'If *you* want,' Peter replied, smiling just as widely, starting a back and forth that happened every time they met there. 'I can see if I could find you a proper job rather than standing behind the counter being a shop assistant for guns.'

'I'm fine,' Marlowe shrugged. 'It's nice and easy. I don't get into trouble. Haven't killed anybody today ... yet.'

Peter, again, had expected this line. Although for the first time, the use of the word "yet" had shaken him a little.

'How long do you think they'll keep you in here?' he asked.

'Honestly, I don't know,' Marlowe looked around the room unhappily. 'Maybe a day, maybe my career ...'

'Well, at least there's no Slough House you can be sent to, some Botany Bay for spies,' Peter smiled, before allowing a horrified realisation to cross his face. 'Oh, wait. There is. It was called Section D, and you were a member of that already, weren't you?'

Tom let the jibe slide.

'I joined Section D because of my mother,' he said. 'Not because I wasn't good enough to do anything else. For your information, we did good stuff there, and it's a damned good department. A department so off the books, people literally removed their identities to move up in there.'

'You mean Wintergreen? I heard she did that to get out of an abusive marriage,' Peter shrugged. His uncle had mentioned this once, pointing out the absurdity of MI5 removing someone's entire life, only to reveal it all again when the next Government came in, or you got promoted too high to keep hiding.

Peter knew little about Tom Marlowe's record, but he'd seen some files, hence the jibes against the man. He knew Marlowe had been involved in several high-profile cases and he was aware that Marlowe had been the man who had thrown a bomb into the Thames from the Houses of Parliament a few months earlier, saving everyone inside. For a man a few years younger than Peter, Marlowe had managed in a short time to do everything Peter had joined to do.

Bloody army rejects again.

In fact, he was still quite surprised Marlowe was reinstated to such a small role, considering the significant number of things he'd done to save the country – most recently, stopping rogue GCHQ analyst Kate Maybury from stealing a list of every agent's true identity and selling it to the highest bidder.

Of course, that was one of the reasons why he was in that doghouse; in doing this, not only had he saved the country, he'd also killed a fellow agent. Some claimed it was in self-defence, which was pretty much one reason he hadn't been thrown into a black site somewhere, but it was still filmed on camera phones on an expressway of the A40 coming out of London, and Tom Marlowe had been all over social media, seen effectively stabbing an unarmed man to death.

'I'm fine with this one,' he said, placing the Glock into a shoulder holster and deciding that the conversation had gone on long enough.

'You take care,' Marlowe said, understanding the banter had run its course, returning behind the Plexiglass counter embedded into the back wall.

As he walked out, Peter saw Lawrence Jackson passing, and nodded to him. Jackson was five or six years older than Peter was, but had been in the Service for about a year less than Peter, entering late in life, another of the "military first" people. Because of this he was the same low rank as Peter, even though he hadn't technically earned it, something that irritated Peter greatly. It also didn't help that Jackson looked ten years younger, with a trendy blond haircut and cool-looking designer stubble.

'You shouldn't be chummy with that man,' Jackson said, nodding back into the gunroom. 'He's got a Midas touch, but in the wrong way. Everything he touches turns to shit.'

'He's harmless,' Peter replied. 'Look at him. He doesn't even know he's done for. They'll just keep him on a nine to five until eventually he quits, and then you won't have to worry about him anymore. He'll end up being a security guard in a shopping centre, or something just as mind-numbingly boring.'

He shook his head sadly.

'From what I've heard, he had a lot of promise.'

Jackson looked at him.

'That "promise" you're talking about is wasted on a rogue operative that killed agents,' he said.

'Who were trying to kill him,' Peter replied defensively. 'Come on. We would've done the same.'

'I wouldn't have killed fellow Orchid agents,' Jackson hissed as they walked along the corridor. 'Even Vic Saeed says he's suss, and that guy's a bloody psychopath.'

At the word "Orchid," Peter looked around nervously. They were alone, but he still wasn't comfortable saying the name, even if Jackson had always been a little more careless with his words.

Peter Lloyd, if you needed to place him in a box, was more *paranoid*.

They'd both joined Orchid at the same time; it was a secret society *within* secret societies, and something that had been around since Victorian times; since before Sir Vernon Kell, or "K" as he was known, created the Secret Service Bureau in 1909 to concentrate on the activities of the Imperial German government. From the start, Orchid had been helping from the shadows, known as a society for entrepreneurs and adventurers at the time that had slowly infiltrated Kell's spy service, it had stayed constant throughout the years. It had faded away completely in the twenties, after the Great War, but returned secretly after the Second World War when a need for more secrecy than the government was able to provide became paramount.

Peter's uncle had been a member when he was at MI6 and had suggested Peter for membership way before Peter had disappointed him by joining MI5. It was a bit like the Freemasons, but super secret and with guns; however, one rule of Orchid was to *never* talk about Orchid, *especially* if the man you just received your sidearm from had stopped Orchid agents from doing Orchid things.

The argument against this, of course, was that Kate was a rogue agent, doing her own thing and making her own money. There were people who believed that once Kate had sold the list, she would pass money back into Orchid, no longer the society it was a hundred years earlier, but you simply couldn't ignore the fact that a substantial percentage of exposed agents around the world would have been affiliated to Orchid as well.

So, in a way, Marlowe had helped Orchid by stopping her. Basically, they probably should have recruited him from the start.

Now it was just too late.

'What do you think they'll do to him?' he asked, as they continued down the corridor.

'Who, Marlowe? I heard a rumour from a sister cell that the High Council hasn't decided yet,' Jackson replied. 'He helped us while he doesn't even know we exist, if we're being honest.'

'Are we sure about that?'

'If he had, he'd have screamed the name as loud as he could, used it to get a better deal,' Jackson pursed his lips as he considered the question. 'MI5 have kicked him out and brought him back. He's worked with American agencies, and saved Presidents. But even with all that? Now he's got nothing.'

He chuckled.

'I mean, come on,' he said. 'He saved hundreds of agents, a President, a Senator and apparently some solicitor in New York, and Home Secretary Joanna Karolides wants to shag him. Most of us would have been knighted for that. But all he did was piss off McKellan and get Curtis shot.'

'I heard the Senator likes him.'

'Kyle? Only because he saved her life. He's a tool. Nothing more.' Jackson turned and started towards the staircase. 'I have a meeting on the third floor. Whatever you're doing, good luck, and I'll see you in Paris, if you can find a way to wing it.'

'Wouldn't miss it for the world,' Peter nodded.

'God, you're so eager,' Jackson grinned. 'No wonder they like you.'

As Lawrence Jackson walked off, Peter Lloyd gave one last sad look to Tom Marlowe, currently waiting for a requisition order from someone new standing in front of him, and carried on with his day. Poor bastard only got a reprieve when someone wanted him to go somewhere and fulfil some menial task. It was embarrassing to watch.

'Just quit, you fool,' he muttered as he started up the stairs to the main lobby.

TOM MARLOWE HAD BEEN WATCHING AS PETER WALKED OFF. He saw him talk to Lawrence Jackson, the pair of them glancing at him as if he was some kind of unclean member of MI5 ... which, in a way, he was.

Once Peter was gone, though, Marlowe let the act slip. He wondered what the next step would be. He'd been building up Peter as an asset for a while now, and he thought he'd finally managed to gain his sympathy, primarily due to pity at Marlowe's current role.

If he only knew, Marlowe smiled to himself.

He looked back at Robbie, the older of the two men behind the counter.

'I'm going to take a break,' he said.

'Do whatever you want. I don't care,' Robbie replied. He was what was known as a "lifer," and had been behind the gun counter for a good five years now. 'You'll be back tomorrow, and the day after, and the week, the month, the year after ...'

'I won't be doing this forever,' Marlowe shook his head at this. 'I know you desperately require my approval and friendship, though, so I promise to come visit you. You know, down here in this hideous hobbit hole.'

'You think you're Colin Farrell in SWAT?' Robbie smiled.

'Why not?' Marlow replied.

'Because you ain't Colin Farrell and never will be,' Robbie shrugged. 'Go on then, piss off, take a long lunch or whatever you want to do. I'll cover for you.'

Marlowe grinned, pulled on his jacket, and left the gunroom. It wasn't called the gunroom; it was just the nickname it had been given. It had something official like "Authorised Requirement and Requisition Counter" or something similar and long winded. Marlowe didn't care. All Marlowe needed to do now was make sure that wherever Peter Lloyd was going, Marlowe was following.

This was his job, given personally by Emilia Wintergreen, and with a team and budget to match.

Peter Lloyd and his James Bond fantasies were just the beginning.

1

NEW BEGINNINGS

MARLOWE DIDN'T NEED TO KNOW WHERE PETER LLOYD WAS going; he'd placed a tracker on his car a few days earlier and was still quite amused that this "elite spy" hadn't even bothered to do a sweep. He was nothing but a small fish, and Marlowe had been befriending him more than anything to build some kind of asset list, rather than throwing all his eggs into one Peter-Lloyd-shaped basket.

Marlowe had rapidly found he wasn't enjoying this mission, though. Although used to working on his own with an autonomy he liked, this was very much a "blank sheet" op; a single target, way off in the distance, and no planned way to get to it.

The largest issue Marlowe faced though, was that although Wintergreen had tasked him with taking down Orchid from the inside, and given him a "black bag" slush fund, it wasn't exactly *Mission Impossible* levels of money. In reality, it was less "fancy sports car" and more "topping up your Oyster card before hopping onto a bus" level. But he'd done more with less before, and he knew he could extend the money he'd been given.

The USB stick provided by Wintergreen during their last meeting had some old cryptocurrency on it, stored in a cold wallet for an op that never happened, and utterly forgotten for several years now. Unfortunately, the crypto currency they'd placed on it was almost as forgotten now, and rather than finding a wealth of opportunity, Marlowe found a healthy, but uninspiring balance to remove. Which meant that currently, Marlowe had to strategise his mission on a budget.

More than anything, he didn't know how long he'd be on this op, or fighting the quiet war he'd been conscripted to fight. The slush fund was likely a one-time deal, and unless Wintergreen had a few of these around, he was looking at a quarter of a million at best with some clever accounting. Which sounded a lot, but not when you had to figure in off-books identities, ammunition straight from the dark-web and black-market intel.

If he could last six months with this, he'd be impressed.

He had gold Britannias in his go bag still, unpacked from his last operation, part of a collection worth several thousands of pounds and amassed over years, with a significant portion gifted by his late mother, who'd done the same for most of her life. Britannias, a coin legally worth only a hundred pounds but consisting of an ounce of gold, could be sold at any reputable coin shop or gold dealer in the world, with no capital gains tax – which, although seemingly dull and financial, also meant no paperwork. Also, with each coin worth almost two thousand dollars, he could sell the coins for a substantial windfall and have untraceable money.

But, that was *his* money and, right now, he wasn't planning on spending his money on Emilia Wintergreen's mission.

So, deciding to do similar with this, Marlowe emptied the slush fund, dividing it into three: some in more reliable crypto, some in gold coins, and the remainder turned into large wads of cash, stashed in various locations – just in case.

Once that was sorted he planned his next moves.

First, he needed a team.

He knew that Trix Preston was up for this as she'd contacted him the day after his meeting with Wintergreen by the Serpentine, suggesting she was ready when he was, plus she'd been the one who'd emptied the crypto cold wallet and repurposed it. Trix's official stance, as far as MI5 was concerned, was that she was still on administrative suspension, set to continue for a few more months. Which meant that while Marlowe went to work daily at the most mundane position he could find, currently a gun cage at the bottom of Thames House, information gathering in a more analogue fashion, Trix sat at home and hacked security systems, searching for information.

For fun.

They had suspect lists, mostly speculative guesswork, though Vikram, or "Vic" Saeed, was high on it. During their pursuit of Kate Maybury, Vic, at the time working in Whitehall for MI5 and a distinguished service officer, had been shot in the arm, but refused ultraviolet treatment for his wound. Marlowe believed it was because of the Orchid-required UV tattoo of their emblem, something all members were commanded to do, and which, when placed under a UV light would show the person was truly part of the organisation. Marlowe believed Vic had a little UV orchid on his arm, and someone would see it if he was treated.

Better to be in pain than to be outed.

However, Orchid, as Marlowe saw it, was somewhat chaotic. Established centuries ago for security, it had fragmented into smaller cells, most unaware of others' activities for safety's sake. Marlowe's first idea was to rock up to Thames House one day, show an Orchid tattoo and infiltrate the organisation from the front. The problem with that, however, was he had been seen killing Orchid members, and had personally stopped what was possibly an Orchid finance operation by Kate Maybury – although he was still convinced that was a rogue operation. He'd decided instead to work a little more patiently, and use the chaos to his advantage. Cells didn't know what each other were planning, the left arm literally not knowing why the right arm was firing a bazooka right now. All he had to do was find a way to slowly build trust in one cell while destabilising others.

Moving back to his plan, second on his list was Brad Haynes, someone he knew was crucial for operations in America, if they came about. While Senator Kyle was an ally, her bodyguard's membership in Orchid, shown when he'd tried to kill her in San Francisco, revealed the organisation's international reach and infiltration of security services. Brad's allegiance to the CIA was ambiguous, particularly after incidents with Sasha Bordeaux, or whatever she called herself today, which ended with the mysterious CIA agent, who had been helping Marlowe, demanding Brad's head on a plate after the New York escapade.

He still wasn't sure about Brad, though. He'd worked with him twice in recent months, and both times had wondered if Brad was actually a threat, rather than an ally. And there had been mutterings Brad had returned to the CIA, likely under Sasha, and she was still an unknown commodity.

Third on the list was Marshall Kirk. He was retired now and had spent a lot of his last few months loudly complaining from his East Finchley home that he was bored. Marlowe knew this because he'd been the one at the receiving end of the conversations. Marshall Kirk was experienced, knew everybody, and was off the grid now, but Marlowe was a little uncomfortable about bringing him in. Kirk posed risks, primarily because of his daughter, Tessa, a former Russian sleeper agent – whether she knew of it or not. Marlowe had once jeopardised his career to shield her, taking the blame for something on a NOC list that should have been aimed at her, purely so she could have a life she hadn't been able to consider previously. Involving Marshall Kirk in this would surely involve Tessa Kirk, complicating matters and likely making that sacrifice in vain.

Marlowe considered others but wished to keep the team compact. The situation amused him; it felt cinematic, reminiscent of Jim Phelps or Ethan Hunt from *Mission Impossible*, assembling a squad against rogue organisations. It sounded like the stuff of movies – and if not for that incident on the A40 flyover, he might've thought it so.

Then there was McKellen, the MI6 chief who had an axe to grind against Marlowe. Wintergreen had assured him of McKellen's allegiance, that he was on his side – in a broad sense of the term – but whether McKellen would prove to be an ally was something that Marlowe reserved judgment on. He decided only to contact him if the world was falling down around his ears. After all, McKellen knew of Orchid, but was convinced this was an MI5 issue as no MI6 agent would do such a thing.

Then there was Wintergreen herself. A friend of his late mother, but someone Marlowe trusted as far as he could throw. Which wasn't far at all, because nobody in their right mind would ever try to lay a hand on Emilia Wintergreen and expect to keep it.

After his shift, Marlowe hinted to Robbie that he might be absent for a few days, tapping his nose and saying, 'secret stuff'. Used to such absences, Robbie didn't think much of it, as often people in the gunroom were seconded for boring "dog work" for the Service; bodyguarding minor dignitaries, backing up agents on ops, whatever it took for somebody who desperately wanted to get back into the Service to show their worth, but who wasn't trusted with the toys anymore.

Someone like Marlowe.

Knowing he could spend a couple of days on this without drawing any attention, Marlowe then returned to his West London residence, a small, old, abandoned "fixer-upper" church he was converting, using the proceeds from selling his mother's house. Empty for a good ten years now, unable to be sold because it was a nightmare to heat, recent months saw the establishment nearly transformed into a large, multi-level studio-style apartment, a construction nightmare thanks to a variety of confusing agreements and NDAs with multiple contractors, with Marlowe changing the blueprints every time a new firm started, often paying teams off-the-books to avoid paperwork, purely to muddy the waters and make sure nobody knew the *true* story behind the building.

As Marlowe entered through the ornate front door, inside was an open-plan lounge, built into a modest-sized space resembling a typical warehouse apartment. It featured a kitchenette at the back and, to the side, amenities including a toilet and a downstairs shower before reaching a back room doubling as a utility room. A mezzanine bedroom overlooked the main area where the high-ceilinged altar once was, stained glass window to the side, kept for aesthetic value, the floor held up by wooden and brick pillars and newly built load-bearing walls, and a bathroom with a comprehensive ensuite completing this floor.

While it seemed perfect for a single man, that was exactly what it was supposed to look like – because this wasn't really where Marlowe had spent a lot of his time over the last few months; in fact, apart from a few items left in the church to make it look as if he was camping there while building was going on, including a lamp, camping stove, small TV, camp bed and sleeping bag on the mezzanine floor, Marlowe's real haven was concealed. A sliding door secret entrance under the stairs, created by Marlowe himself when nobody was around, hidden behind a fake power junction box and not on any of the blueprints, led down some older, stone steps into the church's crypt, where the true home of Thomas Marlowe, and the reason he'd spent good money after bad on this renovation, could be found.

This crypt was Marlowe's true abode, equipped with living quarters, top-tier computer systems that would put most cyber hackers into shame, and an extensive arsenal placed on a pin board armoury to the side. A safe contained his valuables, and was next to a small collection of metal boxes which had been "borrowed" from various MI5 store rooms at some point in the past, and were now filled with his own stores.

If intruders approached, Marlowe could retreat to the crypt and hide out behind a two-inch-thick steel door, once more built and welded together by Marlowe; and if this became untenable, there was a small, hidden exit to the rear of the churchyard, the external entrance half covered with foliage and forgotten. Marlowe had been worried about the exit being so close to the church – this was what had almost killed him in his mother's similar bunker in Old Epping, after all. While investigating the tunnel that led to the exit, he'd found a bricked-up hole leading to an adjacent tunnel, one leading to one of London Transport's Central Line's many service tunnels. Now secured from the other side with another welded, two-inch steel door to match the one at the base of the crypt stairs, and covered with a black tarpaulin to blend it into the darkness of the tunnel, it provided a clandestine route into London's underground network.

The idea of an external underground entrance, akin to *Batman*, amused Marlowe, but seemed overly flamboyant. He had learned the importance of discretion, especially after a previous hideout had been compromised.

But Marlowe hadn't entered the crypt this time; he'd stopped as he entered, closing the door behind him and trying to keep his face bland and emotionless, as he turned to the man in the folding chair facing him.

He was middle-aged, maybe late forties, early fifties at a pinch. His hair, not quite flecked with white yet, was shoulder length and relaxed. He was slim and wore a leather jacket over a polo neck, and jeans.

He didn't look like a spook.

But then the whole point of being like a spook was not looking like one.

'Your security's shit, Mister Marlowe,' he said, as he nodded at the gun in his hand. 'Come, have a seat.'

2

NEW CONTACTS

THE MAN'S ACCENT SOUNDED EUROPEAN, BUT NOT FROM THE British Isles. Maybe there was the slightest of lilts to it. Marlowe didn't react to him, or the Sig Sauer P228 in his hand, which looked strangely familiar.

'I don't think we've met,' he said, walking over to the kitchen area, opening the fridge and pulling out a jug of filtered water.

'Drink?' he asked, finding a glass to pour some into.

'I already have one,' the man said, indicating a bottle of beer on the side table – well, a metal box that had been doubling as a side table – next to his foldable chair. 'Your selection is a bit limited.'

'I don't often have guests,' Marlowe shrugged, continuing the conversation, even though he still didn't know who this man was or why he was there.

As if realising the conversation had moved, the man rose, walking over to the kitchenette area, to stand at the yet-unfinished high breakfast bar.

'That's not what I hear,' he said. 'Trix Preston, Marshall

Kirk, Brad Haynes. You have them all over here from time to time.'

'You seem to know better than I do the names of people I've had in my house,' Marlowe said. 'But I don't think Brad's been here. Or were you just showing how clever you were by naming names?'

At no answer, Marlowe continued.

'So how about we bypass all this nonsense and you just tell me who you are?'

'In time,' the man nodded. 'For the moment, know that I'm one of you.'

'A spook?'

'And I've been watching you, sitting in the gunroom,' the man continued, confirming the question in the process. 'Waiting for your time, sent off on the occasional errands for Wintergreen and MI5, and I'm wondering how long you'll last before you end up shooting someone in the head.'

Marlowe grinned.

'Is this a job offer?' he asked.

The man shrugged.

'More scoping you out,' he said. 'I'm curious why you came back.'

'Want to serve my country,' Marlowe replied.

'This isn't some kind of weird James Bond fetish, is it?' the man asked. 'We have enough of those at MI5 and definitely across the river.'

'No,' Marlowe was trying to evaluate the rank of the man in front of him. He spoke with the casual arrogance of someone high up, maybe a section head or even an ex-spy.

'So, which department are you trying to pull me into?' he asked. 'Or do you have a friend in the private sector who wants somebody just like me?'

'I don't think there's anybody out there who wants someone just like you, Tom,' the man replied, sipping from the beer. 'Ex-Marine Commando—'

'*Royal* Marine Commando,' Marlowe corrected. 'If you're going to give me my greatest hits, you might as well do it correctly.'

The man raised his glass in salute.

'Ex-Royal Marine Commando,' he said. 'It's not quite SAS, but you know, not too shabby.'

'I've been with the SAS too,' Marlowe interrupted. 'I've seen what they do. Cut to the chase.'

The man straightened, eyeing Marlowe up and down.

'I've already asked my question,' he said. 'Why are you back?'

'And I've already given you my answer,' Marlowe replied. 'I have an urge to serve my country. I've had it all my life. It's why I became a soldier. It's why I followed my mum into Section D and it's why, when I was kicked out for something I didn't do, I fought to come back.'

'Why did you take Tessa Kirk's NOC list status as your own?'

Marlowe hid his surprise at the question. This was something only a few people knew.

'I wouldn't know what you're talking about,' he said.

'Yes, you do,' the man smiled. 'There's a NOC list out there with sleeper agents from the Cold War. It's called Rubicon, and your mum's on that list, alongside other operatives, like Bridget Summers and Raymond Sykes. But it's a recent addition. It replaced Tessa Kirk.'

There's no way you know this unless you saw the original list. Who the hell are you?

'Admin issues,' Marlowe shrugged as he considered his options.

'You know that if Kate Maybury had released her stolen NOC list to the highest bidder, the truth would have come out?' the man replied. 'You would have been exonerated. However, by stopping her, you actually lengthened your sentence.'

'True, but in the process, I saved a shit ton of lives,' Marlowe grinned. 'So, I kind of feel it evened out in the end.'

'How do you see that?'

'There were a lot of agents on that list who, if she had sold it to the highest bidder, would be dead by now.' Marlowe shrugged. 'Small price for my career. Do you want something to eat? I'm hungry.'

He opened his kitchen drawer and laughed.

'I thought that gun was familiar,' he said, nodding at the Sig in the man's hand as the man placed it on the kitchen counter. 'So tell me, did you go through all the drawers? Or was somebody kind enough to inform you of where to look?'

'I've been waiting for a while,' the man shrugged. 'You get bored, don't you, on a stakeout? Had to find something to do.'

He reached into his pocket and pulled out a Sykes Fairburn blade.

'This is in case you decide to go to the freezer,' he continued.

'Thank you, that saves me a lot of time.' Marlowe now gave the stranger his full attention. 'But I'm still waiting for why you're here, and don't give me more nonsense about who do I serve and all that. I've told you the truth, and you know it. You've obviously searched me out. You know my backstory. You know more than most people do about me.'

'You're making friends with members of a clandestine organisation,' the man said.

'Orchid,' Marlowe said carefully. He'd assumed this was likely the reason for the visit, but now there was a small piece of him that worried why this relaxed, arrogant, extremely competent, possible hitman was in his kitchen. 'Is that why you're here? To reprimand me? Terminate me? Recruit me?'

Unconsciously, he rubbed at the webbing of skin between his left thumb and index finger, where a small lump was. It had been itching for a while now, like when falling into stinging nettles, but there was nothing to see there.

'How did you hear the name?' the man asked.

Marlowe shrugged. This was a little safer ground to be on as he'd expected a conversation like this from someone. He'd already decided the story he'd use, something simple and incontestable.

'Kate asked me to join,' he said. 'When we were on the run there was a moment I saw her tattoo, and she explained who she was and why she was against the government.'

It was a half-truth and a bluff. Kate had spoken of her tattoo when Marlowe saw it, a small white scar on her neck, but had lied about its true meaning.

'It's just a flower. Means nothing.'

Marlowe knew there was no way anybody could argue with his take on events; Kate Maybury was dead, and could never dispel any of these rumours.

'Kate Maybury was rogue,' the man said, rubbing at his chin, frowning. Marlowe hid a smile; the man hadn't expected Marlowe to claim such an arrogant falsehood, which meant there was the slightest chance it was true. Also, with that one spoken line, Marlowe now knew he was talking to someone not only high in the Secret Service, but who knew Orchid, and well.

'Didn't stop her mentioning it,' Marlowe replied, but the man didn't reply, considering the statement. He pressed his luck here. 'So, her theft of Whitehall data wasn't an Orchid op then,' Marlowe continued, the words more a confirmation of fact than a question.

The man shook his head.

'She was playing someone else's game,' he replied, all semblance of mystery gone now. 'What do you know about us?'

Marlowe took a long draught of water and examined the man in front of him once more.

'You've been around longer than MI5, and you're international,' he said. 'I know that Kate Maybury managed to find a likeminded Orchid cell and turn them on to her side. But, guessing from your appearance here, I also know that you're not happy about that.'

The man nodded.

'There's an ... internal situation within the ranks,' he said carefully.

'You're at war with each other, more like,' Marlowe gave a smile. He was working out who was truly in control here; the man may have been Orchid, but he didn't know what information Kate had, or had passed on to Marlowe.

And that made Marlowe erroneous data.

'You could say that,' the man replied, his face still expressionless. 'There are people who want the status quo to change, who feel now is the time to make their move. She tried to steal a list for them.'

'The NOC list?' Marlowe paused, realising. 'No. She found a different list in Whitehall, didn't she? What was it, a list of possible Orchid Agents? MI5 or MI6 breathing a little too heavily on you?'

Marlowe paced around the kitchen area as he considered this.

'MI5 or MI6 have a list of potential Orchid agents. Kate, being one, knows who is and who isn't – at least, in her cell. Maybe enough to prove what she sees on it is real, through her role as an analyst at GCHQ. A list that, if taken by her, could help her side take down every other cell. Or she could remove her cell from the main NOC list when she sells it, and watch everyone else burn. How am I doing?'

'There's more to it than that,' the man admitted. 'Finances, long-term strategies ... there are old redundancy files that could have been compromised. Gone now, but possibly still taken by Kate, God rest her soul. And there are chances she took some files given to us by an Orchid ally. Someone who you know well. Nathan Donziger.'

The name ran a sliver of ice down Marlowe's neck. Donziger was the billionaire Marlowe had taken down in New York a few months earlier, and part of this had involved a late night trip to Donziger's private blackmail archives, hidden in a salt mine upstate, due to the fact it had consistent temperature and humidity and was naturally free from ultra-violet light, rodents and flooding.

'You had access to Donziger's archives?' Marlowe put the snippet of information – that Donziger was a friend to Orchid – aside.

Of course he was. He was a bloody billionaire. They were probably all members of Orchid.

'Sadly, no. Only you seem to have had that singular honour. But we were promised a file, Mister Marlowe. One we never received, and one now being used to save Donziger's own neck.'

Marlowe knew what the man was talking about – Donziger had a file on someone big, and was using it to gain leniency from the CIA ... or bigger.

'Let's just say Mister Donziger's holding Orchid hostage with this, and only a Presidential Pardon will suffice.'

Marlowe whistled.

'President McKay,' he said. 'It has to be Donziger's file on him. You do move in high places, don't you?'

'Some do, and some believe they're higher,' the man replied. 'There's two sides in Orchid right now ... actually, there are multiple sides, multiple angles, but only two major players. And one of these wants to stop the information coming out, while the other wants to see McKay brought down, for their own purposes.'

'Kate was one of the latter team, I'm assuming?'

The man smiled.

'The question though, Mister Marlowe, is what do you intend to do about it?'

'Nothing,' Marlowe laughed. 'I'm done. I'm stuck in a basement gun room, doing errand jobs. If I'm lucky, in six months, I might be seconded to a Budapest listening station or somewhere fun like that. Probably the best I can ask for.'

'Then why stay?'

'King and Country.'

'You've saved senators' lives, presidents' lives, MPs' lives, and as yet, not one of them has given you help or thanks,' the man shook his head. 'Apart from Karolides, and even as a Government Minister, she almost lost her seat in the last election so she's not exactly a shining example of who you should use as character references. You need friends, Marlowe. You don't have any.'

'I have friends, but I can always do with more,' Marlowe said. 'Are you saying Orchid wants to be my friend?'

'Orchid is a dangerous enemy to have,' the man replied. 'I'm here to tell you that if you think for one second that some chaotic mission to take down an organisation that's been around longer than the Security Service is something you really want to do while the careers of presidents are in the balance, then you might as well take this gun now and shoot yourself in the head, because it will be a far quicker death than the one you'll get.'

'Okay,' Marlowe forced a smile. 'Good talk. Glad we had it. Always fun to make new buddies.'

'Tell Wintergreen she's barking up the wrong tree,' the man said, rising and picking up the almost empty beer bottle, 'You have two choices, Marlowe. You can be our friend ... or ...'

At this, he spun, hurling the bottle at the wall where it smashed against the brickwork.

'Or you can be an enemy and suffer the consequences.'

'You're going to clean that up,' Marlowe muttered, completely nonplussed by this. 'If not, you can piss off right now. Obviously, we're done with the fun conversation part. And in a second we're going to turn to the "I shoot you in the skull" part.'

'And how would you do that?' the man asked, pointing to the Sig on the counter beside him. 'I have your gun.'

'You think I only have one hidden away here?' Marlowe laughed, his hand now under the breakfast bar table. 'There's a button you press on the microwave. When you do so, it opens a secret compartment under the table. You would have missed it because you're too arrogant to think that I'd have something complicated like that. What it means is I have a Walther PPK now aimed at your groin, and I'm more than happy to shoot your cock off.'

He smiled.

'Also, how do you know I'm definitely going against Orchid?' he asked. 'How do you know I'm not one of you already, recruited during the Rubicon debacle, and I killed Casey and stopped Kate because of the same reasons you're here?'

'Which is?'

'To keep Orchid hidden and safe.'

'You're lying.' The man held his hands up. 'But I can't be bothered to find out. Don't cross us, Marlowe. You'll find us a very loyal partner, but a terrible enemy.'

'So, be my friend,' Marlowe gave a salacious, mocking wink.

The man stopped, as if deciding something he hadn't considered before, and then smiled.

'If you are on the level, though, check in on your father, ask what your heritage is,' he said. 'You should help us find what Kate stole from us while on your watch.'

With that, the strange man with shoulder-length hair walked out of Marlowe's church.

Marlowe watched him leave, waiting for the door to shut before taking a breath and bringing his empty hand up from underneath the counter, grabbing the discarded Sig for comfort. It had been a ruse, and it was pretty obvious the man knew this as well, using this as an excuse to leave, his message given

Orchid knew he was coming for them.

They knew he'd be making allies and assets.

And now it seemed a different task was needed.

As if knowing he was alone now, his phone beeped, and a new text arrived. One of the first things he'd done when rebuilding was place signal boosters into the wall, so not only could he get good service in the onetime Nave but also in the crypt.

Looking down at his phone, Marlowe saw it was from an old friend.

FROM: CLEVER GIRL

Watched your friend since he arrived. He didn't drop anything that I could see, but it might be worth doing a bug sweep. When you're ready, come downstairs.

Marlowe chuckled as he walked over and entered the under-stairs cupboard, sliding the fake wall backwards, leading to the steps that brought him to the two-inch steel door at the bottom. Usually locked, Marlowe saw that it was already ajar.

Walking into the crypt itself, he saw Trix Preston sitting at his computer. Young, slim, with blonde hair, no makeup and in jeans and a hoodie, she looked more like a student on a gap year than one of the most promising hackers of the Service.

'How long have you been here?' he asked.

'I turned up about half an hour before your mate did,' she replied, watching the screens as she spoke. 'One of the perimeter cameras picked up the car arriving. I grabbed my things and made for the base.'

'Is that what this is now?'

'Well, I was gonna call it the Batcave, but that's been

taken. Maybe the "Shitty Spy Cave," or maybe "Gopher Cave" because that's pretty much what you're doing.'

She stroked her chin, now deep into crypt-naming mode.

'It doesn't matter. Either way, I came down here and locked up behind me about a minute before he walked into the church.'

'How did he get in?' Marlowe said, walking over to his armoury and swapping his gun.

'He did it without breaking a sweat. It was almost as if he had a key.'

Marlowe nodded absently as he checked the Sig's slide. The key to this church was quite basic, but that was the point of the church. It was for people to come in and find nothing of note.

It was only once they were in the *crypt* that they could find more.

'Did you recognise him?'

'No,' Trix replied. 'Neither does any of my software. That guy's a ghost. If he's MI5 or MI6 as I think he is, then he's scrubbed himself off the records. At the moment, he's Mister Nomad.'

'Why Nomad?'

'Because all the cool names are gone,' Trix shrugged.

'Did you hear what he was saying?'

'Sounded like a job offer. Or a very, very polite message to piss off and not bother them.'

'Kind of feel it was more the latter,' Marlowe nodded, placing the Sig into the back of his trouser band. 'With a caveat that if I did so, maybe there was an opportunity for me.'

'They know you're after them,' Trix was already typing in numbers. 'It's up to you now how you play this.'

'What did you think about his line about the NOC list? Or McKay being in some crosshairs?'

Trix looked up from the monitor, shaking her head.

'Could be a fishing exercise,' she said. 'Fractal Destiny had managed eighty percent of the download when it was stopped, there's every possibility one of the files in it has Orchid names. But we'll never know, as they dumped it in a black site the moment they knew they had a problem. And as for Donziger, that cockroach just refuses to bloody die.'

'I need to speak to Wintergreen,' Marlowe said. 'The plan was to do it quietly, but if they know I'm here, then I can't take them down like that.'

'I think I might have something for you,' Trix looked back at him. 'I've got chatter. I don't think they intend to be quiet much longer. Your mate upstairs said there was a war of sorts going on. It seems there's one of the cells that's decided they want a bigger part of the pie. Or, rather, all of the sodding thing.'

She shuddered.

'I think they're about to make a play against the whole bloody global spy community,' she finished. 'Including any of their brother Orchid agents who go against them, and because of Kate Maybury, we're the catalyst for it.'

She looked up from the screen.

'We're to blame for this, Marlowe,' she said. 'So, how do we fix it?'

3

BOX SEATS

'YOU ARE AWARE, WHEN I SAID WE SHOULDN'T BE MEETING, that it actually meant I didn't want to meet with *you?*' Emilia Wintergreen asked as she stood at the top of the steps of a four-person box at the Royal Albert Hall.

Marlowe shrugged as he walked up to stand next to her, looking out across the auditorium.

'It's the Proms,' he said. 'Who doesn't want to see the Proms?'

'*I* don't want to see the sodding Proms,' Wintergreen replied, looking at him. 'Unless you have tickets to the last night, and they're doing Elgar. Is this an update? Are you quitting already?'

Marlowe leant against the left-hand wall of the box as he watched his boss carefully.

The box itself had seemed a good idea at the time. A friend – well, more of a contact that hadn't tried to kill him recently, so Marlowe considered this the same – a weapons dealer from Serbia, had one of the four-seat boxes in the

Royal Albert Hall on a yearly retainer, and borrowing it for the night had been a simple request.

It was also a perfect place to meet with Emilia Winter-green, because heads of Whitehall departments loved this kind of stuff. Officious non-meetings in opera halls were catnip to Thames House operatives. If asked, Marlowe could claim Wintergreen was just trying to "teach him culture," and people would believe it.

The box was perfect for a two-person conversation; it was narrow and cosy, with deep-red painted walls, a thick red carpet leading to four red and gold seats, two on each row, and a red curtain to pull across behind you as you watched. This curtain, provided for privacy while staff placed food on the table for the interval, also currently shielded them from the watchful eyes of the other attendees of the Proms, which was the reason Wintergreen now joined Marlowe in hugging the walls.

'You could at least have provided catering,' she muttered as she looked back at the table beside the wall opposite them, covered in a red tablecloth and empty of any food or drink.

'That cost extra,' Marlowe shrugged. 'I didn't think you'd be hungry, anyway.'

'Cheapskate,' Wintergreen muttered, and Marlowe almost thought he could see the slightest hint of a smile on her lips. 'So, go on then, why am I here?'

'Orchid,' Marlowe replied. 'I think they might be about to kick off a war.'

'And why would you think that?'

'Because someone connected to Orchid pretty much told me they were about to kick off a war,' Marlowe shrugged, pulling out a printed picture. 'I thought this would be better than giving you anything digital.'

Taking it from him, Wintergreen looked at the picture; it was a screen grab from when Mister Nomad had been in Marlowe's church.

'Do you know who this is?' she asked.

'Well, we call him Mister Nomad, but I'm guessing he's ex-MI5 or MI6, possibly GCHQ, or something along those lines,' Marlowe said. 'He's high up, I think, in Orchid as well. Either that or he's been given permission to talk to them.'

'He's known as the Arbitrator,' Wintergreen replied. 'He speaks for many places. He's kind of like Switzerland for the secret agencies. His name's Sinjin Steele.'

Marlowe knew that even though she pronounced his first name as "Sinjin", this was the pronunciation of "St John," in the same way "She-vaughn" was the pronunciation of Siobhan.

'Steele by name, steel by nature,' she said. 'Or, as others say, Steele by name, *steal* by nature.'

Marlowe looked down at the picture.

'We can't find him anyway,' he said. 'And believe me, Trix tried everywhere. He's completely scrubbed from the systems.'

'He's deep cover – I'd say off grid, but I don't think the grid even knows he exists,' Wintergreen replied as she passed it back to him, almost as if unhappy holding a photo of the man. 'I only ever met him once. And that was a good ten years ago. The only reason I remember is he tried to seduce me.'

Marlowe raised an eyebrow.

'I didn't sleep with him,' Wintergreen snapped in reply to it. 'I knew something was off the moment I met the guy. He was at MI5, then he was bumped to MI6, was seconded into a Black Ops department ... and then one day he disappeared.'

'He turned up at my church,' Marlowe said, pausing as Wintergreen smiled. 'The church I'm renovating, I mean. I don't have my own religion or anything.'

'Shame,' Wintergreen replied, and the slightest hint of a smile crossed her face. 'I'm sure Tessa Kirk and Roxanne Hart would quite happily join it.'

Marlowe ignored the comment.

'He told me, in no uncertain terms, that Kate Maybury went off books. And there's some kind of war going on in Orchid,' he said. 'I also got the impression that someone in the UK is making a play for the entirety of the organisation and Kate was working for them, and that Nathan Donziger is trying to blackmail McKay for a pardon. Orchid are either for or against this, depending on who you speak to.'

'Well, at the risk of making you feel a little superior and massaging your already extortionate ego, we're hearing the same,' Wintergreen nodded. 'It sounds like taking out Orchid might be harder than we thought.'

'Or we let them kill each other and save us the hassle?' Marlowe suggested. 'Whoever wins would be weaker, and easier to take out once they're done with each other.'

'It's a thought, but a war between covert groups within covert agencies? That can get messy fast, especially if they're bringing the President of America into it,' Wintergreen shook her head at this. 'If the options are leaving them be or letting them go to war, I'd prefer for them to stick their head back under the radar, right now. With the war in Ukraine, and ...'

She drifted off, deep in thought.

Marlowe waited for her to continue, before deciding to do so himself

'You stopped before the good part,' he said. 'What did you just think of? What am I missing there?'

'You should watch the news, rather than building your own religion,' Wintergreen walked over to the table. 'Are you sure there's nothing to eat? Not even bread and butter?'

'Emilia ...'

Wintergreen sighed; her attempt at changing the subject failed.

'Senator Kyle's been speaking out against the President,' she said.

'Isn't that her job? With him being Democrat and her a Republican?'

'True, but there's an element of smoke without fire here,' Wintergreen said. 'There's talk McKay might step down if whatever she knows turns out to be career-ending. And there's a primary debate happening at the end of the week, where McKay and any challengers to his throne answer questions from a yet-to-be-decided moderator.'

'Surely he's running for a second term, and even if he doesn't, then the Vice President is the next logical choice?'

'True, but Harrison Caldwell isn't liked, so it's a clown show,' Wintergreen explained.

Marlowe leant against the facing wall, taking this in. Republican Arizona Senator Maureen Kyle hadn't been shy of admitting she was considering a Presidential bid for 2024. Marlowe had removed any blackmail information Nathan Donziger and his corporation had on her, and as a "thank you" she'd brought him in as bait for a meeting with the British Home Secretary, Joanna Karolides in San Francisco; a meeting that hadn't gone well, had introduced him to Kate Maybury and had sent him on the run, in fear for his life.

But since then he'd kept tabs on her and knew she'd been shoring up support in case she did go for the position; it sounded like she was still eyeing the prize.

'Do we know what the issues with McKay are?'

'Well, you've just said Donziger's making a play for McKay, and there's talk he might have been making alliances among the wrong types of people,' Wintergreen replied.

'Orchid?'

'We know they're global, so maybe,' Wintergreen shrugged. 'Kyle was given her life back by you, but maybe someone's whispering in her ear?'

She mused on this for a moment.

'Maybe they *are* going to war. Maybe some want to go public, create some kind of global, unbiased security agency.'

'That sounds a little on the nose,' Marlowe replied. 'Is that their plan?'

'It's always the plan,' Wintergreen checked under the tablecloth for a bottle or two. 'Caliburn tried it, Rattlestone too. Remember how that went for them?'

'That was a mercenary agency.'

'All commercial security services are mercenaries,' Wintergreen straightened now. 'That's the point.'

'And you think McKay is connected to this?'

'It's one of many possible outcomes. Maybe when you stopped terrorists blowing him up in Westminster, you did the world a disservice.'

'I will point out that it wasn't just him being blown up,' Marlowe said as he glanced out of the box from behind the curtain. The orchestra was now walking onto the stage, so he knew that the music would start soon. 'In fact, they wanted to do it *before* he arrived, so he'd be the one pressing the nuclear button. You tasked me on this, Wintergreen. What do you need from me?'

Wintergreen thought for a long moment, stroking her cheek unconsciously.

'There's a UK cell of Orchid; we know that. And it sounds like they're at war with another,' she said. 'Let's pick the lesser of the two evils, and end that war, while keeping whatever Pandora's box they have on McKay absolutely locked shut. Also, let's make damn sure whoever wins knows we helped them. If they go public, let's make sure everything goes public.'

'What about Steele?'

'He turned up to your house unannounced and didn't kill you, so for the moment, I'd say err on the side of caution,' Wintergreen pursed her lips. 'Did he say anything else?'

'He knew you'd tasked me to take Orchid down.'

'That's worrying. Anything more?'

Marlowe wanted to nod, to say he'd been told to contact his father and ask about a heritage, but decided not to. Wintergreen had known his mother well before she died, but hadn't known Taylor Coleman personally. Also, when they'd last spoken face to face, she'd promised to look into his company, called *Arachnis* – named, suspiciously, after the orchid – and hadn't come back with anything.

St John Steele telling him to check in on Taylor Coleman felt like the most solid confirmation you could get that his family was connected to Orchid.

Wintergreen shifted, pulling away from the wall and heading to the door.

'Be careful,' she said.

'Concern for me, or reminding me not to throw you under any buses?'

Wintergreen paused and looked back at Marlowe.

'Your mother was my best friend,' she said. 'I'd rather not watch you buried next to her.'

'Not staying for the concert?' Marlowe decided to change the subject.

Wintergreen glanced down at the stage, grimacing as she did so.

'God no,' she said. 'It's Rachmaninoff. I can't stand Rachmaninoff. If you'd given me Mozart or, say, Handel's "Zadok The Priest," maybe I would have hung around.'

This said, she left the box through the single back door, leaving Marlowe alone as the audience below applauded the arrival of the conductor, and the beginning notes of Rachmaninoff's Symphony Number Two floated across the auditorium.

Marlowe considered staying, watching the orchestra, but he felt an energy, a nervousness he'd felt before; the start of a mission, when you crossed the point of no return and you knew you were committed, no matter what.

Senator Kyle was an avenue he needed to look into, as was McKay, and bloody Nathan Donziger, a man he hoped he'd never hear the name of again. Could he get Brad Haynes to do that? Could he *trust* Brad Haynes to do that? He wasn't sure anymore. Brad had made a deal with an assassin to kill Marlowe in New York, purely and without the assassin's awareness so he could turn up and save Marlowe's life at the last moment while they attacked Donziger, forcing Marlowe to owe *him* a life debt. It was a risky play and one that hadn't worked, explained by Brad when they last met in Bryant Park.

'I had to turn you back to my side of the table and I knew this would put you in my debt,' he'd said. Marlowe had explained that the CIA were hunting Brad, and they'd been called to the park; Marlowe's job to keep him there. But that hadn't been his plan. Instead, he'd offered Brad a six-hour start.

'I know you're packed and ready to go. I also know you probably have someone in the agency who'll go to bat for you while you lie low. So, get out of here and call them up ASAP. And drop me a line when you're okay, yeah? You're a prick, but you're a good man.'

That was the last time Marlowe had heard from him. He assumed this was because Brad was still lying low, but he couldn't be sure.

And he sure as hell didn't trust the man.

Walking out of the Royal Albert Hall, Marlowe was so deep in thought about Brad he barely noticed the man waiting outside reading a newspaper, who started to follow him, folding it away as Marlowe crossed the street, heading towards Kensington Gardens. But even though he hadn't consciously recognised the potential threat, he'd somehow unconsciously done so and before he realised what he was doing, Marlowe saw he was walking now towards the Albert Memorial, allowing the man to follow.

Realising he'd been targeted, Marlowe walked briskly, his footfalls echoing in the still air, eyes darting around in the receding light, looking to see if anyone else was joining this lone tail, but it seemed this was to be a one-man job.

The silhouette of the Albert Memorial rose ahead, an edifice of shadows and history as, from the corner of his eye, Marlowe spotted the figure that had unconsciously kicked him into threat mode, a young man in a suit and tie. Innocuous enough, he looked no more menacing than a diligent office worker heading home after a late shift, in his mid-twenties, and with AirPods in his ears.

But instincts honed from years in the field sent warning chills down Marlowe's spine.

His unconscious self deserved a medal. He was being followed.

The question was, had they been following him, Winter-green, or both? Did they know he'd met her? There were a lot of exits, there was every chance he hadn't seen the Helen Mirren-lookalike walk out if he was here for Marlowe.

Adjusting the lapel of his coat, Marlowe discreetly felt the reassuring weight of the object he had clipped there earlier – a compact telescopic baton. Legal in the UK and often carried by security personnel and police officers, it was a discreet but effective defensive tool. This one had been given to him by Alex Monroe of the City of London Police as a thank you for the help he'd given them. He rarely carried it, usually preferring a firearm, but with the Royal Albert Hall regularly checking ticket holders at security checkpoints, he'd gone low key.

Besides, he didn't think Wintergreen would be attacking him – apart from him forgetting to stock the bar.

As the Albert Memorial loomed larger, Marlowe decided to confront his shadow. He slowed his pace, allowing the man to draw nearer. There, near the base of the towering memor-ial, Marlowe knew the confrontation would take place, and he was ready for it. His baton wasn't as good as his Sig Sauer P228, but it might at least stop the man long enough for a conversation.

He waited for the man to catch up with him, turning to speak—

With unexpected swiftness, the young man lunged at Marlowe, revealing a gleaming blade in his hand, glittering malevolently in the dim light.

Marlowe hadn't expected such a vicious beginning, but had expected something, so quickly sidestepped the initial strike, swiftly pulling out and extending the baton with a practised flick of his wrist.

The two clashed, blade against baton, as Marlowe tried to use brute force to push his rival backwards.

'This isn't the place for a mugging,' he said as he tried to work out the story here. 'Who sent you?'

'Kate Maybury was my friend,' the man said, as he slashed wildly at Marlowe. 'She says hello.'

'If she does, it's from Hell,' Marlowe said as he batted the blow away. 'And I didn't kill her.'

'You were there!' the man exclaimed furiously. Both combatants seemed evenly matched, each parry and strike revealing their skill sets, but Marlowe's every move was calculated, forcing the man to fight on his terms, using the environment – the memorial's steps, the decorative railings – as both weapons and shields. And while the man fought with anger, looking to gain vengeance, Marlowe's reasons for fighting were to stay alive, and he'd do whatever that took.

'Are you Orchid?' Marlowe asked in a rare moment of pause. 'Can we talk—'

The answer was obviously no, as the man attacked once more, the blade darting in and slashing at Marlowe's sleeve – not deep enough to cut into his flesh, but enough to slice the fabric, before trying a second attempt.

In a fluid motion, Marlowe deflected the blade using the baton, twisting the young assailant's wrist.

The blade flew upwards, and with a powerful kick, Marlowe sent the suited man stumbling back, before lunging, reclaiming the knife in mid-air.

Without hesitation, Marlowe drove the blade into the man's chest.

The suited man gasped, a mixture of surprise and pain flashing in his eyes. He crumpled, collapsing to the ground, the memorial casting its long, silent shadow over the fallen.

'Who sent you?' Marlowe hissed, dropping to the dying man's side.

Nothing.

'Come on!' Marlowe hissed. 'You want revenge for Kate? So do I! Help me, even if it's the last thing you do, because whoever sent you, they lied to you to finish the job they started with Kate!'

It was a lie, but it did the job. Marlowe had heard from others that when you were close to death, an unconscious urge to confess would bubble out. Marlowe had hoped this would be the case here.

'... Delacroix ...' the man whispered before slumping back to the ground, his eyes glassy and open.

Marlowe stood, panting slightly, eyes scanning the darkened gardens for more attackers.

Seeing none, he pulled out the blade, wrapping it in a handkerchief, being careful not to contaminate the hilt any more than he could, and searched the body quickly, looking for anything that could give away the killer's identity.

Finding nothing, he pulled his phone out and snapped a quick shot of the dead man's face before rising and heading swiftly off into the park.

The man had no ID; he hadn't intended to be discovered. And if he was taken, he'd have had nothing to give away his identity.

He was a kill squad.

He was a spy, likely MI5 or MI6, and if he was a friend of Kate Maybury, he was likely part of the same Orchid cell.

If he was Orchid at all, that was. This might have been a personally motivated attack.

Either way, Marlowe had been targeted for death.

This wasn't good, he thought to himself as he now broke into a run, now far enough from the memorial not to gather any attention. *This wasn't good at all.*

And who the hell was Delacroix?

4

CHURCH OVERVIEW

ONE OF THE STRANGEST ASPECTS OF WORKING FOR A SECURITY service, no matter which world, no matter which country you worked for, were the odd locations where you'd find yourself during clandestine meetings. As such, it wasn't really much of a surprise for Marlowe to find himself walking around the upstairs corridor of Temple Church in the city of London.

Marlowe knew the church and the area well; his mother had been friends with people who worked for Temple Inn, and he had worked with several of the police detectives that had their base of operations here. But this day wasn't for meeting friends; it was a day of strategising.

The reason for the meet location was mainly because, although the church was a popular tourist location, the upstairs chancel was rarely visited. More an upper gallery, a clerestory around the top of the Nave to add more light in. The staircase to it was almost hidden away behind a nonde-script door half-hidden itself behind a notice explaining about the church's connection to the American Bill of Rights, by way of the Magna Carta. Halfway along the staircase very few people would venture up to see a small wooden door where, back in the days of the Knights Templar, people were placed into the cell for transgressions and blasphemy.

Now, in the upper gallery, Marlowe observed the clerestory for the first time as he looked down through one of the balcony windows over the nave of the church.

Trix was already up there waiting for him when he arrived.

'Any sign of Marshall?' he asked.

Trix nodded, pointing into the church. Sitting at one of the pews near the altar was Marshall Kirk.

'Why isn't he up here?' Marlowe went to wave at him, to gain his attention, but Trix held his arm, pausing him, nodding quietly to the left side of the church. Marlowe followed her gaze and realised that sitting in the pews across from Marshall was a familiar female figure.

'What the hell is *she* doing here?' he frowned.

'Your guess is as good as mine,' Trix replied quietly. 'But my guess is she's come to try to help us, so take that as you will. But we can't let Marshall meet us until we decide what to do about this. You know, with his daughter sitting opposite him.'

Marlowe wanted to scream in frustration, but there wasn't much he could do about this. Tessa Kirk had likely followed her father into the church, and he knew from long experience that once she set her mind on something, there was no getting rid of her.

Well, he could think of a few ways, but they were all violent, and quite permanent.

'Bring them both up,' Marlowe said. 'We might as well get this done.'

Trix motioned with her hand and, in the pews below, Kirk

saw this and nodded, looking questioningly towards his daughter before moving. Trix nodded again, and Kirk understood, this time motioning for Tessa to follow as they walked towards the stairs.

Marshall Kirk looked good for his seventy years, and in fact looked a good ten years younger than his true age. He'd taken up vegetarianism and long-distance running, and Marlowe had heard rumours of an Iron Man ultramarathon in the planning.

Looking at the man as he walked up the staircase, Marlowe could believe it.

Kirk smiled when he saw Marlowe at the top of the stairs.

'I see MI5 haven't got rid of your beard yet,' he said. 'Is that hair regulation-length?'

'I'm playing the role of a pissed-off subordinate,' Marlowe replied. 'They haven't yet told me I need to clean up, but that's because they're expecting me to get fired any day now.'

Marlowe gave Kirk a firm handshake. He'd known him long enough to offer a hug, but at this point, it didn't feel like an "embrace the moment" kind of situation.

This done, Kirk stepped aside, and Tessa walked into the upper gallery clerestory. She looked exactly the same as she had the last time Marlowe had seen her, with short, blonde hair under a battered grey baseball cap. Both Tessa and her father were dressed for comfort, with Barbour jackets, jeans and sweaters on. Marlowe was going to joke about the look, but then realised what it was.

They were dressed for action.

Ready to go immediately if needed – and right now, they didn't know where they'd be going.

Marlowe appreciated the trust, even if he was annoyed at the appearance of one of them.

'Surprised to see you here,' Marlowe stated.

Tessa gave a small, nervous smile.

'Look,' she said. 'I get it. You caused yourself shit with the Security Service to get me out of a bind, and I'll always appreciate that, but you need my help, and I'm here.'

'The whole point of me being on that shitlist is because I helped you,' Marlowe said. 'You shouldn't be here, Tessa. You're supposed to be getting into politics, getting a law degree or something.'

'Well, I am here, and you have to deal with it,' Tessa shrugged, her lips set in a thin line as she looked at him. 'I know what you did for me. But everything that happened made me realise – what I thought I wanted with my life, it isn't what I wanted. Besides, I got a closeup look at what being a politician could mean to me, and I don't know if I want to sacrifice everything. Maybe this is what I want.'

Marlowe had somewhat expected this answer. Having a taste of the spy life her father had for many years, and with the training she'd received as a child – a sleeper agent for Russia because of her mother's background – Tessa Kirk was formidable, and unfortunately addicted to the life.

Which, down the line, if left unchecked, could get her killed.

'Fine,' Marlowe said. 'Let's have a chat.'

'So, no Yank showing up?' Kirk asked, looking around.

'Brad ...' Marlowe paused, considering his words. 'Brad's a bit of a loose cannon. I'm not sure whose side he's really on. The last time we worked together, it didn't end well, and I had to send him on the run, give him a head start before the CIA went after him. If we need him, he's there, and I know he'll always come to our aid, but at the same time ...'

Marlowe didn't need to finish. Marshall Kirk nodded in understanding.

'So it's the four of us?'

'For the moment,' Marlowe confirmed. 'Although I *was* expecting three.'

'Deal with the change of plans,' Tessa said. 'Besides, having a better agent on the team will probably help you "up your game," anyway.'

'Is the better agent you or me?' Kirk asked his daughter, who wisely kept quiet.

Marlowe smiled.

'What do you know about Orchid?' he eventually asked.

At this, Marshall Kirk's eyebrows raised.

'This is about *them?*' he asked. 'Jesus, I thought we were in for some kind of straightforward, non-suicidal kind of task.'

'Go on,' Marlowe encouraged. 'Tell me what you know.'

'Well, it depends,' Kirk shrugged. 'Which Orchid are you referring to?'

'I didn't know there was more than one.'

'Mate, there are at least half a dozen, and they all absolutely despise each other,' Kirk laughed. 'Orchid appeared around the time of the Crimean War. There were a lot of wealthy people back in those days; wars were run by the rich. Land grabs, oil stakes, you name it, they wanted it.'

'Oil stakes during the Crimean War?'

'Shut up, I'm telling a story,' Kirk snapped back. 'Anyway, if you wanted a commissioned career in the army, well, you had to be from a well-connected family. People bought commissions, and the proper soldiers never really made it higher than Sergeant Major.'

'I'm aware of how the military worked back then,' Marlowe interrupted. 'But how does that relate to Orchid?'

'Before the Crimean War began, there were many

holdovers from the Napoleonic Wars that changed the way the rank structure worked. Fewer elites were on the front line,' Kirk explained, scratching his chin as he thought back. 'I suppose they felt wars weren't exclusive enough, or something. Anyway, during the Crimean War, they created their own little organisation, a sort of private members' club called *Orchid*. The problem was, the club wasn't solely affiliated with the British back then, it also comprised their allies. But, over time, wars change alliances, and your friends aren't always your friends. By the start of the twentieth century, we weren't allies with Russia, but now Russia had *their* Orchid while we made friends with Germany. And by the time World War One begun, we weren't allies with Germany either.'

'Let me guess,' Trix interjected. 'Germany had their own Orchid too?'

'Everyone had an Orchid,' Kirk said. 'And, when MI5 began after the war, and the Security Service became more legitimate than they had been for the last couple of centuries, Orchid moved along with them. There were Orchid agents in the KGB, MI5, the OSS, you name it, Orchid was there. And there was a High Council: representatives from each region, who met and tried to negotiate the state of affairs, similar to the fictional organisations in the Bond films, or T.H.R.U.S.H in *The Man from U.N.C.L.E.*. But the problem was they couldn't ever agree, and Orchid returned into autonomous country-based groups, until about twenty years ago.'

'What happened then?'

'Nine-eleven, and the Twin Towers,' Kirk shrugged. 'Now warfare was changing. Orchid realised the world wasn't theirs anymore. Also, by then, many of the organisations were purely financial, connected to some of the richest people in the world. And the last thing they wanted was terrorism to destroy their magic money trees. After decades, they finally talked. And, eventually, they started to reluctantly work together.'

He sighed, the history lesson seemingly over for the moment.

'Well, as far as I knew, that was the case, anyway. So, what have they done now?'

'We think there's an Orchid contingent attempting to assume control of everything,' Trix said, opening a laptop and placing it on a candlelit table. She shrugged at Marlowe, who watched her intently. 'I know whacking it onto some kind of memorial altar isn't the best environment for it, but I need space to work ...'

After a moment she sighed, removed the laptop and slid down the wall, now cross-legged, the laptop in front of her.

'What do you know about Fractal Destiny?' Marlowe asked.

'Only what I saw from the briefings about you and Kate Maybury,' Kirk replied, and Marlowe hid a smile. He knew that even though he was retired, Marshall Kirk still gained classified information from his friends.

'Kate Maybury went rogue from Orchid,' Marlowe said. 'I've pretty much had that confirmed. She was part of a cell that had decided to go against the bosses, create their own army, and take down their rivals.'

'And how did they intend to do that when their rival's army is in the shadows?'

'Fractal Destiny,' Marlowe explained. 'It was supposed to be some kind of weird AI device that could foretell the future by working out algorithms and possible destinations. But in the end, it was purely an AI-driven blunt force *bump* key. She activated it inside Whitehall, and it hacked into and connected to the network, drawing down every piece of data it could find, taking the NOC lists of every spy in the field. Not just MI5 and MI6; we're talking CIA, Mossad, the lot. Anything we'd gained over the years, all taken by this.'

'Jesus,' Tessa exclaimed. 'I can see why people didn't want that news out.'

'But I had it confirmed that it wasn't just a list of all active country-based agents,' Marlowe nodded. 'Somewhere deep in Whitehall, there's a list of Orchid agents from across the globe. It's not a complete list; it's added to as time goes on, but I believe Kate was trying to get this list for herself, and use it to blackmail Orchid agents to side with her.'

'To become her soldiers in the war, or be outed to everyone,' Tessa replied. 'Tough choice. This list – is it just operatives, though?'

'What else could it be?'

'If it's a list of possibles, it might include the people who fund Orchid, who keep it going,' Kirk said, understanding his daughter. 'As you said, it's run by billionaires and oligarchs now. It's not funded by official means, so someone has to be bankrolling it.'

'Possible, but either way, I've been tasked with cutting its head off,' Marlowe said.

'That's impossible,' Kirk interjected, straightening as he spoke. 'You can't do that to an organisation that's been around for over a hundred years. They'll have too many fail-safes, too many intricate bureaucracies you'll have to navigate. Sure, you could cut off the magic money tree, but they'll just grow another. Remove the High Council, they'll just elect a new one. It's like saying to kill Parliament, you kill the PM. It's not the way to do it.'

'He's right,' Trix nodded. 'The best way to kill Parliament is a social media route to kill democracy.'

'It concerns me you've even considered this,' Kirk looked horrified at the younger woman.

Marlowe sighed.

'Orchid is looking to take over,' he nodded. 'I know there are agents in America who are connected; a Secret Service agent named Ford, who wasn't part of Maybury's UK based cell, was assisting her. He tried to take out Senator Kyle for some yet unknown reason.'

'Maybe because they believed she was a rival to President McKay,' Trix offered.

'McKay? Didn't you guys just save that prick?' Kirk cocked his head, glancing back at Trix, who simply shrugged in a "what can we do?" kind of manner.

'He has a presidential election in a year, and there are people already claiming they're going to run against him,' Marlowe ignored the comment. 'He has a debate in Washington in a few days. Kyle seems to have something explosive on him, and there's every chance that whatever Orchid is planning will be unveiled then. However, there's a chance Nathan Donziger has a file on McKay, and is trying to use it as leverage for a pardon, which might be screwing up their work.'

'If Kate was working against Orchid, it makes sense they want Kyle to succeed,' Tessa pursed her lips as she stared off, working though potential threats in her head.

'Hence trying to kill her,' Marlowe nodded.

'Perhaps you should have kept a copy of Nathan Donziger's file on her.'

'Who said I didn't?' Marlowe gave a dark, humourless smile.

'So, in essence, the mission is to take down a global organisation that's been around for over a hundred years by the end of the week, before they do something terrible to the President?' Tessa remarked. 'While at the same time allow them to do the same thing, so Donziger doesn't win? Sound about right for you?'

Marlowe groaned. Tessa was right. There were too many moving parts here. Donziger wanted a pardon, and that was a bad idea. Orchid wanted McKay removed apparently, and that was also a bad idea. Unless McKay *was* actually Orchid, and *not* outing him was a bad idea.

Marlowe hated bad ideas.

'What do we have, asset-wise?' Kirk asked. 'What help can we expect if we need it?'

'You're looking at it,' Marlowe replied. 'Possibly Brad, and maybe a CIA spook who gives fake names of comic-book characters. This operation is off the books. We have a small budget, but it's nowhere near what they'll have. We just need to disrupt them, gain whatever data they have and pull the teeth out of it, push them back into the status quo.'

There was a long moment of awkward silence.

'Do they know we're coming?' Tessa asked.

'Yeah,' Trix said from her spot by the wall. 'Marlowe had someone try to stab him three days back. French DGSE agent by the name of Marc Deschamps. He's dead now. And then there's St John Steele—'

'*Steele's* involved?' Marshall Kirk's face reddened as he bellowed. 'Bloody Steele is involved, and you didn't even think to mention this?'

'You know him?'

Kirk went to reply, opened and shut his mouth a couple of times and then turned away, walking off, then back.

'I give up,' he said. 'So, what's the first plan of action?'

'Kate Maybury stole ID data from global agencies, and probably the Orchid list as well, maybe financials, before escaping,' Marlowe explained.

'We know, you had it all over the bloody news,' Kirk replied. 'When you caused a pileup on the A40. And, if I remember right, it failed, and she died.'

'Yes and yes, but eighty percent of the data still went into Fractal Destiny, before we cut the power,' Marlowe's face darkened at the thought. 'Eighty percent just sitting inside a box, that's not been destroyed yet.'

'No,' Kirk shook his head. 'No, no, no. You're thinking of a heist, aren't you?'

Marlowe shrugged, holding out his hands.

'Did you think anything less?' he asked innocently. 'Come on, Marshall. Come help me steal a NOC list-stealing computer from one of the deepest black archives MI5 has.'

'How long do we have?' Tessa asked. 'We'd need ...'

She trailed off as Marlowe looked at his watch.

'I think just after midnight should do it,' he said. 'Hell, you said you were bored, and maybe this was the life you wanted.'

'Yeah, but definitely not the death I wanted,' Tessa sighed. 'Come on then. Let's go get arrested for grand treason.'

She smiled.

'Also, if we're breaking into a black archive, shouldn't we take a shopping list with us?'

Trix's mouth shrugged, impressed at the idea.

'That might be a plan,' she said. 'And I know just the thing.'

5

GOING UNDERGROUND

'YOU'RE KIDDING ME,' KIRK SHOOK HIS HEAD AS HE STARED AT Trix's laptop screen. 'It's bloody-well where?'

'The MI5 black archive is held in what was once the British Museum Station,' Trix replied, looking back up at him.

'I don't know if you're aware, but there isn't a station there,' Kirk snapped, looking at Marlowe. 'Or are we visiting Narnia today?'

'For your information, there might not be one now, but there was one,' Trix had returned to the laptop now. They'd moved the clandestine meeting to a new location now, a pub at the end of The Strand, south of Kingsway and Holborn Station. 'It was on the Central Line, between Tottenham Court Road and Holborn stations.'

She turned the screen around to show an old photo of an underground station.

'It was opened at the end of July, 1900,' she explained. 'Although Holborn was opened a few years later, it was a different company that did it; the Piccadilly Line, rather than

Central. But when the area's underground was expanded
right before the First World War, Holborn was given priority,
as it was a junction of two lines.'

'I don't need the history lesson,' Kirk grabbed his pint,
sipping it before continuing. 'I know the station's history.
That it was closed in the thirties and used until the 1960s as a
military administrative office and emergency command post.
But I also know the surface station building was demolished
in the late eighties, and now there's a bank or something on
the spot. Which, as I said, means there's no station there. And
with no station, there's no bloody entrance, is there?'

Marlowe smiled at the conversation.

'Looks like he has you there,' he said. 'If only there was
another way to access the underground station, attached to
an underground line ...'

'A portion of the eastbound tunnel is used by engineers,'
Trix smiled in response as she pulled up another window on
the screen, typing into it. 'Officially, it's used to store materials
for track maintenance, and you can see it if you peer really
hard through the window between Tottenham Court Road
and Holborn. But unofficially ...'

'It's the entrance to the archive,' Marlowe continued.
'Made to look like a track maintenance dumping ground.
And, as Marshall so eloquently explained, there's no way to
easily get in from the surface, even though people have tried.
There's a door, but it has Thames House-level security, and a
guard on the other side.'

'Also twenty-four-hour patrols, an airlock system on
arrival, biometric keypad and card entries, turnstile
entrances, CCTV cameras and panic alarms,' Trix added.

'Airlock system?' Tessa frowned.

'Well, it's official name is "thermostatic pressurised

compartment," but it's the same thing,' Trix continued. 'You enter through one door, allow it to pressurise and then emerge out of the other. But, if they think you're dodgy they don't open the second door.'

She mimed suffocating, grabbing at her throat while making "ack" noises.

'Jesus,' Tessa shook her head. 'And this is the straightforward job we can do in a few hours?'

'No, that's us explaining why trying from the top is a nightmare,' Trix replied. 'Everyone goes that way. Or, rather, did. The archive's been downgraded for a few years now, and officially doesn't have anything in it, according to MI5 and MI6.'

'But all spies know other spies lie,' Kirk understood this. 'So what, you happen to have a way into the tunnels that bypasses every bloody security camera in every bloody station?'

At this, Marlowe chuckled.

'Actually, yeah,' he shrugged. 'I do. My new accommodation is built on the western end of the Central Line, and there's a door into the tunnels at the back of the crypt. I haven't walked the length, but I reckon we can make it across London.'

'How do we bypass the platforms?' Tessa now asked. 'You might evade the cameras going in but every time we hit a station, and there's about six or seven to pass through to get where you want to go, we'll hit them. And I don't know about you, but that's a giveaway on any camera.'

'We go late at night – well, more early in the morning,' Marlowe explained. 'Around two, maybe three am. The London Underground is twenty-four hours on weekends, but during the week the stations are closed. We dress like workers, say we're on a maintenance job, nobody would look twice.'

'And bulky overalls and hard hats with torches attached are great at blocking cameras,' Trix said, her head still buried in the laptop. 'Although I won't be wearing that, as I'll be supporting from some underground location.'

'Okay, so what sort of distance are we talking?' Kirk, now looking a little concerned, asked.

'Why?' Marlowe smiled. 'I thought you love your ultramarathons and shit like that?'

'It's one thing to run long distances, and another to traipse through bloody tunnels in hard hats,' Kirk grumbled. 'And unlike you, I don't seem to have a death wish, which I'd get the moment I touched the third or fourth lines.'

'It's about three or four miles,' Marlowe admitted. 'But don't worry, I have another job for you.'

'Wait, so *I'm* walking three miles in the dark with you?' Tessa raised her eyebrows at this, and in response, Marlowe just shrugged.

'You were the one who wanted in,' he replied. 'You get to wear the overalls.'

'So, if you have another job for me, I'm guessing you already have a plan?' Kirk finished his pint and reached for the prawn cocktail crisps Marlowe had bought him.

'This isn't a last-minute idea,' Trix smiled. 'We've been working on it for days now.'

'Days, eh? Oh, well, that makes everything okay,' Kirk mocked. 'Tell me the bloody plan then.'

Marlowe, leaning closer, told them the plan.

IN ACTUAL FACT, IT HAD TAKEN ANOTHER DAY TO GATHER everything together; Marlowe had used another asset, the enigmatic gunrunner Deacon Brodie for the acquisitions, but had also made sure he'd used a couple of other sources to muddy the waters. After all, Deacon wasn't a fool, and could probably work out what was going on once he saw the whole shopping list. And, although there was every chance this was going to burn Marlowe, and he'd be seen while in the archive, he had to at least try to keep his team out of the spotlight.

They'd left Marlowe's crypt, clothed in overalls and with duffel bags over their shoulders, shortly after midnight. Even though it'd take a good couple of hours to get to the station through the dark, almost black tunnels, there were still trains at that point; the last of the night was still running, and the last thing Marlowe wanted was to be splatted by some tired driver heading back to Epping. So, knowing that the last trains were around half-past twelve that night, Marlowe had felt it safe to start shortly before midnight, hugging the main-tenance tunnels as they did so.

Walking through the dimly lit tunnels of the London Underground in the early hours of the morning was like step-ping into a subterranean world, frozen in time. The air was cool and musty, carrying a faint trace of the previous evening on the wind, and the quietness was eerie as the usual cacophony of screeching trains and hurried footsteps, shouting drunks and singing football fans had temporarily given way to an almost meditative stillness.

Marlowe didn't tell Tessa he hadn't walked the route before; he felt that was probably something that could annoy her if she learnt of it, and so he used a maintenance map he'd gained from Brodie. It was one of the whole network, so he'd taken what he needed and archived the rest – after all, you never knew when you might need it – knowing there was no way Brodie could work out what part of the sprawling miles of underground tunnel work he was interested in.

As they moved deeper into the tunnel, the archaic brick walls on either side bore the marks of decades of wear and history. Flickering fluorescent lights cast shadows that danced across the curved surfaces, and the occasional drip of water echoed in the distance. Graffiti art decorated the walls intermittently, its vibrancy contrasting the muted surroundings, as Marlowe's head torch moved across one as he turned his head.

Though the tracks themselves lay dormant without the usual rush of trains, there was not one, but two electrified rails still powered up, and neither was to be taken lightly. The central electrified rail, a crucial component in powering the underground trains, ran between the running rails and was gently crackling with latent energy. Alongside it was the conductor rail, located outside the running rails and at a lower level, providing the return path for the electric current used to power the trains. It was a reminder that this world, while hushed in the early hours, remained charged with the potential to spring to life and kill at any moment. A brief brush against the rails would kill either Marlowe or Tessa instantly; the voltage coursing through them was enough to deliver a deadly shock.

Tessa swallowed, frowning in the darkness.

'Can you taste like a metallic tang?' she asked.

'It's the electricity coursing through the rails,' Marlowe nodded down at them, the light from his torch illuminating them in front of her. 'It's like licking a battery. But I'd suggest not trying it for real.'

Tessa made a face and flipped Marlowe a middle finger as he fiddled with his radio.

'Mic check,' he said, tapping his earpiece as they reached Bond Street. 'Middle of Oxford Street, ETA about half an hour.'

'Got you loud and clear,' Trix said, her voice altered by what sounded to be some kind of voice changer. Marlowe understood this, too. If anyone was listening, they'd recognise her voice quickly – there weren't that many young, female hackers good enough to do what they were about to attempt, and at least the voice changer gave plausible deniability to the sex or even the age of the hacker. 'Big dog getting ready for the bang.'

Tessa glanced at Marlowe, and he grinned.

'Big dog?'

'I believe he wanted it spelt d-a-w-g,' he replied.

'I didn't realise we could change our callsigns.'

'We can't. I allowed him to do it because he couldn't play with us down here and he was very sad,' Marlowe continued, as they followed the tracks into the darkness once more.

After a few minutes, Tessa spoke again.

'What sort of security is this place going to have?'

'Well, it's an archive for some of the darkest shit MI5 has, so I'd say good,' Marlowe replied. 'Even going in from the back door, expect advanced biometric security systems, CCTV cameras, and infrared motion detectors integrated into the walls.'

'And you have a plan for getting past that, right?'

'Christ, no,' Marlowe shook his head, pausing for a moment, listening. Then, with a nod, he continued. 'They'll know we're there the moment we walk through the first door. Even if Trix kills the feeds, they'll see that happen. She can't loop, it's not possible to be done on this system – the feed has to be live, although she reckons she has an AI thing to help her there. And we picked up something from Deacon your dad's going to play with that should help us, too.'

'So, if we're literally announcing our presence the moment we arrive, how do we get in and out?'

'Your dad,' Marlowe paused again, looking down at the map, allowing his hard hat's head torch to illuminate it, looking back to the walls, noticing they occasionally bore signs of maintenance, with brightly coloured markings indicating inspections and repairs over the years, ones that ensured the system's safety and functionality. 'He's about to become very busy upstairs, pulling everyone away as we sneak in downstairs.'

'And then what?' Tessa shook her head. 'We steal some box and run? I'm sorry, Tom, but this seems like folly, no matter how many times you explain it.'

'They'll have locked it up,' Marlowe pulled Tessa down a side tunnel now, away from the tracks. 'But yeah, that's pretty much what we're doing. Yes to the second part, too. This is definitely folly.'

He stopped, crouching, Tessa doing the same.

'Shh,' he pointed up the tunnel. 'There's three mainte-nance men up there, and the schedule you got from Deacon Brodie says there shouldn't be.'

'MI5?'

'Or worse,' Marlowe gritted his teeth, working the situa-tion through in his head. 'The archive is a prime target. If Brodie worked out what we were going for, he might be looking to hit it first. No, it wouldn't be that quick. I think it's a rotation, nothing more.'

He tapped his ear.

'Fingers, tell big dog to start barking,' he said, cutting the feed quickly, looking back at Tessa.

'If they're on the frequency, they heard that,' he said, pulling out tonight's weapon of choice, an X75, police-issue taser. 'Remember, they're friendlies.'

He turned off his torch; Tessa did the same.

'All electronics go dark in three, two, one,' he hissed as he disconnected the earpiece, glancing back at Tessa in the darkness.

'Friendlies,' he repeated.

'You worried I might go feral?' Tessa grinned as she followed suit. 'How cute.'

'Just remembering who trained you,' Marlowe moved forwards – and then fell against the wall of the tunnel as an incredible explosion rocked through the walls, shaking the whole area, and the faint lights either side of the door flickered out momentarily, before restarting.

'Dad?' Tessa gripped a wire on the wall for dear life.

'I think he's just blown up the whole bloody street,' Marlowe hissed through clenched teeth.

TRIX HAD BEEN WATCHING THE JUNCTION OF NEW OXFORD Street and High Holborn through a nearby bank's CCTV, and had seen the van drive up to the front of the building on the corner of Bloomsbury Court, pausing beside a six-storey building on the right-hand corner. Old photos had shown it to be a bank, but Trix could see that now it was some kind of high-tech workspace, with meeting rooms, cafes, even a gym inside for its members.

Trix winced a little as she saw Marshall Kirk, in his overalls and hard hat emerge, duffel over his shoulder, walking over to the corner. It looked like a nice place, and they were about to royally screw it up.

Marshall continued to walk down the alley though, past the workspace building, towards the one behind it, a red-brick apartment complex on Barter Street, to the rear.

The entire building, front and back, had been built over where the British Museum underground entrance had once been, the rear made to match the architectural style of the brick buildings beside it.

Kirk pulled out four packages, placing two on each side, front and back of Bloomsbury Court, and then walked back to his van.

'I could do more,' he said into his earpiece, his voice echoing through Trix's speakers.

'Keep to the mission,' Trix said and was rewarded by the vision of Kirk arriving back at the van, dumping the bag into the passenger side, and returning out with a can of spray paint.

'Keep your eyes peeled,' she said. 'First sound, the police will be seconds away.'

'No, please, keep telling me what to do,' Kirk mocked as he pulled out his phone, pressing a button on an app.

On the closest building, the device he'd placed on the wall flashed into life. Trix couldn't hear through the cameras, but she knew from past experience that right now, the sonic emitters on the device would have hummed to life, their vibrations resonating with the glass, building in noise.

She hoped Kirk was wearing earplugs, as this was about to get loud.

Everything seemed to pause, as if the building was holding its breath – before the glass quivered, then fractured into a spider's web of cracks. The tension snapped like a taut wire as the glass shattered, and Kirk vaulted through the opening, bringing the spray can up and with quick strokes he graffiti'd a circle with an "M" inside it on the wall before running for the van.

'Can you hear the police?' Trix asked. 'That was pretty loud.'

'Not yet, but they'll come,' Kirk smiled as he turned on the engine—

'No!' Trix quickly shouted. 'Keep it off!'

'Oh yeah. Shit. Thanks.' Marshall Kirk turned off the engine and pulled the phone back out, also turning it off.

'Hope you don't have a pacemaker,' Trix snapped as he tapped a button on the screen a second time.

And the screen went dead.

Trix had expected this; the other three devices had been pocket-sized EMP generators, crudely and commercially made, that emitted a controlled electromagnetic pulse upon activation, calibrated to disrupt and temporarily disable a wide range of electronic devices within a specific radius, rendering them inoperable and causing confusion among security systems.

Including Marshall Kirk's van, if it had still been turned on, likewise his now turned-off phone, and the camera she'd been watching through. In fact, if the camera *hadn't* turned off, she'd know there was a problem.

The devices also had a minimal amount of C4 charges within, set to detonate after the pulse went out, a "dead man's switch" keeping them at bay until the connection was lost – then boom - and these would have detonated with a small but directed blast of brick, smoke and noise as the van's engine turned on and Kirk drove away; the amount wasn't enough to destroy any of the buildings, but it was enough to cause a hell of a distraction.

After a minute, Kirk's voice echoed.

'On the way out, the entire block is down and dark,' he said. 'In all directions.'

That had been the plan; to send an electromagnetic pulse into the black archive itself. There would be redundancies, but these would take time to come into full effect, and in the meantime, everything would point to a surface attack – of which there wasn't one.

'Good to go, tunnel rats,' she said.

'No shit,' Marlowe's voice whispered. 'We heard that down here.'

'That was the point,' Trix watched as, on the screen, black SUVs pulled up outside the building. These weren't police, and that'd been a matter of seconds.

They'd probably been on alert since the van arrived and the glass had broken.

'Big dog, go to ground fast,' she said. 'We've got dogcatchers out.'

THE MAINTENANCE MEN GROUPED TOGETHER, TALKING AFTER the tunnels shook, and eventually two of them peeled away, their head lamps now the only light in the tunnels, obviously heading upstairs to see what was going on, leaving one lone worker to watch the tunnels carefully, his fluorescent jacket creating an odd juxtaposition with the grave importance of the place he was guarding.

'Right then,' Marlowe whispered to Tessa. 'We need to get

past that guard and through that door. I can handle the door. Can you distract the guard?'

'No killing?'

'No killing.'

Nodding, Tessa backed down the corridor, moving out into the main track line, now turning her head lamp on and loudly walking towards the guard, feigning distress.

'Bloody hell, what was that!' she exclaimed. 'Sounded like the whole bloody network was about to come crashing down! I think the line went dead! Has the line gone dead?'

The guard, torn between his duty and this new, obviously distressed civilian, approached Tessa cautiously, his suspicions evident.

'How did you get down here?' he asked, eyeing her up and down, noting the uniform she wore.

'How the hell do you think?' Tessa snapped back. 'Are you one of Minty's crew? You're supposed to be Piccadilly Line, you numpty. *We're* doing this stretch. Well, we were until the bloody world fell down on us. Was that you? Did you hit a gas line or something, you bag of clowns?'

She stopped, now shaking her head.

'Nah, man, wait,' she continued. 'I ain't seen you before. You're not TfL. What are you doing down here?'

The guard, instinctively feeling the need to confirm he was indeed a member of Transport for London rather than tell the truth, held his hands up, almost to placate her—

Without breaking stride, Tess closed the distance, pivoting on her front foot, channelling her momentum into a vicious elbow strike to the guard's throat, smacking hard into his exposed windpipe. As he gasped, hands involuntarily flying to his neck, Tessa swiftly moved behind him, delivering a sharp kick to the back of his knees, causing him to buckle.

But she didn't stop there. Using her forearm, she applied a chokehold, the element of surprise aiding her as she used the guard's own weight against him.

Within seconds, the man was unconscious, slumping to the ground.

'I said distract, not kill,' Marlowe whispered as he snuck past.

'I didn't kill him, you old woman. Just gave him a nap-time sleep,' Tessa shrugged, following Marlowe to the door, as he extracted a slim card-like device from his pocket. 'It was that or the taser, and I wasn't sure if the EMP had damaged it.'

Marlowe paused.

'I don't think so,' he said, but his voice was uncertain.

Tessa pulled out her X75, aimed it at the fallen, groaning man and fired. The tines hit him, shocking him, leaving him a quivering wreck as she replaced the magazine.

'Yeah, we're good to go,' she said with a smile.

Marlowe sighed, returning to the door and crouching over it with the slim, card-like device.

'You're using a credit card to pick the lock?' Tessa asked, frowning. 'This isn't a back door of a semi-detached.'

'It's a high-frequency modulator designed to intercept and unscramble encrypted signals,' Marlowe said, sliding it along the door's edge. 'The EMP will have disrupted every-thing. A kind of hard reset. This will get us through while it's still in a "booting" stage.'

After a couple of passes, each one punctuated with a soft expletive from Marlowe, it eventually started humming softly. The LED on the card transitioned from red to green, and the solid steel door clicked open ever so slightly.

'I mean, it's kinda the same technology as using a card to

bump a lock,' he said, placing the card away. 'But now the door's open, every alarm in the place that's still active will go off. Now we really need to hustle – and expect the worst.'

'Like we weren't doing that already,' Tessa sighed as she followed Marlowe inside.

6

PASSAGEWAYS

IF MARLOWE HAD EXPECTED THE INSIDE OF THE BLACK ARCHIVE to look like other MI5 black sites he'd visited, he was sorely mistaken.

There were no elevators or questioning rooms, no break rooms or even security doors to move through. This was an archive site, nothing more, with the bulk of the security way above them on the surface levels of the building. As such, the tunnels of the original underground station, still with their pale ceramic tiles around the sides, had become walkways lined with metal shelving with items in thick, plastic boxes, placed almost randomly upon them, on floor upon floor of the once-thriving station's passageways. Every couple of yards, there was a piece of paper with a number on it taped to the side of one of the shelving struts; four numbers, a decimal point, and then two more numbers.

Marlowe assumed this was some kind of system to plan where the items were, not unlike the way library books were organised, but unfortunately, he didn't have a clue what they meant.

'You'd better be able to solve this,' he said irritably through his earbud, mainly aimed at Trix but open on the possibility Marshall Kirk might be able to answer it, as he examined the first couple of shelves. 'I know what Fractal Destiny looks like, but these are in boxes. I can't go through each one – we simply don't have the time.'

He paused.

'Can we be monitored on this?'

'Not while I have the modulator settings on, but let's keep it quiet in case.'

The lights were still on emergency lighting, a pale pink or red hue that didn't help with things either, as Marlowe rummaged through the boxes in the warm half-light.

'You don't need to look through each one, either,' said Trix, the voice modulator still playing with her voice. 'The tunnels are chronologically organised. The first, the oldest items will have been placed closer to the main entrance, to save moving through corridors of nothing when the archive was empty. It makes sense that as Fractal Destiny was taken within the last couple of months, it'll be right at the end of the row.'

'So, not near the entrance?'

'Christ no,' Trix almost laughed down the line, the voice altering software making it sound more like a cough. 'You're not at the front. You think high-ranking Government officials walk down tube tracks? You came in the tradesmen's entrance. The "stage door," so to speak.'

'Then where the bloody hell do we need to go?' Marlowe snapped.

'I'm working on it,' the voice changer had altered her voice, but it didn't change the tapping on the keyboard he could hear through the earpiece. 'I was connected to the system the moment you swiped the card, but currently I'm screwing with their CCTV.'

'I thought you couldn't loop anything?'

'I have to keep it live feed,' Trix explained. 'But I also took the last hour from their file system, before the EMP wave shorted everything, and then threw it through my AI, so now it's creating its own virtual scenes, linking straight to the monitor screens two floors above you. Now and then someone walks past, and they're a little skewed, being artificial and all that, but it does the job.'

There was a beep on Marlowe's wrist – looking at his smartwatch, he saw a scrollable map appear.

'Staircase to the next level is on the left, then the door to the right, fifty metres along,' Trix said, and Marlowe and Tessa immediately started down the tunnel, taking the steps of the staircase to the side two at a time. 'You'll need to get through a card reader like the last one.'

'Can I use the same card?'

'No need, I already opened it,' Trix's altered voice was sounding remarkably smug right now. Moving through the now disabled access door and walking onto the upper level, Marlowe saw the same tile decoration; this was simply another of the passageways, now covered with more shelving.

'I see another door,' he was describing to Trix as he ran to a solid metal door on the right. 'Looks like a bloody scanner to the side. Is this open too?'

'No, sorry. You'll have to hack it.'

As he stopped beside the scanner, he swore.

'Bollocks, it is a retina scanner,' he muttered. 'Can we bypass it?'

'I've already said no.'

'How about a HD eye scan?'

'Looking at it, we can't use a digital image,' Trix was frantically typing. 'But we thought ahead here. Time to use the box.'

'The box?' Marlowe frowned, but Tessa nodded, pulling a small, plastic, 3D-printed box out of her leg pocket. Opening it up, she almost dropped it as an eyeball stared up at her.

'What the sodding hell—'

'It's Joanna Karolides's eye,' Trix explained, a level of excitement escaping through the voice changer. 'I scanned it without her knowing, and used a 3D ocular printer to work from the scans. It's identical in every way. Just hold it up.'

Tessa grimaced as she grabbed it, but the expression turned into one of surprise as she pulled it out.

'It feels like acrylic,' she said.

'Well yeah, it's not an actual eye,' Trix laughed as Tessa placed it against the retinal scanner. After a couple of scans, with Tessa adjusting its angle, the light turned green, and the door unlocked.

'And you just had this by chance?' Marlowe asked as they slipped into the room behind.

'Oh hell no,' Trix replied. 'I collect eye scans. I have pretty much all of MI5, a few MI6, two CIA, half of parliament, a few exes ... you never know when you'll need one.'

Marlowe shuddered, disconnecting the call by tapping the earpiece.

'Your friend is a little creepy sometimes,' Tessa said as, standing in an identical tunnel to the others, they faced a new line of shelves.

'Other end,' Marlowe was already hurrying. 'Start at the last one, move your way back.'

He paused, looking back at Tessa.

'It's about this size,' he added, holding his hands out to

show a box about a foot in diameter. 'It's black and made of metal.'

Tessa nodded, already pulling open the tops of plastic boxes.

'They're mainly files,' she said with a slight touch of disappointment in her voice. 'I thought we'd find fun stuff.'

'Live with loss.' Marlowe was pulling open boxes on his side of the tunnel, one ear open for sounds of footsteps, alarms, or even gunfire. By now they'd have seen it was nothing more than a diversion, maybe even found the unconscious guard by the door. They had to move fast.

But Tessa had paused.

'Stop,' she said. It was one word, but it was spoken with such gravitas that Marlowe couldn't help but look at the folder in her hand.

PROJECT: RUBICON

'Where was it?' he asked.

'Here,' Tessa nodded at a plastic box. 'I don't understand.'

'When they closed it down, they must have dumped it here,' Marlowe opened the box wider, pulling the lid off, staring into the depths. This was the sleeper list that ended his career, that caused so many deaths.

Left on a shelf for anyone to find.

'Put it in the bag,' he said, opening the duffel. 'All of it. We can have a look later.'

'There's another box beside it,' Tessa continued, looking back. 'It's ...'

Her voice trailed off as Marlowe looked over.

BRIDGET SUMMERS

'It's her go bag, I think,' Tessa said, opening the box and peering in. Marlowe placed a hand on her own to stop her.

'We're on a clock.'

'But this could clear you!'

'I know, and that's why we'll look at it later,' Marlowe said, pulling out the holdall and slinging it over his shoulder, next to his duffel. Bridget Summers was a retired MI5 analyst who'd worked with Tessa's father, but who'd later become a traitor, using Marlowe as a patsy. She'd been captured when Baroness Levin had tried to set off a dirty bomb in Westminster, but had escaped in the confusion.

Was Rubicon connected somehow to Orchid?

Shaking the thought away, he continued to move through the boxes, opening anything that looked big enough to house Fractal Destiny. He was being distracted right now, and the last thing he needed was that.

He stopped – he could hear footsteps, but they sounded like a floor above him.

Pushing onwards, he continued opening another box before pausing. Inside this one was something black and metal, and he could see a power cord at the side.

Pulling the box out from the shelving and placing it on the floor, Marlowe stared down, once more, at Fractal Destiny.

'Got it,' he whispered with a little reverence, picking it up quickly and throwing it into his duffel bag. 'We need to go now.'

And with that, he started back towards the main entranceway—

Which now had two agents standing there, Glocks in hand, looking confused at the appearance of two apparent TfL workers.

Before either of them could speak, however, Marlowe started towards them, his torch still on, shining into the faces and hopefully blinding them from seeing his face properly.

'What the hell's going on?' he yelled, forcing his voice to sound more gruff. 'Who are you? Why are you here? What is this place? You're not supposed to be here! This station's condemned! What is all this shit?'

The nearest agent hadn't expected Marlowe to be so confrontational, nor did he expect the barrage of questions to be thrown at him in a scattershot way. His gun lowered for a split second, trying to determine if this was genuinely a TfL mistake and Marlowe used that moment of distraction of plausible confusion, sliding in quickly and taking the man out at the throat, the fingers of his palm stiff and outstretched, jabbing upwards, similar to how Tessa had taken out the first guard outside.

Well, she had been trained in MI5's fighting techniques by the age of twelve, after all.

As the first agent crumpled, the second turned to fire, only to be hit by the X75 taser, now in Tessa's hand. This done, the second MI5 agent collapsed to the ground, as the lights turned a far deeper red than before, and an alarm echoed through the hallway.

'Go, go, go!' Trix shouted through the earpiece, the voice changer forgotten in her urgency. 'We've got incoming from upstairs! They're done with the distraction. And we've got bogeys coming in from Holborn along the track! Move, tunnel rats!'

Marlowe didn't need a second warning and grabbed Tessa by the arm, yanking her back through the retina scan door, down the staircase at a run, and back out into the tunnel, slamming the door shut behind them, jumping over the still-unconscious guard.

'We need to go now,' he said as they started sprinting down the darkness.

But Tessa slowed, uncertain. 'They'll find us,' she replied, already looking around, as the faint sounds of people shouting could be heard coming from the Holborn direction. 'They'll know where we're going.'

'They won't know anything,' Marlowe replied, pulling her into a side tunnel, leaning up and turning off the torch on her helmet, followed by pulling her helmet off and placing it carefully to the side, making no noise as he reached into the duffel, pulling out a pair of night vision goggles. They looked like binoculars attached to a backing plate that, with straps secured to the head, had been one of Brodie Lee's gifts to Marlowe earlier that day.

'All they know is someone's come in from upstairs. They'll think we're trying to make our way up to the surface, and whatever Marshall blew up when he was buggering around playing activist,' he breathed. 'We don't need to get all the way back. We just need to get …'

Gunfire echoed around the tunnel as he quickly turned his own torch off, tossing the hat to the side as he pulled his own pair of night vision goggles onto his head, turning them on, giving himself a moment to acclimatise to the green-tinted world he was now seeing. Marlowe wasn't sure if the guards were firing blindly or if they could see them, so, hugging the wall even more now, he and Tessa carried on along the tunnel slowly.

'Go now,' he breathed into the earpiece. 'Get to the place. Don't wait for us.'

There was no answer, and Marlowe hoped this was

because Trix had already left. Tessa, through the night vision goggles looked nervous, biting her lip as she kept glancing backwards. Marlowe drew her close to him in a small recess in one of the side tunnels.

'Shush,' he whispered, holding her tight to him, his hand over her mouth.

Tessa struggled briefly and then stopped as she heard the running steps of MI5 agents. Angry voices echoed through the tunnels.

'They got out through the door,' one, a male, snapped. 'They can't have got far.'

'Do we know if they took anything?' A second, older male.

'Of course they took something!' the first voice exclaimed incredulously. 'They broke into a black archive! You think they did that for fun?'

The voices got closer now, as Marlowe squeezed tighter against Tessa, their bodies moulding together as they tried their best to look just like a wall.

Marlowe felt Tessa tense at the action, and then relax into it.

It felt comfortable.

Too comfortable.

'They don't know where we are,' Marlowe whispered after the noise had faded. 'They know we came out into the tunnels, but they don't know what we took, or which direction we went. We'll stay here for a bit, and they'll go on.'

'And what do we do when they pass us?' Tessa asked. 'They'll be in front of us then.'

Marlowe just waited, and the running footsteps slowly disappeared, the angry voices fading as the MI5 agents continued towards Tottenham Court Road.

'They'll leave someone at the back,' he said. 'A minute or so behind them, to catch anyone who thinks it's safe. We'll wait for them. Once they're gone, we'll move and head north.'

He smiled.

'Or we could just stay here like this for an hour.'

'Let's carry on while we can,' Tessa suggested, gaining a little distance from him as they stayed still. They were no longer entwined, but they were still closer than lovers.

Marlowe wasn't sure if he liked this or not. He definitely knew her dad wouldn't.

After a few moments, they heard a third set of footsteps as the third agent walked past. And only after these steps had faded away did Marlowe nod, the two of them slipping out, heading back into the tunnels. This time, they went north towards King's Cross along the Piccadilly line. It wasn't the direction Marlowe had originally intended, but it was a path that took them quickly out of the immediate danger.

'What if they're waiting at the station?' Tessa asked.

'There's two hundred and thirty miles of track down here,' Marlowe replied as he led her down a maintenance tunnel to the left, up three steps and through a battered and soot-covered door. 'They can't police it all. And besides if they do find us we'll just get Marshall to blow something else up.'

Tessa actually snorted a laugh at this.

'The scary thing is you're completely serious,' she said.

'Still want to be involved in all this?' Marlowe asked, pausing and looking back at her, lifting the goggles. There were small lights in the maintenance tunnel; enough to see without them

Tessa took a breath, let it out, and then nodded.

'Yeah,' she said. 'Let's get on with this.'

Marlowe patted her on the shoulder and passed by, heading towards a ladder.

'They'll expect us to come out at Russell Square or Covent Garden,' he said. 'But we can pop up here, move to a line closer to the surface, and head to the Northern Line instead.'

'I bet you loved this shit as a kid, didn't you?' Tessa asked with a smile. 'Train tunnels and junctions and all that.'

Marlowe didn't reply, having stopped in the middle of the tunnel, the ladder still ahead.

'You okay?'

Marlowe shook his head.

'My mum died down there,' he said. 'Train going southbound from King's Cross, on the Piccadilly Line. It blew up before it hit Russell Square, but it would have been down this tunnel.'

He looked at the floor.

'I've never seen the site,' he whispered.

'And you want to play tourist now?' Tessa pulled at his arm. 'Come on! Your mum wouldn't want you captured because of her.'

Snapping out of whatever this was, Marlowe nodded. Far down the tunnel, there was the slightest hint of newer shouting voices.

More agents.

More extremely pissed-off agents.

'Come on,' he said, heading towards the ladder. 'Let's go.'

7

TURN IT OFF AND ON

'THERE'S NOTHING ON IT,' TRIX SAID AS SHE STARED UP FROM Fractal Destiny. 'Literally, it's dead.'

'What do you mean "nothing on it?"' Marlowe stepped forward. 'I saw it working.'

He had been the last arrival with Tessa to the safe house, with Trix and Marshall Kirk arriving half an hour earlier. The house, a long-forgotten hideaway for MI5 witness relocation was a onetime showroom for a King's Cross apartment complex which, since she'd joined the service had been carefully removed from all records by Trix, purely to offer her a hiding place and a location to get away from it all if needed. It had been a selfish decision, made when she was still working out who worked for who, and was short of allies, but it was a solid location to be used right now. With the recent rebuilding of the surrounding area, should any unwanted visitors arrive, Marlowe and his friends could easily escape through a myriad of mazes and alleyways, regrouping at a secondary location.

After a three-hour walk through tunnels – doubling back and taking secondary paths to confirm they weren't being followed – when Marlowe and Tessa arrived, dirty, tired, and carrying a duffel bag containing Fractal Destiny and a wealth of other secrets, the room's sentiment was jubilant. They had successfully executed a heist against MI5 with no major casualties, and there was no way they could be pegged for it. Trix had monitored the systems since arriving and could hear through the chatter that MI5 believed, thanks to the strange logos Kirk had spray painted, that this was some kind of new anarchist terrorist organisation. Whereas any anarchist organisations in London, immediately hoovered up by MI5 operative-led Special Branch teams in the early hours of the morning, didn't have a bloody clue what was going on and started turning on each other. Within hours, splinter groups would claim credit for the vandalism, purely to get some kind of reputation, each one leading the case further and further away from Marlowe and his team.

Marlowe knew the connections between the heist and his current connection to Orchid, tenuous as it was, might eventually be made, but for now, he could relax. However, after Trix had spent half an hour examining Fractal Destiny, this first spoken review of the item was not what he had hoped for.

Trix looked back at Marlowe, obviously frustrated.

'There's nothing,' she declared, discarding the small screwdriver she'd been using. 'Zero. Zilch. Nada. Choose your term; it's utterly inert.'

'Kate downloaded data onto this,' Marlowe countered, perplexed. 'How can it be dead?'

Trix, removing the casing, revealed the inner workings of

Fractal Destiny, as if showing the remains of the device in the middle of a courtroom trial.

'Because of this. See? No hard drive, no motherboard. It's a mere shell.'

'Could there be a tracker on it?' Kirk frowned. 'This was a honeypot trap?'

After inspecting it, Trix shook her head.

'Even if there was, this room acts as a Faraday cage. I set it up before we all arrived. No signals enter or leave, including from your phones.'

'Could that be why it's not working—' Marlowe began, but flinched as Trix spun back to face him, her eyes flashing in anger, staring at him as if he was some kind of idiot schoolchild.

'Did you miss the part where I mentioned *the absence of the hard drive and motherboard?*' she snapped. 'The memory, the "brain" has been removed. It's likely in some secure server room in Thames House as they try to pick out what they can from it.'

She looked back into the empty device.

'What I will say, though, is there's no way this held all the data Westminster had,' she said, looking back at Tessa and her father. 'You weren't there when it happened, but I was. This box, which we believed at the time to be some kind of AI algorithm device that could foretell the future, it was nothing more than a bump lock to gain information from Whitehall. And when Kate used it, she gained the information of every agent, of every international network, that Whitehall had on records.'

She waved her hands, as if trying to visualise something massive.

'That's terabytes upon terabytes of data.'

'But terabytes can be quite small now, right?' Kirk interjected. 'I have a NAS server unit at home and we have four SSD twelve terabyte hard drives in it.'

'Are some of those for redundancies?'

'Two of them, sure,' Kirk nodded. 'But that's still forty-eight terabytes, in a box no bigger than that.'

'Forty-eight. That's adorable,' Trix smiled. 'Here though, I'm talking hundreds, thousands of terabytes' worth of data. Think of an entire wall worth of NAS drives. Even with current tech, this device couldn't have stored more than a few hard drives' worth inside it. Even if we filled this with Nimbus ExaDrives, which are a hundred terabytes each, that's costing forty grand a drive, so they're already over a hundred grand in, cost-wise before they started, with maybe three, four hundred terabytes total gained. Still too small.'

'And you didn't think of this before we went for it?'

'I knew the size, as Marlowe and Kate ran around the world with the bloody thing,' Trix snapped. 'I just didn't...'

She blushed with embarrassment.

'I didn't think about the size,' she admitted. 'I got caught up in the whole bloody thing, like everyone else.'

'They would have made billions, so maybe the payout for the drives was worth it?' Marlowe suggested.

Trix didn't reply, but mouth-shrugged an acceptance of the point as she picked up the screwdriver again, prodding at something inside it.

'What it has, though, is state-of-the-art, high-frequency transmission tech inside it,' she eventually said after a couple of minutes' worth of poking around.

'What does that mean?' Marlowe asked.

'It means it wasn't using Wi-Fi,' Trix replied as she started prying something from the inside of the box. 'We assumed it connected to a Whitehall network server and downloaded the content onto the machine, but I reckon this is just a junction box. The data was likely sent elsewhere using hard-link satellite Wi-Fi. Basically, satellites in low-earth orbit, enabling low-latency internet access from space.'

'How fast is that?' Tessa now entered the conversation.

'Starlink, that's the one by Elon Musk, they reckon two hundred megabytes a second. But, if it connected directly to the Whitehall hard-link satellite network instead, which she had time to do, they could download everything in a couple of hours. And the original plan was to turn it on under the story of "showing it," and then probably leave it rumbling in the background while they escaped.'

'Come on,' Tessa shook her head. 'Even if they had a ten gigabyte speed, that's a couple of minutes a terabyte, so about eighteen, twenty hours to download everything.'

'She's right,' Marlowe said. 'Kate had the device on for a couple of hours, tops, and managed eighty percent of the data she stole.'

Trix was still playing with the box.

'But if she used the tech to hot-wire straight into the ethernet, it changes everything,' she said. 'It's Wi-Fi enabled, but I wasn't in the room during setup. I know the US has a high-speed system at the Energy Sciences Network that downloads at forty terabytes a second, and I think we have maybe ten terabytes a second through the hardlines at Whitehall. Which means she could use that to download the data in ...'

'In the time she had with Karolides,' Marlowe's lips

thinned in anger. 'But if that data wasn't stored here, though ...'

'This is just a dummy device,' Trix agreed. 'MI5 will realise this once they examine it closely.'

'Why haven't they examined it yet?'

'Probably because Orchid are muddying the waters, in case it reveals more about them,' Trix shrugged. 'It doesn't matter, though. The data ... it was transmitted elsewhere.'

A determined glint appeared in her eyes.

'But if it was sent, I can trace it.' As she pulled an item of circuitry out of Fractal Destiny, connecting it to her laptop with a cable and a bulldog clip to ground it, lines of data scrolled on her screen.

'How long?' Kirk asked.

'Give me a couple of minutes,' Trix muttered, already typing.

Realising they weren't going anywhere for the moment, Marlowe pulled up Bridget Summers' go bag holdall.

Tessa was already reading through the Rubicon notes.

'Anything?' he asked her as he unzipped the bag.

'Well, I think it's all connected,' Tessa replied, looking up. 'Bridget was using the Rubicon list to help Baroness Levin. They were part of some unnamed organisation that wanted to cause anarchy.'

'Sounds familiar,' Marlowe stroked at his chin. 'Do they mention Orchid by name?'

'Here and there, yes,' Tessa nodded. 'But it's in passing. They don't state outright Orchid was behind the mission.'

Marlowe looked over at Kirk now.

'You worked with Bridget for years,' he said. 'Did you ever see anything that looked out of the ordinary?'

'Sure,' Kirk shrugged. 'Bloody everything was out of the ordinary. It's spy craft.'

Marlowe glanced back at the bag as he opened it up.

'She's in the wind, still,' he said. 'She escaped after Westminster, in the confusion, but she never grabbed the go bag.'

'She probably had a dozen,' Kirk chuckled. 'That bitch was always three steps ahead of everyone.'

Marlowe understood the resentment from Kirk. Although they'd worked closely together, Bridget's plan relied on Kirk being blamed for the deaths at Westminster, found dead at the scene. He was going to reply, but instead whistled as he pulled out a wad of passport blanks.

'These are service quality,' he said, flicking through them. There had to be at least fifteen there. As he moved them to the side, he saw ammunition, small gold bars, each one an ounce in size and around the width and height of a credit card, wads of hundred-dollar bills, some fifty-pound notes he quickly pocketed, and three USB sticks, one a cold wallet for cryptocurrency.

There was also a notebook, but it only had one page written, and it was a long paragraph, written completely in code.

'Got some things for you,' Marlowe said as he passed the sticks and the book to Trix. However, Trix was leaning closer to the laptop screen, narrowing her eyes.

'I recognise this,' she said. 'It's the same data stream of code Kate was using when she broke into our system. I've been checking that source code for a while now and I think I can ...'

She paused, tapped a few times on the keyboard, and then started entering large sections of code into the middle of it, seemingly from memory.

After a while, some new numbers appeared on the screen.

She started writing sections of these down, not all of them, though, and to Marlowe it gave the impression of deciphering some kind of secret code, which he assumed she probably was. After half an hour of constant work, and just as the morning dawn was appearing through the windows, Trix slammed back into her chair, whistling with relief.

'I know where it went,' she said. 'It was sent to a server farm in Switzerland, linked to a shell company connected to a French billionaire named Lucien Delacroix. After that, it could have gone anywhere, but he would have had to have signed off on this.'

'That's got to be the same Delacroix the killer named,' Marlowe leaned closer to stare at the screen, even if he couldn't read half of it. 'He got away with eighty percent of the world's secret agent data.'

Kirk's face paled.

'Wait, are you suggesting a substantial chunk of the world's agents are currently endangered by a French billionaire?'

'No,' Trix shook her head. 'The main packet, the core data, didn't get through. It was halted in a buffer, probably when their plan went to shit and wasn't completed. They lacked the power supply to reconnect it. I mean, being stopped in the middle of a motorway stops any convenient spot you can plug a three pin adapter into.'

Marlowe stared at the device, contemplating.

'So, Delacroix didn't obtain it?'

'No, but they did capture some packets,' Trix replied, working on her computer. 'I can't see what they are, but they could be very interesting. And there's a file, which was likely within a restricted server in Whitehall titled "Orchid," that was snapped up, and one ...'

She stopped.

'Rubicon was taken,' she said. 'The original list.'

'Probably how Steele knew,' Marlowe muttered.

'I only ever met the prick once, but it was enough to make me decide to never look for him again,' Kirk added. 'Guy's a sociopath.'

'Delacroix has the list,' Marlowe muttered. 'But more critically, we know Kate had to be working for him, if she was uploading to him.'

'Sounds like he aimed to sell it,' Kirk added. 'The whole thing could have been worth billions. Trillions, even.'

'Why? He already has billions. Why do all this just for money? No, he must have a different use for it,' Marlowe growled. 'Can we get into the server farm? See what it took?'

Trix shook her head.

'It's in Saanen, in Bern,' she said.

'So?'

'So, I know the location,' Trix leant back in her chair. 'It's known as the "Swiss Fort Knox" as it's based in a decommissioned nuclear bunker, literally built into the Swiss Alps. And we can't try to requisition the data, because of the Swiss Data Protection Act, which protects all personal data, including digital data.'

Her hands clenched into fists as she continued.

'That means that under Swiss legislation, nobody has unauthorised access to data legally stored in Swiss centres – whether in physical or digital format.'

'And if we go in under the radar?'

'I just said it's called the "Swiss Fort Knox," Marlowe,' Trix shook her head. 'It's impossible.'

'We just broke into a black archive.'

'That nobody gave a shit about.'

Marlowe sighed, changing the subject.

'Okay, so if we can't hunt the server, we hunt the man. Where's Delacroix now?'

Trix paused from replying as she pulled up some windows.

'MI5 are being really twitchy, right now,' she said. 'Probably because some bastard broke into the archive. I have a couple of aliases I created when I joined Wintergreen's crew, but I have to be careful they don't lead back to me.'

She stopped, nodding as some more data appeared on the screen.

'Okay. He's currently in Paris, hosting a grand event the day after tomorrow. It's a big bash, and the guest list is extensive. It's a literal *who's who* of every major player in the world. Both white hat and black hat.'

'We need to get into it,' Marlowe said. 'Can you get us into the event?'

'It looks like it's invite only, very exclusive,' Trix typed. 'You'll need a connection to an already invited attendee.'

'MI5 won't permit you to leave,' Tessa added. 'Especially given your situation, and anyone who betrayed Kate Maybury is probably not high on Delacroix's Christmas list.'

Trix was scrolling down the list of names.

'Oh, that's clever,' she said. 'It's *two* parties. One is the public face, lots of dignitaries, very visible, and then there's another event, a more *behind closed doors* sort of thing. Looks like that's the one we need to get ...'

She stopped.

'Actually, we might be able to get you into that one,' she said to Tessa, pointing at a name. 'Viktor Orlovsky. Spetsnaz grey man from Averkyevo. That's where you trained, right?'

Tessa nodded.

'Viktor was one of the men who taught me,' she said. 'But I haven't spoken to them since I was a teen.'

'Maybe it's time to reconnect,' Trix was looking again at the list. 'I mean, we're running out of options here. Currently, it's the man who made you a Russian sleeper agent killer, who apparently now runs a deli in Croydon, and ...'

She stopped at another name.

'... your dad,' she said to Marlowe as he looked over at the screen.

TAYLOR COLEMAN

'Steele mentioned my father,' he said as he leant back.

'Do you think he was hinting that, by calling your dad, you could have found out what we needed to know and avoided all of *this* shit?' Marshall swatted at the machine as he said. 'If so, I'm going to be really pissed at you.'

'If we hadn't taken the machine, we wouldn't have known that Delacroix only had a percentage of the data,' Marlowe replied. 'It's helped us, just not as much as we wanted.'

He frowned as a new thought came to mind.

'Do we need IDs for this?' he asked. 'Because MI5 isn't going to let us have anything. We'd be in Paris, so we could go see Helen Bonneville, take the blanks—'

'No,' Trix interrupted. 'I know what you're going to say. If you want to bring Helen in, that's fine, but I think this event is going to want a more official angle. The question here is whether MI5 is going to let you go out to another country when you're supposed to be on some kind of gopher job.'

She smiled.

'Luckily, I know a gopher job that can help in both cases,' she continued, tapping another name on the first party's list.

SENATOR MAUREEN KYLE, REPUBLICAN, USA

'I reckon a call to either Kyle or your nameless friend in the CIA could get you a bit of help here,' she said. 'Kyle is attending the public party, so we get her to ask for you as a consultant bodyguard, part of the whole "special relationship" we're supposed to have. She requests you, Wintergreen allows you to go, everything's sweet. And then, after you're through the door, we get you into the other meeting through Daddy Dearest.'

Marlowe sighed. As much as he didn't really want to phone the CIA agent known only to him as Sasha Bordeaux, an agent so dark and off the books that even Trix couldn't find her identity, there was a chance here that they were working on the same side. Even though she had helped him – but then betrayed him – the last time he travelled to France, he knew she was possibly his only option to get through to the Senator without setting off warning bells from here to Langley.

However, before he could do that, his phone vibrated. He'd turned the ringer off and now pulled it out of his pocket, staring down at the screen.

Caller: Vic Saeed

'Do I answer it?' he asked.

'If you don't, they'll see it as suspicious,' Trix was already typing. 'I'll bounce your trace off a nearby tower. They'll think you're in the train station down the road.'

Taking a deep breath, Marlowe forced himself to relax.

There was no way Vic Saeed knew he'd stolen Fractal Destiny.

There was no way Orchid knew he'd stolen Fractal Destiny.

'Marlowe,' he said, answering. 'What can I do for you, Vic?'

'Did you do it?' Vic Saeed almost shouted down the phone. 'Did you steal the box? Because if you did? You've now got a nice big kill order on your head. Well done.'

8

MEETINGS

'Okay, how about you back the hell off and explain to me what you're talking about?' Marlowe snapped as he faced off against the other agent in the main ticket hall of King's Cross. 'It's early in the morning, and I haven't had my coffee yet.'

'Why meet here?' Vic Saeed asked, his voice a little more suspicious now. Marlowe understood the concern, though; he knew Vic was a fellow MI5 agent, but he was also a believed member of Orchid. After all, this was the man who, when Marlowe had taken over MI5 briefly during the case – *Maybury's* case – had refused ultraviolet assistance on a wound, a refusal that made both Trix and Marlowe believe he had a small UV tattoo of an orchid around the wound area.

'I'm popping up to drop flowers on my mum's grave before work,' Marlowe waved around the station. 'If you wanted to speak to me privately, you should have called me at home earlier.'

When Vic had called, the first thing Marlowe had done was create a meeting location for them that explained why he was in the area, keeping his current colleagues in the wind, while giving an open space with a healthy amount of witnesses, even at this hour of the morning, right before the start of rush hour.

That Vic could be there within minutes showed he'd been hunting for him, and that he'd been in the area.

Which wasn't optimal.

'We tried going to your weird church thing,' Vic replied. 'You weren't there.'

'Because I'm here.'

'We tried—'

'Vic, am I under investigation again?' Marlowe sighed, interrupting, intending to throw Vic off balance. 'Because this is sounding a lot like an interrogation.'

Marlowe knew Vic didn't believe him, or his reasons for being there. But Marlowe, being at a train station, could be for a multitude of innocent and innocuous reasons, including the one he'd given, and there was no conspiracy that could be taken from the location.

'Did you hear about last night?' Vic eventually asked.

Marlowe considered his answer here. He could play dumb or instead, he could push buttons and see where it took him.

'Do you mean the bombs in Holborn?' he asked. 'Yeah, I heard about that.'

'They weren't bombs. They were sonic EMP devices.'

'That went "boom" like bombs,' Marlowe decided to be obstinate here, to see how far that took him.

'Did you hear where they were in Holborn, Marlowe?'

Marlowe shook his head. Trix had already checked, and apart from a couple of small news outlets, there'd pretty much been a major media blackout on this. If anything, the story being used was there had been some kind of gas explosion.

'A few hours ago, somebody went into Bloomsbury Court and blew out the windows of all the surrounding businesses,' Vic narrowed his eyes, watching Marlowe. 'Do you know any organisations that have a symbol of a circle with an M inside?'

Marlowe gave it a moment, as if working through his own thoughts to see if he could think of anyone.

'It's a French Metro sign, isn't it?' he asked.

'Yes, but I don't think this is the French Metro blowing things up.'

Marlowe held up a hand, as if a thought just came to him.

'You said it's on the junction of Bloomsbury Court and Holborn,' he said. 'Could it have been an attack on the Black Archive?'

It was a risky statement to make; by stating he knew what the Black Archive was, he could have been placing himself as a suspect. But if he had played complete ignorance, and it'd been found out he knew, he would instantly have been placed in the crosshairs of a dozen different agencies.

There was a long, uncomfortable silence before Vic spoke again.

'What do you know about the Black Archive?'

'I know there's one in an abandoned tube station around there,' Marlowe replied, keeping his expression blank. 'Never been inside, but I know you can get down there from one of the doors on Bloomsbury Court. Don't know which one, though. Above my pay grade.'

'Yeah,' Vic replied, his suspicion lessening slightly. 'It is. You're right though, there was an attempt on the Black Archive. Two guards are dead, and we're now hunting who we believe are terrorists, Marlowe.'

Marlowe kept his face calm as Vic mentioned the two dead agents. They'd not killed anybody, and Marlowe wondered if this was some kind of line to make him react, a story to give MI5 a "shoot to kill" remit, or whether someone had actually taken out the two guards to make sure they couldn't tell the truth of what had been stolen.

He really hoped it wasn't the last of these. *Nobody should have died for this.*

And if they did, and it was Orchid, he'd be having words.

'Did we lose anything?' he asked.

'I don't know,' Vic watched Marlowe, before looking round the station, possibly searching for either other members of Marlowe's team, or his own agents on the upper levels. 'What do *you* think we would have lost?'

Marlowe knew Vic was fishing. There was no way they could know it was Marlowe; they could suspect, but there was no proof.

'Vic, if you think I'm involved in this, you're barking up the wrong tree,' he said. 'And believe me, you *are* barking. Big and loud.'

He looked around the station again, trying to spy any faces he recognised.

'You phoned me,' he snapped now, deciding to go on the verbal offensive. 'I'm trying to fix my career, and the last thing I want is someone going cowboy, and me getting blamed for it. If someone's shooting agents, I'm probably in the crosshairs as well. So why don't you stop with all this secrecy bullshit and just tell me what's going on?'

'They stole Fractal Destiny.'

Marlowe had been waiting for this, and he prepared his voice with the right amount of outrage and surprise.

'You *kept* it?' he asked, his voice incredulous. 'Christ, you absolute bunch of clowns. Why? You thought you could keep it a secret? The bloody thing should have been destroyed, torn apart, cut into scraps.'

'It was,' Vic replied, now backing away slightly, holding his own hand up to calm Marlowe down before he made more of a scene. 'Don't worry, it was nothing more than a shell. Whatever they did, whatever they took, they'll gain nothing from it.'

'Orchid,' Marlowe said the word, not as a question, but as a statement, a naming. 'Kate Maybury's got friends. Maybe they assumed the data she'd stolen is still there, and they're still trying to make money from it.'

'I don't think it's Orchid,' Vic shook his head.

Of course you'd say that, Marlowe thought to himself. *Fly into my trap, little wasp.*

'Of course it's Orchid,' he argued. 'It's the kind of thing they want. The data will help them take over the world. It's the same reason Kate—'

'It's not Orchid!' Vic snapped, interrupting him, and Marlowe smiled inwardly, still keeping his face emotionless. *He was finally getting under the agent's armour.*

'If you're so sure it's not Orchid,' he said. 'Who do you think it is?'

'It was a small team,' Vic explained. 'Man and a woman coming in through the underground, dressed like TfL workers. Older man at the door blowing up windows and spray-painting symbols, and someone on a computer using a voice changer until the very end when we hear their voice and realise it's a female.'

Marlowe almost grimaced at this. He'd hoped when Trix had forgotten to use the voice changer, it hadn't been picked up.

'Okay,' he replied. 'It could still be an Orchid cell. We know there were older members of Orchid. Maybe this is something McKellen knows something about.'

'McKellan's clueless,' Vic shook his head. 'This personal trip you're taking ... are you coming into the office afterwards?'

Marlowe smiled. He knew Vic was playing with him. They knew enough, but couldn't quite prove it.

Yet.

Plausible deniability.

'No,' he replied. 'Wintergreen has me on some kind of babysitting duty. I'm finding out more about it today, but I think I'm off—'

At this point, he decided to play a hunch.

'—to Paris,' he finished. 'I think I'm helping some US Senator, maybe Kyle? I dunno, it's something in Paris. That's all I know.'

'Maureen Kyle?'

'Yeah,' Marlowe shrugged. 'Which is weird because I don't think there's a summit going on. I'm assuming Karolides is trying to have another one of her secret meetings.'

'Probably,' Vic said, and for a moment Marlowe wondered if he'd actually convinced the agent. 'Do me a favour, Marlowe. Keep your ears open and keep your nose clean.'

'Of course,' Marlowe feigned innocence. 'When haven't I?'

Time for another reach.

'I'll see you in Paris,' he finished.

'You think I'm going to whatever this is?' Vic registered surprise at this.

'I believe MI5 might be at the same event, yeah,' Marlowe nodded, tapping at his chest. 'If they're sending the screwup, they're definitely sending the superhero. So, feel free to send me anything you have. Because I don't really want to go in empty-handed or uncocked.'

Vic didn't reply to this, and as usual, didn't even say good-bye, simply nodding at someone on the upper balcony, and then turning and walking off towards St Pancras.

'They're trying to track you,' Trix said, a sudden voice through his earpiece. 'He might have left you alone, but looking at security cameras, I can see there are agents everywhere watching you.'

Marlowe went to nod agreement, but stopped himself – the agents watching him didn't know he had a voice in his ear.

'Looks like I'll be shaking some tails,' he said, scratching his lip to hide the movement of them as he turned from the station platforms and headed towards the underground entrance and the Piccadilly Line.

THE LAST TIME MARLOWE HAD TRAVELLED FROM KING'S CROSS while being tailed, he'd also been going to a secret meeting. But that time he was doing his best to avoid his trails. This time, he felt he could bluff his innocence, as even if Vic still suspected him, he still couldn't prove it. So, as he started down the steps towards the underground station he paused, looking at a poster to the side, waiting for the agent that was following him to catch up.

There were two agents: the first was a tall, middle-aged man with short cut greying hair, slim in a suit, while the second was a younger woman, around the same age as Marlowe, her hair pulled back and in what looked to be a floral summer dress. It was probably to blend in as she followed him, and Marlowe appreciated, on a professional level, the effort made.

He waited, and as the first of the two agents walked past, he grabbed him by the arm.

'I don't appreciate being followed,' he said.

'I don't know what you mean,' the man pulled away from Marlowe's grip.

'Vic Saeed told you to follow me,' Marlowe continued with mock indignance. 'I've got nothing to hide, and I don't appreciate you tailing me like some asset. So you have two choices: you can either go tell him you've lost me, or you can explain to my – and his – boss, Emilia Wintergreen, why you're using me as some kind of training exercise.'

The man glowered at Marlowe.

'I was catching a train to work,' he sniffed. 'You know, Whitehall.'

'Good,' Marlowe smiled. 'We'll be on different lines then. Have a good day.'

With that said, Marlowe gave a nod and walked into the station itself, keeping the agent within his peripheral vision. He saw the agent pull his phone out and angrily make a call, probably to a second team. He knew he'd been burnt, and now it was time to pass the baton on.

Let them come, Marlowe thought to himself.

King's Cross underground station was a rabbit warren of tunnels and passageways, and from walking into one entrance to the south, you could find yourself exiting in St Pancras Station, or even on both sides of the Euston Road. Marlowe used this to his advantage quickly, doubling back on himself, making sure the man who was now outed couldn't do anything about this.

Marlowe knew the woman would still be there, and

others would have been alerted now to take over, but Marlowe was already working on his next step.

As he walked to the stairs heading down to the underground entrance, there was a cupcake stand to his left with a bored teenager selling cakes to morning commuters, a company baseball cap on his head, thick, black-framed glasses on his face and an apron around his neck.

Marlowe threw one of Bridget Summers' fifty-pound notes down.

'Hiding from an ex-girlfriend,' he said. 'Can I put that on for a second as she goes past?'

The teenager, happy to make a little money, quite happily passed over the baseball cap and apron, and Marlowe threw them on, also taking the pair of thick-rimmed black glasses as well. He knew the beard was a giveaway, so instead, he kept his head down, watching as the floral-dressed woman walked past, now frowning as she tried to see where her target had gone, completely oblivious to the cupcake seller to her left.

As soon as she passed, heading through the gates to the underground platforms, Marlowe pulled off his hasty disguise, thanking the teenager before returning the way he'd come.

The last time he'd done this, he had a go bag waiting for him on the south side of the Euston Road, and it was only while travelling he'd realised that MI5 had learned about this at some prior time, and placed a tracker inside it.

This time he decided to go a more improvisational route, so as he walked through St Pancras Station he popped into one of the many shops that lined the side, grabbing a brown suede bomber jacket, a new baseball cap and a pair of aviator glasses, paying once more from Bridget's money. He knew she would have made sure the serials couldn't be connected to her when she set the bag up, so he knew they were okay to use. Items purchased, he threw them on quickly and headed out of the station, walking swiftly across the Euston Road, and south down Judd Street.

As soon as he reached Tavistock Place, he walked over to a selection of push bikes attached to locks. Known as "Boris bikes" in London, these were bicycles you could rent by the hour, placing your credit card details into the keypad locks to open them. But Marlowe didn't do that, instead placing his phone against the lock, pressing a button on an app that quickly ran through a million different combinations before unlocking the bike. With bike in hand, he started cycling quickly, heading out of Tavistock Place, and towards Goodge Street.

There was a man on a Brompton folding bike who was matching him as they cycled, and Marlowe didn't know if this was a commuter or another agent, so he decided it was best to err on the side of caution. Stopping on Tottenham Court Road, leaving the bike outside Goodge Street Station, he quickly jumped the barriers and ran down the stairs. The station was one of the few in London that still relied on elevators to move passengers up and down from platform to ticket hall, but the staircase, effectively circling around them was only a hundred and forty steps, and honestly, at a downward run, was way faster. And it meant he could watch the elevators from a place of hiding, checking if the Brompton bike rider was following.

He wasn't.

Deciding he was safe for the moment, and leaping onto a Northern Line train, Marlowe stayed on it until Leicester Square, where he emerged back into the fresh air, hitting the early morning tourist crowds.

At this point, he noticed the woman with the floral dress again.

He hadn't lost them, and this was annoying. These people were good – although if Vic sent them, the chances were they were the best of the best. She hadn't been on the train, he was pretty sure of it; she must have travelled straight down the Piccadilly Line. There was probably an agent outside every station.

Dammit.

There was a buzz on his burner phone – a message. He looked down at it.

FROM: CLEVER GIRL

Serpentine Bridge

Marlowe deleted the message and, pulling the phone apart, discarded it in a rubbish bin as he continued heading down through Trafalgar Square. He didn't need it anymore, and he'd buy a new phone as soon as he got out of this current predicament.

He'd lost the floral dress for a moment, and looked for a new angle to play here. There was a German tour group walking along beside him, the tour guide speaking excitedly as he waved his hands around. Marlowe didn't really understand much conversational German, but he knew enough to walk up to the speaker when he took a moment to pause, passing him another fifty-pound note and saying in German, 'I join you, please?'

With the jacket taken off and in just a white t-shirt with a baseball cap, Marlowe mingled into the tourists as they walked through Admiralty Arch and down the Mall, towards Buckingham Palace. He was still heading in a direction he needed, but he was also concerned he was being watched.

He knew he couldn't have been tracked as he had nothing that was trackable on him. Looking around, he couldn't see floral dress anymore; she'd probably headed towards Whitehall, hoping to catch him before Thames House.

As they finally reached the end of the Mall, heading up towards the twenty-five-metre-tall Victoria Memorial, Marlowe quickly used some cyclists riding past to block him from view as he left the tour group with a quick 'Danke,' running across into St. James's Park.

By now, he'd been playing hide and seek for well over an hour, and finally in the park, he used the myriad of narrow paths to slip across it, quietly keeping an eye out as he did so. Nobody was following him that he could see, and if they were, they were doing a bloody good job of hiding.

Arriving at the Serpentine Bridge, an arch and stone balustrade bridge that spanned the two ponds that created the Serpentine Lake, Marlowe saw a man standing, waiting for him.

He was tall, painfully thin, his Adam's Apple jutting out, and his thinning hair was slightly too long for the haircut he had been trying to rock, and artificially old, looking in his forties, but possibly no older than thirty.

He reminded Marlowe of the cartoon character Ichabod Crane.

Marlowe smiled, walking up to him.

'I'm guessing you're here to see me?' he asked.

'I'm here to tell you your father doesn't want to talk to you,' the man said. 'And I suggest you never call him again. Whatever you're doing right now, whatever game this is, it's over, Thomas.'

9

FAMILY REUNIONS

'LOOK,' MARLOWE SAID. 'I GET THAT WE'RE NOT TALKING. I'VE had my last conversation with Taylor, and I'll be honest, I'm not that bothered about speaking to him again. But you have to understand I've been told to speak to him by somebody very important. Somebody even he might work for—'

'Your father, working for somebody else?' The man, who as of yet still hadn't given his name, and now would be called Ichabod by Marlowe until he gave his real one, laughed.

'You don't work directly with my dad, do you?' Marlowe asked.

'I don't think you have a right to call him your dad,' Ichabod replied. 'And you certainly don't have a right to say there's somebody bigger than—'

'St John Steele.'

Marlowe spoke the word calmly, with a slight smile on his lips.

'The Arbitrator? What about him?'

'He's the one who told me to call my dad,' Marlowe

replied casually. 'I think even you'll agree that if someone of his level tells you to do something, you kind of do it.'

'Even if we wanted to, your father's not around,' Ichabod was now looking around the park as he spoke, possibly wondering if Steele himself was about to appear. 'He's not back in the country.'

'He's in Paris,' Marlowe interrupted, tiring of this now. It was only a matter of time before Vic Saeed's attack dogs gained his scent again, and he really didn't want to be seen on the bridge with this gangly servant. 'He's at a party tomorrow. Lucien Delacroix's party. Why do you think I'm talking to you right now?'

Ichabod stopped himself from replying, pausing as he mentally went through his options. Marlowe could see he hadn't expected Marlowe to be in control here. But then he'd never spoken to Marlowe, and probably hadn't expected anything more than some loser burnt spy, based on the information he'd probably been told by people connected to Taylor Coleman.

'It's really simple,' Marlowe said. 'I've been told I have to speak to Taylor Coleman. I'm guessing because I can't be invited into the more exclusive part of the event in Paris, I'm guessing I have to be invited by my father, rather than Steele.'

'Why can't Steele invite you?'

'Because I'm an active MI5 security services agent, and Steele's a goddammed ghost,' Marlowe snapped, his tolerance finally thinning. 'I can't be invited to a little backroom shindig at some political event by some random billionaire. But I can be invited by my estranged father, who just wants to make up.'

'But your father doesn't want to make up.'

'You know that, and I know that,' Marlowe sighed. 'But MI5 doesn't know that. And neither does Orchid.'

He'd thrown the word out as a Hail Mary, testing the waters to see what happened. What he hadn't expected was for Ichabod to instinctively reach for what looked to be a hidden gun inside his left jacket pocket before stopping, realising it was just a name.

'Why did you mention that ... that word?' he asked, looking around, as if expecting snipers to start shooting at any moment.

'You know why I said it. You know what Delacroix's position in Orchid is, you know what my father's position in Orchid is, so right now, you know as much as I know about this,' Marlowe leant closer. 'So how about we cut this crap? I've already got an invitation to the less exclusive part of this party, so tip him the nod that at some point, I'll turn up to have a chat with Dad, keep Steele and Delacroix happy, and then I'll leave him alone.'

'Why do you care about keeping Delacroix happy?'

'He's a billionaire with a possible list of agents' names and addresses,' Marlowe shrugged. 'Why do you think I'm gonna do it?'

Ichabod considered the words and then nodded.

'I'll pass it up the chain,' he said. 'But I can't guarantee you anything.'

'That's fine,' Marlowe replied. 'I'm on a plane in three hours, and I'll be in Paris no matter what. But trust me when I tell you – I *will* be at the party, one way or another. It's up to you to decide whether my father is an enemy or an ally.'

'Your father's not well,' Ichabod added. 'This might not—'

'Are you about to tell me that seeing me might cause his

cancer to end it all?' Marlowe laughed. 'I'm good, but I'm not that good. Remember what I said. Paris.'

This threat stated, Marlowe then turned, walking off the bridge and away from Ichabod, who stared after him, scratching at his balding head, unsure of what deal he'd just made.

Marlowe hoped Tessa's conversation had gone a little better.

MARSHALL KIRK HADN'T BEEN HAPPY ABOUT THIS. TESSA GOING over to Paris was one thing. Tessa going as part of some clandestine mission to take down a top-secret organisation was another, but Tessa, using the people who trained her to be a sleeper agent to do so, was *way* off the board.

'We can find another way of doing this,' he said as he sat in the passenger seat of Tessa's car, staring at the Eastern European deli they'd parked down the road from.

'You can't,' Tessa replied, currently in the driver's seat. 'I need to have somebody there who can vouch for me. Otherwise, how are we getting in?'

Kirk shook his head.

'It's a bad idea,' he replied coldly.

'Is this because it's dangerous? Or because I'm returning to a life that my mum gave me?' Tessa snapped, and Kirk looked hurt at the accusation.

'I've never stopped you from doing anything,' he said. 'Don't think for one second that what your mum did to you would affect my thoughts about that.'

Tessa reached across, grabbing her father's hand.

'I never did,' she smiled, before straightening, taking a deep breath and exiting the car. 'Wait here. I mean it.'

Kirk grumbled something about not promising anything, and Tessa let out the breath, walking across the street towards the Eastern European deli. It was a nondescript doorway sandwiched between a tattoo parlour and a vintage clothing shop, the flickering sign reading "Miroslav's Deli," the letters tinged with a patina of age and the colours of the Czech Republic's flag.

Tessa almost laughed at this – *Miroslav* was Slavic for "one who celebrates peace," and she hadn't considered Viktor Orlovsky to be someone like that for a long time, if ever.

Stepping inside, she was greeted by the aroma of pickled vegetables, smoked meats, and freshly baked rye bread – a scent that transported her momentarily to far-off places she'd rather forget, ones filled with moments of pain, and a mother's displeasure. Rows of glass jars filled with marinated olives, sauerkraut, and dark-red beetroot lined the rustic wooden shelves. A display case showcased a surprisingly lacklustre array of sausages and cheeses, while an old television set perched in a corner broadcast news in a Slavic language, its staticky audio filling the small space with a haunting undertone.

Behind the counter stood an ageing man with salt-and-pepper hair, his eyes narrowing, wiping his hands on his soiled apron as he looked up to notice Tessa.

'Can I help you?' he asked, his voice heavily accented.

Tessa forced a smile and pointed to a jar of pickles on the top shelf.

'I'll take one of those,' she said, her voice a careful blend of detachment and curiosity. 'And some information, if you're willing to part with it.'

'What kind of information?'

'I want to speak to Viktor,' Tessa replied.

'Many Viktors here.'

'Viktor Orlovsky.'

The man didn't change his expression on hearing the name, but Tessa definitely felt the temperature drop.

'Who are you?'

'Tessa Kirk, my mother was Angela Kirk. Before that she was Angela Weber.'

'Common surname.'

'Not to Viktor,' Tessa sighed. 'Look, if he's not there, just be honest. I don't have time for this. It's about Rubicon.'

The man went to reply, but Tessa saw a movement behind the door at the end of the counter – she was being watched. Deciding to ignore the older man behind the counter and concentrate on this new angle, she started towards it.

'I need to be on a plane in a couple of hours,' she said. 'I need safe passage to Paris for something. Something Viktor has an interest—'

She didn't finish; taking her eye off the old man, she'd shown her back to him, and the moment she did so, he lunged at her, brandishing a hidden filleting knife from beneath the counter. His move was swift but weighted, his age slowing him down. Tessa had expected this, however, and sidestepped just in time, the blade narrowly missing her abdomen and slicing through the air where she had stood a moment before.

As she pivoted, her left hand shot out to grab the old man's wrist, her thumb digging viciously into the pressure point to loosen his grip on the knife. With her right arm, she shifted her weight and executed a quick elbow jab to his face, disrupting his balance and his grip on the weapon. The knife clattered onto the wooden floor as, using her grip on the old man's wrist as leverage, Tessa twisted it back sharply, forcing him into a vulnerable position. With a sweep of her leg, she took his feet out from under him, and he went crashing down, disoriented and winded.

Tessa's foot came down on the dropped knife, kicking it out of his reach, and for a brief moment, their eyes locked – his filled with a volatile mix of surprise and grudging respect, hers icy and calculated.

'I expected that, Fyodor,' she said, emotionless. 'You were always a backstabber when you taught me during my holidays in Averkyevo.'

The old man, now named Fyodor, stared up at Tessa in recognition, and in return she straightened, allowing him to clamber to his knees. However, as she did this, she felt the cold metal of a gun barrel rest against her head.

'And you would always rely too much on guns,' she smiled. 'Shall I remind you how fast I can take it from you?'

The gun disappeared, and Tessa turned to face a short, squat, bald man in his seventies. He was five feet six at best, brandishing a bushy dyed-brown beard that didn't match his wild, salt and pepper eyebrows, the left one split in two by a vicious-looking scar.

'We've been here seven years,' Viktor Orlovsky said, his English accent perfect. 'You never visited.'

'I had no need to,' Tessa replied, helping Fyodor up to his feet.

'We see your father is in the car outside,' Viktor added. 'Shall we invite him in?'

'I think that's probably unwise,' Tessa said, glancing through the window at the car. 'I have fond memories of you, but he still hates you.'

'Understandable, but he must know we never killed your mother.'

'Being my mother killed my mother,' Tessa replied, leaning against the counter. 'And that almost killed me.'

'I heard,' Fyodor now picked up the blade, placing it behind the counter again. 'You were almost outed. How did you change the list?'

'I was helped by an old friend of my father's,' Tessa looked from one to the other as she spoke. 'I'm not here to rejoin, but I need your help.'

'Paris, tomorrow,' Viktor nodded. 'I know what you want. And I won't be there to help.'

'But your name's on a list?'

'It might be, but just because I was invited, doesn't mean I'm attending,' Viktor's face darkened as he spoke. 'I left that life. This is my world now. The only flesh I slice into is dead, the only lies I tell are to customers on where I source it. Orchid wants me there because of my connection to Rubicon, but that died many years ago. And the Russia you see on the news now, that's not my Russia.'

He looked away.

'My Russia is dead now.'

'Then let me go on your behalf,' Tessa continued, not believing a single word of Orlovsky's sob story. 'Tell whoever invited you that Angela Weber's daughter, a true child of Rubicon will be there to speak for you.'

'But you are not a child of Rubicon anymore,' Viktor replied, almost sadly. 'Your name was removed from the list.'

'The public list,' Tessa snapped. 'You think Whitehall, or even Orchid doesn't have the real one, with my mother's name on it? Be honest, it's just a matter of time before I'm outed. So what's the point in trying to build a life, just to see it broken down?'

She leant closer.

'This is an opportunity for me,' she said. 'Something my training was built for. Let me do your bidding.'

'My bidding?' Viktor Orlovsky laughed. 'Child, the only bidding I have is to see Lucien Delacroix brutally murdered, and I wouldn't wish that task on my greatest enemy.'

'Why?' Tessa raised an eyebrow at this. 'I thought you'd be friends.'

'With a billionaire? We have enough oligarchs we have to suck up to,' Viktor smiled. 'But as I said. I am out of this life you seek. If Delacroix wishes to send killers after me, then so be it. I won't stop them. If anything, their vengeance is my payment to cross Charon's ferry.'

'But it won't be vengeance,' Tessa snapped back. 'It'll be killers working for a payout, terminating a target they have no knowledge of.'

'And why do you care again?' Fyodor asked, the slightest of grins on his face. 'You allowed another to take your heritage, remove you from a list.'

'Because I thought I wanted that.'

Viktor moved back to the counter.

'The spetsial'noe naznacheniya are nothing but dreams now, and Averkyevo is long gone,' he said. 'Agents, created to be nothing more than rumours, are just that now. Bogeymen for children's stories as our leaders squabble for lost land, killing mercenary leaders when they bite their hands, and hiding from drone attacks from countries they should have overcome years earlier. I will not return to that life, or be acknowledged by it.'

He reached under the counter and pulled out a folded sheet of paper.

'This, however, states that you will,' he said. 'It also says you speak on my behalf.'

Tessa took the folded sheet, opening it up and reading it.

'You already knew,' she said. 'All this, and you expected me. You even signed my name on it.'

'I would be a rather lacklustre spymaster if I couldn't work out how to spy now, wouldn't I?' Viktor gave a resigned shrug. 'But know that once you walk this path, you cannot leave it, or turn back the way you came. You can only move forward. Tell me, are you the daughter of Angela Weber, or Marshall Kirk?'

'Can't I be both?'

Viktor considered this.

'Maybe you can,' he said. 'But only if you can come to peace with both. Can you?'

At this, Tessa wasn't sure.

10

OLD FRIENDS

Following his meeting with Ichabod Crane, or at least the suited man who bore more than an unfortunate resemblance to the character, Marlowe had returned to his West London church. He knew he was being watched, so he played it as casually as he could.

It had been broken into.

The furniture had been tossed, the boxes of unpacked items scattered across the floor. Someone had been looking for something, most likely Fractal Destiny. However, they hadn't found the staircase and the route downstairs.

Even if they had, they wouldn't have found what they wanted, he thought to himself with a dark smile. That was still with Trix, and even he didn't know where she was right now.

He tidied up as best as he could, grateful the location was still mainly under construction, checking the spare Sig hidden in the kitchen drawer was still there; he'd replaced it after Steele's visit, but there was a nagging suspicion someone may have removed it, or even tampered with it. The last thing he wanted was to grab it when being attacked and find the firing pin, or something similar had been removed.

The gun was still there.

There was a small digital recorder in the drawer, and Marlowe could see it'd been moved, probably listened to. There was nothing on it, so whoever entered wouldn't have heard anything; but this wasn't because the recorder hadn't been used, but more because this wasn't a digital recorder. In fact, three quick presses on the side button turned it into a highly effective bug sweeper, and Marlowe took the opportunity to use it, sweeping each room for new arrivals into his church. He found three, one upstairs, one in a lamp by the TV and one in the kitchen. He didn't remove them – after all, why would he do such a thing if he had nothing to hide, but he noted down where each one was, before heading downstairs.

The crypt was untouched. They hadn't made it down. But, even so, he still made a pass with the scanner, just in case, only relaxing once he was completely sure. Then, sitting down at the computer monitors, he started to scroll back through his security footage, taken from the same camera, almost hidden in a corner of the main area, that Trix had watched Steele, days earlier.

It was a two-man team, and Marlowe recognised one of them immediately.

Peter Lloyd.

The other man was younger and Indian in looks, his black hair and beard trimmed short with a gradient done with clippers in what was probably a trendy style. It made Marlowe scratch at his own beard, realising it probably needed a trim itself. However, on the screen, the younger man seemed to be in charge, pointing areas for Peter to check.

Marlowe leant back in his chair as he watched the footage. Was this Orchid, or was this MI5 controlling the op? They obviously thought he was connected to the heist, which was probably a wise move on their part, but Peter Lloyd was a nobody. He was picked by Marlowe because he wanted to get out but *hadn't* been allowed.

Well, someone was allowing him now.

There was a beep from his new burner phone, picked up after the meeting with Ichabod – he'd immediately passed the number to Trix and the others, but hadn't heard anything back until now.

FROM: CLEVER GIRL

As we thought – Hotel Bed up for more security. News later.

Marlowe smiled. He knew Trix would have gotten through to Senator Kyle, named as "Hotel Bed" because the first time they'd met had been when Marlowe broke into her hotel room in New York in the middle of the night, but he wondered whether this had been through official channels, or rather through some other back channel route, perhaps with the CIA agent known only as Sasha Bordeaux.

Quickly, he typed a reply.

Get D's file on her. Check for anything.

The "D" here stood for Donziger; Nathan Donziger, in fact. He'd been the one holding an analogue file on Kyle in a salt mine depository, and although Marlowe had returned it to her after stealing it, he'd still taken a copy of the file for his own reasons.

Or, rather, Trix had.

There probably wasn't anything there he could use, but he'd met Kyle a couple of times now, and even though he'd saved both her career and her life on several occasions, he still didn't fully trust her.

This done, he took the back passage out of the crypt, exiting out into the back of the graveyard that came with the building. The graves had been emptied; the coffins removed to newer, larger cemeteries years earlier, but the gravestones had stayed, possibly for aesthetic value. And, behind one of these, Marlowe pulled out Bridget Summers' go bag, placed there by either Tessa or Marshall Kirk before they went to their meeting, knowing Marlowe would return here rather than King's Cross after his meeting in case Vic Saeed was still tracking him.

Returning to the crypt, making sure nobody *was* monitoring him, Marlowe placed the bag on the table, opening it up. They'd only managed a cursory look earlier, but Marlowe had been curious about what else Bridget would have had in here – and what MI5 would have left in it when they stuck it in the archive.

There had been USB sticks; Trix had copied them and placed them back into the bag. A cold ledger, something to hold crypto in. Pulling out more items from the go bag, Marlowe inventoried it: she had a change of clothes, a thin-bladed knife, a second, folding butterfly knife, some ammo for a 9mm revolver, a lockpick set that seemed better than Marlowe's own one, a burner phone still in its blister pack, pepper spray, some protein bars, a box of matches, water purification tablets and a portable charger, with USB-C cables.

A look into she side pockets revealed basic medical supplies, in case she'd been injured while escaping, the wads of dollars he'd seen earlier, the fifty-pound notes already gained by Marlowe, the handful of small gold bars, each less than an ounce in weight, but likely gathered for the same reason as Marlowe collected Britannia coins, a satellite phone and a clear bag filled with fake IDs. Flicking through them, Marlowe saw at least three new identities for Bridget, each with a couple of additional credit cards in the new ID's name.

On the top were the passport blanks Marlowe had seen before. They were from a variety of different countries, and with them Bridget could have become an American, a member of the EU, even an Australian if she'd so wanted. Marlowe had been pretty close in his assessment, as when counted, there were sixteen of these. And, attached to them by a rubber band, was the same notebook he'd looked at earlier, a single page filled with a paragraph of code.

Marlowe sat back, staring at it. *What was the code here?*

Giving up, he tossed the notebook onto the table as his phone, his "normal" one, left here since before the heist, rang. He'd forwarded all calls and messages through some ghost servers, so he knew nobody had been trying to contact him during his time off the grid, and he rose quickly, answering the CALLER ID WITHHELD number.

'Marlowe. It's Wintergreen.'

'Ma'am.'

'You're on babysitting duty, I'm afraid,' Emila's voice was apologetic, but suspicious. 'Senator Maureen Kyle has asked for you to run point on her security while in Europe.'

'Kyle's in Europe?' Marlowe tried to sound surprised.

'You know damn well she is,' Wintergreen muttered. 'I don't know what you're playing at, but I've sent you an encrypted file with where to meet her tomorrow, in Paris.'

'Trix?'

'Strangely, she'll be there on the Home Secretary's coin,' Wintergreen replied, obviously irritated she didn't see what was going on here. 'I also hear Marshall and Tessa Kirk will be there on behalf of some Russian interest. I thought they were friendlies?'

The line was spoken casually, but Marlowe knew what Wintergreen was really asking.

I told you to create a team, but are they compromised?

'I know,' he said. 'I suggested the linkup.'

'Well, I hope to God you know what you're doing,' Wintergreen replied and, with her usual friendliness, disconnected the call before saying goodbye.

Marlowe placed the phone down and returned to the computer monitors, where he pulled down Wintergreen's message. It had been sent through official channels – after all, it was an official meeting, and he noted down the times, places and items needed.

He was booked to leave on the Eurostar in four hours. Barely enough time to prepare. But then Wintergreen was never one for long waits.

Sighing, he started to pack his own duffel.

———

MARLOWE HAD BEEN MET AS SOON AS HE GOT OFF THE Eurostar.

Before leaving, he'd told the team to go dark, and only

connect through secure channels while in Paris; the black archive heist was still a raw wound in the security service's side, and he was worried that anything they did to throw any kind of spotlight on them would not end well.

He'd met with a CIA agent named Dickinson, a slim man with almost prematurely white hair, giving him the look of a man far older than he truly was. Dickinson had passed Marlowe a manila envelope containing keys to a hotel room, the Senator's itinerary, and a list of things he needed to purchase before the party: tuxedo, tie, grooming, all the usuals.

Marlowe had thanked the man and carried on, already noting Vic Saeed emerging from the station a few moments behind him; quick enough to catch up, but long enough to miss Dickinson.

Or was that deliberate?

'Where are you staying?' Marlowe slowed down, letting the other agent join him.

Vic, surprised at the question, shrugged.

'Karolides tells us nothing,' he said. 'But I know there's a government office nearby. They'll have sorted it. You?'

Marlowe waggled the manila envelope.

'Apparently I have a suite,' he lied.

'If that's what playing with Americans gives you, where do I sign up?' Vic smiled. It was supposed to be disarming, a relaxed comment to lead Marlowe along a path of friendship and support, but Marlowe wasn't in the mood to play nice right now.

'Peter Lloyd,' he said, as they walked out of the station and towards the taxi cab rank to the right. 'He's one of yours, right?'

'Sometimes. Why?'

'He was in my apartment earlier,' Marlowe replied matter-of-factly.

'And how do you know that?'

'I have a video doorbell. It picked them up,' Marlowe lied again. 'Peter and another fellow. Didn't recognise him, but I would if I saw him again. Indian. Clipped beard.'

'I don't know anything about that, and I'm not sure of the other guy,' Vic shook his head, and Marlowe wasn't sure if Vic was lying or not. 'But Peter will be at the event tonight. He's part of the Karolides contingent. You can ask him yourself.'

Marlowe smiled.

'I'll take you up on that,' he said as he climbed into a car. 'Can I drop you off? US Government is paying the tab, it seems.'

Vic shook his head, and Marlowe wondered if this was because he didn't want to be in an enclosed area with him, or whether he didn't want to be seen gaining anything from the US. Either way, Marlowe had lied again; he was paying for this himself, even if it was with Bridget's own money.

The hotel Kyle had set him up in was *Le Meurice*, overlooking the Tuileries Garden in the first arrondissement, a stone's throw away from the Louvre. A blend of traditional French opulence and modern luxury, with a two-Michelin-starred restaurant, Marlowe was almost disappointed he wouldn't have time to spend there. As soon as he'd reached his room, finding nothing more of note waiting for him, he quickly changed clothes, slipping back out. If anyone asked, he was on a shopping trip for the following day's event, but in actuality, he had a meeting to attend, one with an old friend.

He hadn't noticed the *other* old friend waiting for him

beside the door of the hotel until he'd exited the building, finding the muzzle of a revolver pressed against his spine.

'Hey, buddy,' Brad Haynes hissed. 'Missed you.'

Marlowe froze, frantically trying to work out what was happening here. *Was Brad here to kill him? Was he with someone else? An ally?*

'So what the hell's going on?' Brad asked as he walked Marlowe towards a black limousine, waiting patiently outside the hotel, gun still jammed into the small of Marlowe's back. As ever, Brad gave the appearance of a middle-aged man in good condition, a black suit open over a collared sports shirt, a lack of tie completing the casual ensemble. His hair was thick and dark, his body stocky, as solid as a prize-fighter.

'I need a little more here,' Marlowe played for time.

'Why are you meeting with Orchid in Paris and using a US Senator to do it?' Brad said as he rapped on the window of the limousine. The tinted window slowly slid down, and Marlowe gave out a groan.

'Hello, Sasha,' he said.

The woman in the car was in her mid-to-late thirties, red hair in an overgrown bob style, with minimal makeup over an attractive face and a navy business-suit over a pale blouse. Marlowe didn't know her name, only that she called herself Sasha Bordeaux when meeting him, based on a DC Comics character, and had also used the alias Diana Prince with someone else, the secret identity of Wonder Woman.

Marlowe looked back at Brad.

'I see you finally reunited,' he said, banging his head as Brad pushed him into the vehicle through the now open door, sitting opposite Sasha as Brad, gun in hand, moved in behind him, gun still trained on him.

'Last time we worked together, I brought you to Paris,' Sasha said. 'And now you're back.'

'Let's be honest here,' Marlowe shook his head, waggling his finger in an accusatory manner. 'Last time we worked together, you informed on me while I was in the air, and I only just got out.'

'I had to keep my cover,' Sasha shrugged. 'That of a loyal US servant. Just like Braddy boy here.'

Brad grimaced at the name; Marlowe realised this wasn't the first time he'd been called it.

'So why don't you cut the crap and tell us why we don't send you back in a body bag?' Brad snapped.

'Is that the way to treat a friend?' Marlowe snapped back. 'I gave you a head start.'

'You almost ended my career.'

'Yeah? Well, you almost ended my life, Brad, so I think in the great list of cock ups, you're way higher than me.'

Brad didn't answer this, leaning back on the car seat.

'You're trying to get a meeting with your father,' Sasha continued, and Marlowe wasn't surprised she knew this. 'Why?'

'Lucien Delacroix,' Marlowe replied. 'He's Orchid. I'm trying to take down Orchid.'

'God, is this one of Wintergreen's suicide missions?' Brad almost laughed. 'If you want to die, I can easily help you out.'

'It's not just me,' Marlowe watched Brad as he continued. 'It's a team of us. Me, Trix, Marshall and Tessa.'

'You dragged Marshall Kirk into this?' Brad's eyebrows almost shot off his forehead, he raised them so high. 'And not me?'

'Again with the "tried to kill me" part of our last mission,'

Marlowe narrowed his eyes. 'You're untrustworthy, Brad. I spent half of New York wondering if you'd screwed me.'

'And had I?'

'Only at the end,' Marlowe admitted. 'And only when you thought you had no other option. But it doesn't explain why you're here.'

He'd aimed the last part of this at Sasha now, who mouth shrugged disinterest.

'It's a party filled with the richest and most influential people in the world,' she said. 'It's Davos meets the Met Gala. Why wouldn't I be here?'

'Because it's exposed.'

'I like bright lights.'

'Says the woman in the car with the blacked-out windows,' Marlowe smiled. 'Or are you telling me you've taken a side in this?'

'The CIA has their own agenda—'

'Come on, Sasha, or whatever your real name is, we both know you've not played by CIA rules for years. You play more by Cold War Moscow rules. Watch your back whenever you're exposed. Find people who owe you to work for you.'

This last line was now aimed at Brad.

'As fun as this reunion is, I'm bored now,' Sasha interrupted. 'The event's tomorrow. You're here in Paris, looking shifty as hell, Tom. I'm guessing you have a plan?'

'Depends if I'm passing it to Orchid.'

Sasha looked genuinely hurt at the accusation.

'I thought we had a connection,' she complained.

'We do, and he's still aiming a gun at me, while looking like he's eaten a mouthful of wasps,' Marlowe leant back on the chair. 'So if you think we're all friends, tell Brad to grow up and put the bloody gun away before I make him eat it. Slowly.'

Chuckling, Brad did so before being asked.

'There,' he said. 'All friends together. So, tell us what you're doing?'

Smiling, Marlowe told them.

11

FAKERY

If he was being brutally honest, Marlowe hadn't expected Helen Bonneville to stay in the Parisienne forgery den she'd been in the last time he had visited. In fact, he assumed, probably quite legitimately, that she'd moved out of the building within hours of Kate Maybury and Tom Marlowe's pickup of their passports. After all, she probably had three or four locations that she could work from, and Marlowe had given her several grands' worth of passport blanks for the work she had done.

What Marlowe hadn't expected was for the building to still be standing.

The Helen Bonneville Marlowe had once known, would more likely have set the place on fire to remove any trace of evidence, or even set an explosive device inside it – maybe even use some kind of satellite, nuking it from space just to be sure.

Although *that* was a bit extreme.

Either way, Marlowe hadn't expected to find her at the same location, and he wasn't surprised to find she was gone.

But Helen was a forger, and a popular one; she had a clientele that would have needed to know where to go to find her again. So Marlowe spent the next hour walking around the block, looking for clues that would tell him where she was going next – clues she would have deliberately left for her own clients.

He found them in the form of painted squares, left here and there on the walls of the buildings. As Marlowe walked around examining them, he realised that when placed together in a three-by-three grid, these squares would create an effective QR code, which considering the fact they were painted on the side of a building was a digital answer in an analogue form.

Marlowe had taken photos of all nine of the items, and then used software to stitch the nine squares he'd photographed together, trying them in a variety of different combinations until one worked, the now-fixed QR code opening a website. The website itself was a forum and on the forum was a single post, an image of a dog, a breed known as a "Sheltie." Inside the image was code, and Marlowe recognised it as a hidden message, embedded using a technique called steganography.

Steganography involved hiding information within another medium, such as an image, in a way that wasn't immediately apparent. Marlowe had seen Trix use the same thing to work out a code while hunting Rubicon a few months earlier, so piece by piece, Marlowe followed this digital treasure hunt, each step taking him closer to the forger he wanted to find.

Eventually, he gained GPS coordinates that, when placed into Google images showed him a building on the Rue de la Roquette, a narrow road near the Bastille, with a blue-painted door leading up to floors hidden from view by faded-white-painted wooden shutters.

Arriving there two hours after he first started looking for her, he found a place to sit; a small corner bar thirty yards down the road, with pavement tables under a canopy that boasted "Cafe Biere Limonade," where he ordered himself a small beer and waited, watching the building while pretending to read a magazine.

He had waited, partly because he wasn't sure if he was being followed, but also because he didn't trust where he was going. There was every opportunity for a rival of Helen to place the images on her building after she went, and send Marlowe in a completely different direction – in fact, any of the stages of his treasure hunt could have been corrupted by enemies, rivals, or even security services.

However, one of these processes had used a Vigenère cipher at one point, something he hadn't expected to use, but something he also knew well. A Vigenère cipher was not only a complex adaptation of a Caesar cypher, it was also rather apt, created by Blaise de Vigenère in the sixteenth century, as he returned from his travels to live in Paris.

This was one of the few things that allowed Marlowe to believe he was actually following Helen Bonneville, as not only had she used this cypher before, but she had used the name of her long passed dog, Alfie, as the cypher.

The same dog the picture Marlowe had first found was taken of.

When Marlowe typed "Alfie" into a code solver app he had on his phone, the line of garbled text he had found on the last clue was revealed to be the coordinates of her new location, across the street from where he now sat.

Few people knew of Alfie, let alone knew to use him in a

cypher. The only reason he did was because his mother, a long-time friend of Helen, had dog-sat for her frequently, and this more than anything had made Marlowe feel more comfortable about using this address. But he still wasn't comfortable enough to walk in without spending at least ten minutes checking the place out.

After a while, a familiar face appeared at a doorway. It was a muscled black teenager in a puffer jacket, an obvious pistol in his inside pocket – the muscle that Marlowe had seen the last time he'd spoken with Helen.

Marlowe knew that the chances of him being involved in some kind of trap were small; Helen wasn't a poor judge of character, and if he worked for her then, he likely still worked for her now. With this raising the percentage of the tattered building being Helen Bonneville's new location, Marlowe finished his drink and, with a smile, started across the street. The puffer-jacketed muscle, seeing Marlowe walking towards him, groaned visibly and re-entered the building, moving quickly to shut the door behind him. Marlowe, however, had gained the distance between them even quicker, and placed a foot in the doorway.

'That's no way to treat paying customers,' he said. 'I'm here to see Helen.'

'Helen don't want to see you,' Puffer Jacket said grumpily. 'Not after last time.'

'I'll let her tell me that,' Marlowe pushed past Puffer Jacket, entering a hallway with a narrow staircase in front of him. Walking up the stairs two steps at a time, paying close attention to the faded, peeling wallpaper, Marlowe wondered whether Helen had lowered her expectations of locations, or was picking the first place she could find.

He entered a large, upper-floor warehouse space, with

brick walls and wooden floorboards. It looked simplistic, almost like a turn of the century office. But the thick power cords and Ethernet wires Marlowe could see running along the walls where they met the ceiling showed him there was something far bigger going on. In fact, by simply following the cables, Marlowe found himself in a second, harder to find, office.

Helen Bonneville glowered at him from a table. A middle-aged, dumpy woman with wiry grey hair, chain-smoking cigarettes and wearing a fluffy dressing gown as some kind of housecoat, she looked nothing like the archetypical image of "ID forger" you'd expect to see when hunting a passport.

'You are kidding me,' she said, leaning back and placing down the magnifying glasses that she'd been wearing. 'You're a prick, Thomas. Why in God's name are you here?'

'A pleasure to see you too, Helen,' Marlowe smiled, wondering whether he'd made a big mistake by turning up.

'Because of you, I had to run,' Helen replied coldly. 'I did what I did to help you, but you didn't tell me you were helping some bloody rogue spy try to take down Whitehall.'

'I didn't know at the time either,' Marlowe held up his hands in a peaceful gesture. 'Kate played us both.'

'No,' Helen stood now, facing Marlowe, anger emanating from her every pore. 'She played you, and *you* dragged me into your bloody mess.'

'Fair point,' Marlowe nodded, accepting the blame. 'I didn't mean to cause you any problems, Helen, you must know that.'

'I had Whitehall here for a week after that debacle,' Helen snapped. 'Bloody Joanna Karolides took great joys in auditing me. I think she thought it was Christmas. A chance to take down Helen Bonneville.'

'Yet here you stand,' Marlowe said, looking around. 'Seemingly having done quite well for yourself.'

'Don't take the piss, Thomas,' Helen snapped. 'I lost clients and work because of you. I am *not* in the mood.'

'I paid you for the work you gave me,' Marlowe said. 'And I gave you blanks, professional grade ones that you could use. I'm sure you've made your money back since—'

'I had to use those blanks to gain favours to bring back clients!' Helen snapped. 'Do you know how many forgers live in Paris? How many forgers work around here? It's a cut-throat industry, and I didn't have a single bloody thing I could use to my advantage after you came by!'

'I get that, and I'm here to help you,' Marlowe outstretched his arms. 'A guardian angel returning a favour, so to speak.'

'Yeah, yeah, whatever,' Helen sat back down in the chair, slumping back as she stared at Marlowe. 'What do you want this time?'

'Behold, I bring you gifts,' Marlowe pulled out the wad of blanks, passing them to her. 'There are sixteen government grade blanks here. I need eight used, the rest are yours.'

At this, Helen's eyes narrowed. She knew very well the cost of each of these blanks.

'Quality work,' she grudgingly admitted. 'Taken from several times and locations, too, as I can see there are different print marks. She's been amassing these for a while, I'd say.'

She looked up, as if realising she was speaking out loud.

'Where did you get them?'

'Bridget Summers' go bag,' Marlowe replied, being honest. 'So you know from that, they're solid. They're MI5, and they're from before anybody started itemising them. She went on the run without them. She probably had other bags ready, with more blanks.'

'Ah, Bridget,' Helen replied with a slight smile. 'I hope she's safe wherever she is.'

Marlowe watched Helen as she worked through the blanks. 'You didn't seem surprised at these,' he said. 'You knew exactly where they were from before I even told you.'

'I guessed.'

'Did you guess the sex, too?' Marlowe asked. 'You said "*she's* been amassing these." I never said I got them from a woman. Which makes me think you've seen these, or something similar, before.'

'Well, of course I have,' Helen said, looking back at Marlowe. 'When you came to me with Kate Maybury. I thought these were more from her collection.'

'But this feels different,' Marlowe said. 'When I mentioned Bridget Summers, you didn't ask if she was in prison, as the official story goes. You said, "I hope she's safe wherever she is." You knew she escaped.'

He leant closer.

'Did Bridget Summers gain an ID from you?'

Helen glared at Marlowe. 'I don't appreciate someone asking me – even if I know them well, as if they were my own son – about other potential clients, fictional or real.'

'Apologies,' Marlowe nodded. 'But down the line, if Bridget is out, I am going to have to have a conversation with her.'

'And when you do, I'm sure it will be a fun one. You just won't involve me,' Helen muttered as she flipped through the pages. 'Go on then. What do you need? You're giving me these lovely gifts, but you said you needed eight of them used.'

'Two passports each for four people,' Marlowe nodded, understanding that Helen wanted the subject changed, and for the moment complying. 'I'm one. Trix Preston is another, and ...'

He paused, almost wincing, realising he had to admit this.

'The other two are Marshall and Tessa Kirk.'

'Marshall bloody Kirk is involved in whatever bollocks you're doing?' Helen laughed now. 'And you've dragged his daughter in too?'

'I didn't drag anybody in. But this is important, Helen. It's important enough that by the end, there's a very strong chance we might be burned and on the run,' Marlowe explained, leaning against the desk now. 'I need some solid IDs that we can go to ground with if we need to.'

'Who are you going for?'

'Orchid.'

It was a risk, but one Marlowe felt he could take here.

Helen whistled at this, saying nothing as she stared at the blanks for a long moment.

'I'll only take six,' she said. 'I'll give you ten.'

'Why ten?'

'Because although I haven't heard any of those three mentioned on any back chatter, I've heard your name everywhere, Thomas,' Helen said, looking back at him. 'You want two IDs? Brilliant. They'll be burned before you have time to have breakfast if you're taking on Orchid. I'll give *you* four different IDs. At least that way, when the shit hits the fan, you can leave the others and go take your stupid bloody war somewhere else.'

She started flicking through the blanks.

'I think I might make a couple for myself as well,' she

added. 'All you seem to do is bring bloody trouble down on me.'

'If it helps, I'm willing to soften the blow,' Marlowe smiled, pulling out one of Bridget Summers' wads of hundred-dollar bills, tossing it onto the table. 'There's at least five grand there, maybe even ten. I haven't counted—'

'If you haven't counted, it means it's not your money,' Helen said. 'But I appreciate the gesture. When do you need them by?'

'When can you do them by?'

Helen scratched at her chin.

'I'll need all new photos, data, you know the deal.'

'I can get you that tonight.'

'You manage that, I can have them for you by tomorrow. Say midnight?'

'That might work,' Marlowe nodded as he worked out the timings. 'I'm at a party tomorrow, and after that, things might be a little hot.'

'What a surprise,' Helen said. 'Lose my address, Marlowe. I'll send you a place to meet for these. I'm not moving again.'

'Understood,' Marlowe leant over the desk, writing a number on a notepad. 'That's my new number. Where do you want the images sent?'

Helen considered this, then wrote a website URL down.

'Cloud drive, encrypted, do it from a web cafe within the next couple of hours,' she said.

Taking the address, Marlowe held his hands out.

'Hug?' he asked. 'For the son of your best friend?'

'Piss off, Thomas,' Helen chuckled, already lighting another cigarette up. 'Go cause whatever trouble you're causing again and leave me out of it.'

'Karolides is involved,' Marlowe teased.

'If you kill her, I'll do the whole thing for free,' Helen smiled, the first time since he'd arrived. 'Now bugger off and let me get to work.'

12

PARISIAN PARTY

MARLOWE ASCENDED THE WIDE, MARBLE STEPS OF THE Château de Versailles under the dim glow of gaslit lanterns, each flicker casting elongated shadows onto the ancient stone. A light mist currently hugged the ground, lending the slightest of ethereal airs to the French opulence that stretched as far as the eye could see. He adjusted the black silk tie of his tuxedo, deciding he wasn't going to go "full Bond" for the night, preferring the straight tie to the bow tie and felt the reassuring cool metal of his defence bracelet around his wrist. He knew he wouldn't get a gun through security – even if he was being classed as security himself that night – so the metal chain around his wrist gave him at least some level of comfort.

Each step he took across the courtyard leading to the main entrance resonated with the weight of history; wars had been declared, treaties signed, and kings toppled right here. The grand façade loomed ahead, golden details glittering in the night, as if winking at the cloak-and-dagger games that had unfolded under its roof for centuries.

As expected, security was tight. Men in tailored suits discreetly armed with concealed Glocks and Sigs stood guard at regular intervals, their eyes sweeping the crowd with military precision. Marlowe's eyes met one of the guard's – a tacit acknowledgment of abilities and skills passed between them.

Well, Marlowe had tried to give that impression, anyway.

The guard had given a pretty disdainful look in return. But he hadn't moved towards Marlowe; probably because Marlowe was at the entrance to the event, which meant he'd been through security several times by this point, checks that had actually started the previous day when he first arrived at Gare du Nord Station.

They'd already vetted his invitation, his identity confirmed through layers of digital and human scrutiny before he'd even reached the Palace of Versailles. He couldn't help wondering, however, whether this was protocol for a billionaire's black-tie event, or an overture to something far more clandestine?

Perhaps both, he supposed.

He walked through the towering, intricately carved doors, held open by the uniformed doormen, and stepped into a different world altogether. The Hall of Mirrors beckoned, a spectacle of grandeur and illusion, its expansive mirrored walls reflecting endless crystal chandeliers that dripped from vaulted ceilings like a cascade of golden rain. For a moment, he lost himself in the illusion of infinity these mirrors cast, a never-ending pathway of light and shadow that became a backdrop to the surrounding guests.

Gathering his senses, Marlowe took a flute of champagne from a passing server, still subtly scanning the room for familiar faces. Diplomats, tycoons, politicians, even celebrities, they all stood there; pieces on a chessboard they didn't even know was under them.

It was time to start.

A woman, surrounded by tuxedo-clad men nodded at him from across the hall; she wore a buttercup-yellow evening dress, contrasting with her short, gunmetal-grey hair, a small clutch purse in her hand, which Marlowe knew probably held pepper spray or something similar. Ever since a stranger had appeared in her hotel room, Senator Maureen Kyle had been more than a little paranoid, and for good reason.

'Marlowe,' she said as he walked towards her. 'Is he dead?'

Marlowe smiled at this.

'Ma'am?'

'Brad Haynes. I heard he met you at the hotel,' Kyle replied.

Marlowe nodded at this; that Kyle knew Brad had met with him outside his hotel meant she'd been keeping tabs on him. Which also meant he'd not seen anyone keeping tabs on him, meaning they were better than him.

The thought gave him a brief shiver; not that there was someone out there better, but because he'd not seen them while travelling to Helen's. And, if he'd missed a tail while travelling to Helen, he could have brought a whole world of shit on her head.

'And how did you hear this?'

'I pay the doormen an extortionate amount of taxpayer money,' Kyle replied, a slight smile crossing her lips. 'I've become incredibly paranoid at hotels these days. If you still want him dead, let me know. He's also part of my detail.

Somewhere around here. I'd rather I knew if I was going to have to hide a body.'

Marlowe forced a chuckle, shaking his head.

'We're good,' he replied. It was a simple comment, made to put her at ease, but he was still wondering how much Senator Maureen Kyle truly knew.

She looked across the ballroom, and Marlowe followed her gaze; there, standing with some East European delegates, was Tessa Kirk, Marshall standing behind her, working as her muscle.

'Your friend seems more comfortable with the Russians. Your hacker friend is also here, perhaps?'

'Trix Preston is here somewhere,' Marlowe replied, nodding at her. 'Although I believe she's personally requested for by Joanna Karolides. Will you be talking with her tonight?'

Kyle shook her head.

'Too public,' she said. 'Although I hear there's a more exclusive meeting here this evening. You found your invite for that yet?'

'I couldn't possibly confirm or deny what you mean, Ma'am.'

Kyle actually laughed at this.

'Damn Brits,' she said. 'Always so polite when telling you to piss off and mind your own business. You know "we cannot confirm" is CIA code for "yes," right?'

Marlowe grinned, looking at the agents around the Senator.

'I see you listened to me, and changed your detail,' he said.

'When enemy agents try to kill you, it's time to listen,' Kyle replied. 'These came from a mutual friend in the CIA.

It's why I knew Brad Haynes had spoken to you. And ... our friend.'

Marlowe understood the comment. Sasha Bordeaux was covering Kyle's security while she was here. He wondered briefly what name she gave Kyle, but this was put aside by the sudden realisation that Bordeaux, the woman who claimed she had no skin in the game, was working either on behalf of, or with, Senator Kyle, the Republican from Arizona.

'Maybe we'll talk about it later,' he replied. 'When I've had a drink or two.'

Kyle sniffed, irritated at not getting what she wanted, but not stupid enough to argue for it at such an event.

As the orchestra stirred to life, Marlowe felt the sharp prick of intuition run down his spine, settling in his gut. In a setting designed to overwhelm the senses, his were zeroing in, sharpening and as he glanced around the Hall of Mirrors, Marlowe couldn't shake the feeling that they weren't the only things in the room hiding more than they revealed.

Tessa, doing the same, locked eyes with him – it was only for a moment, but the message was given. *She was ready, and she was nervous.* Marlowe had hoped to keep her out of this, but he knew her father, a few steps behind her and looking like hired muscle, would keep her safe.

Across the ballroom, he saw Ichabod – he still hadn't learnt the poor man's name – who had looked around and also seen Marlowe, his face darkening as if he'd hoped Marlowe wasn't actually going to be there. Marlowe smiled, mentioned to Kyle he was off to get a real drink from the bar, and started walking across the hall – after all, although he was there officially as Senator Kyle's security liaison to the UK, he wasn't expecting to do any liaising on her behalf any time that night.

This was what he was there for.

Ichabod sighed audibly as Marlowe approached.

'Your father will see you now,' he said.

'I never doubted it,' Marlowe replied, looking around the ballroom. 'Shall we move on with things? I'm on the clock here.'

'So we hear,' Ichabod started towards one of the side rooms. 'So we hear.'

The two of them walked across the room, and Marlowe tried to warm the atmosphere between them.

'I never took your name,' he started.

'Because I never gave it.'

'What do I call you?'

'Nothing. By the end of tonight, you'll never need to speak to me again.'

'I've been calling you Ichabod. In my mind, when thinking about you. Based on Ichabod Crane.'

At this, the tall, gangly man stopped, turning in utter confusion.

'Sleepy Hollow?' he asked. 'You see me as the Disney character, or the actor in the recent crime show?'

'Which one's the more capable?' Marlowe smiled innocently. 'Go with that.'

Ichabod didn't believe Marlowe, but he obviously didn't have the time to argue this, and so continued on across the dance floor, Marlowe following behind like a subordinate. They were hurrying towards a corner of the room where a small army of tuxedo-clad guards stood around a booth.

In the booth was a wheelchair, an expensive, electric one. And, sitting on the chair, an oxygen mask strapped to his face, was Taylor Coleman.

Marlowe's estranged father.

Marlowe hadn't expected such a drastic physical change in the man since the last time they spoke, in the Tick Tock Diner in New York only six months or so earlier, and he almost stumbled, catching himself as the guards opened up for Ichabod and Marlowe to sit the other side.

The Taylor he'd met in New York had been more tanned, his hair greying, and even with suits and watches that were worn to give the impression of a man better off than he really was; Taylor still gave an arrogance that made Marlowe fight the urge to strangle him. He'd hired a terrible hitman to try to kill Marlowe, purely to get his son's attention. And then, when facing him across a similar table, he'd given his bombshell statement.

'I have cancer. It's eating away at my lungs. The annoying thing is it wasn't actually from smoking. It was from various carcinogenic shit I've inhaled while working on weaponry. But it doesn't matter now, the doctor says I've got weeks, months, maybe years if I'm super lucky. No one seems to know. Nobody wants to give me a solid diagnosis just in case I prove them wrong and take them to court. But chances are, by the end of this year, you'll be an orphan.'

Marlowe had found any concern for his father – no, he still hadn't earned the right to be called that – for Taylor lasted about half a second, or until Taylor continued with his next comment.

'I brought you here today, because I wanted you to know that when I die, I'm not leaving you anything.'

Now, Marlowe stared at the shrivelled figure in front of him, desperately sucking on an oxygen bottle while talking to another white-haired man, and realised the diagnosis had been pretty much spot on. Taylor Coleman's hair was now also white and thinning, his eyes bulging out of his almost skeletal face, his fake tan now forgotten.

Seeing Marlowe, Taylor spoke to the man, finishing a conversation. The man nodded, rose and walked from the chair. Marlowe looked after him, frowning. He'd seen him before.

'Sit,' Taylor wheezed, waving Marlowe to a seat. 'You wanted to see me. Here I am.'

Marlowe glanced around, realising the guards had all turned their backs. To them, this was a private meeting.

'I need to get into the other meeting tonight,' he said, deciding to cut to the chase. 'St John Steele said I should speak to you.'

'And the other meeting ...'

'Lucien Delacroix, and Orchid,' Marlowe continued. 'And don't tell me you're not part of it, I already know you are. *Arachnis*. Named after the orchid.'

Taylor chuckled weakly.

'You want to deal with Lucien?' he asked softly. 'That can be done. Do you remember my last words at the Tick Tock diner?'

'You told me you let Mum and me down, and you'd send me a gift I wouldn't want.'

Taylor nodded.

'*You will never get what you hope for. Instead, you will always get what you deserve,*' he intoned. 'That's what I said. My last apology to you. And when you got it, I said I hoped you'd use it.'

He waved around, and even this seemed like way too much effort.

'You won't have to wait until I'm dead, Thomas,' he

wheezed. 'You'll get your gift tonight. Yes, I'll be in Lucien's meeting, and yes, you'll be with me.'

He looked at Ichabod, who didn't look happy at this.

'He's your older brother,' he said to Ichabod. 'It's his by right. And you never wanted it, anyway.'

'Wait,' Marlowe looked at Ichabod. 'Are you my half-brother?'

'We're done here,' Ichabod replied, rising from the booth, walking through the guards as they adjusted their jackets, probably making sure any small hidden weapons were easy to grab. 'The second party is about to start.'

Standing up as two of the guards wheeled Taylor, his oxygen tank strapped to the side of his chair, towards a door at the side, Marlowe couldn't help but look over at Ichabod. There was nothing familial about him, and if Taylor had said nothing, he'd never believe they were related.

But, apparently, Ichabod didn't want to be. Which, in a way, was fine.

As they walked through the crowds, Taylor looked back at Marlowe.

'My company has been linked to Orchid for many years,' he explained. 'And I, as my father before me, have been a member of Orchid's highest echelon. Technically, by heredi-tary rules, as my oldest son, you would have been my successor in the organisation, if you weren't a bastard.'

'I don't recall asking to be—'

'You don't get to choose if you're in or out of a secret organisation,' Taylor snapped, wheezing. 'I told you that you wouldn't want it. Yet here you are, asking all about Orchid.'

'Because I'm trying to take Orchid down,' Marlowe hissed, no longer caring if anybody heard. 'I'm not here because of anything that you give me. Orchid is—'

'Orchid is the future,' Taylor interrupted, holding a hand up. 'Do you know who won the war? Americans will tell you they did. The British will tell you it was *Operation Mincemeat* and D-Day that turned the tide, but the fact of the matter was it was Orchid, working with the Office of Strategic Services. Do you know who won the First World War?'

'Let me guess, Orchid?'

'Exactly. Orchid agents have been involved in every single military and espionage activity for the last century,' Taylor was coughing now, waving for someone to twist the nozzle on his oxygen bottle. After a moment, he continued. 'Whether they fought for one side or the other – on most occasions, they fought for both – that's the problem when you have a global organisation built of separate cells, each with their own interpretations of what the rules should be. Even Presidents need to listen when Orchid speaks.'

Marlowe knew this was a comment about McKay, but it brought back the image of the white-haired man Marlowe had just seen, and suddenly, he knew where he'd seen him before.

Harrison Caldwell. The Vice-President of the United States.

They paused as they reached a set of steps; the guards moving to each side and picking the wheelchair up with ease, putting Taylor back down at the top.

Before he moved on, though, he looked back at Marlowe, following up the steps.

'If you think they're the only people who do this, you really should have a chat with the various international orders of Freemasons out there,' he coughed.

They were now beside an almost hidden door leading to the Gardens of Versailles, and a line of guards were checking passes before allowing people through, taking phones and placing them into gold-lined Faraday bags, stopping them from being able to be connected to anything, before passing them back. Marlowe knew nobody would be stupid enough to pull their phone out while in the meeting and, as he looked about to see if anyone was, he saw Tessa ahead, moving through after a few spoken words, before the party with Taylor arrived.

'Arachnis,' Ichabod explained to the guard, passing his phone across.

'We know Mister Coleman,' the guard said. 'But the security can't come in. And neither can *he*.'

This was aimed at Marlowe, and he tensed.

'Mister Coleman's eldest son has an invitation by right of blood, as have I,' Ichabod continued, giving the impression of a man not taking no for an answer, even if he didn't want to be in any room with Marlowe. 'Do you really want to cease tradition on such a night?'

The guards looked at each other, and then turned back into the gardens, where Marlowe saw St John Steele standing, watching the exchange.

He gave a brief nod and then slipped back into the crowd.

'Helps to have high-up friends,' the guard muttered as he waved Marlowe past, placing his phone in a Faraday bag, passing it back and allowing him to join Taylor and Ichabod.

'You're in,' Taylor croaked, waving around the scene. 'Well done.'

The Gardens of Versailles were a sprawling labyrinth of foliage under the moonlight's glow. Lit paths branched off in multiple directions like tendrils, drawing guests deeper into its snare. Marlowe couldn't help himself; he straightened his jacket, the air suddenly chill against his skin, laden with the scent of damp earth and blooming roses.

Statues of Greek gods and goddesses loomed around him, their stone eyes casting judgment, or perhaps sharing silent secrets. The hidden groves and alcoves, which once provided seclusion for royal affairs and covert negotiations, were now awash with a different intrigue, as Orchid agents and allies spoke with subdued whispers floating from the shadows; unspoken alliances and quiet betrayals were taking shape.

Clusters of guests had drifted from the chateau to share in less discreet conversations. Low wrought-iron tables, covered in white lace, were arranged sporadically along the paths, each holding an array of fine cognacs and chocolates. Marlowe knew that right now, the decisions made in these moonlit gardens would send ripples through capitals and war rooms across the globe, and amidst the grandeur and the treachery, he couldn't help but marvel at the paradox, of such beauty serving as the stage for human cruelty.

In the middle of the garden, with a spotlight-lit fountain behind him, Lucien Delacroix stood alone, his hands outstretched in a gesture of friendship.

'The meetings are already beginning, but today is about family,' he exclaimed to the watching guests, looking around. 'This family.'

Marlowe did the same, looking around the gardens, realising Tessa had entered, but now stood alone, while none of MI5 or MI6 seemed to be there.

No.

To the side, Marlowe was surprised to see Peter Lloyd. However, the moment they clapped eyes on each other, Peter seemed to merge back into the bushes, likely embarrassed to have been seen at an event he really shouldn't have been at.

It made Marlowe wonder, though, whether he'd underestimated the man; was Peter larger within the organisation? Or was everyone connected to Orchid here?

Marlowe looked back over at Lucien, realising the man hadn't finished.

'Out there, in the Hall of Mirrors, the greatest minds on the planet mingle with the most powerful politicians and the richest people, all meeting to decide the fate of the world, while we meet here, deciding what to allow them to do,' he said. 'The real power behind the thrones stand right here, and the global population lives or dies at our command. It's an intoxicating feeling, yes?'

There was a murmuring of agreement around the gardens, and Marlowe wondered how many of these Orchid agents actually felt the same. For a clandestine organisation, Delacroix seemed to want to shout it out from the highest mountains.

'For decades, centuries, even, we have been the voice in the shadows, the whispered ideas that shape the planet,' Delacroix smiled. 'We have raised empires and toppled them when they no longer suited our purpose. However, there is talk that it's time to move into the light, and reveal ourselves.'

The murmuring around Marlowe wasn't as enthusiastic as he'd expected. Many of the people here didn't want to out themselves, it seemed.

'The High Council will decide, though,' Delacroix continued. 'And we will comply with their wishes.'

Marlowe liked the "we" added in, as if Delacroix was placing himself with the surrounding people, rather than dictating a remit he was pushing personally.

'We can't go public when we're at war,' a woman, unknown to Marlowe, spoke up now. She was in her fifties, and like Delacroix looked like she came from immense amounts of money, her accent sounding a little West Coast America, maybe Beverly Hills. 'And McKay has told his advisors he wants us removed.'

'All wars end,' Delacroix smiled back at her. 'And this one will end sooner than people think, with McKay no longer a threat to us.'

Until the moment you blackmail everyone's identity with a list, and out whatever secret you have on him, Marlowe thought to himself, watching the surrounding people. He'd noticed that several of whom he'd already decided were security guards were now walking through the gardens, examining the people in there. They were checking Faraday bags, but they were distracted, looking for someone.

They were looking for him. Had his father set him up?

Marlowe slowly clasped his hands together, feeling the steel defence bracelet on his wrist. There'd been confusion at the entrance about it, but he simply explained it was his religion, a strange metal rosary he kept at all times, and they reluctantly let him through. He assumed the guards had guns, but all he needed was to take one gun, and he had a fighting chance.

'We will inform you of our decision in the current days—' Delacroix continued, but paused as Taylor, leaning forward in his chair started to cough, Ichabod frantically adjusting oxygen levels, and placing blood pressure gauges on his father's fingers, examining them as he did so.

'If he's going to die right now, could he do it elsewhere?' Delacroix asked with a hint of amusement.

'He's High Council!' Ichabod shouted back. 'Give him some respect.'

Before Delacroix could reply, however, St John Steele approached.

'He is right,' he said. 'The High Council will gain the respect it's due. From all of you.'

'So speaks the Arbitrator,' Delacroix mocked. 'Well, if we can't remove one thorn from my side, perhaps we can remove another.'

He clicked his fingers and as one, the guards who'd been walking through the gardens suddenly turned to face Marlowe, Glock 17s now in their hands, aiming directly at him.

'We have a sheep in wolf's clothing, an imposter here,' Delacroix smiled. 'Tell me, people. What shall we do with Thomas Marlowe?'

13

JOB INTERVIEW

As Marlowe stared at the guards now surrounding him, guns aimed directly at his face, he realised this wasn't going quite the way he'd expected.

He had, however, considered this as a potential outcome.

'Why the weapons?' he asked with mock innocence.

'Because you are an enemy to Orchid, and everything we stand for,' Delacroix said, shrugging. 'You killed Kate Maybury and Oliver Casey, both upstanding Orchid operatives. Because of that, blood demands blood.'

There was a grumbling around him, as the Orchid agents surrounding him realised who was in their midst, but instead Marlowe straightened, shaking his head.

'I didn't kill Kate,' he replied. 'Someone else did that, stopping her from killing me.'

He deliberately ignored the fact it was Trix, using the special branch gun she'd taken before they'd given chase across London – the last thing he wanted was for Orchid to look to another target to kill. Instead, he gave a small half smile.

'But sure, I killed Oliver Casey. He was a prick and the pair of them were going into business for themselves.'

He turned, looking around the garden now.

'You claim to be loyal Orchid agents,' he spoke loudly now, making sure everyone could hear him. 'But none of you know what you're doing. Every left hand here isn't paying attention to the right hand. Every cell works its own beat.'

He pointed at Delacroix now.

'Only him, sitting in the middle of the web like Professor Moriarty knows what's going on,' he continued. 'And he's decided you're all expendable.'

At this there was a slow muttering of dissension; Marlowe had most likely vocalised what many members had been thinking of late, and the guards raised their guns a little more intently towards his face.

'Let the boy speak.'

It was Taylor Coleman, taking his mask away from his face to wheeze the words.

'You vouch for this man?' Delacroix was quite surprised at the outburst, such as it was. 'You've had nothing but derision for him since I've known you.'

'I would like to know where he's going with this,' Taylor shrugged. 'I have my reasons.'

'Family isn't a reason.'

'Didn't you just start your bullshit speech talking about family?' Marlowe knew he only had one chance. To the side he saw St John Steele watching him curiously and wondered if this was the reason Steele had wanted Marlowe there. To the other side, he saw Tessa slowly moving through the crowd, grabbing a bottle of champagne from a table, holding it by the neck, ready to fight if needed.

'Kate Maybury was part of a splinter cell of Orchid,'

Marlowe said, raising his voice again so everyone could hear. 'They deliberately went against you and tried to steal the data of all agents of all agencies—'

'Why does that involve us?' The older woman spoke now.

'Because it included a list that named every known Orchid agent, and financials connected to anyone funding Orchid,' Marlowe replied. 'Her plan was to take Orchid and control it, blackmailing the agents and financiers to follow her plans.'

Delacroix hadn't moved to stop him, and so Marlowe continued.

'Every one of you lives by secrecy,' he said. 'Imagine being told you'd be outed unless you helped Kate's rogue group? What would you do?'

'They would do whatever I requested,' Delacroix finally replied. 'I'm on the High Council.'

'We've already mentioned you're not the only member of the High Council here, so here's the problem with your statement,' Marlowe shook his head, looking back at Delacroix. 'I was there when Fractal Destiny was used. I saw how Kate was uploading the data to a Swiss server farm that you own—'

'Lies,' Delacroix interrupted, waving his hands almost lazily.

'You were good, but I'm better,' Marlowe ignored the comment. 'I know exactly where the data went, as it all leads to you and your server farm bunker in Switzerland. Or are you about to tell me you don't own a bunker in Saanen, in Bern? You controlled Kate Maybury, and she confirmed it before she died.'

This was a play on Marlowe's part; Kate had never mentioned Delacroix. In fact, until an assassin stated his name, Marlowe hadn't even heard of Delacroix. But now it was time to press forward, keep Delacroix on the defensive before he survived this.

'But you knew this anyway,' he carried on. 'That's why you sent an assassin to kill me outside the Royal Albert Hall.'

There was another grumbling at this point. Marlowe wondered if this was because they were classical music lovers. Some might have even been inside, listening to Rachmaninoff.

'I could show you photos of him,' he said, looking around. 'Many of you have probably met the guy. French DGSE agent by the name of Marc Deschamps. You could probably also confirm which cell he works for in your secret cabal.'

'You talk a good talk, Mister Marlowe, but you don't explain one thing. Why would Kate have told you this?' The West Coast-accented woman asked now, as Delacroix lazily grasped a champagne flute, sipping at it.

Play the card now.

'Because I'm Orchid,' Marlowe said as clearly and as loudly as he could, and, as expected, he heard the loud intake of breath from the people in the garden.

'Bullshit.'

'I was brought in by Bridget Summers.'

'Summers?' Vic Saeed now appeared, confirming Marlowe's earlier suspicions as he stepped from the bushes and into the conversation. 'She wouldn't have done that. You stopped Rubicon. She'd worked for years to get that going, and you told me personally you weren't Orchid.'

'Yeah, she did, and yeah, I stopped Rubicon. For the same reasons that Kate Maybury was stopped. For screwing around with lists. And no offence, Vic, I didn't know who you play for. Why the hell would I mention my position here to an MI5 operative? To someone who might be helping Delacroix blackmail a US President?'

There was an expected intake of breath from the party-goers around Marlowe as he said this, and Vic looked at Delacroix.

'Summers escaped after the Westminster attack,' he said. 'I'm sure we can get a message out, see if she can confirm this from wherever she's hiding.'

'Bridget Summers wasn't Orchid,' Delacroix said firmly, but Marlowe could see his voice was less sure now. Marlowe had hoped for this; he was playing on a hunch, rolling dice that Orchid was so broken into small cells and secret cabals, that nobody really knew who worked for who – even the High Council couldn't be a hundred percent sure.

'Sorry, Mister Delacroix, but yes she was,' Steele spoke now from the side. 'Take my word for it.'

'Bridget Summers worked for Orchid, but also worked with Rubicon,' Marlowe said, looking around, mentally filing away Steele's statement – nothing but a comment, it wasn't conclusive proof, even if spoken from the Arbitrator – and he wondered if it was a lie, stated to give Marlowe time to continue. 'I was brought in to ensure that—'

At this point, he pointed across the garden at Tessa Kirk.

'—*she* wasn't revealed to be a sleeper agent for Rubicon, and an Orchid agent.'

Now, the others turned and looked at Tessa, and Marlowe hoped to God she understood where he was going with this.

'I speak for Viktor Orlovsky,' she said. 'I'm Rubicon, and I confirm what he, and St John Steele, tell you is true.'

'This is nothing but story time!' Delacroix was angry now, and Marlowe, expecting this, held his hand up.

'If I may?' he asked, reaching carefully into his tuxedo.

There was a tense moment as the guards trained their guns on the hand in case he was pulling a weapon. But instead, Marlowe pulled a small penlight torch.

'Ultraviolet light reveals all,' he said, turning on the torch and shining it at the external skin between his thumb and index finger. It still itched now and then but that's what happened when you have a tattoo that's still fresh, and in the light, the people standing closest to him saw a tiny UV tattoo.

Of an *orchid*.

'I tried to stop Kate Maybury because she was working against the interests of Orchid,' Marlowe held the hand up for all to see, the torch shining on the tattoo. 'But I also killed Oliver Casey because he was a traitor and a prick and I won't apologise for that.'

He looked at the stunned Delacroix.

'I killed Deschamps because he tried to kill me, and I got burnt from MI5 for saving a Rubicon operative. You might not like it, but I'm one of you and I'm here to call out your games, Mister Delacroix.'

The guards, now confused on whether they should be aiming a gun at him or lowering their weapons, glanced back at Lucien Delacroix, who started to laugh.

'This is just a joke,' he said. 'This isn't true.'

'Did you take the list?' Taylor now wheezed.

'What if I did?' Delacroix snapped. 'I'm High Council—'

'As am I, and about half a dozen other people in this garden right now,' Taylor croaked, his breath shortening as he half doubled over in his chair. 'Remember that. You need *Arachnis* as much as you need any of the people in this garden right now. But it sounds to me like you've decided many of us have outlived their usefulness.'

Delacroix laughed.

'Mister Coleman, you outlived your usefulness the day you started sitting in a wheelchair with an oxygen bottle strapped to your face. You've got what, weeks? Days to live? Be careful of what you say, lest it become hours or even minutes.'

'I'm dying. That's true,' Taylor said, unconcerned by the threat and strangely, he looked back at Marlowe. 'When I saw you in February, I told you that when I died, you'd get a gift. I told you it would be something you wouldn't want.'

Taylor looked back out at the Orchid agents facing him.

'When I die, my place on the High Council must be filled,' he said loudly, and obviously with great effort. 'And as per tradition, I choose my replacement. I choose my eldest son, Thomas Marlowe, to take my spot on the High Council of Orchid in my place, effective immediately.'

At this, the garden erupted into anger and shouts. Many of the people here had issues with Marlowe, and probably didn't believe what was going on – which, to be frank, Marlowe agreed with. But the chaos that came from this didn't seem to affect Taylor, who looked up as Ichabod replaced his mask on his face, allowing Taylor to gulp in some oxygen.

He then slumped forward in the chair.

'I have last words,' he said, his voice almost inaudible.

Delacroix couldn't help himself. He stepped closer.

'And what would they be, old man?'

'They would be that your time in Orchid is over,' Taylor said, his eyes still bright as he looked back up, his hand moving out from underneath his blanket and a gun in his hand.

Marlowe realised that this must have been what Ichabod had been doing when he'd been adjusting parts of the wheelchair. They'd brought the weapon in past the multiple levels of security, helped because Taylor Coleman was a member of note and part of the High Council. He probably hadn't been examined as strongly as people like Marlowe would have been, and Delacroix must have realised this at the same moment Taylor Coleman fired dispassionately into his chest at close range, three times.

Delacroix seemed surprised and then crumpled to his knees, sliding down, falling onto his side, his eyes still open.

The guards leaped into action, moving on Taylor, yelling for him to put the weapon down. But by now, Marlowe and Tessa had stepped in front, Marlowe dropping his chain from his wrist, and Tessa wielding the bottle like a club.

'This man is a member of the High Council,' Marlowe snapped. 'Drop the guns.'

'He gave up his spot! We heard him.'

'True,' Marlowe shrugged. 'He gave it up for me. So if you're going with that tradition, *I'm* a member of the High Council, and *I'm* telling you to drop your guns.'

The guards looked confused at this, and Marlowe pushed on.

'Delacroix was a traitor to Orchid, and I can prove everything I said,' he lowered the chain, holding up his free hand. With this, the guards, looking for an option to get out of this without dying, looked at each other, confused, and nodded.

The guns lowered, and Marlowe turned back to look at Taylor Coleman.

Taylor had fallen back into his chair now, his eyes shut and a brief staccato wheezing coming from his chest. It took a couple of moments before Marlowe realised he wasn't wheezing or having any kind of attack; Taylor Coleman was laughing. Laughing at what he had done to his bastard son.

It was a gift, and one Marlowe didn't want.

As Taylor Coleman, in one of his last acts on this planet, had not only saved Marlowe's life, but had also destroyed it in the process ...

For Thomas Marlowe was now one of the High Council of Orchid, the organisation he was tasked with destroying.

14

GET OUT NOW

HISTORICALLY, WHEN A KING DIED, HIS SECOND IN COMMAND and advisors would all fight amongst each other to see who would rule if there was no heir. In a contemporary secret society it seemed the tradition continued, as the moment Lucien Delacroix fell dead to the floor every Orchid agent and probable High Council member in the garden realised their future had radically changed. Allies of Delacroix were now looking at rivals, expecting to fight, weapons were being revealed where weapons were not supposed to have been placed, and gunshots – suppressed after all, they didn't want to affect the party inside – could be heard echoing throughout the garden.

Marlowe didn't have a gun, and Taylor's gun had already disappeared, taken by one of his own men, probably now in the garden and guarding their boss. But Marlowe was a man who didn't need a gun, the metal chain bracelet still in his hand. Usually secured by a dragon-head clasp, it was something that not only deflected knives but also, when held loose, became a metre-long whip of vicious steel, a vicious whipping tool he could use as people tried to take him out, a tool he now held waiting for the first attack.

He guessed that in the realm of targets right now in the garden, he was high on everyone's list and the chances were that Taylor had taken this moment to effectively throw Marlowe under the bus, knowing it would cause chaos at a time he wanted to leave. Taylor Coleman had just given everything to his bastard eldest son, whether or not he wanted it.

Tessa grabbed Marlowe by the arm, pulling him away as somebody swung a vicious looking axe-like weapon down towards him, the metal causing sparks to fly as it slammed onto the flagstones of the garden.

'Marlowe!' she screamed. 'We need to get out now!'

Marlowe nodded, still trying to get his head around what had happened. Looking around, he spied St John Steele, watching him from a place of concealment as the chaos raged around him. The man was sipping at a cocktail, and looked like he was actually enjoying front row seats for the show.

Marlowe stormed over to him.

'This was you,' he retorted. 'You knew by talking to my father, I'd set this off!'

'How could I?' Steele smiled. 'I am just an arbitrator. I know nothing of what goes on in a dying man's mind.'

'You lying bastard!' Marlowe wanted to punch the man, but settled instead for knocking the glass out of his hand, sending the drink splattering onto the grass. 'What have you got me into?'

'Well, that was rude,' Steele looked down sadly at the spilt cocktail, before turning back to Marlowe. 'You wanted to take down Orchid. Here's your opportunity. Delacroix was taking it in the wrong direction. Your father ... well, it looked like he just readjusted the course.'

He leant closer.

'But the data is still out there. And whoever gains it will decide what happens. To the agents, to the President, to everyone.'

'Why do you even care?' Tessa, now joining Marlowe, asked. 'What's this to do with you?'

'I've been a loyal member of Orchid for close to a decade,' Steele said. 'But now, it isn't what I joined. The war in Ukraine, the cyber "world wars," this isn't what I expected to see happening now. Everything's moved too far to the left, or to the right. There's no central ground anymore. And an arbitrator needs space to move.'

'Are you telling me you did all this purely to help you defect?'

Steele shrugged.

'You can't defect from a secret organisation,' he said. 'You can only leave. Usually, feet first.'

There was an explosion to the side, where a small gas tank, heating food on hotplates had been struck by something, and now people were running around in chaos. Wives and husbands of members, now realising this wasn't quite the fun secret society shindig they expected and that things were turning fatal, hunting salvation that wasn't coming.

'I think it's time to leave,' Steele said, as if this was the end of a pleasant day, rather than a brutal attack. 'I'll be in touch, Marlowe. Look for Benjamin's Quill.'

This said, he pressed what felt to be a bullet casing into Marlowe's hand, and then sauntered off through the chaos as if he wasn't involved in any of it.

With a silent nod, Marlowe started leading Tessa through the maze of hedges and exotic plants of the garden.

'We need to get out before someone realises we're best left dead beside French billionaires,' he said, but drew to a stop as a dark figure burst from behind a giant fern – one of the guards who'd stood beside Delacroix, now with a vicious-looking knife, glinting under the moonlight. Without breaking stride, Marlowe flicked out his wrist, sending the chain whirling. It wrapped around the assailant's knife-wielding arm and, with a sharp tug, the knife clattered away. Marlowe yanked again, sending the man sprawling into a thorn bush as Marlowe didn't break stride, punt-kicking the attacker in the head.

'Keep going!' he ordered.

They made it another twenty yards before a second assailant, this time a woman, sprang from behind a marble statue, garrotte wire gleaming. Tessa ducked just in time, but the wire wrapped around Marlowe's arm, cutting into the tuxedo sleeve like a cheese wire cutting through a lump of cheddar. With a fluid motion, and ignoring the pain, Marlowe pulled, using the motion to yank his enemy off balance, sending her tumbling into a decorative pond with a splash.

To the right was a wrought-iron gate that led to the main courtyard, but before they could continue a gunshot echoed, a round chipping the stone fountain, next to Marlowe's head. A third assailant, gun in hand, stepped into the moonlit clearing.

Lawrence Jackson. The MI5 operative Marlowe had seen in the Gun Room corridor.

'You're not Orchid, Marlowe,' he hissed. 'You're nothing but a cancer.'

Marlowe pushed Tessa behind the fountain, motioning for her to follow it around. And then, with a grunt, Marlowe swung the chain in a high arc, letting go of it, sending it like a missile at Jackson's head.

It didn't fly true; it was in effect a desperation move. However, instead, it struck the Glock 17's barrel, and was enough to distract Jackson as, using the momentary distraction, Tessa lunged from the other side of the fountain, spearing the rogue MI5 operative before he could turn to her, sending them both to the floor, the Glock now dislodging from Jackson's grip and flying into the air, descending grip-first into Marlowe's waiting hand.

'Stay down, Lawrence,' he said. 'I don't have an issue with you.'

Jackson went to rise, to attack again, but slumped to the ground after Tessa slammed her elbow into the back of his head.

Tessa and Marlowe didn't pause as, using the crowds still running for the exits to their advantage, they slid out through the main entrance, back out into the courtyard that led to the palace itself.

To the right, Marlowe saw Senator Kyle being ushered into a car and knew that at least she was okay – but he couldn't see Brad Haynes, and wondered if the man had even turned up as expected. Also, MI5 and Karolides were missing as well, so the chances were the event had been classed as some kind of terrorist attack, and everyone was getting the hell out of Dodge.

Carrying on, Marlowe now hid the Glock in the waist-band of his trousers, wondering idly if Jackson had run in from outside when things had gone south, or had been inside and grabbed a gun somehow, as either of these were better than the third option; that Lawrence Jackson had been allowed to have a gun in Lucien's presence.

That would be concerning.

The crowd still around them, they ran out of the palace looking for a car, anything that could take them out of here. Marlowe hadn't really considered he'd reach this far, so he hadn't planned that much into this.

'Trix, get us out of here!' he screamed into his phone, as on the other end, a far calmer Trix replied.

'Look to your left, oh grand high wizz wozz.'

Marlowe bit off an answer as he glanced quickly to the left where, avoiding a discarded motorcycle, a limousine pulled up with a screech. The driver's side window, currently a dark screen wound down and the familiar face of Brad Haynes stared at them.

There you are, Marlowe thought.

'Come on,' Brad said as from somewhere else in the garden another explosion went off. 'We need to get you out.'

Marlowe paused, and Brad laughed.

'If I wanted you dead I'd leave you here,' he said. 'Besides, I like Tessa more than you, so just get the hell in.'

Reluctantly Marlowe climbed into the limousine; Tessa getting in on the other side. Brad drove it through the crowds, beeping the horn, and gaining distance from whatever was going on in the palace behind them.

Marlowe slumped back in the seat, nodding at the man sitting opposite him.

'Did you get what you wanted?' Marshall Kirk asked. 'Because it looks to me like all hell broke loose in there.'

'It's a long story,' Marlowe replied, staring down at the

bullet casing Steele had passed him. 'And I need a lot to drink before I can talk about it.'

'Yeah,' Tessa smiled darkly. 'Marlowe's some kind of *king* now.'

15

THE KING IS DEAD

ALTHOUGH TRIX HADN'T BEEN AT THE LOCATION, SHE HAD BEEN involved with monitoring everyone, which meant she'd had to stay connected to the systems, making her way in through the servers, doing whatever magic Trix did to listen in on what was going on. Now, sitting in the limo as it drove through the Parisian streets, Marlowe redialled her number, placing her on speakerphone.

'We need to get somewhere safe,' he said.

'This isn't going to end tonight. Your hotel room or mine?' Trix said down the phone. 'I will point out mine is really cheap, whereas yours seems to be some kind of massive suite.'

'My hotel, different room,' Marlowe smiled. 'You know how I work.'

Trix knew. It was a thing that Marlowe always did. When he was in a strange country, he would book a backup hotel. Sure, it cost him money, but he'd rather spend a few hundred pounds for peace of mind in case something went wrong, and currently, he couldn't be sure whether or not this job had gone wrong. The hotel he'd been booked into by Senator Kyle was extravagant and swish; after all, senators didn't enjoy sleeping in travel lodges or pay-by-night locations. So, Marlowe found a backup room in the same location. Before leaving the hotel, he'd even taken his items and placed them in this additional suite, booked through one of his few remaining pre-Helen Bonneville meeting names.

Marlowe had always followed one rule when booking a backup room; he never went for the cheapest. It was where anyone hunting him would look immediately. After all, if you didn't think you needed the room, you wouldn't look at spending that much "wasted" money on the room. And when hunting a rogue agent, agencies would instantly start looking for the cost-effective options, mainly because of tight operational budgets.

But Marlowe never did that. He'd look for opulent suites and locations that he could book, usually at full price, not even looking at vouchers or codes that would give him discounts.

He wanted to stand out as by doing so he would be ignored.

Amusingly, the suite he'd booked was literally across the corridor from the room he'd been given. Trix knew the number; he had passed her the details. All he had to do was gather a key from reception, placed in an envelope addressed to his fake name.

Once more, altering the situation was Marlowe's speciality.

Arriving at the hotel, Marlowe glanced back at Brad.

'Coming up?' he asked.

Brad thought for a moment and then nodded.

'If you think you can use me,' he said.

'I thought you might have to ask your boss,' Marlowe smiled.

'She ain't my boss,' Brad snapped back. 'I'm my own man. Always have been.'

'Of course you are,' Marshall Kirk smiled in the back of the limousine. 'You've always been your own man. Especially when you're stabbing someone in the back.'

Brad paused and then shrugged.

'Scorpion and the frog, my friend,' he said. 'Never more so when you're talking to spies.'

Allowing the others to park the car in the underground car park, Marlowe had entered the hotel, watching as he walked across the lobby to see if anybody was paying attention to him. It wasn't paranoia if they really *were* looking to kill you and Marlowe was now probably quite a high target, especially as half of Orchid now believed he was the one that was destroying them, while the other half wanted to save his life as some new king in their organisation. Yet another reason to thank his father, preferably with a bullet.

At reception he asked if there was any mail for him using his fake identity and he was passed an envelope containing a key to the suite. Taking this, he waited for the others then made his way up to it, ignoring the room that Kyle had given him.

He quickly opened the door and ushered everyone in, closing it behind him.

The suite was larger than the room on the other side of the corridor and was, in some effect, mirrored. After a second, someone knocked on the door. Marlowe checked through the peephole seeing Trix standing on the other side looking uncomfortable, being so exposed.

He opened the door and Trix entered past Marlowe, as he closed the door behind her.

'This hotel is hot,' she said. 'It's on a few watch lists.'

'How recent?' Marlowe asked.

'Since whatever you did at the party,' Trix smiled. 'You really shit the bed with whatever it was.'

'Marlowe became king,' Tessa grinned. 'It was quite an interesting experience.'

'I know,' Trix replied, already opening her laptop, connecting it to the Wi-Fi with a variety of different devices attached to the side, devices Marlowe assumed hid their location if anybody found them poking around in the servers of some company or organisation. 'While you were having, well, whatever fun you were having, playing spies in ancient and historical gardens, I was linking onto your landline connection to worm myself into their servers.'

Marlowe nodded. This had been the plan from the start, to use the same technology and plan Kate Maybury had used against MI5 and Whitehall, to use against Delacroix. On entering, Marlowe didn't have a weapon on him, but what he did have was a USB receiver built into the base of the UV torch, one that had been filled with data-crunching algorithms and Wi-Fi attachments that could latch on to anything nearby, in the same way that Fractal Destiny had connected through to the servers and started uploading anything they could find.

By the simple act of Marlowe being near Lucien Delacroix with it, Trix had managed, through the UV torch, to hack his phone, his accounts, and the systems that connected him to his personal computer. It was likely the same server farm in Bern they'd discovered earlier, and Delacroix's phone was the perfect conduit. They'd gambled that as the host, he wouldn't have lowered himself to the levels of the others there, placing his phone into a Faraday bag - and this arrogance had been his undoing.

Trix had been there from the start, worming her way into his servers while he spouted platitudes.

'What did you get?' Marlowe asked.

'No money, which is annoying,' Trix shrugged as she was typing. 'I kind of hoped I might be able to get a billion or two before someone realised, but I did find something interesting. The data's definitely in Saanen, which means it's still impossible to get to, but there is coding.'

'What exactly does that mean?' Brad asked, as he opened the minibar and pulled out a beer.

'You know, when you write a cheque,' Trix replied. 'You still use cheques in America, right?'

'Well, we do, but we don't spell them the way you Brits do,' Brad smiled, toasting her.

'Well, in the same way that you sign a cheque to show it's yours, or you sign a contract or anything like that to prove your identity, coders have signatures as well,' Trix explained. 'Things that use – if they need to – lines of code as a kind of digital proof of authenticity.'

'It also helps that coders are arrogant little pricks,' Kirk added, accepting a beer from Brad.

'Well, there is that,' Trix admitted. 'Hackers can be a load of bitchy little queens, but the best hackers out there can't help but put their signature coding into anything they do. Sometimes it's as simple as a small virus which opens a backdoor, allowing them to return into whatever they created, sometimes just to tinker around and see what's been going on. Often it's purely architecture, the way things are built.'

'And the coder who built Fractal Destiny signed it?'

'In a way,' Trix nodded as she typed. 'There're a few complicated automations that divert the data. Custom stuff. And one of these has a coding signature. Coding that leads to one man: Phoenix Elite.'

'Phoenix Elite,' Marlowe repeated. There was something odd about the way she said it, as if disdainful.

'Obviously, that's not his real name,' Trix said. 'In fact, nobody really knows his real name, apparently. He uses it as a moniker, as a denominator. The "o" and "e" in Phoenix are a zero and a three.'

'Of course they are,' Tessa nodded, as if understanding. 'Because just using normal letters is so annoying.'

Trix glared at her.

'You remember when we first met, you aimed a gun at my head?' she asked icily. 'I still haven't forgotten.'

'So what you've found is that the code was created by a ghost?' Marlowe asked, deciding to move the conversation away from the inevitable rematch.

'Yes. But by tracing the coding here, I can see when he last logged into the Bern server, which means he has a backdoor past all the Swiss security, and this gives me a location,' Trix was still typing. 'He won't have been guarding his IP that much, as he's going through a backdoor he doesn't think anybody knows even exists. He always was like that.'

She sat back, a triumphant smile on her face.

'It's linked to a game server,' she said. 'Which means I now know he plays on a particular game server frequented by people based on a GMT time zone.'

'Hold on, what do you mean, "he was always like that?"' Marlowe held a hand up. 'You know him?'

'By rep,' Trix nodded. 'He was part of the same hacktivist group as me about four years ago. Cocky bugger, but probably the best coder I know. And, I'll admit, I only knew the coding signature because I recognised a shortcut he always uses.'

'Will you have a problem when we find him?'

'Christ, no. I haven't seen him around since I started with MI5.'

'So, where are we going?' Kirk sat up. 'Because I'll be honest, I think it's time to dip out of this bloody city.'

'Dublin, by the looks of things,' Trix said.

Marlowe was pacing now, as he thought through the situation.

'Unless you can find out anything else before we have to leave, I think we need to get to Dublin and then to America,' he suggested. 'It's a matter of days now before President McKay has this debate, and if Phoenix Elite has any way of revealing what's going to happen there, we have to get to them fast.'

There was a general nod of consensus to this.

'One other thing,' Marlowe said, holding up the bullet casing. 'St John Steele gave me this.'

Trix took it, examining it.

'Give me a moment,' she said, sitting back, reaching into her laptop rucksack and pulling out some kind of electronic magnifying glass, using the device to examine the casing closely.

'So, what actually happened at the meeting?' Kirk finally asked as he sipped at his bottle. 'I saw you chatting to the Senator, I then saw you chatting to your dad and some white-haired guy, who looked real familiar—'

'Actually, hold that thought,' Marlowe interrupted as he looked back at Brad. 'The white-haired guy. Did you know your Vice President was there?'

'Harrison? He's in Delhi.'

'No, he was there, as I caught him talking to my father before we entered the party,' Marlowe replied. 'Didn't see him on the other side, in the super-secret meeting, but smoke and fire ...'

'Shit,' Brad muttered. 'He's in India. Publicly, anyway. To come here off the books. That's risky. Means something bad's happening. He's a shifty-looking prick at the best of times.'

Marlowe nodded back at Kirk to continue.

'Anyway, I see you talking to your dad after the apparent Vice President of America buggers off and the next thing I know, you, him, and that gangly bloke are going straight through, while I'm being told I can't enter with my daughter.'

'Lucien Delacroix wants to take over the world,' Marlowe said. 'Well, I should say wanted, because Delacroix is now dead.'

'Was it you?'

'Surprisingly, no,' Tessa replied for Marlowe. 'It was his father, Taylor Coleman. Taylor and his company are members of what was called the High Table.'

'The High Council,' Marlowe corrected. 'I'm guessing it's some kind of ruling elite, a group of powerful people from each cabal meeting together. You know, *evil society of evilness* and all that kind of thing. But it seems that when Taylor Coleman said he was going to give me a gift I didn't want, the gift was his position on the Council.'

'Shit,' Kirk said. 'So what, you're super-powerful now, and in with the secret societies?'

'I don't think they're happy I'm a member, if that's what you mean,' Marlowe replied, taking off his tuxedo now, checking the slash on the sleeve from where the garrotte wire cut in, wincing at how close it'd almost been before cutting into skin, changing from his shirt into a dark-blue sweater.

'But you have power now?'

'I genuinely don't,' Marlowe said. 'All hell broke loose before I could ask about it, and I don't think they give instruction manuals.'

'Maybe they do,' Trix said, looking back over at Marlowe. 'You said St John Steele gave you this. Maybe he was working in his role as the Arbitrator.'

'And how do you see that?'

She held up the cartridge.

'Kirk?' she asked. 'You're a gun expert, right?'

Kirk took the cartridge carefully, examining it.

'This is old, Marlowe,' he said. 'I can't be sure, but I'd even say this is an original cartridge, not a replacement.'

'Original what?'

'A 12mm Lefaucheux pinfire,' Kirk replied. 'You can tell by the little metal pin on the side. But it's been altered.'

'There's what looks to be soldered circuitry inside it, and around the edge there are filings. Like someone's stamped a code into the inside,' Trix added.

'I'm not an expert on guns, so what the hell is a Lefaucheux pinfire?' Brad asked.

'It's a pinfire revolver invented by the Frenchman Eugène Lefaucheux in the 1850s,' Kirk replied. 'Unlike the percussion revolvers of the era, the Lefaucheux was loaded with a metallic cartridge with pinfire ignition. That's the little pin on the side, which would be struck into an inverted percussion cap. This allowed for easy loading without the use of fragile paper cartridges, loose caps and ramrods. Didn't last long though as they soon upgraded it to the more common centre-firing bullets.'

He pursed his lips.

'It's the sort of bullet they reckon Van Gogh took his life with,' he added.

'So when would this bullet be used?'

Kirk shrugged.

'In 1858 France became the first country to officially adopt a metallic cartridge for military use, but the Lefaucheux M1854 was around four years earlier, so around then.'

'When did you say Orchid was created?' Marlowe asked.

'Around the time of the Crimean War, which was 1853 until 1856 ...'

He paused.

'Shit,' he said. 'The bullet is probably from the date of Orchid's inception.'

'And the dents around the casing? Deliberate or from firing?'

'This bullet casing was never fired,' Trix shook her head. 'This is completely different. I think this is a key. A circular key that, when placed into a particular lock, takes the information and connects to whatever the circuitry is at the bottom of the cartridge. The circuitry at the bottom opens something.'

'Opens what?'

'If I knew that, I wouldn't be mysterious. I would say this opens a particular box, and we should go there now and see if there's billions of dollars inside.'

At no immediate move to leave the room, Trix sighed.

'I'd say this probably opens something quite bad and important to Orchid. Something that you, as the heir apparent, seem to require. Did Steele say anything else?'

'Yeah, he made a comment about hunting "Benjamin's Quill," or something like that,' Marlowe replied. 'He wants to get out. He's very much "enemy of my enemy" and made a point of saying that you don't defect from a secret agency, you leave, usually feet first. And this isn't the Orchid he wants people to join.'

'So, he was happy when it was some kind of weird boys' club, but now it's trying to take over the world, he doesn't want to play?'

'Pretty much.'

There was a moment of sombre reflection, only broken when Brad smiled.

'I know this one,' he said, looking around. 'I bloody know it!'

Marlowe raised an eyebrow at this.

'You got any dollars on you?' Brad asked.

Marlowe considered this, and then nodded.

'Yes, actually,' he reached into his wallet, pulling out one of Bridget Summers' hundred-dollar bills. 'Like this?'

'Exactly like that,' Brad said, taking it from Marlowe. 'We call these "Benjamins." You know why?'

'Benjamin Franklin,' Marlowe replied. 'On the bill.'

'But that's not the only thing on the bill,' Brad continued, tapping the note. 'Look. Next to him, an ink pot and a quill. Benjamin's Quill.'

Before Marlowe could say anything, Brad slipped the hundred-dollar bill into his pocket.

'So how does a hundred-dollar bill help with the key?' Marlowe asked, ignoring the blatant theft, considering he'd done the same effectively to Bridget.

Trix, on her computer, shook her head, but it was a motion of disbelief.

'Montmartre Cemetery,' she said. 'The Lefaucheux mortuary chapel is there. It holds Casimir and Eugene

Lefaucheux, and it lies on the south-east side of the cemetery ... at plot number *one hundred.'*

Marlowe nodded.

'Where's the cemetery from here?'

'Two miles north.'

Marlowe took the cartridge.

'I'll go look before I sort the next stage out,' he said.

'We'll go look,' Tessa interrupted. 'You might be king for the day, but people still want you dead. And the police will be all over the place.'

'Versailles is fifteen miles to the west,' Marlowe shook his head. 'We'll be safe for the moment.'

'I'm still coming.'

Marlowe sighed, then stopped, holding his hand up for everyone to be quiet. Trix, understanding what Marlowe meant immediately, flicked the light switch, turning off the suite's desk lamps, leaving only the glow of a laptop screen and a small side lamp left on.

Slowly, and grabbing his stolen Glock 17, Marlowe motioned for Brad to pull out his own gun, as he slid across to the main door, peeking through the peephole into the corridor.

Two men stood on the other side.

But they weren't outside his door; they were outside the door they believed he was staying in. One of them was fiddling with the lock, the other one standing guard, watching down the corridor. After a moment, the first one opened the door, the two entering quickly, the one behind already pulling out what looked to be a weapon.

Marlowe looked down at the Glock in his hand; it matched the one the man outside now held, as it was the one Marlowe had taken from him only an hour earlier. He watched once more as, after a minute's wait, it opened again, the two men returning into the corridor.

Peter Lloyd and Lawrence Jackson.

Apparently, MI5 and Orchid's finest.

'Find out if he booked any other rooms,' Jackson hissed as he looked around the corridor. 'I want this ended swiftly and with extreme prejudice.'

'But he's High—'

'I don't give a shit about the word of a dying arms dealer,' Jackson whispered coldly. 'Thomas Marlowe is a traitor, a spy, and tonight he dies.'

16

GRAVEROBBING

'YOU NEED TO CALL THEM,' JACKSON SAID, AS MARLOWE watched through the peephole. 'Tell them we want the whole bloody place under guard.'

'We don't even know if he came back here! We should tell Vic we're doing this!' Peter replied.

'Do you need to tell Vic everything?' Jackson answered mockingly. 'You said you were ready for Orchid. Are you telling me now that perhaps we should just let you go?'

'He's a member of the High Council now.'

'His father made him nothing. He's no more Orchid than the Rubicon bitch who stood beside him.'

At this, Marlowe saw Tessa straighten out of the corner of his eye, and he waved her down.

'As you said, she's Rubicon. You can't deny that,' Peter argued through the door.

'I can deny whatever I damn well want to,' Jackson was looking up and down the corridor now. 'I came into the service with Oliver Casey, and he killed him, unarmed and in cold blood, on a motorway in front of witnesses. He was trying to bring us down, destroy us. You've been in Orchid what, ten minutes? Don't start telling me what Orchid wants to or doesn't want to do. What they want is Marlowe dead, and McKay kept in power until the election.'

'You don't know that.'

'Caldwell said it himself, right before Delacroix started talking,' Jackson hissed, confirming Harrison Caldwell had been in the gardens that night. 'McKay's useful until the debate. After that it's anyone's guess.'

'Well, we'll find out when the debate happens, won't we? If the High Council want him gone, he'll be removed. Simple as that.' Peter was strangely argumentative, and Marlowe wondered whether this was because he didn't like Jackson, or because he believed what he said.

They both looked down the corridor now and as Jackson looked around his eyes scanned across the door opposite him.

Marlowe wanted to shrink away as Jackson's gaze met his eye. He knew that if he moved, a slight change in light might reflect through the peephole, and Jackson would know he was being watched.

'Find out from the hotel where they'd be staying,' Jackson said, looking away. 'Marlowe likes to book backup rooms. Check if there's one here. Or if he's gone somewhere else, find out where Marshall and Tessa Kirk are staying. He may have gone with them, too. And check that computer bitch. She'd go for something stupidly cheap, even though she has expensive tastes.'

Trix, who could hear what was being said across the door, glanced up indignantly, but had the good sense not to reply.

Marlowe waited, watching the two men leave before turning back to the others.

'We give them ten minutes, and then we leave. This is serious now.'

'Where do we go?' Marshall said.

'Helen Bonneville has identities for us,' Marlowe replied. 'We take them, we use them to go to Dublin.'

'What about me?' Brad asked.

'You're not technically part of this, Brad,' Marlowe said. 'Go back to Sasha, tell her you met with us, and tell her what you think she needs to know, especially about Caldwell. Against my better will, I trust you to do the right thing. Then find your own way to meet us in Dublin. Sorry, but I didn't think of making you a fake ID.'

'Why would I need some Brit fake ID when I could have just gained one from God's greatest agency, the CIA?' Brad smiled. 'So you want Sasha on board, or to leave us alone?'

'Depends on whose side she's playing for,' Marlowe said. 'It looked like she was playing for Kyle's team tonight. We're giving you the benefit of the doubt because we know you. But, at the same time, I'm cautious about what you'll do ...'

'Because you know me. I get that.'

'If you're on our side, that's great. But if you and her are playing us, it *will* end badly.'

'I'll not go to Paddy land. I'll go back to Washington and find out what's going on with the debate,' Brad nodded. 'It sounds like something's going to be aimed at it, and I'd rather we didn't kill the President.'

Marlowe grabbed his bag, pushing his tuxedo into it.

'Grab your items, children. Meet me at the Bastille just after midnight,' he said. 'Leave anything you don't need, but don't leave your passports. We want them to think we're still travelling on IDs they could find.'

'What are you going to do?' Tessa asked.

Marlowe considered the question.

'You and me? We're going to pay our respects to the dead,' he said coldly. 'Because I think I'm not being told the whole story.'

MARLOWE'S FOOTSTEPS ECHOED AS HE AND TESSA APPROACHED the green metal gate of Montmartre Cemetery. The entrance was deceivingly basic, a stark contrast to the intimate tangle of plots and pathways that lay within. However, the gates were out in the open, on a corner of the road that led onto the Rue Caulaincourt Bridge, which, even at eleven-thirty at night, was still busy.

Marlowe, however, had been here before, and even though he knew the south-eastern plots were only a matter of moments along the pathway the other side of the gate, this was too open. Instead, they carried on south, over the bridge, turning right at the end, entering a twenty-four-hour multi-storey car park that at this time of the night had nothing entering, and used the raised sides of the ramp to give them enough height to climb over the wall, landing on the south side of the cemetery, just south of the Chemin Saint-Eloy. There was a staircase heading down on the other side, leading to another entrance, but that was guarded by an even higher wrought-iron gate that was impassable from this side of the wall.

Luckily, now they were here, they didn't need it.

Without speaking, they immediately took the descent down the stairway to their right, the one that offered a view of the sinking lower levels of the cemetery, where the terrain itself seemed to fold inward. The vertical layout of this place was a unique trait, lending it a strange sense of depth and layers, as if the dead themselves were stacked upon each other, watching them walk past in tiers. Montmartre Cemetery had been built on an abandoned quarry, after all, and the terrain matched what was once there, rather than trying to change it.

Marlowe's shoes crunched on the gravel path as he navigated around clusters of closely packed graves. Here, the tombs were not spread in regimented lines but assembled like a tightly knit community; old crypts and newer gravestones intermingled, each trying to claim its own space in this finite place of rest.

They paused before they passed beneath the stone bridge that connected two sections of the cemetery, the bridge that moments earlier they'd walked across, convinced they heard someone nearby, but it was just people walking past on the bridge above them, laughing at some conversation Marlowe would never know of.

Walking under the bridge, following the path up and to the right as it wound through the cemetery, arriving at the south-east corner, the Cheim des Gardes, Marlowe's eyes fell upon a narrow mortuary chapel. Above the green door was a single name.

LEFAUCHEUX

At the base of the door was a symbol, a wreath with winged pillars within. However, there was no visible keyhole that fitted the cartridge and the door was locked.

'We can pick it?' Tessa suggested, but Marlowe was already frowning as he looked at the chapel.

'I don't think it's inside,' he said. 'Look around.'

Using the light from the street on the other side of the wall, Marlowe walked around to the back, where he found another message, chiselled into the stone.

CONCESSION A PERPETUITE
N. 100 ANNEE 1849

Marlowe knew enough French to know what this meant; "the tomb and its contents remained here forever."

And its contents.

Marlowe knelt, brushing away the base of the stone, looking for something.

The chapel had a two-foot-high base of stone, a different style and slightly wider than the ones above it. As he looked up, he saw a small circle about a foot from the join, about half an inch in diameter. Pulling out the cartridge, he placed it against the hole, a literal "O" shape with a centrepiece of stone in the middle, and saw it fitted perfectly. Sliding it in, he found the pin stopped the cartridge from entering all the way, and he could use the pin as a lever to twist the cartridge in a clockwise direction. As the pin hit twelve o'clock, there was a flash of light, some kind of slight electrical discharge, and he heard a gasp from Tessa at the side.

'The door just opened,' she said.

Quickly, Marlowe removed the cartridge and walked around the chapel, pausing at the door and carefully opening it, turning on a torch, quickly scanning the room. On the wall was a list of the dead inhabiting the chapel, likely buried inches under their feet. On the back wall were three stone friezes of flowers.

The middle one consisted of orchids.

Marlowe walked over to it, picking it up. At the base was a

similar circle to the one on the back of the chapel. He placed the cartridge in a second time, twisting like he had before, and there was a click, and a small cavity opened up at the base of the stone.

Looking into it, Marlowe could see a list of numbers and letters painted onto the base, so quickly took a photo before closing it back up.

'I'll guarantee someone just got an alarm we're here,' he said, pulling the door closed, and looking around. 'We need to get out fast.'

They moved back the way they came, but stopped as the harsh lights of a car's headlights started approaching them down one of the wider roads.

'Quickly,' Marlowe pulled Tessa to the side, behind one of the tall chapels that lined the edges of the Cheim des Gardes, dragging her deep into the shadows.

'Security guards?' she asked, curious.

Marlowe shook his head.

'If they were doing a pass, they would travel a particular direction; work from north to south, east to west, something like that. Those guys? They're coming straight for us, almost as if they knew we'd be here.'

He looked back at the mortuary chapel.

'Looks like somebody did get an alarm,' he said.

The car pulled up outside the mortuary chapel. Marlowe held up a hand to stop Tessa from replying to his comment as, outside the chapel, men climbed out of the car. Both were in security uniforms, and both held what looked to be large Maglite torches, shining them around the cemetery.

Walking towards the door, pushing at it, they were quite surprised that the door was open, and the torches were aimed into the chapel, the two men speaking rapid and argumentative French.

Tessa glanced at Marlowe.

'I don't speak French,' she whispered.

'I do,' Marlowe held a finger up to silence her as he listened, straining his ears to hear what was being said.

The two men talked to each other, turned around, shone torches over the cemetery again and then climbed back into the car, driving off.

After a couple of moments, Marlowe nodded to Tessa. It was safe to move.

'What did they say?' she asked.

'They were surprised the door opened,' Marlowe replied. 'But they kept saying "they did it." As if they knew there was more than one person in there.'

'Camera?'

'Maybe. Hopefully, we'll be nothing but shadows. They went inside and somebody said, "the orchid has been moved." Which suggests they knew that was the important thing.'

'Shit,' Tessa swore. 'How many of these keys do you reckon exist?'

'That's a question we might hear the answer to soon,' Marlowe said. 'Because another word I heard as they were walking off was "arbitre," which in English means arbitrator.'

'They know St John Steele still has one of the keys?'

'Possibly,' Marlowe replied. 'Or they're going to contact him about this. They're security guards. They're probably not that high on the food chain.'

He tapped her on the shoulder.

'We should go now, though,' he said. 'They'll be looking for us.'

'How do we—'

Tessa didn't finish what she started, as suddenly they were hit with bright lights as the patrol car, having turned around, sped towards them, a siren on top blaring.

Marlowe, cursing his idiocy pushed Tessa to the side, pulling out the Glock he had stolen from Jackson earlier that evening and fired three shots, the rounds hitting the driver's side tyre. The driver, not expecting this swerved hard to the left, and the car flipped, rolling onto its side, slamming against a row of monuments and gravestones.

'Now!' Marlowe yelled, pulling Tessa behind him. The two of them sprinted away from where the car was, down the Cheim des Gardes, towards the tunnel under the bridge. Marlowe knew they didn't have time to go any further before the guards started following, so instead of going for the tunnel, he pulled her to the right, towards the green door that guarded the entrance to the cemetery. He was relying on the cemetery doors being closed and padlocked to stop people entering rather than letting people escape; after all, the people in the cemetery weren't likely to be getting up anytime soon.

And he was right. The door was locked with a bolt, a lock that could be opened from the inside, with the key still in it, and a small bar across the middle. And with some effort, Marlowe could push the door wide enough for the two of them to escape through.

Now out onto the main street, Marlowe pulled Tessa quickly along the road, away from the entrance to the cemetery, deep into the narrow Paris streets. In the distance, the two-tone siren of the French police could be heard approaching. Marlowe paused for a moment, trying to triangulate it, but the tall buildings made it sound like it was coming from all directions – which possibly it was, as he had no idea how many police cars were now approaching them.

Running quickly, the two of them slid into a dark alley. Running to the end and, with nowhere else to run, climbed up a fire escape, moving on to one of the buildings' long, grey, sloped roofs, following it along for half a block before finding themselves at a dead end.

Climbing down by moving from balcony to balcony, as they dropped the four storeys, they realised they'd made enough distance away from the sirens, and for the moment, they were safe.

Taking a deep breath, Tessa laughed, as the adrenaline left her body.

'I've never been so scared about breaking into a graveyard,' she said.

Marlowe raised an eyebrow.

'Something you do often?' he asked.

'Tom, I come from Essex,' Tessa chuckled. 'All the churches there had graveyards I'd hang out in as a kid.'

She leant closer, giving a salacious wink.

'I even lost my virginity on a raised gravestone,' she said. 'But don't tell Dad, yeah?'

Marlowe didn't want to know any more, so quietly and stiffly nodded.

Tessa, giving him one last smile, strolled off back towards the Bastille.

Marlowe tried to shake the image of a younger Tessa on top of the gravestone. She was attractive, and the last thing he needed was a distraction, especially when the object of his affection had been trained by Spetsnaz from the age of ten. So, shaking himself back into reality, Marlowe checked his watch and called out.

'Meet your father. I'll find you afterwards.'

'Not coming with me?'

'No,' Marlowe said. 'It's time for me to see an old friend about some passports, and maybe have a little chat. We're being chased all over the place, and it's starting to piss me off.'

17

PASSPORTS

MARLOWE HADN'T HEARD FROM HELEN BONNEVILLE, AND THE clock was now past midnight. So, deciding not to wait for whatever location she was going to give, he headed down to the same location he'd found her before.

Puffer Jacket was standing out in the front.

'She said she'd send you a location when she was ready,' he said.

Marlowe nodded.

'She also said she'd be ready by midnight,' he said, tapping his watch. 'We've gone past midnight. So, I'm not the only one who broke a promise today.'

Puffer Jacket nodded and tapped into his phone. Marlowe hadn't checked as he did it, but he guessed it was a message to Helen, informing her she had a visitor.

After a moment, another text arrived. Puffer Jacket looked at it and showed it to Marlowe.

'You know the address?' he asked.

'My phone has a map app. I can find it.'

'Then she'll see you there in ten minutes.'

Marlowe looked up at the building behind Puffer Jacket.

'I could just go in and see her,' he said. 'I'm on a bit of a deadline right now.'

'She's not here,' Puffer Jacket replied. 'She's with a friend.'

'At midnight,' Marlowe smiled. 'I'm so glad to see she's paying attention to my work.'

'Your work was finished hours ago,' Puffer Jacket smiled back in response, but his voice didn't emanate any warmth. 'Looks like you're not as important as you seem to think.'

'You'd be surprised how many people have told me the opposite today,' Marlowe replied, tipping his imaginary cap to Puffer Jacket before walking off. 'I'll meet her at the location, it seems.'

He wondered if this had been deliberate – Puffer Jacket waiting for him to arrive, the address not being sent until now, constantly making sure Marlowe couldn't arrive early to check out the location. As it was, the meeting was in ten minutes, and going from the map app, he had just under nine and a half to get to it, meaning Marlowe arrived effectively at the time he was supposed to, with no chance to look around, or check for traps, enemies, or double crossing.

The meeting was in a sheltered courtyard next to St Margaret's church, on the Rue Saint-Bernard, the spires of the neoclassical, minimal building casting a shadow against the night sky. The night was turning cold. It was the early hours in the morning, and Marlowe regretted not picking up a jacket. He did, however, have a weapon tucked into the back of his trousers, just in case, but even that offered no comfort against the cold.

There was movement beside the church, and Marlowe saw a woman walk out of the shadows, heading towards him. It wasn't Helen Bonneville, but it was a woman he'd not expected to see again – no, actually, it was a woman he *had* expected to see again, but in an off-the-grid MI5 black site down the line.

She was in her late sixties, maybe early seventies, and the asymmetrical haircut she'd had the last time she'd seen him was now growing out, the white, buzz-cut side on the left now almost as long on the right. No expression on her face; no revelation of whether she was happy or angry to see him, although even in the dark, he could see her green eyes were as piercing as ever.

Marlowe waited for her to stop in front of him before he nodded.

'Bridget,' he said. 'I'm guessing you're now the go-between for Helen Bonneville?'

'Only in passing,' Bridget Summers replied softly, keeping her voice low. 'I asked to be the one who met you. I needed to speak to you.'

'You and I have nothing to say. What you tried to do—'

'Is nothing compared to what Orchid is going to do,' Bridget interrupted. 'Did you think I didn't know about it? I heard what happened in the Gardens. How you showed your little fluorescent orchid tattoo. If you want, I can show you mine. It probably means as much as yours does.'

She gave a smile, half-mocking, half-rueful.

'As I understand, you're going up in the world these days. Long live the king and all that.'

Marlowe glared at Bridget. She might have seemed innocuous, but she was a Rubicon agent who'd worked with Raymond Sykes, Martina Shaw and Baroness Levin to take down the government with a dirty bomb in Westminster, while trying to frame Marlowe and Marshall Kirk for the attack. He'd thought Curtis had taken her in after Tessa and

Emilia Wintergreen had halted her and Shaw in the Gardens, but recently had realised that obviously hadn't been the case.

She was still on the Rubicon list, though; Marlowe's sacrifice had been for Tessa, not for her.

'How did you get out?' he asked.

'While the chaos ensued at the end of the Westminster attack, I was able to slide through the cordon before anyone realised. An elderly lady, hunched over and terrified, is often ignored when police run around looking for suspects. And I'm very good at playing parts, as I suppose you know. I understand Marshall's here?'

'He's around.'

'Can you pass him a message for me? Tell him it was nothing personal.'

'Sure,' Marlowe growled, tiring of the dance. 'I'll tell him how you're terribly sorry for what you've done and how you promise never to do it again.'

Bridget just watched Marlowe, as if expecting him to say something more, before shaking her head.

'The wisdom of youth, convinced that you know everything. Well, young king, it seems you don't know *anything*.'

'You're right,' Marlowe replied. 'For a start, I don't know if you're an enemy or an ally right now. You've been both in the past.'

'Are you looking to take down Orchid?' The question was basic, blunt, and emotionless.

Marlowe considered the question.

'The thought had crossed my mind,' he replied carefully. 'And Wintergreen would like nothing more than to see them destroyed.'

'You still dance to Emilia's drum?' Bridget shook her head sadly. 'After everything that bitch did to you.'

Marlowe shrugged.

'What can I say? King and Country always rang true for me.'

'It was Queen and Country for me,' Bridget snapped back. 'I've told that lie to myself for decades. Don't use that one on me. Come back to me when you've walked as many miles in my shoes as I have.'

She looked around, as if deciding she'd also had enough of the conversation, pulling an envelope out of her pocket.

'This is from Helen. I've not looked at it. I don't care what's going on.'

'Then why are you here?'

'I know you took my go-bag,' Bridget shrugged as she looked around again, and Marlowe wondered if she knew something he didn't. 'I recognised the blanks. And if you took these, then you took my crypto wallet – a chunk of money I'd like back. Trix Preston is probably trying to break it, but only I know how. You can keep the dollars and the pounds. You've probably already spent them by now. I'd like the cryptocurrency, to give me a little "retirement fund," so to speak, and the gold bars. You have enough bloody gold already. You don't need mine.'

'Trix was thinking of starting a collection.'

'Tell her to do it with her own money.'

Marlowe considered this, and then nodded.

'We don't have it here. It's back in London.'

'That's fine by me,' Bridget smiled. 'I'm going back tomorrow. Where would you like to meet to drop it off? And my notebook?'

'Your notebook is empty, apart from one page.'

'Then send the page,' Bridget shrugged. 'You know, when you pick them both up in "London."'

Marlowe smiled. Bridget knew he was probably lying. And he was. The stick was back in his bag.

'Give me your number, and I'll send you a location.'

Bridget's lips thinned as she worked through the situation, and Marlowe knew she was thinking the same thing he was wondering. *Would she be walking into a trap? If she arranged a separate trap for Marlowe, who would double-cross whom? And how would they play it?*

Eventually, she nodded.

'Tell Marshall to use the ways we used to connect,' she said. 'That's all I ask.'

Marlowe nodded, placing the passports into his pocket.

'Thomas,' Bridget's voice was crisp, melancholy, and Marlowe looked back up at her. 'It wasn't personal, you know. You were a means to an end – an asset to be stripped. That's what they trained us for, in Rubicon. In MI5, too. No matter who you are, it's purely business.'

She turned to go and then stopped, looking back.

'I saw Tessa is with you,' she said. 'Saw her photo. I also heard she spoke to Viktor Orlovsky. You should be careful of that, as Orlovsky's very good at finding stray dogs, and bringing escaped ones back under his care.'

'We'll see,' Marlowe said, turning now and walking away from Bridget. He felt her staring at him from behind, hoping she hadn't arranged for a sniper to be watching him as well. But there was something she had said at the end, something that rang false. She claimed she hadn't looked at the passports, so wouldn't know the names, but just admitted she'd seen Tessa's photo. Marlowe was pretty sure that Bridget had flicked through the passports and now knew every single one of the names Helen had used. That worried him, especially as two of her last words rang through his head.

'You were a means to an end – an asset to be stripped. That's what they trained us for, in Rubicon. In MI5, too.'

'Orlovsky's very good at finding stray dogs, and bringing escaped ones back under his care.'

Marlowe trusted Tessa, and he was pretty sure this was an attempt by Bridget, for some reason, to cause discord in the group.

But he was only pretty sure, not certain.

And that worried him.

MARLOWE HAD HIS LATE NIGHT MEETINGS, BUT TESSA KIRK HAD hers as well. She didn't head to the Bastille immediately. Instead, she diverted east, heading more towards The Basilica of Sacré-Cœur de Montmartre and the Place du Tertre. She'd been given the address of a small Armenian delicatessen there, one that stayed open into the early hours of the morning. Upon arrival, she saw it was still open, with a couple of elderly men sitting outside playing chess, even though the party goers were now starting to go home.

She was still wearing the party dress she had worn to Versailles, now a little muddy and scuffed following her clamouring around Parisian cemeteries, and as she entered the cafe, she assumed that she probably looked a bit of a state.

The woman behind the counter, a standard deli-style barrier that showed a variety of sandwiches and rolls, probably ones that had been there for days and were purely "display purposes only," glanced up as she entered, her eyes narrowing. She was middle-aged, stocky and gave the impression of someone who, if you didn't pay the right amount of money, would take you apart with a meat cleaver. She glared at Tessa as she arrived, as if expecting some kind of confrontation, but Tessa knew that even with her battered dress, she probably looked a little higher class than the usual clientele.

'What can I get you?' the woman asked, her accent heavily French. It was almost as if she knew who Tessa was.

'Thank you for speaking English,' Tessa smiled.

The woman, in return, gave a non-committal shrug, as if she couldn't care less what the new customer wanted. Tessa walked to the counter, lowering her voice.

'Orlovsky sent me,' she said.

At this, the woman's demeanour changed. No more was she grumpy or annoyed at this guest; now, she suddenly smiled, her posture changing, now deferential to Tessa.

'Have you travelled far?' she asked.

'There and back again,' Tessa replied. 'Crossing the Rubicon many times.'

The woman now beamed widely.

'Where did you train?' she asked.

'Averkyevo.'

'Spetsnaz?'

'Among others,' Tessa shrugged.

'Awakened?'

'No,' Tessa shook her head. 'I work for myself and others.'

'And Viktor has brought you to me because ...' The woman was still a little suspicious.

'He told me if I was in trouble, I should contact you,' Tessa explained. 'To pass a message back to him.'

The woman nodded, motioning for Tessa to join her at the back end of the delicatessen. Tessa followed her and it was only as she reached the other end, she realised the woman held a snub-nosed Walther PPK aimed directly at her.

'Tell me your message,' she said coldly.

'Do we need the gun?'

'Viktor and I ... well, we have had our problems over the years,' the woman smiled. 'Your message could be something I don't like. Maybe an action. Maybe you were sent to kill me —'

'Orchid.'

It was one word, but it was enough to pause the woman.

'You are one of them?'

'No,' Tessa shook her head again. 'Orlovsky's name got me into a meeting. You will hear later the billionaire Lucien Delacroix was shot—'

'Oh, I know he's dead,' the woman held her hand up to stop Tessa. 'We already have that information. But it wasn't a gunshot that killed him. Apparently, he suffered a heart attack.'

'If a heart attack can be caused by a bullet, then sure, why not,' Tessa smiled. 'The truth is, he was shot by an Englishman named Taylor Coleman, shortly after Taylor Coleman gave his position on Orchid's High Council to his son, Thomas Marlowe. Also, Harrison Caldwell was there.'

'Is this a report or are you telling me this to prove your loyalty?'

'Can't it be both?'

The woman lowered her gun, deciding finally that Tessa was obviously some kind of ally.

'What do you need?'

'A contact in Dublin and one in Washington,' Tessa replied. 'That's the journey we're going to be taking. And tell Orlovsky he needs to be ready, because something bad's about to happen in America – and I think it will affect him in the process.'

The woman nodded, and asked for a number that she could pass the details across on, and Tessa gave her a proton email address. This was something that Trix had suggested they all should do – it was an old email app, older than Gmail or many of the others, but it was known as the "hackers email," as it gave a far more enhanced level of anonymity and privacy to the user.

This given, the woman, who still hadn't given her name nodded, placed the gun away, reached behind her and picked up a paper bag.

'Here,' she said. 'You look famished.'

'It's been a long day,' Tessa grinned, taking the bag, and with a final nod, walked out of the delicatessen, noticing as she walked across the street that the two men hadn't moved a single piece since she'd entered.

They weren't there to play chess. They were there to keep an eye out. I wonder how many of these Orlovsky has. Maybe this was why he now ran his own deli? Is this a mafia of delicatessens?

A block away from the delicatessen, she finally glanced into the paper bag. In it were three small pastry rings – poppy-seed sushki, from the looks of them – and a USB stick.

Placing the stick into her clutch bag, and tossing the paper bag of sushki into a bin, Tessa continued towards the Bastille, and the others.

18

IRISH EYES

RATHER THAN TAKING THE EUROSTAR TO LONDON, THEY'D flown from Paris to Dublin the next morning, using the first of their fake passports. As some of the passports were European Union ones, they had an easier journey getting through customs, with Ireland still being part of the EU after all.

Marlowe had felt this was the better of the options they had, as standing in a longer queue meant more chances to be picked up. Even so, the paranoia of wondering whether everyone in authority were part of some secret society started to weigh heavily on him for the entire journey. He had been like a bear with a sore head, glaring out of the window, only really speaking to Marshall to inform him that Bridget Summers was alive, on the loose, and expecting a message sometime soon.

The first thing they did upon arriving in Dublin was book a hotel, once more under fake names and picking the nicest suite they could find while Marlowe picked a second one down the road under a more recognisable name – well, to a particular person – just in case. Trix then disappeared off into the Temple Bar, looking for an old hacker friend she had once dealt with to help with the codes she had; the ones from both the orchid stone and the notebook, while Marlowe sat down and worked through what they had.

The news was already reporting a terrorist attack at the Château Versailles. The story, however, didn't mention secret organisations meeting in gardens. Instead, it aimed at the more political guests within the outside party, explaining that these were likely the targets, with some nameless organisation trying to make some kind of statement.

According to the news, Joanna Karolides, Senator Kyle, Chancellor Kohl and half a dozen other various dignitaries had likely been the targets of the event, all of whom had escaped, thus proving the terrorist attack had been effectively a failure, the only casualty being Lucien Delacroix, who had unfortunately suffered a cardiac arrest while there.

Marlowe wondered if this was a story given by the government, or by Orchid. After all, if you're a top-secret society, the last thing you want people to know is that you're having problems.

Maybe it was by the government ... and Orchid?

Marlowe shook his head, trying to shake away the conspiracy thoughts from his head, and started to doom scroll through the internet, looking for information he could find. He had a page open, a server Trix had organised, where anyone who tried to contact a long dead number could leave a message if it was still available, allowing Marlowe to keep in contact with assets while on the run.

He saw he had a voicemail on there from his now forgotten phone. Playing it, he heard the voice of Vic Saeed.

'Marlowe, I don't know where you are, but we need to talk. I

don't believe you're Orchid, and you've got yourself into a position
you won't be able to get out of. You know where to find me.'

Marlowe leant back as the message ended, idly scratching at his hand. He'd had the tattoo placed there the day after Wintergreen tasked him on this mission. He knew it'd take time to find his way in, and that time would reduce the inflammation on the tattoo, making it look like the tattoo had been there longer than it really had.

He was glad he'd done it. He felt the tattoo saved his life, as nobody had been able to prove he'd been lying.

It still itched terribly, though.

Tessa and Marshall were in another room down the corridor, and Trix had taken a room on another level, claiming that the Wi-Fi was better on the second floor. Also, if somebody was going to turn up and kill everyone, as she stated it, she wanted to be as far away from Marlowe as possible, which he understood.

In fact, there was nothing more to do until Trix could speak to this mysterious hacker friend of hers, hopefully to not only find the location of Phoenix Elite, and work out Bridget's notebook text, but also work out what the code in the Paris chapel had meant.

So Marlowe took a break and saw the sights. Of course, he wasn't actually intending to *see* the sights. This was just what he told himself as he traversed the streets of Dublin. What he *really* wanted to do was work out if he'd been followed from Paris, and the easiest way to do that would be to place himself as a target and see who followed.

After several streets, he started to relax; it seemed nobody had found him, after all. Currently, he was off the grid.

He didn't have any euros; he'd spent the ones he had in Paris, and Dublin, being part of the EU took those rather than dollars or British pounds. So, he took some dollars he still had from Bridget Summers' stash and changed them up in a bureau de change.

While he stood there facing the woman on the other side of the glass window as she counted out a wad of twenty-euro notes, the reflection on the glass caught somebody on the street, a young man, no older than his late teens, standing for a moment watching him, a phone in their hand. It looked like they were taking a photo of him, but he wasn't sure, so grabbing his money quickly, thanking the lady but not waiting for a receipt, Marlowe exited the bureau de change, moving onto the street.

Looking right, there was a young man walking off, wearing a black hoodie with some kind of band logo painted on the back. He was the teenager Marlowe had caught in the mirror, and he was more focused on his phone than on the traffic in front of him, as a car horn beeped, pausing him in mid step from walking onto the road.

Marlowe started after him, walking until they paused at the crossroads. The man was still looking at his phone, and Marlowe was worried he was typing something about the man he saw in the bureau de change, so he quickly stepped forward, grabbing the wrist from behind.

The teenage lad started to say something, but then paled as he saw Marlowe.

'Tell me you haven't texted anything,' Marlowe said calmly.

'No, no, I haven't,' the lad said, shaking his head. 'I haven't at all. I was going to, but I didn't, yet.'

'Good,' Marlowe nodded. 'How did you find me?'

'I wasn't looking,' the lad continued. 'We were just told to keep an eye out if we saw you.'

'Who's "we"?'

'We're a gang,' he said, but the way the teenager said it made it sound like the most ungainly gang Marlowe could think of.

'What kind of gang?' Marlowe questioned.

'It's not a real gang,' the teenager said quickly. 'It's a *game* gang; we're a gang in a game.'

'I guess that's what "game gang" means,' Marlowe smiled, recalling what Trix had said about Phoenix Elite working from a game's server.

'Did Phoenix Elite send you?' he asked.

'I can't say,' the teenager replied.

'Oh, I think you can,' Marlowe said, tightening his grip, knowing he'd caught one of the pressure points on the teenager's wrist as he pulled him away from the road, guiding him towards the wall behind them. 'You didn't tell me exactly who told you to look. How many of you are doing this? Who are you?'

It was a rapid fire questioning, aimed at putting the teenager off balance, and it seemed to work.

'Woody,' the teenager said.

'Like the cowboy from *Toy Story?*'

'I think so. I never really saw it as a kid.'

Marlowe nodded.

'So your game – it's on a server?'

'It's a game called *Crime City*. We drive cars, rob banks, steal cars … commit crimes,' Woody replied nervously, and Marlowe laughed.

'Of course you do. Why else would it be called *Crime City*,' he paused, looking around. 'You do all this on a fictitious server?'

'Well, yeah,' Woody looked at Marlowe as if he was mad. 'If we did it in the real world, we'd go to jail.'

'Well, I couldn't argue with that,' Marlowe said. 'And Phoenix Elite is on the server?'

'He runs it, owns it. It's his roleplay server; we pretend to be police officers and EMTs and stuff like that,' the teenager said. 'A few of the bigger people stream their days, do YouTube videos, because it's really fast and super secure, especially with the upgrade a few weeks back. It's fun. It's really cool, you know. We have fun.'

'I can tell,' Marlowe smiled darkly. 'Your conversations standing around in this fake world must be amazing.'

He scanned the street, making sure they weren't drawing a crowd.

'How many people are on the server?'

'Hundreds,' Woody implied. 'But they're not all on there at the same time. The Americans come on very late in the day, you know? The Brits and the Irish are usually on in the evenings.'

'And Phoenix Elite?'

'Yeah, he's usually on the server around UK time.'

Marlowe scratched his neck.

'And he told you all to look for me?'

'He gave us a list of faces,' Woody said, reopening his phone. 'Look, this is the Discord chat.'

On the screen, Marlowe could see some kind of text-based chat. There was a thread on it titled:

Find these people. Lambo for the winner.

'What does that mean?'

'It means if we find you, he gives us a Lamborghini,'

Woody explained. 'Not a real one; it's one in the game, but they're expensive and in-game credits are hard to get.'

'So you're looking for some kind of virtual reward?'

Woody nodded as Marlowe scrolled down the thread, seeing a collection of four pictures, and winced. The images were the ones he'd given Helen Bonneville that were being used for their passports. Ones he was sure Bridget Summers had seen. They weren't originals, either, these had the reflective tape of the passports on them, so had to be scanned from the page itself.

Which meant either Helen or Bridget set them up.

'How did he get them?' Marlowe tapped at his picture.

'I don't know.'

'How well do you know Phoenix Elite?'

'I don't. I've only met him twice. One time, they were doing this thing for YouTube with exploding cars and stuff. I came along, and they said to go away. The other time, they needed me as a hostage for a robbery.'

He spoke as if it was the greatest thing he'd ever done.

'Did it succeed?'

'Nah, they accidentally blew the gas station up, and we all died,' he said. 'Made great content, though.'

'Of course it did,' Marlowe said. 'Well, here's your opportunity to become super popular with your game server. Would you like that?'

'Sure. What do I need to do?'

'It's very simple,' Marlowe smiled. 'All you have to do is get Phoenix Elite to meet with me.'

'But he just wants to know where you are.'

'And if he meets with me, he'll know,' Marlowe applied a little more pressure. 'You see, this isn't like a game, Woody. This isn't where if you crash your car, you get a big sign saying "game over" above your head and you start again, or your server crashes and you have to wait for your computer to restart. If you die right now, there's no save point, and trust me when I say you're getting very close to *losing* that save point.'

'What do you want me to tell him?' Woody whined, finally getting the gist of the severity of his situation.

Marlowe tapped at the screen.

'I want his little minions not looking for us anymore. And I want to have a chat with him. Tell him if he doesn't, I'll make sure that everybody knows who he was working for. Because as you say, your code shows who you are. Okay?'

Woody nodded, tapping on his phone.

'I'll message him in the Discord server. We talk there a lot. Or, at least he does.'

Marlowe saw the message typed.

I have one of them. He wants to speak with you.

Marlowe waited after Woody sent the message, keeping his hand on Woody's wrist. After a couple of minutes Woody checked his phone as it made a *ding* sound.

'He'll speak to you,' he said. 'Not in person. There's a cyber cafe half a mile down to the right, on the south side of the Liffey, opposite Ha'penny Bridge and upstairs above a tanning salon. If you go there and type in this URL, it will lead you to a chat room where he'll contact you.'

'No, I wanted face to face.'

Woody smiled weakly.

'That is face to face, or at least pretty much in his world,' he said.

Marlowe realised he wasn't going to get a better offer, and

so he nodded, taking a photo of the URL number with his phone.

'And is he stopping his friends?' he asked. 'I don't want my friends to be in a Dublin version of Where's Wally.'

Woody nodded, pointing at the chat app.

'He said the bounty's off until you've had your conversation.'

'Good.' Marlowe passed a twenty-euro note across to Woody. 'For your Lamborghini fund.'

With Woody gratefully taking it before running off, heading as far away as he could from this terrifying stranger, Marlowe headed to the Liffey and the cyber cafe above a tanning salon, sending the photo of the URL to Trix.

She called a moment later.

'What's this?'

'The address I'm about to speak to Phoenix Elite on,' Marlowe replied.

'You bloody what?' Trix was outraged. 'Me and my mate have only just hacked into the game server! How did you get him so quick?'

'I'm a spy,' Marlowe said casually, deciding to omit the fact he'd been spotted. 'It's what we do.'

'You're also supposed to be able to shoot a gun, and I'm still not sure you understand that part,' Trix muttered. 'I'm guessing you want me to piggyback the chat, see if I can track him?'

'No idea,' Marlowe smiled. 'That's your world.'

Trix ended the call with a stream of expletives, telling him to wait until she was ready before connecting, and Marlowe headed to the cafe. It was lunchtime, and although the salon was packed, the upstairs cyber cafe was quite empty, with most of the people probably coming in during the evening shift. Paying a man at the counter, and taking an offered stick of gum, Marlowe chewed hard on it as he looked at the room, filled with triangle tables with three monitor sets on each one. After a moment's decision, he walked to the corner, a seat far from anyone else, and with no way to stand behind him. This done, before typing anything, he took the gum from his mouth, and mushed the wad of sticky residue over the webcam on top of the monitor, blocking any view. This done, he typed in the URL, checked his phone, waiting for Trix to give the go ahead that she was now tracking the link. He could see she was typing, the three dots taking ages for the single word that came through.

Now.

Marlowe hit return and waited. A server chat window opened, and Marlowe could see from the cursor flashing that someone was there.

Hello, Mr Martin.

Marlowe smiled. *Brian Martin* was the identity he'd used to enter Dublin, probably named after some traitor that Helen thought would be funny – she had a love of throwing in jokes into his IDs. Marlowe started to type, but a second line appeared.

You can speak. I can hear you.

Marlowe looked around. Although he had covered the camera, the microphone was obviously still active.

'Am I speaking to Phoenix Elite?' he asked.

This is Ph03nix Elit3.

Marlowe smiled at the "leet speak" style of the name, remembering Trix's line about zeroes and threes.

'How do I know you're who you say you are?'

You don't.

Marlowe smiled. This was going to be an interesting conversation.

Why are you after me?

Marlowe raised an eyebrow at this.

'As far as I've seen, you're the one sending your people after me,' he replied. 'Your friend Woody found me at a bureau de change.'

This is because you're hunting me.

'I'm not hunting anyone,' Marlowe replied. Well, that wasn't exactly true, and it probably showed in his voice, because the next word that appeared on the screen knew it as well.

Liar.

'Let me rephrase that,' Marlowe said. 'I'm not hunting you. I'm hunting Orchid.'

There was a long pause following this, and Marlowe wondered for a second if the mysterious Phoenix Elite had actually left the chat.

'Are you there?'
After a moment, one word appeared.

Yes.

'We know you worked on Fractal Destiny,' Marlowe continued, lowering his voice. 'We know you worked with Orchid. My hacker found your signature code, and it led us to Dublin to speak to you.'

I worked on Fractal Destiny. And I've worked for Orchid. I do not believe in them, and I am not a member. Everything I have done has been work for hire.

There was a pause.

You still haven't explained why you want me dead.

Marlowe frowned at this.
'We don't want you dead,' he said. 'We need your help. There's something happening in America—'
He was interrupted as extra words appeared.

Liar.

Twelve hours ago the man who hired me was murdered at a party.
Six hours after this, I'm told I have a kill order placed on me.
Then, four brand new identities turn up in Dublin.

'I've placed no orders,' Marlowe's mind was spinning with this new piece of information. 'But you do raise an interesting point. How did you have our photos? Only one, maybe two other people knew those.'

It wasn't difficult. People with fake IDs – even good fake IDs – won't use the biometric scanners. They prefer to let a human eye examine the passport as it is more likely to be let through.

When four people travel in from the same airport, arriving in Dublin, all claiming to be different yet all having been seen together on CCTV at Gare du Nord, you realise something is going on.

'So you weren't given the pictures?'

No.

'How can I trust you?'

How can I trust *you?*

Marlowe smiled. *Phoenix Elite had a point.*

'Look,' he said. 'I'm not beating around the bush here. I want Orchid gone, and so do my friends. Yes, we're here under fake IDs. And yes, I'm sure that if you tried hard enough, you would find out who we are, really.'

I know who you are. Thomas Marlowe. MI5 agent currently disavowed, working his way back in. You worked for Section D under Emilia Wintergreen; you work with Trixibelle Preston. Who is also one of the four people who entered the country.

'Few people know that much about me,' Marlowe narrowed his eyes.

I also know that your father is Taylor Coleman. That your mother died during the seven seven attacks and that you are a patriot for your country. I also know you're not Orchid, even though you have claimed to be.

'That's a subject for debate at the moment. But let's get back to the important part. We haven't got a kill order on you. Which means if someone's put one out, then it's someone else, probably someone who's trying to close off any loose ends,' Marlowe leant closer, lowering his voice. 'You worked for Lucien Delacroix? Well, somebody wanted him dead. Orchid is at war with each other. And you, unfortunately, seem to be in the crosshairs. But we can get you out.'

There was a long pause, before any more text appeared on the screen:

I can find my own way out.

'You'll need friends,' Marlowe pressured. 'Let me help you.'

This said, the chat ended abruptly, a box appearing to inform Marlowe of the fact. He leant back, considering what he'd learned.

There was a kill order out. That would have been from an agency: CIA, MI5, maybe MI6. A dozen other firms out there. It didn't matter who it was, but it was something that was enough to spook Phoenix Elite.

If he'd been involved in coding for Orchid, somebody was definitely silencing people involved.

A message from Trix appeared.

> Clontarf. Got the bugger. Real name Ciaran
> Winston. Sending address now.

Marlowe rose from the chair, closing everything down.
He needed to find this "Ciaran Winston," before Phoenix
Elite's "severance package" arrived to take him out.

19

BRAM STOKER

As Marlowe steered the rental car into Clontarf, with Dublin Bay stretched out to his right, he couldn't help but marvel at the view; the waters tinged with the hues of the sinking sun. This suburb of Dublin had an air of quiet affluence, where the Irish Sea met leafy, residential tranquillity. St. Anne's Park lay somewhere to his left, its expansive grounds home to rose gardens and duck ponds, a pastoral respite amidst the still-building urban sprawl.

But Marlowe wasn't here for the scenery.

The road he now drove down, heading towards the address Trix had passed him earlier, was lined with a mix of Edwardian and modern houses, their exteriors well-kept, and the gardens manicured. The area had seen the comings and goings of history, from Viking invasions to the Easter Rising. But what concerned Marlowe now was the modern underworld hidden behind the façade of this charming suburb – specifically Phoenix Elite – who had made the grave mistake of crossing paths with the wrong people.

As he followed along the Clontarf Road, with its

sweeping view of Bull Island and the distant Howth Penin-
sula, he couldn't help but laugh at the scene before him. This
was a place where family SUVs and sailboats at the local
yacht club represented the everyday, yet yards from them was
a man preferring to live in a virtual world while working for
the worst people imaginable.

His destination was a nondescript apartment building on
the right; it was modern, but not ostentatiously so. It stood
sandwiched between a small grocery store and a quaint
coffee shop that looked to be in the process of closing for the
night. Apparently, it was the coffee shop's IP address that had
been the last one used by Phoenix Elite or, to use his real and
less exciting name, *Ciaran*, and Trix was pretty convinced he
was in the building between the two.

The problem was, she couldn't work out which of the
apartments within the building he was actually in.

Marlowe pulled the car into a vacant spot, the engine's
hum dying down as he killed the ignition. As he sat there
gathering his thoughts, he glanced at the rearview mirror. His
own eyes, wary and intense, stared back at him. Since he'd
faced Lucien, since his father had committed murder in front
of him, he'd been constantly on the go. Now, finally finding a
moment to relax, instead he was driving a car under a fake
name, to find a hacker who didn't want to be found, before
killers he thought were friends came to end his life.

He needed a new line of work. This one was *tiring*.

Watching the apartment and considering his next steps,
Marlowe thought back to Vic's comments earlier. Orchid
knew he wasn't a member, but they weren't unanimous in the
thought. There was still plausible deniability, and Marlowe
knew this had to wind up Vic Saeed, in the same way it'd
wound up Jackson and Lloyd, back in Paris. He idly

wondered if they were still there, hunting the streets, unaware their target was now closer to MI5 than they were.

No. Wait. Paris was about two hundred miles from London as the crow flew, while Dublin was closer to three hundred. In a way, he'd got further from Thames House.

As he watched the apartment, he saw a red SUV pull up and three men climb out. They were wearing jeans and T-shirts, casual denim or leather bomber jackets over the top. They looked like a "dog squad" in MI5, the grunt workers, ex-soldiers sent out to do the off-the-books jobs operatives shied away from. They could have been Special Branch officers, though, although Marlowe wasn't sure if Special Branch actually existed in the Irish Garda. One thing was sure, though, these three men, all in their thirties, all with short-cut hair and muscles bursting out of their tees, and attitudes to match were definitely there for somebody, and not for a passing visit.

With no gun, Jackson's having been left in Paris, Marlowe picked up a tyre iron he'd grabbed from the back and climbed out of the car. If they were coming for Phoenix Elite or, rather, his real life persona, he needed to get there first.

He hadn't seen the men knocking on the door to the apartments, instead, they stood near the door, watching nervously around until it opened after a couple of seconds. Marlowe knew this meant they'd used some kind of device to open the main door, and this, in turn would take them into the entrance hall, after which they'd be able to find the apartment of Ciaran Winston. Time was running out, so he quickly hurried across the road. He needed to take out the third man, the one who was now standing guard outside the doorway.

He decided instead of going straight at him to divert him

away. Placing the tyre iron down and weaving a little as he walked towards the man, he gave him a smile and a wave once he was spotted.

'All right, lad?' he said in his worst possible Irish accent, even though he was trying his best. 'I'm lookin' for Bram Stoker. Do you know where he is?'

Expecting something worse from the obviously drunk man approaching, the man loosened his posture, relaxing.

'Bram Stoker's dead, mate,' the man replied, his accent British, maybe Essex or Kent based. 'You're a little too late.'

'I know that, you eejit,' Marlowe slapped the guard lightly on the shoulder, partly to play the part of the friendly drunk, but also to subtly check if there was a Kevlar vest underneath. 'But he lived around here, in Clontarf. Fifteen Marino Crescent. His house has got a little thingy on it, you know, the round things ... the coloured things.'

'You mean a plaque?' the man asked, now leaning into the conversation.

Marlowe nodded vigorously. 'Yeah, that's the word. A plaque.'

The guard shrugged.

'Sorry, mate, I don't know where he—'

He didn't get any further. So distracted by thinking about the house, he hadn't realised that Marlowe had moved close enough to strike. Quickly driving his fingers into his throat, Marlowe used the Yonhon Nukite, or "four-finger spearhand" movement, to hit a nerve point that sent him to the ground.

Moving quickly, frisking the guard and taking a Glock 19 from his waistband, Marlowe pushed at the main door, which had been held open just in case. He used that to his advantage, moving into the building. Upstairs and to the left, the two men could be heard further on.

'Open the door, Ciaran. You know this isn't going to end well if you don't,' one of them was saying.

'Ciaran isn't here. You've got the wrong place,' a terrified male voice came from inside.

As Marlowe walked up the staircase onto the first floor, he saw the first guard look at the second and pull out a Glock. Marlowe, knowing what was going to happen, hid his own gun behind his back and stepped up.

'Could you keep your bloody noise down?' he said in his most annoying, outraged accent. 'Some people are trying to sleep, you know! We work the night shift on the docks and you eejits are waking us all up!'

'Piss off, mate,' the second guard said.

'I'm not your mate,' Marlowe retorted. 'You leave that poor lad alone.'

Underestimating Marlowe, and like the outside guard, not realising he was using this to get within a few feet's reach, the second guard turned around, allowing some kind of extendable baton to slide out of his jacket sleeve, most likely hoping Marlowe would see this and back off. Like Marlowe, he also didn't want a gunshot to alert the local Garda.

Marlowe had expected this, however, and had already unlinked his security chain. The bracelet now sliding down, a vicious looking, metal whip, he quickly slashed upwards before the guard could react. The dragon-headed clasp smashed into the man's jaw with tremendous force, sending him backwards, his teeth now a mass of blood as he screamed.

Marlowe didn't need to do anything else with him. He simply pulled out his stolen Glock as the first guard briefly allowed his attention to be diverted to his companion, and less bothered about the police now, fired three times, taking the first guard in both legs and the second guard in the arm as they both went down, moaning in pain.

'Phoenix, get your arse out here. Now,' he said as he quickly rummaged through the men's pockets, taking phones and wallets. 'It's Marlowe and we need to run.'

The door opened, and a man, ginger-haired with a wispy beard, slim, in his twenties and with the body of somebody who led a sedentary lifestyle, stared at him in utter shock.

'How did you find ...'

'Same way they did. Go! Now! This isn't the only kill squad that's coming for you.'

Ciaran nodded, running into the room. A moment later, he came back out with a giant rucksack on his back.

'It's got my gaming laptop and all my hard drives in it,' he exclaimed. 'We've got to go.'

'Really?' Marlowe with mock surprise. 'I hadn't guessed it.'

THE NIGHT AIR WAS HEAVY WITH THE TASTE OF SALT AND THE smell of rain as Marlowe and Ciaran burst through the back door of the apartment building. They'd barely cleared the threshold when the first rounds thudded into the wall behind them, and the sound of screeching brakes could be heard out the front.

Their pursuers were close, too close. And it sounded like there were more of them.

'Move!' Marlowe growled, his Glock aimed behind them, ready for whoever appeared first.

Ciaran, out of his depth but now fuelled by adrenaline,

kept pace, even with what looked to be a stupidly heavy, bulky rucksack on his back as, running across the rear street, they plunged into the labyrinthine tangle of Clontarf's backstreets and alleys.

The neighbourhood's dual nature – part quaint suburbia, part urban grid – offered both sanctuary and danger to them as they continued through. Marlowe had checked the map before arriving, and knew there was a maze of interconnected shadows he could hide in, where one wrong turn for the hunters could mean finding or losing their prey, while for Marlowe and Ciaran, one wrong turn meant the difference between life and death.

The quaint Edwardian homes that lined the quieter roads seemed to gaze down at them with a silent judgment as they hurried down them, Marlowe looking for a car to hot wire. To their left, an alley opened up, a narrow corridor framed by wooden fences, and overrun with ivy and brambles. Without a second thought and already committing to the change of route, Marlowe led them into it. Behind them, the guttural growl of an engine told Marlowe whoever these mercenaries were, they weren't willing to give up the chase just yet.

'Who are they?' Ciaran asked, terrified.

'I'd reckon they're Orchid, looking to clean up,' Marlowe replied, calmer than the man he was with. 'Probably hired killers. They look the type.'

'Orchid wouldn't kill me!' Ciaran whined. 'They know if they did, they'd never open the vault!'

'I don't think they care anymore,' Marlowe replied, wondering what the vault was and where it could be found.

They emerged near the cricket grounds, crossed under the dim glow of a streetlamp, and veered right, back towards the estuary, where the sloping land met the waters of Dublin

Bay. It was dangerously close to the apartment and his parked rental car, but Marlowe knew that was probably still too hot to return to. He had a snapshot of the area mapped out in his mind; if they could make it to the shoreline, the tide and darkness could offer cover.

Another shot rang out and a round whizzed by, perilously close, shattering the night's deceptive stillness.

'We need to split up,' Ciaran gasped, his face flushed and beaded with sweat.

'No,' Marlowe replied curtly, his eyes scanning the terrain. 'You stick with me if you want to get out of this alive. It's not like your game, is it?'

Ciaran shook his head, almost yelping with fear as, from the side a feral cat darted out from beneath a parked car as they sprinted past. Up ahead, the mouth of another narrow alley beckoned. It led to a residential cul-de-sac, the sort of dead-end trap Marlowe usually avoided.

But sometimes the obvious risks were the least expected.

He pulled Ciaran with him into the shadows. They'd done this before whoever was shooting came back into view. The shooter paused at the entrance to the cul-de-sac and watched the street for a moment. Marlowe knew what the man was thinking – *going down there was suicide for them. Nobody in their right mind would do it.*

He hoped that, anyway.

After a moment of consideration, the gun wielding mercenary continued on, and after a moment, listening to hear if anyone else followed, Marlowe decided the coast was clear, and pulled Ciaran deeper into the cul-de-sac.

The cul-de-sac ended at a small house with a wooden gate to the side, latched but not locked. Marlowe unfastened it and eased it open, cringing at the faint creak of the hinges.

They slipped through, finding themselves in a garden, the outlines of flowerbeds and a shed just visible in the darkness.

'Come on,' Marlowe hissed, his nerves electric, listening out for anything. The sounds of cars had faded now, the shouts of anger no longer heard.

Had they lost them?

Breaking through a low hedge, Marlowe was surprised to see they'd finally reached the shoreline, where the brackish waters of Dublin Bay greeted them with undulating waves. A small boat, a thirty-foot trawler, with a red base and white deck moored and bobbing gently, offered a slim chance at freedom. As Ciaran clambered in carefully, holding his ruck-sack like a baby, Marlowe took one last sweeping look at the terrain they'd traversed, checking one last time for anyone following, before he untied the boat, and they drifted out into the black, ink-like waters, swallowed by the darkness.

As the boat's engine roared to life, Marlowe couldn't help but think that sometimes, even in the most unassuming places, danger lurked where one least expected it.

Maybe Bram Stoker's memory lived on after all.

API CODES

Ciaran Winston wasn't anything like the supercool persona he pretended to be online as he sat on a chair in the Dublin suite, staring nervously around the room. Trix sat at a laptop, half watching him while typing, while Marshall Kirk sat on a sofa opposite the hacker, smiling at him now and then before returning to sharpen a wicked-looking hunting knife, while humming "He's got the whole world in his hands," like some insane serial killer.

Marlowe let him continue for a few minutes more, as the whole point was for Ciaran to realise how precarious his position truly was.

'Tell us about Orchid,' he eventually asked, walking over and sitting next to Kirk.

'They hired me for a couple of jobs, nothing more,' Ciaran replied nervously.

'They did? Or someone in Orchid did?' Kirk stopped singing now. 'Because from what we hear, there's a lot of little groups involved.'

'High Council,' Ciaran nodded eagerly. 'Lucien Delacroix.'

'From what I hear, he wasn't Orchid,' Marlowe added. 'He was actively creating an op against them. And you created the device he used.'

'There was this analyst guy, Brian Tooley,' Ciaran looked away, nodding. 'He was building some AI thing and contacted me, asking if I was interested in joining him on a project. He didn't know me, but my rep had obviously spread that I was elite.'

There was a snort from the laptop, and Trix turned it into a cough, keeping her eyes locked on the screen.

'Go on,' Marlowe brought Ciaran's attention back to the subject in hand.

Ciaran swallowed as he considered his next words.

'I said I was interested,' he continued. 'I asked for more details. About a week later, a car turned up outside my flat in Clontarf. A limo. They said that the man organising everything wanted to meet with me. I'd never had a limo sent for me before. It was both scary and exciting.'

Marlowe didn't reply. For a man who crashed cars and robbed banks in a virtual world, it sounded like anything was exciting in the real world, no matter how pedestrian.

'Go on.'

'So we went into Dublin and Lucien Delacroix was there. He'd booked out the entire floor of some hotel. Not this one. It was a better one.'

Marlowe ignored the jibe, realising Ciaran hadn't meant it in any form of attack. He was simply being blunt and to the point.

'And what happened in the hotel?'

'Well, it wasn't like *Indecent Proposal* or anything like that,'

Ciaran laughed. 'They needed my skills. They had a device that was going to perform the ultimate hack. And because of that, they needed the ultimate hacker.'

'And this was Fractal Destiny?' Trix asked, finally looking over from the laptop.

'It didn't have a name then, but I assume so,' Ciaran said. 'It was supposed to look pretty when it was opened. Like holographic tech that made it look like you were in some kind of virtual room. All smoke and mirrors and not really doing anything, while in the background it punched through any security on the Wi-Fi and stole whatever it could find.'

He shrugged, a slight hint of arrogance now taking over.

'I've got experience doing that kind of thing. I think that's why they wanted me there.'

'So, you're behind Fractal Destiny,' Marlowe nodded. 'The device that would have outed thousands of spies real names and addresses, putting their families at risk.'

'No,' Ciaran waved his hand. 'I'm not a coder like that. I mean, I have experience in the way things look. I'm a designer. I make the UI interfaces for people. The software was almost finished when I got it, so I created the holograms you saw when it was turned on.'

He glanced around the room nervously.

'I didn't know what he wanted it for,' Ciaran straightened, as he realised the severity of the accusation here. 'And, as I've already said, I'm not Orchid. I don't believe in what they believe in. I don't even know *what* they believe in. I was paid seven figures to create a code they could use that could make the software they already had look super pretty as it smashed through any cyber wall. I had several I could alter for the situation. Many came from Russian hackers.'

Marlowe understood this; Trix had mentioned in the past

that Russian hackers had some of the best skills in the industry. After all, when your hackers had actual *tech support* for the hacking software, you knew you were pretty much screwed when they attacked your systems.

'What about the key?' he asked, changing the subject.

Ciaran paused, frowning for a second.

'What key?'

'An old bullet with a little pin in the end,' Marlowe spoke now. 'You place it into a small mortuary chapel in Paris, and a magical door opens.'

'Oh, that was nothing,' Ciaran started to laugh. 'He just wanted a cold drop location for the meeting link, and he gave me an opportunity to play with it. He needed something in Paris and I've always had an interest in guns. I thought it'd be quite cool to use the creator of the metal cartridge, like, with a cartridge, you know?'

'Did you come up with the idea, or did they?' Kirk asked.

Ciaran thought about it.

'He did, actually,' he admitted.

'How many keys did you make?'

Ciaran didn't seem to understand the question, staring confused at Marlowe.

'How many keys?' Marlowe continued.

'One,' Ciaran replied, as if this was the most obvious answer. 'This wasn't for Orchid. This was for Steele.'

Marlowe sat forward.

That was why he was saying he, and not they.

'You worked for St John Steele?'

'Well, yes,' Ciaran looked around the room as if realising he was telling them things that nobody seemed to know. 'You know he's a big fella in Orchid, right?'

'We also know he's trying to leave Orchid.'

At this, Ciaran laughed harder.

'Christ, no, if he said that, he's playing you! The guy's a lifer. He was more of a zealot than bloody Lucien was, and the harridan that came with him.'

'Describe the harridan that came with him.'

'British, white hair. Had a kind of weird haircut, you know, short on one side, longer on the other?'

Marlowe held up a finger to pause Ciaran, scrolling through his phone, pulling up a picture of Bridget Summers, and showing it.

'Yeah, that's the one,' Ciaran smiled. 'Right wicked piece of work. Real "Lady Macbeth" vibes. You know her?'

'Far too well,' Marlowe replied. 'So let me get this right. You created this lock for Steele and this woman, and when you get there, there's a stone orchid this key unlocks, and when you pick the orchid up, it shows you coding.'

Ciaran mouth shrugged, or it was a damn good impression of Robert De Niro as he settled back into the chair.

'I just created the key, not what it opens,' he admitted.

'So you didn't create the coding?' Marlowe continued, scrolling to an image of the text at the base of the stone orchid.

Ciaran peered at it and then smiled. Another element of smugness now coming over him, as he looked lazily over at Trix.

'Why don't you ask your hacker there?' he asked. 'Yeah, I know who you are. You left *Unifyre* to run off to MI5, right? I've seen your work recently.'

'And how would you have seen her work?' Marlowe asked.

'Because she used to work for Trisha Hawkins.'

'That's a lie,' Trix said, spinning around. 'I worked for

Frankie Pierce. Trisha Hawkins was her assistant. I was Pierce Associates—'

'Which then turned into Rattlestone, which then turned into Phoenix Industries,' Ciaran interrupted with a smile.

'You worked for Trisha Hawkins?' Marlowe wondered if he had made the right decision, bringing the man in.

'Among others,' Ciaran was settling in nicely into his new position of *whistleblower to the stars.* 'Hawkins gave me work here and there. I'd seen *her* work there, back in the server archives; must have been created when Frankie Pierce ran the town, but I remembered her style from when we hung around the same circles.'

'You know, for somebody who likes to play games in a fake world, you seem to know a lot about these people,' Marlowe replied.

'Have you got the game anywhere?' Ciaran now asked, looking over at Trix.

'No,' she replied, folding her arms irritably. 'I don't play games.'

'Shame, it might take the stick out of your wee arse,' Ciaran nodded at his rucksack. 'Do you mind?'

Marlowe waved his hand to go ahead, and Ciaran, gently, to make sure nobody thought he was making a fast movement, opened up the rucksack, pulling out his laptop. It was a gaming one, and high-spec; you could see from the moment he turned it on, with LED lights along the hinges that lit up as he opened the screen.

'I run a server,' he said. 'Based on *Crime City.* It's a really popular game that's been out for years, and there's a lot of PC modifications you can use on it.'

'Which means?'

'Basically, if you have the code, you can create things in

the world,' Ciaran was beaming now, proud of his creation. 'It's also a place where people can run around and blow things up and not die and genuinely have fun being criminals. Or cops, we don't differentiate.'

'Get on to the good part,' Marlowe growled.

Ciaran nodded, booting up his computer.

'Can I log on to the internet here?'

'No,' Trix said, passing him a piece of paper. 'That's what you'll use. It'll bounce you around a dozen different networks for a good half an hour. No offence, but I'm not just ... I'm not trusting you with anything.'

Ciaran accepted this by tapping the numbers in.

'Brian Tooley learnt about me from my server Discords,' he said. 'That's how they first contacted me.'

This was the second time Ciaran had mentioned Tooley. Marlowe knew the name well – he'd been to the shallow grave that Foster and Peters had left the long dead Tooley in with Kate, when he still believed she fought for the good guys, taking his prosthetic arm, finding the clue he'd been led there to find, like a dog being led by a lead.

He must have darkened his expression, as Ciaran had paused, watching him nervously.

'You know Brian?'

'I visited his grave,' Marlowe spoke angrily. 'Go on.'

'Damn, I didn't know he was dead,' Ciaran looked genuinely saddened at this. 'Okay, so I sorted out Fractal Destiny for them to prove my worth, and the tech they gave me, this virtual holographic tech that they asked me to use? I copied the code. I thought I could use it myself to somehow create my *Crime City* server's world in reality. You could stand in your room and move around the world with no need for a VR headset or anything like that. I could make millions.'

'And then what happened?' Marlowe asked.

'They offered me another job,' Ciaran replied. 'They wanted some kind of practice location, somewhere they could repeat the same actions, time after time, *Groundhog Day* style, until they knew they'd get it right. A couple of them had met me in the servers, and they'd seen the possibilities. They gave me blueprints of a building, along with 3D scans taken while walking around the inside, and asked me to create it, like a virtual model of it in my server.'

'And that's possible?'

'Oh, hell yes,' Ciaran laughed. 'You can buy entire city models in Blender now. And Las Angels, the location setting for *Crime City* is effectively Los Angeles. You can even drive up Santa Monica pier.'

He clicked his neck to remove some tension as he straightened now.

'But the server I was on wasn't good enough for what they wanted,' he said. 'They needed it to be way more secure and faster. They gave me a super-fast server of my own on their own network—'

'In Saanen, Bern?'

Ciaran nodded.

'Massive speeds kept the frame rate high. Makes the YouTube videos pop, you know?'

Marlowe nodded, even though he didn't know.

'I created the building just outside of town, so nobody could really play with it. Put it into an old military camp in the game, with big fences all around. People would come and look about; but as far as they were concerned, all I was doing was creating new ideas for YouTube videos, and they left me alone in case I got pissed at them and banned them from the server.'

He now leant forward.

'But what I was doing was bringing Orchid agents into the system through the game server, giving them all the in-game equipment they needed, and allowing them to play, running around the rooms, learning the layout based on the rendered images I'd been given. They played it like the game was played; some played it first person, some third person, some even used VR headsets. I didn't really care what they did, but all I know is that for about a month, Lucien had people, his Orchid people I suppose, learning every inch of this location.'

Marlowe knew something more was coming and waited.

Ciaran shifted in his seat and then sighed.

'It's the Willard InterContinental Washington,' he said. 'I don't know why they wanted to know all about it; I didn't care. Some would play police and SWAT and soldiers and agents, and some would play terrorists, and then they'd swap over and play the other way around. They learnt every single way to take over that hotel and every single way to stop them.'

'Couldn't an AI have done these scenarios just as quickly? Quicker even?' Trix asked.

'I asked the same question,' Ciaran said, looking back at her. 'But they said they didn't need to know the answers, they needed to go *through* the answers. They needed their people to understand what to do whenever they found one of these obstacles.'

'Why not just go to the hotel?'

'You can scope a location, sure, but they wanted to work out kill shots and shit like that. They wanted to know lighting and wallpaper, the whole lot.'

'Jesus Christ ... it was a role-play,' Marshall said.

'Well duh, old man, I've told you a dozen times I run a role-play server.'

'I don't mean your server, I mean what they're doing,' Kirk looked over at Marlowe. 'The Willard InterContinental Washington is where the presidential debate is being held later this week, in the Crystal Room. CNN mentioned it earlier. There's McKay, his only current rival, and a moderator panel facing them.'

'And Orchid's been learning every single inch of it,' Marlowe understood where his onetime mentor was going with this. 'They know the layout, they know the physicalities, they know where they can place things, where they can hide. They know every obstruction aimed against them.'

'We knew they were aiming at the debate, but not what they were aiming with,' Trix whistled.

'Are they trying to take down the president?' Marlowe asked.

At this, Ciaran laughed, and Marlowe clenched his fists, finally having enough of the attitude. Without speaking, he pulled out the Glock and aimed it straight at Ciaran's head.

Ciaran said nothing, the laugh dying in his throat as a small patch of darkness appeared around his jeans' groin area.

'Nice,' Marlowe indicated the stain. 'You can add that to your game avatar. Want to answer the question now? Or do you still want to piss about?'

He winced.

'Maybe not "piss" anymore, though, yeah?'

'Dude, I was laughing at the absurdity, not at you,' Ciaran held his hands up to ward off the gun. 'Orchid won't attack the president. Nobody's that stupid.'

Marlowe leant even closer, now almost face to face with the hacker.

'Orchid might not be that stupid, but there are many

Orchid cells out there,' he said. 'Lucien's cell – which was also Kate Maybury's one, it seems – is trying to tie off all loose ends. Violently. You'll probably find at the same time another Orchid cell needs to keep you alive. There's a war happening, and if they want McKay dead, or Harrison Caldwell, who seems to definitely be singing from the Orchid song book in power somehow, then they'll have to fight each other to do it, with all these cells, all these countries, all fighting for power.'

He stopped as he suddenly realised something.

'Trix,' he asked, looking over at her. 'When you called Senator Kyle, it was because she was on the Paris party list, right?'

'Not for the super-secret bad guy party, but she was there for the outside event,' Trix nodded. 'She was supposed to be speaking to Joanna Karolides.'

Marlowe nodded. This would have been a continuation of the conversation she couldn't have in San Francisco, when she was shot by her close security guard Ford, an Orchid agent working with Kate Maybury.

But what if she wasn't as innocent as she claimed?

At the time, they thought this was a plot by a think tank named Caliburn – at no point was she asked about Orchid.

What if she was a rival cell to Kate, and Lucien?

'Did she have that conversation?' he asked, a looming dread rising.

Trix now turned in her chair, looking at everybody else.

'I'll be honest, I don't think she even tried,' she said, her voice lowering as realisation seeped through into her brain. 'Oh, shit.'

Marlowe looked back at Ciaran.

'Did you ever deal with Senator Maureen Kyle?' he asked.

'I don't recognise the name,' Ciaran replied honestly. 'But

then, just because I don't know her, doesn't mean she wasn't involved.'

'What's the code? The code in the orchid?'

'It's an API key,' Ciaran said, looking back at her. 'As anyone with hacking skills would know.'

'I know it's an API. I don't know what it's for,' Trix half rose and then caught herself.

Ciaran pulled himself back into the chair, as if scared she was about to attack.

'We're not hackers,' Marshall Kirk growled, his hunting knife gleaming in the knife. 'So explain to *us*, yeah?'

'API keys? Okay, they're an acronym for "application programming interface," a software intermediary that allows two applications to talk to each other,' Ciaran replied nervously, licking his dry lips. 'With it, you could open another piece of software up.'

'But only with the key.'

Ciaran nodded.

'So, Steele was the key holder?'

'No, man, the entire High Council had the code. I never knew what Steele wanted with a key.'

Marlowe narrowed his eyes at this. Steele was creating his own API shaped "go bag," it seemed.

'And where's the software?'

At this, Ciaran shook his head, staring in turn at the scary hacker, the mad old man with the knife and the pissed-off spy aiming a gun at his face.

'What do I get if I tell you?' he asked. 'You all look pretty heated.'

'For a start, we've saved your life,' Marlowe smiled. 'If you don't tell us what's going on, we'll throw you out that door, and within five minutes, Orchid will find you and probably kill you. Or, if you're lucky, they'll take you and use you as bait against the other cells. And then kill you.'

Ciaran nodded at this, accepting it as the truth.

'Okay,' he reluctantly sighed. 'If you promise to keep me alive, I'll tell you everything I know about what they're doing. It all goes around some weird shit anyway, so maybe you can even answer some questions for me.'

'How do you mean?' Trix asked from the desk.

'Well, for a start, can someone please tell me what the hell *Rubicon* is?' Ciaran asked. 'Because I'm hearing that word a lot. Ever since Steele and the harridan – I mean the woman you all seem to know turned up.'

Marlowe looked at Marshall.

'What's Tessa up to right now?' he asked.

Marshall didn't know, and showed this by shrugging, dropping the knife and trying to call her.

'She went for a walk,' he said. 'Like you did. She was annoyed she couldn't come with you to pick this guy up. That's all I know.'

After a moment of silently waiting for her to answer the phone, he looked up.

'She's not answering,' he added, looking around. 'She knows to answer unless she's in a bind.'

'Or, if she's meeting someone she doesn't want us to know she's meeting with,' Trix said, looking back at Ciaran. 'So, why don't you tell us who it is?'

Ciaran checked his nails, considered his options, but only when Marlowe placed the Glock against his skull did he tell them everything.

21

PRETTY BITTY BANG BANG

It was late in the evening when Tessa Kirk finally saw the woman she was waiting for.

The Book of Kells exhibit, nestled within the hallowed walls of Trinity College in Dublin, was an enclave of history and artistry, with its primary attraction an intricately illustrated manuscript dating back to the ninth century, a masterpiece of medieval art that's stood the test of time. The room itself was dimly lit, safeguarding the delicate, ancient pages encased in glass displays. Dark wooden panels lined the walls, and placards detailing the historical context and artistic significance of the artifact were strategically placed around the room.

Tessa stood amidst a crowd of awe-struck academics, each shuffling quietly through the room to get a glimpse of the manuscript's fabled illuminations. There was some kind of evening event on and Tessa had used this to her advantage, mingling in with the crowd while she'd waited. Whispered discussions about the artwork's symbolism and the history of early Irish Christianity filled the air, but this was just white noise to her as she started towards her contact.

'When you contacted, I was a little surprised,' she smiled. 'I thought you were going back to London.'

Bridget Summers raised an eyebrow.

'Why would I do that, when I knew you were going to Dublin?' she said, matter-of-factly. 'Okay, I might have seen the names on the passports Helen made. And I *may* have run them through various servers until I found four of you heading here. And then of course there's you, messaging me the way your father would, forgetting to hide the ping location.'

'Who said I forgot?'

Bridget smiled at this and looked around the exhibit.

'So, do you want to kill me for what I did to you?' she asked.

Tessa understood the question; Bridget had tried to kill her father, and out Tessa as a Rubicon agent, while one herself. And, despite its reputation as a tourist hotspot, the high-ceilinged room, with its academic ambiance, gave enough shadowed corners to kill a rival and leave before they found the body.

Tessa reached into her pocket, noting Bridget step back, expecting a blade or something to appear, but relaxed as a USB stick was brought out.

'I understand you warned Tom about me?' Tessa held out the stick.

'I was looking to cause dissent,' Bridget shrugged. 'I wanted this back, and I thought it'd make me look to be on his side.'

She took the stick with a sigh of relief.

'The crypto's not been touched?'

Tessa shook her head, and Bridget quickly pocketed the stick.

'I'll get you the gold when this is over,' she said. 'And the page of random letters. It's easier to swap a stick right now.'

Bridget puffed out her cheeks – this irritated her, but not enough to stop her.

'Orlovsky says thank you for the Paris information,' she said, watching Tessa. 'That's what you wanted to know, right? Whether I was still in touch with him?'

'Actually, I wanted to know who the players are in this little war,' Tessa shrugged. 'I guessed you'd be my Dublin contact. I know Orlovsky's one player, that Delacroix was—'

'Was?' Bridget raised an eyebrow.

'I saw him killed, Summers.'

'Come on, Tessa. You're a spook, whether or not you like it. Did you really see him killed? Or did you just see someone shoot him three times at close range before all hell broke loose?'

Tessa paled as the additional consideration crossed her mind.

'Taylor Coleman wants out,' she said, working through it. 'Lucien wants out. Taylor gives Marlowe his position, then "kills" Lucien. Orchid goes to war, and the two of them disappear, never to be heard of again.'

'It's an excellent theory, but misses one important fact, apart from the glaring error that Lucien Delacroix could ever stay quiet,' Bridget shrugged. 'Their egos are too large for them to spend the rest of their lives hiding. Also, what does Lucien gain right now by everyone thinking he's dead?'

'So, what's the plan?'

'Are you sure you really want to know what happened at Versailles?' Bridget looked around. 'The party's getting a little loud. And once you pass through the door, you can't walk back.'

'I do,' Tessa nodded.

With this tacit agreement given, Bridget walked close, as if to whisper a lover's secret to Tessa, pulled a small pistol out from her pocket—

—and shot Tessa Kirk three times in the chest.

As Tessa fell back against the wall, three growing stains of blood staining her blouse as she gasped weakly, trying to gather a single breath as the room erupted into terrified chaos, Bridget smiled, placing the pistol away.

'Well, now you know,' she said.

22

AVENGE THE FALLEN

By the time Kirk and Marlowe arrived at Trinity College, the police cars and ambulances had already taken up prime locations. In fact, if they'd thrown in a couple of fire engines, you'd have had the whole trifecta.

Marlowe patted Kirk on the shoulder as he climbed out of the driver's seat. It'd taken a while to get back into Clontarf to pick it back up, but it was easier than renting a new one under a new name, and Marlowe had liked the steering, anyway.

'She's fine,' he said, unsure whether or not he was lying. 'I'll check first. Stay here.'

'Stay here?' Kirk glared at Marlowe. 'No bloody way, Tom.'

Sighing, Marlowe allowed Kirk to join him, as they walked over to one of the Irish Garda officers standing guard at the police cordon.

'Sorry, no civilians,' the officer said. Marlowe considered playing one of his many identities, but he had nothing on him at that moment, apart from something real. So, he pulled a wallet out of his back pocket, showing his MI5 identification.

'Marlowe, Security Service,' he said, knowing he'd pretty much outed himself right now. Although, from the looks of things, Orchid already knew, what with Marlowe removing Ciaran Winston, and Tessa …

Well, whatever had happened here.

The Garda officer examined the ID, nodding. He was in his forties, and Marlowe assumed he'd been around the block for a while.

'We rarely get your type around here,' he said, nodding at Kirk. 'Granddad with you?'

'Yeah, and I think one of my assets is in the building,' Marlowe replied. 'Can you give me an update?'

'Aye, there was some kind of bloody stupid protest or something, like those kids when they throw soup on paintings, yeah?' the officer replied. 'Two women doing some kind of silly street theatre, until it went wrong.'

'Wrong?'

The officer nodded at the ambulance.

'The younger of the two is in there,' he said. 'I'm guessing she's your asset. She's pissed.'

Marlowe nodded at the cordon.

'Can we?' he asked.

'Go wild,' the officer nodded, raising it. 'And don't take any offence at this, but once you're done, head back to wherever you came from, yeah? This is Dublin, not London. And we don't need any spy shite around here.'

Marlowe smiled.

'Noted,' he said, ducking under the cordon and heading over to the ambulance.

Tessa was on the gurney inside, a paramedic over her.

'Tessa!' Kirk shouted, seeing his daughter in pain, climbing into the ambulance.

Tessa, however, pushed herself painfully up from the bed, waving him back.

'I'm fine, Dad,' she said. 'It's just a couple of cracked and bruised ribs. Nothing more.'

'What the hell were you doing?' Marlowe asked, climbing in behind Kirk. 'Bridget Summers? Really? Have you been working with Rubicon?'

'You know I spoke to Orlovsky,' Tessa replied. 'I had to get into the party.'

'Have you spoken to him after that?'

Tessa didn't reply, and after a moment, Kirk leant over his daughter.

'Why did she shoot you?' he asked.

'She was proving a point,' Tessa groaned as she straightened. 'She was showing me that Lucien Delacroix may have faked his death.'

'By shooting you.'

'She knew I was wearing a vest,' Tessa replied. 'She moved in close and fired three times, but the bullets were faked. They had gel tips that provided bloodstains, and the whole thing looked legitimate. And it hurt like hell, even through the vest.'

Marlowe nodded as he leant back.

'So, Taylor faked Lucien's death,' he said. 'Can we be sure?'

'I didn't really get to ask many questions,' Tessa gingerly eased herself off the gurney. 'But there's more going on here than we know.'

'Oh, we can guarantee that,' Marlowe smiled, looking at Kirk. 'We've been hearing a lot of secrets, too.'

THE JOURNEY BACK TO THE HOTEL HAD BEEN LONGER THAN usual, mainly as Marlowe now knew Bridget Summers was in town, and there was every possibility they were being followed. In fact, Marlowe and Tessa even took separate routes at one point, her father going with her, just to flush out any followers.

Surprisingly, there didn't seem to be any. Or they were better than Marlowe was.

Back in the hotel, Marlowe had already informed Trix to move suites, now in the second of three backups he'd arranged. Things were heating up, and they didn't have enough of an armoury here to fight back. Also, the following day they needed to fly to Washington, and that was going to be difficult enough as it was.

In the suite, one reserved under the name "Garth Fleming," Marlowe passed Tessa a cold soda as he sat in his chair.

'So, do you want to explain why you're flirting with Rubicon?' he waved a hand for her to continue.

In return, she glanced at Ciaran, sitting opposite Trix at the suite's dining table, working on his laptop, frowning.

'With the asset here?'

'Trust me, that "asset" knows more about what's going on than we do,' Trix replied from her dining chair, looking over. 'And currently he knows we're his only chance to stay alive, so you're golden.'

Tessa considered the situation, nodded, and then opened the soda, taking a sip, wincing as she held her ribs.

'Wintergreen told me to do it,' she said. 'She told me you needed help, and I was off the grid, and had a particular set of skills and connections you might need.'

Marlowe didn't react; he'd actually expected this. Marshall Kirk, however, exploded.

'That's why you came to the church?' he exclaimed. 'That's why you begged me to get involved? None of this "bored with the life" bollocks, but because you were told to by Emilia Bloody Wintergreen?'

'No, she spoke to Emilia *because* she was bored,' Marlowe replied. 'That's right, isn't it? When Wintergreen tasked me to do this, she already knew what I was going to need better than I did.'

He recalled the conversation he'd had with Wintergreen on the banks of the Serpentine. She'd informed him that Trix, still suspended, would be his "point man" of sorts, but had then discussed a team.

'I've already contacted Marshall Kirk and told him he should expect a call from you. I'm expecting you'll probably also go and find your drunk friend in America, Brad Haynes. And I would probably assume that Sasha Bordeaux, or whatever name she's going to use this week, will be looking out for you as well. She seems to know about more leaks going on than we do.'

'She told Marshall I'd be calling, but she told you to get in on this without my knowledge. Why?'

'Because she'd had intel that Orchid and Rubicon were connected,' Tessa shrugged. 'And, without tooting my trumpet that much, I was pretty much the only agent on the list she knew she could trust. She said if I helped you close down Orchid, she'd get me in.'

'Into the service?' Kirk shook his head. 'You *know* what Tom there did to keep you out of this?'

'I know, and part of the deal was she'd fix Tom's position too,' Tessa argued. 'Not in a bloody gun room, but actually out in the field.'

'Tessa,' Marlowe shook his head. 'After this, do you think we're seriously going to be allowed out there? This was always a suicide mission, career wise. Wintergreen knew it, I knew it, even Trix knew it.'

'I didn't like it, but yeah,' Trix nodded. 'I can get some leeway as I'm not the one seen in gunfights during Orchid meetings, and Marshall there's already on the pension, but when this ends, you'll still have people like Vic Saeed or Lawrence Jackson in the service ... and they have long memories – plus they are really petty.'

There was a moment of silence, and Marlowe held his hand up.

'Okay, so as we can't look more into that, let's try moving on,' he said. 'Wintergreen set you on this and told you to see Orlovsky for more than just the party. I'm guessing there's a reason?'

'Chaos,' Tessa gave a weak smile. 'She knew there were cells, and thought it'd be good to turn them onto each other a little more, especially with Lucien's one – or, rather, Kate's one at the time – kicking off against others.'

'Little did you know, they were already doing that,' Ciaran commented from his laptop. 'You could have stayed at home.'

'Being shot actually helps, in a way,' Marlowe smiled as he walked to the fridge, grabbing water. 'We now know Lucien could still be alive. And if Taylor wanted to give me his position in Orchid, it makes sense to go out in a blaze of glory. He's not faking the illness he has. He's not long for the earth.'

'Bridget said there was a reason for Lucien to need to be dead right now, but wouldn't say what it was,' Tessa added.

'So, let me get this right,' Marshall said, counting off his fingers as he did so. 'Taylor and Lucien want out. Taylor, so his other kids don't have to deal with all this once he's dead, and Lucien for reasons yet unknown. So, they plan together this ruse, a big public spectacle where Marlowe turns up, having been forced by the situation to speak to him—'

'It wasn't the situation,' Marlowe shook his head. 'Sure, we knew we needed this help to get in, but it was placed in my head by Steele when he turned up in my house, and we all know he gave me the key because he wants out, too. And he met with Ciaran originally, with Bridget beside him.'

Marlowe returned to the sofa, sitting on it.

'Steele sends me to my father. Who brings me to watch Lucien die, while placing me publicly as his successor,' he said. 'Knowing half of Orchid wants me dead, for what happened with Kate.'

He looked back at Ciaran.

'Tell Tessa what you told us,' he said.

Ciaran turned on his chair and quickly explained how he'd been hired to not only create Fractal Destiny, sending the data to Lucien's Swiss server, but had also been paid to create a scale model of the Willard InterContinental Washington in a game server attached to the same Swiss bunker, just so people could get used to it.

'I'm guessing that's the place the debate is?' she asked.

'As far as we know,' Marlowe nodded. 'Although they're still keeping tight-lipped on what's actually happening.'

'Not so much,' Trix looked up. 'They just announced the debate schedule for the day after tomorrow. It's President Anton McKay and Senator Ron Tyler.'

'Tyler?' Marlowe frowned at the name. 'I had a file on him back in New York. He was being blackmailed by Nathan Donziger.'

'Well, now he's free and wants to be President,' Trix replied. 'And, more importantly, the people moderating and asking questions are CNN anchor Ricky Morgan, Vice President Harrison Caldwell, and Arizona Republican Senator Maureen Kyle.'

At the last name, Kirk whistled.

'She's going for McKay,' he said. 'She's going to out him on live TV.'

'But why Caldwell? He wouldn't publicly go against a sitting President,' Marlowe scratched at his UV scar again as it'd starting itching. 'That's career suicide. People would always remember he bit the hand of his boss.'

'But he could do the debate in the name of "balance," and if McKay shit the bed, then he could offer to take over.'

'Which means Orchid takes over,' Kirk nodded. 'As it looks like he's Orchid, after all.'

'How does this relate to the other thing, though?' Marlowe looked back at Ciaran now. 'Did you—'

'Did I ever watch them in the hotel?' Ciaran second-guessed Marlowe's question correctly. 'Yeah. They wanted NPCs in the game server, so they could practise hiding from normal people. I logged in, put an NPC skin on and walked around dressed like a chef.'

'And they never realised?'

'You don't speak, and when someone knocks you, they don't pay attention when you walk into a wall a few times,' Ciaran shrugged. 'They've got more important things to worry about. But one thing I can say is they looked for the security room, called the "communications" room when they discussed it, the Crystal ballroom and the main entrances. The plan was to storm communications and the stage at the same time. They weren't attacking McKay, but I got the impression they wanted him outed on stage, and wanted to hack the live feed to upload data.'

'Why that feed though?'

'It's a Presidential debate,' Tessa replied. 'Even a first round one would still have millions watching.'

'They also had another coder in there, an expert on Deepfake face swapping. They were creating a perfect replica of McKay, but it wasn't looking good enough to fool anyone when I last saw it,' Ciaran said. 'But then all I ever saw it do was shoot itself in the head.'

Marlowe thought back to a line St John Steele had said back in his renovated church.

'We were promised a file on one of our own, Mister Marlowe. One he never received, and one now being used to save Donziger's own neck. Let's just say Mister Donziger's holding Orchid hostage with this, and only a Presidential Pardon will suffice.'

'Steele warned me of this,' he sighed. 'And I think I know what the plan was. Nathan Donziger had files on everyone, probably including McKay. Which meant McKay was likely doing whatever Donziger said, in the same way Kyle was. And, when Donziger was captured, he knew he had enough on McKay to gain a presidential pardon.'

'But it's been weeks and we've heard nothing,' Trix shook her head. 'Surely to keep it quiet, he'd have done this fast.'

'Yeah, but there's the problem,' Marlowe said. 'It's coming up to election year. Pardoning Donziger would go bad for McKay in the polls. He was probably kicking it down the street—'

He stopped as Trix waved, staring at a news page on her screen.

'Or he was being stopped by someone else,' she said. 'There was a task force set up after Donziger's arrest, one that confiscated everything from the salt mine. Caldwell was in charge of it.'

She turned her laptop around to show an image. On it was a photo of Harrison Caldwell and Lucien Delacroix.

'Lucien's a long-time friend of his, and there was an issue last election; Caldwell had to admit Lucien gave him millions towards his run, and as it was foreign money, it had to be returned. It's one of the reasons he stepped out of the running, and McKay got the nomination.'

'What if Donziger's realised McKay isn't playing, and so he's gone to Caldwell?' Tessa asked. 'If McKay is removed, then Caldwell pardons him for helping take McKay down or something.'

'Donziger gives McKay's file to Caldwell, and he passes it to Lucien,' Kirk nodded. 'Who uses it to wipe McKay out, allowing Caldwell to step in. But McKay is aware he's a target. Maybe the debate is his way of bringing everyone down, as he knows he doesn't have a hope of getting out now? Admit to everything, but point out every other person in the room is owned by Orchid or Donziger?'

'And if Lucien's dead, then McKay might relax a little,' Marlowe nodded. 'Giving Orchid enough time to somehow switch a fake into the system, fake a suicide on live TV and change the narrative?'

'They asked if I could work out a way for their communication room – the one in the game – to use Fractal's algorithm to punch into a remote server feed,' Ciaran offered.

'Why would they want that?'

Ciaran shrugged.

'Honestly? Only thing I could think of was if they wanted to hack the feed of the hotel, and replace it with the server, which is exactly what you're talking about here,' he said.

'So you could swap feeds of the actual Crystal Ballroom to the *Crime City* one, and they wouldn't notice?'

'Could work, especially if the audience has watched half an hour of real people. Swap the feed, people won't immediately work it out if the setting is exact, have a massively explosive moment, the shock kicks in, especially if you filter it with network issues, pixelating it a little,' Trix suggested. 'Shoot McKay in the face while people see the fake screen, then cut back to chaos and a real dead President.'

'But there'd be witnesses.'

'All Orchid,' Kirk suggested. 'Or, who still have Donziger files held over them. Probably even the CNN guy.'

Ciaran shrugged.

'Depends how bothered they were,' he replied. 'But they'd have to make everything in there exact. And they could definitely do it. I created an in-game version of Fractal Destiny, cut down and able to be used in game. They take it in, connect it, it'll punch through the network feed, once they connect it to the hardline in the security room, which in turn will be connected to the network running the debate.'

He shook his head in realisation.

'But all they could do with the feed is hack it,' he added. 'They don't have access to the vault.'

'Vault?'

Ciaran grinned.

'So, I knew Orchid were sketchy, right? And they had this server they'd given me access to, yeah? I knew they'd cut my feed to the juicy areas the moment I finished, so when I built the hotel in the game, I added an underground vault. I mean, the hotel has something like that on the plans, so I said I was just being thorough. But then I placed an in-game hacking terminal in there, one that links directly to the server, and all of their information.'

He leant back, proud of this.

'The ultimate back door, because it's literally a door,' he continued. 'And once you get through the main vault door, you can use the API I gave them for their secret meetings to link in and grab every piece of Orchid information you can find.'

'Then why haven't you?' Kirk asked.

'Because they'd know immediately and kill me.' Ciaran looked at the older man as if he was mad. 'And I ain't into that.'

'Explain more about the API and the secret meetings?' Marlowe eventually asked.

'It's hard to explain without seeing it,' Ciaran shifted in his chair now. 'You see, API's usually link one app to another. What this code does is, well, more link coding to a server.'

Marlowe waited, and Ciaran eventually sighed and leant back on the chair.

'So I didn't just build a hotel at the start,' he explained. 'One of the first things I was asked to create, mainly as a kind of audition, was a meeting room. A nice, basic, simple one in the middle of the city, one that only people with access, with that particular API code attached to their game avatars, could enter.'

He looked around the room, explaining to everyone.

'Like players using code and mods to make them invincible, able to fly, yeah? This coding, this API gave them the ability to enter a secret location. The way the game works is you arrive at a building and there's a jump point that you can move on to, okay? It's like a little glowing circle, and that jump point takes you to the next level in the building, but only if you have the right credentials. If you don't, then that jump point's invisible and if you walked over it, it's just pavement.'

'So anyone who has the API could do this,' Trix added.

'They're just like modifications or mods in the game,' Ciaran nodded. 'Almost impossible to hack into, unless you know what's going on and you have the right code.'

'So the API is a hack?' Now it was Tessa asking.

'No, the API links you to software that provides the hack,' Ciaran replied. 'What it means is if you create a character in the game – actually to be honest, it's one I create for you – your character, when you log in, has the API in its coding, and this creates a mod that means you can go to this location. Simply walk onto the spot that nobody else can walk onto, and whoosh! You find yourself in a meeting room.'

'And members of Orchid would do this?' Kirk asked. 'They wouldn't rather meet personally?'

'This is a global organisation. If they're seen to move physically to one location, not only would people see it, half the agencies in the world would probably try to nuke it,' Ciaran shrugged. 'This is a far more simple way. A virtual chatroom nobody can see. I provided each member with their own personalised gaming PC, created in such a way that nobody can get to it, and filled with coding linking the API to the Saanen server, and the game I had set up there.'

He scratched at his head.

'That's why I do the YouTuber stuff,' he said. 'Gives me a reason for demanding the security and speed, as some of these guys have millions of followers, and I claimed it's all to keep their data safe, while giving them a reason to have it.'

'So, an Orchid High Council member takes this PC, turns it on, the API and the character created by you then appears in the game, where they walk to the door, and boom, they're in a super-secret meeting,' Marlowe nodded, understanding. 'Pretty clever. And if anyone asks, they're simply gaming?'

'Basically yeah, and they'd sit there at their PC, with a headset on and talk to each other in effective secrecy. Nobody recording, nobody able to monitor or tap the line like a phone call. They're completely off the grid.'

'It's the real world equivalent of the holographic meetings you see in films,' Trix was impressed. 'And on a gaming server? It's so low key, it's ingenious.'

'Thanks,' Ciaran said with a hint of pride.

'I wouldn't be too happy,' Marlowe added. 'Your great idea here might have led to a coup, ending with taking down the President of the USA.'

'That only becomes a problem if they don't succeed,' Ciaran shrugged. 'After all, that's the problem with coups.'

For once, Marlowe couldn't argue with this.

23

GAME SERVERS

As everyone in the suite considered Ciaran's words, Trix, still staring at the server data on her screen, whistled.

'Ballsy,' she said. 'I've heard of people using games to launder money, but nothing like this.'

'Oh, it's more common than you think,' Ciaran noted in response. 'There was money laundering in games like *Second Life* and games like that, where you could buy in-game money with real money, and then give that to other people in the game for services, who could then, if they wanted to, cash it out for real money.'

He smiled.

'Some of these games used it as a way to make people want to play. People would create amazing items in these worlds because they knew they'd make dollars for them. People did this for a living. *Crime City* is no different. There are people in the game world that fix cars, who run coffee shops, who create clothing, modifying specialised costumes to make you look the way you want, create vehicles and weapons ... the list is endless. These people get given in-game money, and in some servers you can then cash that into real dollars.'

He nodded at Marlowe.

'On that point, I messaged Woody, gave him the lambo for putting us in touch,' he smiled. 'You ever want to play, he'll show you the ropes. I told him I vouch for you. After all, you did help save my life.'

Marlowe smiled, amused by the "help" in the comment.

'It's the ultimate money laundering scheme,' Trix nodded. 'Someone in South Korea, for example, can place half a million dollars into a particular game's currency. They then buy a house in the game from somebody else for half a million dollars, paying them in the game currency, and then have a house that's nothing more than code and probably is never even looked at again. But the money's been passed, the transition has been sorted.'

'Is it just money?' Marlowe asked Ciaran now.

'Christ no,' he said. 'Although it's an opportunity for Orchid agents to meet and do that. But it's bigger. They can bring any digital items into the game world. Data mainly, and it can be swapped from avatar to avatar – especially in this room.'

He smiled.

'After all, that was the plan with Fractal Destiny. It's a little all over the place, really. Kate Maybury tried to upload the data to Lucien Delacroix's servers, but the data's source code corrupted as it went up—'

'Probably when we stopped it around eighty percent,' Trix suggested.

'Exactly. So, once the source code corrupts, you can't get anything out of it. And whoever she was stealing from, they were very good at stopping it once they knew,' Ciaran nodded. 'But even though they stopped the main file, thousands of terabytes in size, there were still a few files that went through, smaller ones it'd been tasked with gaining first.'

'Orchid agents.' Marlowe spoke it as a statement.

'Among other things. Kate wanted the world's intelligence agents, but Lucien at the time was creating a census of his own, one of Orchid agents,' Ciaran looked nervous now as he glanced at the window. 'He knew that several global intelligence agencies had their own lists, and they'd been working together with MI5 on them, pooling data. So, the moment Fractal Destiny punched through the security, he effectively gained the list from every single agency out there. His plan was to take those lists, combine them together, and compare it to his own. He'd have a master list of everybody he could blackmail.'

Marlowe had already guessed this was part of the plan.

'Gain the IDs, especially the more secretive cells, and then force them to do what he wanted, or he'd "out" them. And you were okay with this?'

'I didn't know what they used it for until after it happened, I swear. But, the thing they didn't realise, though, was any data that went through the server had a thirty-day archive section,' Ciaran looked back at Trix. 'Are you sure we won't get snipered in here?'

'Pretty sure,' Trix replied, but Marlowe noted she shifted her laptop slightly further from the window now. 'And for the cheap seats, what that thirty-day archive means is any data passed from agent to agent, any of these items created for the game and based on real-world data or file folders, they would stay in the servers buffer, in this mysterious vault, where I can now grab it.'

She grinned.

'With the help of the great Phoenix Elite, of course,' she said, and Marlowe saw that Ciaran didn't know if she was applauding him or mocking him.

Probably a mixture of both, judging from the blush and the confused look.

'Basically, we had the archive in case the game crashed while you were playing, and it took a while for you to get back online,' he explained. 'Your inventory needed to still be there, so you didn't lose anything vital. It was mainly created for the YouTubers, as some of their videos used dodgy mods that often glitched them out, even crashed the server down once, but what it meant was for a few weeks after the transaction, there's a kind of limbo file with a copy in it.'

'How many times did they meet in this world?'

'No more than a handful,' Ciaran admitted. 'A lot of them didn't like it. As the old man there said, they preferred face to face. They felt they were less "watched" that way. Even though my server was the most secure way they could go.'

'Apart from the fact that we now know you watched them,' Kirk smiled.

Ciaran, at this, gave a mocking bow.

'Well, if they hadn't tried to kill me, I wouldn't have given up their secrets,' he said matter-of-factly.

'Is Brad Haynes involved?' Marlowe asked.

Ciaran paused mid flow.

'I don't recognise the name,' he said.

'You should ask him yourself,' Trix suggested, tapping on her screen. 'He landed at Dublin Airport two hours ago. By now, he's in town.'

She checked something else, frowning as she did so.

'Vic Saaed's also heading here as well, with his buddies Lloyd and Jackson,' she continued. 'Probably called up the first plane after your name was picked up by the Irish Garda, landing just before midnight.'

Marlowe leant back on the sofa.

'Tomorrow we fly to Washington,' he said. 'Ciaran, we'll find you a place that's safe in Dublin—'

'Hell no,' Ciaran replied. 'I'm coming with you. You're the only people so far that haven't tried to kill me.'

He grinned.

'Also, you still need me,' he continued. 'Bridget Summers, she was here because she followed your identities, right? She knows the names? I've got a little app, might help. A tiny bit of code that gets inserted into your passport's biometric data. Customs and everybody sees the name on it, as eyes are, well, analogue. But if anybody looks for the name on a manifest from an online source, they see a different name. You don't show. It's a glitch, but it means you're invisible.'

Marlowe looked back at Tessa.

'The moment we got on that plane they knew,' he said. 'But, if Orchid are fighting, we should be taking a side. St John Steele gave me the key for a reason.'

'He wants out,' Kirk added. 'If Lucien and Taylor Coleman are doing the same, there's a chance they're looking for Orchid to explode, possibly on an international stage, and hoping to get out in the rubble. Or get Caldwell to pardon them, too, when he's President.'

Marlowe walked to the window, looking out.

'Lucien wants McKay to think he's safe from harm,' he said. 'He's hoping he'll out the others during the debate, and cause a war. One which Lucien, if he is still alive, will swoop in, offering agents their lives back.'

He spun back to Ciaran.

'Your little piece of code. Did Delacroix ever use it? Can it be reverse engineered? To actively look for the code to see where someone could be?'

Ciaran nodded with the slightest hint of a smile.

'It's in PCs I created, so yeah, it can be hunted down, provided you keep them online long enough.'

'How does this meeting thing work?' Marlowe asked.

'You call a meeting,' Ciaran said, as if it was the easiest thing ever. 'You use the API and the software sends a message. Orchid High Council meetings are important, so people don't usually miss them, and then you all turn up and talk. But no one's used it for a while.'

'Perhaps as the newly crowned King of Orchid I should have a chat with my people,' Marlowe smiled. 'Do you have a gaming PC that I can use with the API attached?'

'Dude, this laptop will get you everything you need,' Ciaran grinned. 'Give me ten minutes and I'll give you an entire world.'

24

MULTI-PLAYER

Marlowe hadn't played games for a long time, but he knew the basics of them. He'd grown up playing *Lara Croft* and racing games, and once you had a vague idea of how the controls worked, it wasn't too difficult to remember them after years away from them.

Now he sat, facing Ciaran's laptop screen, controller in hand and microphone earpiece over his head. The laptop's screen had been sent by some screen mirroring app to the hotel suite's TV, which meant everybody in the room could see and hear what was going on.

'Remember, it's a mixture of two things,' Trix said as she was fine-tuning Marlowe's avatar in the game. 'The controller works for your basic movements, but we have macros in the keyboard's shortcut buttons; to take an item from someone it's Ctrl+A, etc. There's a list I've written out beside you in case you need it.'

Marlowe looked at his character on the screen. It had unkempt brown hair and a shaggy beard.

'I don't look like that, do I?' he asked.

'No, but that's the joy of having a computer avatar,' Trix smiled. 'You can be whatever you want.'

'Well, I want to have less shaggy hair and I need to be taller,' Marlowe smiled. 'I am a king, after all.'

He was standing in what seemed to be a virtual boardroom and, as he waited, slowly, other characters appeared. It had been about half an hour since the call had been made for the meeting, and Marlowe was impressed enough people still had these gaming PCs around. Although, if they had laptops like Ciaran, they could log in from anywhere.

The call had been sent out to the High Council; *Marlowe had the API, and Marlowe wanted to talk.* They weren't sure who would turn up, but Marlowe wondered whether whoever did would be part of the new brood of Orchid, younger people who probably wanted to see a regime change, and, for him, that meant people he was probably going up against.

He noticed, however, that they didn't have their names attached to their bodies. In most games you could click on someone and at least you could get some kind of gamertag. Here, all you could see were numbers. Trix had explained when they first arrived that some cells still relied on privacy, so secret that not even other cells knew their names – hence Lucien's census list – so characters in the game were named by what order they arrived at, rather than their true identities. The first person to arrive was "01," the second "02."

Marlowe didn't know what he was named as, and clicked a button.

00

Well, it was better than being zero-point five or something.

The problem for the others, though, was that Ciaran, having the source code, knew exactly who was in the room and who wasn't.

A third person appeared on the screen saying nothing. Like the others, a little note appeared above their head.

03 has entered the chat.

Number One, a woman in a business suit, now stood next to Number Two, an older man with what looked to be balding hair, but that could have been some kind of glitch with his head, if Marlowe was being honest. Number Three, an individual with a turban, stood alone to the side, waiting for someone to speak. Marlowe wondered if this was the avatar of the Indian who'd searched his room with Peter Lloyd, but guessed it probably wasn't as the High Council wouldn't lower themselves to menial tasks.

Also, assuming the one person with the turban he'd seen was the avatar here, was a teeny bit problematic.

Marlowe also waited. It was said he would start at ten pm GMT and there were still a few moments left. In the final few seconds, two more faces appeared as their avatars popped into existence; one, a black man dressed as some kind of South African warlord and the final one, a man in a black hoodie, with what looked to be a Friday the Thirteenth "Jason" mask on his face.

Ciaran, seeing the time, pressed a button on the keyboard. There was a *dong* that rang through Marlowe's headphones, and probably on the TV in the suite as well.

'I've locked the door,' he said. 'Anyone who turns up now will find themselves barred. They'll be annoyed, but I'll have their details.'

Marlowe nodded.

'Do they know who I am?' he asked.

'You're seen to them as "zero,"' Ciaran added. 'But they'll guess once I press this button here, as you'll be unmuted, and they'll hear everything you say.'

Ciaran looked around the room.

'Remember how microphones work, people? If you talk in the background, they'll pick that up too.'

He glanced back at Marlowe.

'There's a notepad in your itinerary where you can write text-based notes on and pass them to people. Those notes will be only read by that person.'

'I thought this had been decommissioned,' a woman's voice, middle-aged European, spoke through Marlowe's headphones and on the screen, the woman in the suit, Number One, waved her hands.

'I wouldn't know,' Marlowe replied, allowing his voice to speak through the system. 'I'm just relying on what my father gave me in the gardens of Versailles.'

'So, it's Marlowe,' the hooded man with a mask, Number Five, spoke, his voice obviously speaking through some kind of voice modulator. 'Give me one reason we need to stay.'

'Because I'm High Council, according to tradition.'

'You're High Council because your father didn't want it,' this was the balding man, Number Two.

'I wouldn't know what my dad wanted either,' Marlowe said. 'I'm not part of his crowd. But whether or not you agree with this, I'm in a situation where I need to know what my options are. I've not really been given any kind of manual on how to do this.'

'You sit down, you shut up and you let us get on with our jobs,' Number Four said, a hint of arrogance in their voice.

'Yeah, you know, that's not going to happen,' Marlowe replied. 'Especially with the fact that St John Steele gave me the details purely so I could connect to this lovely decor, and tell you that Lucien Delacroix is still alive.'

It was a play mainly to cause dissension, but it looked like it worked, as the others in the room didn't move, their real-life counterparts probably muting their mics and asking their people to check into this.

'Delacroix was shot at close range,' Number One now snapped. 'I was there. I saw it.'

At this point, Marlowe realised this was probably the older woman who spoke earlier at the party.

He remembered her comment.

'We can't go public when we're at war.'

Could she be an ally here? If he could convince her the upcoming civil war was better off elsewhere, that would be a massive win.

'What you saw was what they wanted you to see,' he replied. 'Don't you think it's strange that the only weapon allowed in – well, before all the security ran in and started shooting - was one that my father smuggled in? A weapon that, when put together, wasn't seen by anyone to actually fire, but was placed against his chest at close range?'

Again, silence.

'I believe, thanks to a Rubicon agent working for Orlovsky, that Lucien was shot in the chest with gel-tipped bullets, providing the blood we all saw, while a vest, worn underneath his shirt, took the bulk of the damage.'

He smiled, fitting better into his role.

'We also did an experiment to test this,' he said. 'I can guarantee you the person shot in the same way survived.'

'Viktor Orlovsky sent one of your friends to the event,

yes? I wonder why he didn't come himself, or even turn up here?' Number Four asked with mock innocence, now sitting in one of the chairs around the boardroom table. Marlowe hadn't worked out how to make his avatar sit yet, so he decided just to stand at the end and ignore the comment, apart from the confirmation that Viktor Orlovsky was High Council.

'He didn't feel safe going along, I think.'

'Of course,' Number Four carried on. 'He and Lucien hated each other since Sarajevo.'

Marlowe had no idea what this was, so continued.

'Lucien wanted out, and my father wanted out. From what I can work out, these two were some of the earliest members of Orchid. Christ, my dad's company was even named after an orchid. Yet they don't want to be here right now. Steele is still the Arbitrator of the organisation, and *he* doesn't want to be here right now. What does that tell you about Orchid? Because to me, it says that you're about to die. And whatever Kate Maybury and Lucien Delacroix were doing, it wasn't just about grabbing details of agents and shoring up some kind of blackmail power base. It was about McKay, and the upcoming debate.'

He paused and played his card.

'Fractal Destiny wasn't just about grabbing agents' details,' he said. 'Many of you are aware of this. But what you might not be aware of is when they started the upload, the first thing they got out were the names of every single known Orchid agent. Every agency's guessing list.'

'Agencies don't know anything,' Number Five said, his voice still modulated.

'True. But if you've got a name that's on three agency lists and is a possible name on your own one – and we all know

Lucien had his own one – the chances are they're probably Orchid,' Marlowe smiled. He wondered whether his character, in the *Crime Town* virtual server smiled as he spoke. He had noticed, as the avatars' owners replied to him, that their characters made some kind of weird open-and-shut mouth noises. 'You know he's got his own little hotel complex on this server, right? Where he's been practising time and time again to take down McKay in his debate tomorrow night. That Donziger was pressuring McKay, saying he had files on him, and Harrison Caldwell went into the salt mines and confiscated them.'

Nobody replied. Marlowe knew he didn't have to explain more about Caldwell to them.

Then, finally, the masked man with the hoodie started to clap.

Ciaran leaned over, muting Marlowe, as he stared at the screen with horror.

'Bloody Mary, that's Delacroix,' he whispered. 'When he flies, his satellite IP uses a VPN that gives him a particular address. Bugger's turned up to his own wake.'

'Could it be someone working for him?'

'If it's not him, it's definitely somebody who was working with him ...' Ciaran agreed, but he let the statement trail off as he stared wordlessly at the figure on the screen.

Marlowe pressed the button, unmuting himself.

'It would be far easier if I knew the full story,' he said. 'What's going on and why there's a fight. I'd also like to know what side each of you is on. I noticed that not all the High Council turned up, which gives me an idea that some of you either don't like this as a meeting place, don't like me as a potential member, or aren't around to answer.'

He turned his character with the controller now, walking over to Number Five, the masked and hooded character.

'How about you start?'

As Number Five spoke, exclaiming how ludicrous this was, Marlowe wrote on his virtual notepad, giving it to the hooded and masked avatar in front of him.

I know it's you, Lucien.

He looked back at his virtual audience, having passed the note to Number Five. And then, in a moment of mischief, he walked up to each one of the four others, pausing in front of them, as if doing the same.

'Lucien Delacroix is going to kill President McKay before he outs his role in Orchid,' he said. 'He's using Senator Kyle and Harrison Caldwell to do it, and it looks like he'll switch feeds right before the moment, and throw McKay to the wolves, faking a suicide, allowing Caldwell to take over.'

Nobody spoke, and again, Marlowe assumed there was a lot of muting going on.

'On the table will be a note, something that all of you can read. I ask you to look at it, and if you can answer, reply to the address.'

He placed another note on the table. It was very simple.

One of you here is a traitor to Orchid. And I've already told them I know who they are. It's Lucien Delacroix. Your choice is whether you stand with a man who's already left you for dead.

Underneath it was an email Trix had arranged for him, one that couldn't be traced. And, by walking up to each of them, nobody knew which avatar was told.

Paranoia would now run rife in the virtual boardroom.

This done, he manipulated his character to step back so the others could move close enough to grab the item and read it.

'Be aware. I know who all of you are,' he said ominously. 'And if Orchid kills the President, it will turn the world into chaos. Something I can't allow.'

However, as he turned back to the table, he saw Number Five reach behind his back and pull out a gun.

'Really?' he asked, glancing at Ciaran, but from the face that Ciaran had, Marlowe realised this was possibly something that wasn't good.

'You're playing the wrong game,' Number Five said sadly. 'Even though you've been spoon-fed the walkthrough.'

As the masked and hooded man raised a pistol and shot him several times, the world went grey, faded, and the blue words "GAME OVER" appeared on the screen.

And then the server collapsed into blackness.

'What the hell happened?' Marlowe said, looking around in confusion and anger as he pulled off his headset.

'If you die in the game, you have to start again,' Ciaran was typing frantically on the laptop now, having turned it away from Marlowe. 'So, by shooting the person who created the meeting room, Lucien Delacroix effectively ended the scenario. The meeting is over. Everyone's been booted from the server by you dying.'

'You could have told me this!'

'There was no need to,' Ciaran shook his head. 'He shouldn't have had a gun. There's no way there was a gun. No weapons allowed is one of the core bases of the building.'

'Then how did he have a gun?'

Ciaran hissed as he read a line of code.

'He's altered the bloody coding,' he said. 'Or at least he hired someone to. When he arrived on the server, he didn't come to the meeting, he stole a car, ran over a cop and stole their gun. It didn't matter if he was being chased for it, they wouldn't be able to find him once he stood on the spot.'

'And brought a gun into the meeting room,' Marlowe leant back. 'Well, at least we know something. We've definitely gained his attention.'

He rose, grabbing his jacket.

'So let's go gain it some more,' he said.

25

AIRPORT PICKUP

Vɪᴄ Sᴀᴇᴇᴅ sᴛᴀʀᴛᴇᴅ ʟᴀᴜɢʜɪɴɢ ᴀs ʜᴇ ᴡᴀʟᴋᴇᴅ ᴏᴜᴛ ᴏꜰ ᴛʜᴇ Dublin airport terminal, seeing Marlowe standing in front of him with a sign in his hand.

Welcome to Dublin, MI5 Agents
Vikram Saeed
Peter Lloyd
Lawrence Jackson

'I see Trix has been playing with the flight scanner app,' he said as he paused, placing his duffel bag down. He was dressed in a suit and shirt, no tie; Marlowe assumed that everything else he needed was in his overnight bag. Peter had a hard-case four-wheeled cabin bag, and Jackson some kind of backpack rucksack.

They hadn't come for a holiday; they were here for business.

Of course, the reason they hadn't turned up with anything was because they hadn't had the chance to receive what they needed yet, having only just got off the last flight of the day. Marlowe had hoped, planned even, for this.

'Thought I'd give you a welcome,' he said. 'Guessed you'd be coming.'

Vic nodded and accepted the outstretched hand from Marlowe, as he folded the sign up with his other hand. This was a calculated risk on Marlowe's part. He didn't know if they were turning up as Orchid agents or as MI5 agents, and Marlowe wasn't sure whose side they were on. However, currently, none of them had tried to kill him as of late.

'Clever move,' Jackson muttered. 'Meeting us here before we can meet anybody and gain weapons. I'm guessing you're armed.'

'Always,' Marlowe replied. 'In fact, I think I have your gun.'

With a smile, he passed it across in full view of all the cameras. It wasn't Jackson's Glock – that was still in Paris, and this had been taken from Clontarf – but it didn't matter to the cameras. All they saw was the action.

'Now, if anybody sees you, they'll have to come and have a chat about why MI5 are here and taking second-rate Glocks from me,' he said. 'I'm sure if you were here on Orchid business, you'd have to explain it to a completely different set of authorities.'

Vic nodded, motioning for Marlowe to follow them out of the building.

'I don't think so,' Marlowe replied. 'I like being where the cameras are.'

'We like cameras too,' Vic said. 'After all, we didn't follow you all this way just to kill you.'

'I wasn't sure,' Marlowe replied. 'Why did you fly all this way?'

'We got your message. The one at the Trinity College, where you waved your badge when you could have done a dozen different things instead.'

Marlowe knew this had been a mistake, but was quite surprised MI5 had taken this as some tacit message to them.

'Are you here on behalf of the government or for other entities?' he asked.

'Well, if we were here as other entities, you're technically our boss now, aren't you?' Jackson replied, his voice tight and clipped. He was angry, and Marlowe understood it was from more than the gun he'd been lumbered with. 'We understand Bridget Summers shot Tessa Kirk.'

'Bridget's on our list,' Vic added. 'We've been tasked with getting her. You wouldn't know where she is, would you?'

'She was in Paris, she's connected to Orchid with Orlovsky, and we all know she's Rubicon, but apart from that, I don't know anything,' Marlowe said.

It wasn't too far from the truth, and he didn't want them to know it seemed for the moment she was allied with St John Steele.

'We heard she shot Tessa beside the Book of Kells, right before you turned up as a white knight and waved your ID.'

'Yeah, Tessa's injured badly, but she's not dead.'

'I don't suppose you'll tell us where she is?'

'Resting up under a fake name,' Marlowe replied quickly. 'That's all you're getting. Can we wrap this up quickly though, because I have to stop her father from going on a killing spree because of it.'

'I get that,' Vic nodded. 'I really do. I also know you're not Orchid.'

He pointed at Marlowe's wrist.

'A few weeks after Casey died, you came back to MI5,

brought into the shit jobs by Wintergreen,' he said. 'At the time, you had a wrist bandage on. The tattoo you now have? Fits around the same time. What did she say, "get a tattoo and I'll let you back in?" That's the Wintergreen way, usually.'

Vic smiled now, looking around.

'Also, if Bridget Summers brought you into Orchid, why would she be shooting people who are helping you? I think you were telling the truth in our first chat, and now you're just running for cover.'

Marlowe was silent for a moment, working out what to say now. *Vic was good. Too good.*

'I know Orchid's in the middle of a civil war,' he said. 'I know Kate Maybury's cell decided they'd tired of waiting and wanted to go further. I know Lucien Delacroix is still alive, and his death – or pretended death – was basically created with Taylor Coleman for some yet unknown reason. I also know that Bridget Summers is connected to this somehow, that it's connected to President McKay and the debate in Washington tomorrow, and I know that they're going to kill him – or at least fake his own suicide.'

'You found out a lot,' Vic said.

'I was hoping you could confirm or deny what I know,' Marlowe replied.

At this, however, Vic shook his head.

'Unfortunately, I'm not as involved as you seem to think I am,' he said. 'Unlike you, I'm not some nepo baby who had Daddy give him a role in the company.'

Marlowe chuckled at the jibe.

'What, so you're a blue-collar worker, moving his way up the industry?'

He now turned to Peter.

'How about you? You're recent, right? Five months, only been to a few meetings ...'

'How do you know this?' Peter looked nervously around. 'How does he know?'

'Because that's why he was in the gunroom,' Jackson snapped back. 'That's why he constantly talked to you about his guns and got you to talk to him. He was turning you into an asset.'

Peter Lloyd paled, and Marlowe knew that, finally, his dreams of being James Bond had crumbled to dust.

'You'd know though, right?' he said, his voice getting colder as he turned to Jackson. 'What was it you said in Paris, while outside my hotel door? "Thomas Marlowe is a traitor, a spy, and tonight he dies. What they want is Marlowe dead, and McKay kept in power until the election – Caldwell said it himself, right before Delacroix started talking?" That's pretty correct, yeah?'

Jackson smiled darkly at this.

'You misheard,' he replied. 'I'm guessing you were nearby?'

'You'll never know.'

There was a long, awkward moment of silence.

'Tomorrow we fly to Washington,' Marlowe said, risking giving away the information. 'We have the data and a plan we think could stop Lucien from killing the President and destroying the debate. What I want to know now is, are you – or is your Orchid cell – for or *against* the attack?'

Vic watched Marlowe for a long moment, seconds passing as the two men stared at each other.

'You should stay with Orchid when this is all done,' he said. 'Even if it's based on a lie, you still have a position there.

It might help you get work, because you're sure as hell not coming back to the service after this.'

'Wintergreen's promised me a full pardon if I can bring down Orchid,' Marlowe replied. 'Trix is doing this as part of some kind of suspension task. And Tessa Kirk was informed by Wintergreen that she'd get *into* the service if she helped.'

Vic laughed.

'Emilia Wintergreen is temporary at best,' he said. 'When Curtis returns, she'll be dumped back into Section D. And Curtis, for all his great sayings and motivational speeches ...'

He leant closer.

'He's Orchid too.'

Marlowe shook his head.

'Now you're reaching,' he said. 'Telling me horror stories, hoping I'll run away. Curtis isn't Orchid. I don't think McKellen's Orchid either.'

'Worth a try,' Vic shrugged. 'But either way, Wintergreen will screw you over, no matter what you do.'

'I know,' Marlowe nodded. 'And I've been thinking through the same scenarios you have. But you know what? There's a lot of things someone can do if he has his own secret society. All I have to do is remove the problem people.'

He leant closer to Vic.

'Are *you* a problem person, Vic?'

Vic grinned.

'I can be the best asset you'll ever have,' he replied. 'All you need to do is make sure we keep this secret—'

He stopped as he saw a red SUV pull up just outside the main doors to the terminal.

He glanced back at Marlowe.

'You backstabbing bastard,' he hissed. 'Is this why you

wanted to stay here in the terminal? So we didn't spoil your reveal?'

'Oh, hell no,' Marlowe looked around and frowned as Brad Haynes climbed out of the driver's seat. The blacked-out windows behind pretty much explained who the other person in the car was. 'I wasn't expecting this, and to be perfectly honest, they're not that welcome right now.'

He sighed.

'Shall we go and have a chat?' he asked. 'This has, unfortunately, made everything a little more public than I was hoping.'

Marlowe, Vic, Lloyd, and Jackson walked out to meet the smiling Sasha Bordeaux, who now stood behind her SUV, waving like a friend meeting someone from a plane.

Again, although he'd made out this wasn't expected or wanted, the sudden CIA appearance was something Marlowe had hoped for. He knew that Brad would have been monitoring him, and probably within ten minutes of landing in Dublin, he would have known where Marlowe was staying.

This had been deliberate.

Marlowe had been given fake names in New York when last working with Brad, and had deliberately used one of those names, "Garth Fleming," when booking a backup suite. He'd relied on Brad seeing this, and he relied on Brad recognising the name, one he'd given him personally in New York, and knowing what this meant – *that Marlowe wanted his help, and was still an ally.*

Even though Brad had left on okay terms in Paris, Marlowe didn't know what would happen the moment Sasha Bordeaux got involved. Especially as Brad had been planning on going to Washington.

It seemed that at least Sasha was enjoying the moment.

'Well, look here,' she said, as Vic and the others walked out behind Marlowe.

'Vic Saeed, have you met—'

'Cassandra Cain,' Sasha said quickly, interrupting him from saying the name he knew her under, and Marlowe had to force himself from laughing once more. Cassandra Cain was the other alter identity of *Batgirl*, the one that replaced the more famous Barbara Gordon. Cassandra Cain was the daughter of a ninja, had been trained by the best agents in history, and was the most badass non-powered character in the DC universe.

Of course, Sasha Bordeaux, or whatever her real name was, would use it.

Vic, who had been briefed about her, probably after the Donziger affair, smiled warmly, already turning on the charm.

'So you're the one that likes the comic book characters,' he said. 'I'll play with that. This is Jackson. This is Lloyd. You know where we're from?'

'Oh, that depends if we're playing nice, or if we're playing *spies*.'

'MI5 has come to assist an agent,' Peter said, stepping forward. 'Why are the CIA here?'

'The CIA has come to assist an *asset*,' Brad said, stepping forward now, eyeing each of the MI5 agents up one at a time. 'Marlowe has helped us frequently. And we understand he could be in a bit of trouble with you.'

'And what kind of trouble would that be?' Jackson asked, wide-eyed and innocent.

Brad smiled, and Marlowe could tell that he already didn't like the MI5 operative.

'The kind of trouble that brings cocksuckers like you to

find him,' he said. 'Now get back onto your little Ryanair flight, piss off back across the Irish Sea, and go tell Mummy and Daddy in Whitehall you're not needed, as the CIA have pulled the big toys out of the box, and you're too small to play with them.'

Marlowe, for the most part, had kept quiet up to now, enjoying the banter, but at this he held up a hand.

'Look,' he said. 'We've all got the same enemy here.'

'Do we?' Sasha said, looking at Vic. 'Because I reckon if I wave a nice UV black light around, I'm going to see a ton of little flower tattoos.'

'True,' Marlowe replied quickly. 'Including on my arm. And Vic's. We both took the tattoos as part of an undercover sting.'

'Convenient.'

'If you think having a UV tattoo put on your arm for fun is convenient, then sure, why not?'

'And the other two?' Sasha seemed amused by the quite obvious lie.

'I wouldn't know what Vic suggested to them as part of an ongoing mission,' Marlowe said. 'After all, I've been off books for quite a while, being one of your assets, remember? We could always ask why you allowed Orchid agents to hang around US Senators, if you really want to start waving the flashlight around. We could even look higher. You know, *Vice President* level.'

He took a deep breath, letting the tension move out of his system, and saw Sasha pause, possibly for the first time actually lost for words.

'It's very simple,' he continued before she could catch her breath. 'Tomorrow I'm going to Washington because President McKay is going to be assassinated by Orchid. But it's not

Orchid as a full-on attack, it's a few pissed off malcontents. At the moment, the Orchid agents who don't like these pissed off Orchid agents are allies, so it doesn't matter if someone's got a UV picture on their skin or not. What matters is if they've got a gun in their hand and they're trying to kill President Anton McKay.'

'He's telling the truth. They are looking to kill McKay,' Jackson said suddenly, his voice cutting across the conversation.

'How do you know this?' Marlowe turned to face him.

Jackson looked uncomfortable, pausing as if choosing his words carefully.

'I've been undercover with a cell,' he said, giving context to the information he was about to give, a context that Marlowe knew was given to him under his role as an active member of Orchid, as he turned to face Marlowe. 'That's why I said what you heard. I've been close to the source, becoming trusted by Lucien Delacroix, who had a mission planned, basically to "out" any of Orchid's agents who weren't siding with him, and kill McKay live on air, throwing the blame on them. However, it failed.'

'Because Mister Marlowe's father shot him,' Sasha replied.

'Actually, we think that was a fake out,' Marlowe added. 'He's still alive. I spoke to him an hour ago. Kind of. It was weird, to be honest.'

Jackson glared at Marlowe for a moment, almost as if surprised at the revelation, and maybe angry he hadn't been trusted with that part of it, and then continued.

'The plan was to fill the debate with people who either hated McKay or who were Orchid, and before McKay could "out" them, knowing he had no other option, they'd use deepfake or something to change what McKay said, admitting to everything instead, before grabbing a gun and shooting Kyle, and then himself. Then they'd cut back to the real McKay, dead on the floor.'

'Jesus,' Brad muttered.

'I think they're going to allow Senator Kyle to ask some kind of question, something about McKay's connections to Orchid, something that's been fed to her and utter bullshit, and then they'll kill her off screen, same time they kill McKay,' Marlowe added. 'They'll claim Kyle was part of some conspiracy led by Orchid mercenaries, and that Harrison Caldwell, now President by default, will clean up the now corrupt government.'

Sasha nodded at this.

'There'll be enough high-ranking members of Orchid – people Caldwell would know – on Capitol Hill who'd help convince the people they must listen to everything they say,' she said, already working through the nightmare scenario. 'Within hours, they'd have full control. And then they could start a war, outing every enemy Orchid agent that they know, and forcing the biggest manhunt ever using the death of the old President to fuel anger and rubber-stamp resources, allowing their own puppet one to continue. And, once we get to foreign countries having Orchid agents ... Jesus, it's World War Three.'

'But that's easy enough to stop,' Brad said. 'We still have a day. We tell Kyle not to ask the question.'

'Doesn't work that way,' Sasha shook her head. 'She already believes she has a killing shot on McKay. You can tell her what you know, and she'll still take it. She's thinking of her own politics. In fact, hearing she might be attacked for making McKay look bad, that makes her the Republican frontrunner next year, guaranteed. She'll actively aim for it. Also, if she doesn't, they'll change the plan to something we *don't* know. And that's worse.'

Brad sighed, nodding.

'As much as I hate to admit it, she's right. We could try to keep her out of the room, but it wouldn't matter. He's got Ron Tyler going against him, who's another person who was owned by Donziger, and who you gave his file back to in New York. And, let's be frank here, the files you gave Tyler and Kyle, they weren't the only ones in existence. If Kyle tries to back out, someone else will force her back in. Pearson, maybe. She's a dark horse Democrat.'

'I don't know Pearson,' Marlowe frowned. 'Could she be Orchid?'

'Oh, I reckon so,' Vic passed a photo on his phone over to Marlowe. 'Recognise her?'

Marlowe stared at a photo of a Democrat senator, and instantly recognised her.

She was the woman at Versailles, who'd spoken to Delacroix. The woman he thought had been at the High Council game server meeting.

'Let's hope that's not the case,' he said. 'But we need to get there and stop this.'

'Agreed,' Vic replied. 'Although we would really like to sit down before we end up having to work out our travel plans.'

'There's a flight leaving for Washington at ten thirty tomorrow morning,' Marlowe smiled. 'We're already on it.'

'Listen to you Brits and your ways,' Sasha laughed. 'It's all – oh, what's the term you'd like to use? A "load of bollocks." Is that correct?'

She nodded at Brad, who turned back to face them all.

'We have a plane on the landing strip, fuelled and ready

to go,' he said. 'If you want to bring your friends out from the hotel they're hiding in, we can fit you all in and go as one big, happy family.'

He grinned.

'As I said, the CIA has big boy toys.'

'I will say one thing, though,' Sasha added. 'It's a long flight to Washington from Ireland. And if I find out during the time that any of you are working against the global good? We're going to throw you out over international waters.'

'That works for me,' Marlowe smiled, looking momentarily at the glowering Jackson. 'Let's gather the troops.'

26

MILE HIGH CLUB

THROUGHOUT MARLOWE'S LIFE, HE'D PLAYED MANY PARTS. BUT he hadn't travelled on a private jet that many times and, if he was being honest, it was quite an experience.

He'd gathered up his remaining team members from the Dublin hotel and, after making a quick stop, journeyed back to Dublin Airport where, true to her word, Sasha Bordeaux had a small jet fuelled and ready to go in one of the back hangars.

Marlowe knew this was the right gameplay, partly because he knew Bridget Summers wouldn't be able to follow him, but there was a niggling worry that by doing this, he was placing his head in the jaws of a lion. He hoped Sasha was on his side, especially when he was going into war with a ragtag collection of people that, if he was honest, bar a couple, he wasn't too sure if he could trust.

Trix seemed to feel the same way and spent most of the flight sitting in a chair with a laptop aimed away from everybody else, doing whatever magic she was doing. The CIA had a Starlink connection that was faster than most house broadbands. This was used quite a lot over the flight, especially with Ciaran opening up his gaming PC laptop, connecting to the *Crime City* server and allowing Marlowe, Vic, and Jackson to repeatedly play through the hotel scene, learning where the shortcuts were and being led by Ciaran to where the Orchid agents had stopped while playing the game, meaning they were possibly of importance ... anything that could help.

As for Jackson, Vic, and Peter, they seemed happy to be helping and, for the moment, seemed to play on the side of the angels, continuing even when Marlowe wandered over to talk to Trix about a couple of things. Likewise, Sasha who, as they were about to land in Washington, had pulled Marlowe to the back end of the private jet, sat down at a rear table and faced him.

'How far would you trust them?' she asked, pointing back down the plane.

'Honestly, I don't know,' Marlowe replied. 'All three of them were hostiles at some point. Jackson tried to attack us in Paris, it's how I grabbed his gun. But he was defending his life. I think ... I hope he wasn't deliberately trying to take me down, no matter what I think.'

He looked back up the plane at Jackson, currently trying to play a normal level of the game, driving a car around the streets of a fictional city.

'But let's put it this way,' he continued. 'I wouldn't be putting my back in front of him, lest he stab it.'

'I didn't mean your MI5 boys, I meant all of them,' Sasha said, looking at Marlowe. 'How do you feel about Braddy Boy?'

'You've got him with you, so you must trust him.'

'Or am I keeping him close in the same way you're keeping your MI5 friends close?'

Marlowe watched Sasha for a long moment.

'Are you?' he asked.

'He has his uses,' Sasha smiled. 'I think he's a blunt tool to be used. Likewise, your friend Marshall Kirk, seventy years old yet still healthier than men half his age. But he's distracted.'

She looked back at Marlowe.

'And his daughter is solid Rubicon, born and bred.'

Marlowe leant back in the chair, glancing out of the window at the clouds beneath them. He hadn't known Sasha Bordeaux when he was fighting Rubicon, but it wasn't surprising that she knew about it.

'I like this plane,' he said, trying to change the subject. 'I'm a little annoyed you didn't give us this when we needed to fly from San Francisco to Paris.'

He was commenting on the fact that the last time he had flown, with Kate Maybury, Sasha had given them passage in the luggage hold of a *FedEx* cargo plane.

And then gave them up on the other side.

'This time you're not on the run,' Sasha smiled, and gave a little nod at this. 'And you don't have a rogue Orchid agent with you.'

She paused, making a pointed look at the three men.

'Or maybe you do,' she added. 'It seems to be a thing for you, after all.'

Marlowe acknowledged this.

'Do you have a plan for Kyle?'

'We could just take her out?' Sasha replied, holding a hand up to pause Marlowe. 'I don't mean like that. I mean injure her, make her say publicly she can't do the talk.'

She shook her head, though, and Marlowe knew she'd

already decided the answer, and was pantomiming this for his own benefit.

'No. That would just get somebody else in charge. Pearson, maybe.'

She stared out of the window.

'We could kill them all,' she mused. 'That'd be an easier option. Although you might not like that. You've saved her life a couple of times.'

'She also helped me,' Marlowe pointed out. 'Offered me a job when MI5 wanted me forgotten.'

'Did she, though?' Sasha looked forward. 'Look at it this way. You helped her out by stealing her file from Nathan Donziger. But she had been corrupt for years, doing whatever he'd said to do.'

'She was being blackmailed,' Marlowe pointed out.

'That's one side of the coin,' Sasha pursed her lips, nodding. 'The other side is she did what she needed to survive. She was quite happy to vote the way Donziger wanted. Now, consider the next time you saw her, bringing you to San Francisco, having you assist her ... just in time to be contacted by Kate Maybury, on her own little Orchid-based mission, a mission I'll point out again, that Kate had pretty much decided you were going to be the patsy for from the moment she saw you.'

Marlowe straightened in the chair.

'Are you telling me that Kate Maybury sought me out at the hotel because Senator Kyle told her I was going to be there?'

'It makes an interesting narrative, doesn't it?' Sasha, watching him work though this shrugged, the point made. 'I understand she made a speedy recovery, after all.'

'Trix helped her survive assassins.'

'True,' Sasha opened up a small bottle of water, taking a long draught of it. 'But I mean, let's be frank here, she was taken out in the middle of a conference, with heroic actions in a hospital, defending herself against assassins ... it didn't exactly hurt her presidential nomination chances, did it?'

She now steepled her fingers.

'Her husband was cheating on her. Did you know that? It was a scandal in the making. Then three years back, he dies in a helicopter crash. She gained a ton of public sympathy and removed a potential problem.'

Marlowe stared at Sasha Bordeaux. This was everything he'd seen, but through a different, less cynical set of eyes. The problem was, he could see every play as it happened. He could agree with Sasha's twisted point of view.

As if reading his mind, Sasha sighed, placing the bottle back down as she glanced out the window.

'Buckle up,' she said. 'We're heading into Washington. We'll find a place to grab some sleep, and then hit her this afternoon.'

Marlowe glanced back at the other three men.

'And those guys?'

'Don't worry about them,' Sasha grinned. 'We have a CIA welcome party waiting for them as we arrive. They'll be looked after nicely until we've fixed all this.'

SASHA HADN'T LIED; AS THEY CLIMBED OUT OF THE JET, Marlowe saw three SUVs waiting for them, each with a black-suited CIA agent in front of it. It was about four in the morning; the jet had taken just under eight hours and Washington was five hours behind GMT so the debate was fifteen hours away.

As everyone walked out of the jet, many rubbing their eyes after grabbing an hour or two's worth of sleep, Sasha turned to Marlowe.

'This, unfortunately, is where our paths diverge,' she said sadly. 'I'll take your game hacker, but the rest of you will have a spa day while we fix things for you.'

She nodded, and the three agents pulled out Glock 19s, aiming them at the new arrivals.

At this, however, Marlowe shook his head sadly.

'Oh, Sasha,' he sighed. 'Double-crossing me yet again. Did you really think that I would let you do that after the various times you've screwed me before?'

He raised a hand, clicked his fingers, and the three suited agents now turned their guns on Sasha.

'Thanks for the Starlink internet on the flight, by the way,' he said with a smile. 'It allowed Trix to contact a few people. You see, before I met you, I had a meeting with the High Council of Orchid, and gave them an option; if they wanted to get out of whatever was going on, I left them a way they could contact me to get them out of the way. A couple of the High Council agreed. One of them offered their services.'

He waved at the men.

'Services I'm now making use of. But don't worry, I'm sure your real CIA will be arriving soon.'

He looked at the three men.

'Hold them, get out of here before you're taken, and let them out tomorrow,' he replied. 'By then we'll have sorted it, one way or another.'

'You're making a mistake, Marlowe,' Sasha pouted. 'We could work together.'

'You were literally doing the same to me a minute ago,' Marlowe said, as he now looked at Brad. 'Your call if you want to come with us, or stay with Sasha.'

Brad looked conflicted, glancing back at his boss before nodding and walking over to Marlowe.

'I want to end this,' he said. 'I don't want to sit it out on the bench.'

'Shame,' Sasha nodded at the entrance to the runway, where two police cars and another large van were smashing through the gates. I kind of guessed you'd try something. Here are my people.'

Marlowe looked back at the Orchid agents who had come to save him.

'Go,' he said. 'Tell your boss thank you.'

As they ran to their vehicles, Marlowe took the third and closest of the SUVs, with Brad, Kirk, Tessa, and Trix following. Ciaran looked a little lost, standing still, looking from Sasha to Marlowe, and although Marlowe wanted to go back and grab him, he could see the oncoming cavalry was getting closer. He wouldn't have a chance to do it.

'Good luck, Sasha. I'll see you at the hotel. Look after Ciaran!' he shouted as he leapt into the driver's seat, gunning the SUV away as the police cars approached. The van had stopped at the plane; one police car started chasing the two Orchid SUVs in the other direction, and the other one followed Marlowe's car. Though he knew they weren't going to stop just to confirm that Sasha was okay.

MI5 would be under wraps for the next day, which was good – but if he didn't do something fast, he was going to join them.

'I don't know Washington!' he shouted, gripping the steering wheel of the SUV, his knuckles white, the sirens of the police car behind wailed into the early morning light as they roared past the private jet hangar after Marlowe. The city of Washington lay ahead, a maze of streets and alleys that, although they bore the history of power and secrets, were a complete unknown. His eyes darted to the rearview mirror, where the flashing red and blue lights were becoming distressingly larger.

'Get onto Aviation Drive!' Brad leant forward from the back seat, pointing off vaguely forward. 'I was stationed here when I started in the CIA! It's the quickest way into the city!'

Marlowe did what Brad said, taking a route leading him straight onto Aviation Drive, followed by a sharp turn onto the Washington Parkway, as Brad's intimate knowledge of Washington's arteries and veins, shouting directions like a hysterical sat nav voice into his ear, became his only advantage over his pursuers.

He burst onto the Parkway, the SUV's tyres screeching in protest as he navigated the twists and turns with a brutal precision. The police car followed, relentless, an angry hornet buzzing at his heels, causing more than a few swear words from Kirk, beside Brad, as he offered to shoot the car before being shouted down by everyone in the SUV. Every so often, the police car's spotlight would flick over the SUV's interior, blinding in its intensity, before disappearing again.

At another overly loud order from Brad, Marlowe turned hard onto 395 North, the barrier walls now closing in around them, trapping them in a concrete valley filled with fast moving obstacles. He could feel the police car gaining, and visualised the other driver's breath on his neck until he realised it was actually Brad's, the American close to hyperventilating now.

Keeping a steady speed, they blasted through the Third

Street tunnel, apparently an artery of the city's circulatory system according to Kirk, now being some kind of magical tour guide, reading from his phone.

'Get ready to slam the brakes,' Brad was flicking his eyes from the road ahead to the car behind, jousting distances. 'Let them get close and then take the Massachusetts Avenue exit at the last minute.'

Ahead was the exit, a quick jut off the tunnel's path. As they almost reached it, the police car nearly on top of them, Marlowe slammed on the brakes, the SUV screeching and shuddering under the brutal deceleration, the police car violently swerving to avoid it. At the last possible moment, Marlowe jerked the wheel, throwing the SUV into the exit.

The police car shot past, its driver unable to stop in time, and unable to follow as Marlowe sped up Massachusetts Avenue. The sirens faded, but Marlowe didn't slow, *couldn't* slow, not until he was certain.

'There!' Brad pointed, and Marlowe gratefully turned into an alley, killing the SUV's engine. They sat, and Marlowe's breath came in ragged gasps, listening to the sound of the ticking of the cooling engine and his pounding heartbeat.

The five of them waited in the SUV, every second stretching infinitely as Marlowe strained his ears for the tell-tale wail of sirens, but none came.

'We've lost them,' Brad whispered. 'At least for now.'

Marlowe stepped out of the SUV, his legs shaky but functioning. He could still hear the distant siren, a mournful wail in the Washington night, but it was moving away, not towards them. He knew he had only bought them a few minutes, maybe less. The city was a grid, and eventually his determined pursuer would gain friends as Sasha brought in whatever she needed.

'Phones,' Trix said, pulling out her own and breaking it apart, tossing it aside. 'We were on a CIA plane, so they probably know how to find us through them. And we need to leave the car.'

Marlowe nodded, doing similar as he looked out towards the early lightening of the morning sky.

Later that very day, Orchid was making their move.

Somehow, he needed to stop them – while keeping MI5, Orchid and the CIA off his back.

But first, they needed a base.

So, picking up his duffel, he led his team into the Washington backstreets.

27

ELEVENTH HOUR

'OKAY, WE NEED A PLAN,' MARLOWE SAID AS THEY SAT IN THE far corner of a diner, out of the way enough to avoid attention, and one that looked too old and dishevelled to care too much about CCTV. It was seven in the morning now; in just over twelve hours all hell was going to break loose, and they needed to find a place they didn't need to move from every half an hour.

'I have an idea,' Tessa said, working on a laptop. 'Orlovsky gave me the contact details of assets in Dublin and Washington. We could use them?'

Everyone turned and looked at her.

'Seriously?' Marlowe shook his head. 'You think they'll help us?'

'I didn't say ask them for help, I said use them,' Tessa smiled. 'I'll contact one, ask to meet, say there's a few of us, so don't be scared when we all rock up, and then we go the opposite direction as Sasha gets everyone down on them.'

'Harsh for the asset.'

'You work for someone like Orlovsky, you expect to get screwed over,' Tessa shrugged. 'Doesn't mean it's a bad idea.'

'It's quite genius,' Kirk smiled. 'So, where do we aim them?'

'The Willard is right next to President's Park and the Washington Monument, so we know we need to get there eventually, and there's a Marriott we can get into literally across the street,' Trix was checking a laptop screen. 'I can book us a suite through another identity. One of my old ones.'

'So, we go to the Marriott and aim them all where?'

'Capitol Hill,' Brad suggested. 'Far enough away to give us breathing space, and also plausible enough if we're trying to contact Kyle.'

'Works for me,' Marlowe looked at Tessa. 'You good to do this?'

'Already done,' Tessa looked up. 'It'll come from a new number but has the right codes.'

This done, Marlowe paid the bill with another hundred from Bridget's stash, and rose.

'We get to the hotel, check in, set down and work out what to do,' he said. 'One thing that I'm really annoyed about, though, is that we lost Ciaran to Sasha. Because you know more than anything she's going to have him going into his server right now.'

'I'd be impressed if he could,' Trix smiled. 'After all, I have his laptop.'

In shock, Marlowe turned to look at her.

'What do you mean you have his laptop?'

'I did it when I saw all the people around, right before we were getting off,' she said. 'He was distracted, so I slipped it out of his rucksack and into my bag. I don't think he even realised.'

'So, Sasha has nothing?' Marlowe smiled. 'Well, we might have a fighting chance after all.'

WITH A FEW OF BRIDGET SUMMERS' HUNDRED-DOLLAR BILLS discreetly passed to the receptionist and the duty manager, Marlowe had enabled them to get an extremely early check-in to their suite at the Washington Marriott.

Nowhere near as stately and important looking as the hotel across the road, it was more than good enough for the task required.

Staring out over the Willard InterContinental Washington opposite through one of the corner windows of the suite, he knew what he had to do.

Trix was at the main table, working on two laptops; hers and Ciaran's, linked with a variety of hubs and cables. Somehow, she had broken through Ciaran's encryption, and Marlowe didn't really want to know how considering the last time she had shown him how she'd done such a thing, it had involved gruesome looking fake eyeballs.

Brad was staring out over the street from the other corner window, probably concerned about his own career, and watching for the inevitable Sasha Bordeaux, while Kirk and Tessa watched a news channel, currently showing the setup for the evening's presidential debate.

'I've got an idea,' Marlowe said finally, turning to face the others. 'But you're not going to like it much.'

'Tom, I don't want to spoil your fun, but you've never had

a good idea in your life,' Kirk sighed with a mock mournfulness. 'You usually end up being attacked, hunted, and I usually get battered about, so spit it out and we'll tell you if you're trying to kill us again.'

Marlowe laughed.

'We know McKay is gunning for Orchid,' he said. 'We know Donziger has blackmail information about him. McKay also knows Lucien has it too, but he thinks he can keep them both at bay. He doesn't know Donziger's made a deal with Caldwell, instead thinking he still needs a pardon from McKay, and won't do anything until McKay's no longer President, and as far as he's concerned, Lucien is dead. The one thing he *doesn't* want is to be removed and have Orchid agent Harrison Caldwell replace him as President.'

Everybody nodded at this.

'However, he's going up against Ron Tyler in a Presidential debate,' Marlowe continued. 'He knows Caldwell *should* be the heir apparent, but only if he doesn't run; he's probably unsure who's going to aim at who, and he's hoping to dispel some dissension and chaos in the process.'

'Kyle has a question she's going to ask,' Kirk added. 'We don't know what it is.'

'Even if we did, we're not going to be able to stop it,' Marlowe shook his head. 'It'll be something that probably connects to the Donziger file. The moment it's asked, McKay will know it's too late, and at that point he's likely to reveal everything, go out in a blaze of glory, explain to the world how Caldwell is Orchid, how there's a huge organisation out there taking over, etc etc.'

'Followed by "bang,"' Tessa mimed a gun to the head. 'This'll be when Orchid agents come in to stop him.'

'The feed by this point will already have been taken over

clandestinely, and they'll switch to an identical room in a computer world, where a computer version with a deepfake face will shoot himself in the head right before his file is leaked out somehow. Or Caldwell explains how he's been secretly investigating because of it.'

'A file that will be heavily doctored,' Marlowe nodded. 'Removing anything to do with Orchid, Caldwell, or anyone else Orchid can use. He doesn't really have a way out here and in the deepfake video, he'll probably shoot Kyle, explaining her death. Maybe even the CNN guy. Then the only witnesses in the room will be Orchid-friendly.'

He looked back out of the window, across at the other hotel.

'But there are a lot of things they're relying on here,' he said. 'First off, that the feed is split and they can cut away from McKay. Second, that McKay in the computer world is ready to shoot himself in the head.'

'I'm guessing there's an avatar that's going to do it, but if something happens to the server, surely that can go wrong?' Tessa looked at Trix. 'How could we make something happen to the server?'

'I don't know, as I haven't looked at it, and it's in a Swiss server, so not known for crapping out at the best of times,' Trix ran a hand through her hair as she considered this. 'That said, Ciaran spoke about servers collapsing and everything going down.'

She thought about this for a moment, recalling the moment.

'He said some of the YouTubers used dodgy mods when recording their videos, ones that often glitched them out, even crashed the server down once.'

She grinned.

'Dodgy mods. That's what we use.'

Marlowe smiled in response.

'So *there's* the plan. We get the server to crash,' he explained. 'If the server crashes, they can't fake McKay's death – they'd have to do it live, and there's no way they do that. But before this, we need to get into Ciaran's vault under the fake hotel and take every piece of information that we can. We need to make sure that if it does go wrong, we can still prove that Orchid's behind this.'

Tessa leant back.

'This is a multi-level problem,' she said. 'You need someone to get into the security room in the hotel and stop the Orchid agents from splitting the feed for as long as you can. Which is effectively a suicide mission, as they'll aim everyone at you. You need someone to make sure McKay isn't attacked and defend Kyle. You need to get Trix into the vault —'

'Why do *I* need to go into the vault?'

'Because you're the only one who understands how this stuff works,' Marlowe said.

'I'm not a gamer,' Trix replied. 'I don't know how to glitch a server.'

Marlowe thought about this.

'I know a gamer who would,' he said.

TRIX HAD MANAGED TO BOUNCE THE IP AGAIN AND CONNECTED to the server in the same way she had watched Ciaran do the first time. This time, however, Marlowe didn't step onto the magic circle that led him into the High Council strategy room. Instead, he turned, using the buttons on his controller, and his avatar walked off towards the square.

'This must have been what Lucien had done before the meeting,' Marlowe said aloud, knowing the others were once more watching him through a TV in the suite, pulling out his in-game phone and checking it. He had contacted Woody through the Discord channel a half-hour earlier, explaining that he needed him for something, it was important, and it connected to Phoenix Elite's life.

Woody had replied, saying that once Marlowe was in the game, to give him a call, which Marlowe now did.

After a few minutes of standing around on a digital street corner beside a virtual park, complete with swings and a slide, Marlowe watched as a human with a cat head and blue hooded top arrived in what looked to be an expensive in-game Lamborghini.

'Woody?' Marlowe asked.

'They've made you pretty accurate,' Woody said as he climbed out of the car, walking up to Marlowe's avatar. 'I'm guessing this was Phoenix's work?'

Marlowe pressed the "nod" emotion button shortcut.

'I need your help,' he said. 'But it's going to be a tough one. However, it will make all your YouTube friends incredibly popular when they go viral.'

The YouTuber friends Marlowe mentioned were also there in the park with other gamers, waiting for Woody to vet the new arrival, and once he'd done so, their avatars walked over. One had a donkey mask, another wore the clothes of a Revolutionary War Confederate soldier, another a balaclava with antlers, a fourth dressed like a pink SWAT officer – it seemed that in *Crime City*, style choice was open for everyone.

'Hey man, we understand Phoenix is in trouble,' Donkey Head said. 'What can we do to help?'

'Phoenix has gotten himself into trouble with some billionaire-owned secret cabals,' Marlowe explained, adding a little flair to the conversation. 'He's been working with them for a while. It's how he got the super-fast server you all use, but now he's caught up in a massive conspiracy and needs help getting out.'

'I knew it,' Confederate Soldier did a little dance, hopping from leg to leg. 'I knew he'd done something shifty. He wouldn't tell me, but there's no way we'd be getting this kind of frame rate if it wasn't owned by a corporation or two.'

'Phoenix has been taken, and we don't know who by,' Marlowe continued. 'He needed help, and he knew I could get it for him. That's why he had you all looking for me. Woody here put me in touch, and we were able to help. But when we got him out, they caught us.'

'Where is he? We'll go get him,' Pink SWAT spoke, and Marlowe wasn't surprised to hear a female voice in his headphones.

'It's not in the game, Lyra,' Donkey Head replied.

'Oh, yeah, of course. Sorry.'

'Thanks for the enthusiasm, but that's already been planned,' Marlowe said. 'Don't worry about it, we're getting him out. All you need to know is there are some bad people using your server for something incredibly terrible. And if it comes out it's been used, not only will the server be closed down, but you could all be classed as accessories, because they won't know whether or not you were involved.'

This did not go down well and Marlowe could hear every player complaining through their headphones, although it was mainly anger at the possibility of getting strikes from

YouTube if they were accused of terrorism. It was strange; even though he was looking down on himself, it felt like a normal conversation, and he could understand why people played this game.

'Listen,' Woody waved a hand. 'The guy's got a plan, he told me when we spoke earlier, and it's one we've done before, even if by accident.'

'Phoenix told me you'd once broken the server?' Marlowe continued. 'By screwing around with some modifications or something?'

'Yeah, man,' Donkey Head laughed. 'That was when we had the giant spaceships in the sky. Oh, the server did *not* like that.'

'We need to do it again,' Marlowe said. 'But it needs to be timed. Can you do that?'

'How do you mean?' Pink SWAT asked, and Marlowe noted more gamers approaching.

'There's a military compound somewhere in the desert,' Marlowe said. 'I don't know the map of this place so I can't tell you where it is.'

'Near the airport?' Woody said. 'The one with all the big fences?'

'Ah man, I know the one,' Donkey Head said. 'I even tried to parachute in – you just get bounced off.'

'Because you don't have a piece of code in your Avatar's coding,' Marlowe said. 'Once you have it, you can get into this location.'

He allowed this information to settle in.

'In the compound is an exact replica of a Washington Hotel,' he carried on. 'Probably not from the outside, but definitely on the inside. And, in the basement is a vault Phoenix Elite created, without anyone's knowledge, leading directly into the servers. I have a hacker going in to open it in-game because in there's data we can use to help Phoenix. Once they've got it, we need to break the server before the suits can retaliate.'

He pressed the button to hold a hand up, as the others started talking through the headphone again, waiting until they stopped.

'Phoenix told me there was a thirty-day redundancy, which means if the server goes down, it'll come back up within a matter of hours, saving everything. But you're going to need to do this together, and work it to the second.'

'We could live stream it, maybe even Twitch it,' Balaclava with Antlers said. 'Get it really going, make a point of saying that we're helping Phoenix against the suits. More views and crazier Mods.'

'How crazy are we talking?' Confederate Soldier asked.

'I don't know, how crazy can you get?' Marlowe replied.

'I'll be honest, man,' Pink SWAT stepped forward. 'I mean, Woody vouches for you, and that's nice, and you're talking about Phoenix, but how do we know you're on the level here? You could be deliberately trying to kill the server for the authorities.'

Marlowe had expected this question.

'Let me prove it to you,' he said. 'Does anybody here know Phoenix Elite's real name?'

There was a pause, and Donkey Head held his hand up.

'I do,' he said.

Marlowe walked forward and passed him a note.

CIARAN WINSTON

'Well, he knows his real name,' Donkey Head said after

reading the note, turning in a circle, looking at the others. 'He's just shown me it.'

'I can show you more,' Marlowe said. 'Come with me.'

He walked them away from the corner park, over to one of the nondescript buildings at the side. It was the one he'd appeared at when he logged on, the one where a magic circle could be seen at the doorway.

'Watch,' he said. 'Try to follow me.'

He walked to the door, stepped onto the circle and in the game, after a moment of blackness, the screen resetting, he appeared in the boardroom. It looked a little different now, though, because Trix, earlier on, had used an avatar she'd just created, complete with API code, to enter and change the look of the place using Fractal Destiny's original coding. Now, the room looked like the holographic crime scene wall that Kate Maybury had first shown Marlowe in a motel room weeks earlier, with papers showing Senators being shot and algorithms showing the world collapsing soon.

It was all smoke and mirrors, using information that had once carried Marlowe along a pre-destined path, and he was hoping it'd do the same for the others.

After a couple of seconds, confirming everything was prepared, he turned around and walked back to the circle beside the door. There was a black screen, a flash, and Marlowe appeared back outside the building, the YouTuber crowd backing off as he did so.

'How did you do that, man?' Confederate Soldier asked. 'We couldn't follow.'

'Because, as I said, you don't have the correct code.'

This time, he walked up to each of the gamers, passing them a note containing the API code.

'If you know how to mod, you know how to use this,' he

said. Modify your character with this code, and pass it on to anyone you trust,' he instructed. One by one, the gamers froze in place, probably as their code was altered, then, walking to the door, they disappeared, phasing out of existence.

When the last of them had gone, Marlowe walked into the circle and stepped through.

Now the boardroom was filled with avatars. Every gamer who had been given the text now stood stunned, staring at the walls that Fractal Destiny had manipulated in the game server.

'You weren't lying,' Donkey Head said, as he turned in a slow circle around the room, before walking over to a wall.

'This was Phoenix's crime board,' Marlowe explained. 'It's also where the shadowed organisation trying to kill democracy held their meetings while you played outside. These guys decided how to run the world.'

'Jesus,' Balaclava with Antlers said.

'There's data in this server that could cause them major problems,' Marlowe said. 'It's all connected to tonight's Presidential debate. Now I know, at the moment, for some of you, it's late. But we need you to step up here. We need to break this server, so when the go command is given, you need to go absolutely crazy.'

He paused.

'But know this,' he said. 'I understand a lot of your videos are roleplay ones, where you rob banks and get chased by cops who are played by other members of the server. That might not be the case today. There's a very strong chance you might face off against players who are here to stop you, kill your characters, save their server. They might find ways to delete your characters off the server altogether, to glitch you, to have your PCs crash. So you need to be careful, and you need to be quick. Can you do that?'

'Hell yes,' Donkey Head said, determined.

'Give the details to Woody when you have them, and we'll go get this done.'

28

MERRY GO ROUND

THE NEXT PART OF THE PLAN CAME QUITE SURPRISINGLY, WHEN Trix, thanks to a message from her Dublin hacker friend, worked out what cypher the code in Bridget Summers' notebook was; and once worked out, they found this was actually sixteen random words.

Sixteen random words on a page was used as a seed phrase for a crypto wallet and, upon checking into it, they found it was indeed the seed phrase passcode for Bridget Summers' crypto wallet, the one Tessa had passed her. Bridget hadn't got into it yet, so now connected to the portal, they could see the crypto was still there – all *seventeen million dollars'* worth of Bitcoin, Ethereum, and half a dozen other stable coins.

'No wonder she wanted it back,' Marlowe whistled as Trix showed him the screen. She had suggested a new plan here; to divert the money, withdrawing it from Bridget's account and placing it in crypto funds in the names of Viktor Orlovsky, Lucien Delacroix, Taylor Coleman, and more importantly, St John Steele, each of whom gained four million dollars, with the rest being spent up in transfer fees, leaving a few thousand in the account. This done, she leant back and smiled, sending Bridget the code through the same message route she'd asked Marshall to contact her, marking it URGENT.

She knew Bridget would regain her seed phrases, use them to log in and then see the withdrawals of her rather extensive retirement fund before following the codes back. Trix hadn't covered her tracks as well as someone would usually do while doing this, and with a good hacker, Bridget would see who benefited from the deposits, and go to war against these onetime friends, who in the meantime wouldn't understand what was going on, as the wallets, although under their names, weren't even connected to them. They'd believe Bridget was trying to play her own game here, mainly because Trix had also started passing messages around through the other High Council members of Orchid, the ones who'd messaged the email, saying they didn't want to be involved, asking them to leak out that Bridget was starting a private war, as well as hinting that each of the others were pushing for their own power. Within an hour, the two warring sides of Orchid had turned into *seven*.

She hadn't mentioned Lucien being alive; she wanted that still to be a surprise as they knew he'd not be able to keep away from the Willard debate. Right now, chaos was the name of the game.

With this done, and the YouTubers and gamers now preparing some stupidly large, server-breaking items, all taking this as some kind of challenge to beat the others, Marlowe then moved on to phase two.

He knew Sasha would be annoyed that Trix had taken Ciaran's computer and so Brad had left a message for her, asking them to meet in a nearby, public location, somewhere where Marlowe wouldn't be taken by CIA black-bag agents. Who, by this point, were angry they'd been made fools of.

By the time they met, it was three in the afternoon, outside the Lincoln Memorial. Marlowe and Brad were alone; Sasha was too, but they knew this was definitely not the case, and that most of the casual tourists around them probably had weapons aimed at them as they spoke. It made for a tense encounter, especially with Sasha arriving with a face like thunder.

'Give me one reason why I don't stick you in a black-bag cell in Guantanamo Bay with your MI5 friends,' Sasha growled as she stared at Marlowe.

'Because I have a plan in action,' Marlowe said. 'And I'm offering you a very nice, career-enhancing treat.'

'Go on,' Sasha said.

'We can get into Lucien's vault in Switzerland,' Marlowe explained. 'We can do it through Ciaran's server, which we will then blow up, killing any remote feed Orchid has set up.'

'You can't blow up a server from inside a game,' Sasha retorted.

'You can if you break the server to the point it can't work anymore,' Marlowe replied. 'I've got the means to do that.'

'Maybe we're planning that too.'

'You've got Ciaran, so sure, go for it, knock yourself out,' Marlowe grinned. 'But there's not a lot he can do without his laptop.'

Sasha sucked at her teeth.

'You prick,' she muttered.

'We have a plan to get in. It would be great if we could have Ciaran help us,' Marlowe said. 'We don't *need* him. But we could use your help.'

'Okay, so going in, what's your plan?'

'I need you to get me and Brad into the hotel,' Marlowe said. 'Only people you trust can know. I need to get to the security room. Brad needs to go to the stage.'

'And what about your friends in MI5?'

'Honestly, I could use them,' Marlowe admitted. 'We thought we might do this alone, but if they're on the side of the angels on this one, Vic and his friends could help run interference.'

Sasha sighed, looking up at the statue of Lincoln, sitting in his chair behind them.

'I was thinking the same thing,' she said. 'But when this all goes south, they're gonna have to pay for their crimes.'

'That's your choice,' Marlowe said. 'I won't really be caring by then. By the time this is over, I don't think I'll be MI5 anymore.'

'Or maybe even breathing,' Brad added, helpfully. 'Going to the security room is definitely the short-straw suicide mission here.'

After a moment of silently glowering at the pair of them, Sasha finally deflated.

'Call me when you are ready,' Sasha said. 'We'll get this done. Tell me where you need the hacker. He's bereft without his bloody laptop, anyway.'

'He'll be even more bereft when he sees what they've done to it,' Brad chuckled.

'I've got one more call to make,' Marlowe replied, ignoring Brad. 'And then we'll have that conversation.'

'A friend? Or foe?'

'I think possibly both,' Marlowe stated, turning and walking down the steps, away from the others.

SENATOR MAUREEN KYLE WAS SITTING AT HER DESK IN HER hotel suite when she started to laugh. 'You know, you really need to stop making a habit of this,' she said, looking over at Marlowe, standing in the entranceway. 'How the hell did you get past my guards this time?'

'Your guards have a kind of "gang" loyalty,' Marlowe said. 'And amazingly, it's one I now find I can bypass.'

Kyle leant back on her chair.

'Are you telling me that my guards, my new heavily vetted guards, are Orchid?' she asked.

'U-S-A, U-S-A,' Marlowe smiled. 'Maybe I've just asked a mutual CIA friend to help?'

Kyle rubbed at the bridge of her nose, obviously tired.

'I can't do this right now, Marlowe,' she said. 'Whatever plans you've got, whatever world-changing elements you have in mind right now, you're going to have to leave me out of it. I have an opportunity here to take down a dangerous man and I intend to do it.'

'You've got McKay's file, I take it?' Marlowe asked.

Kyle went to reply automatically, but then paused, narrowing her eyes.

'How would you know about McKay's file?'

'Because it was found in the same place I found yours,' Marlowe said. 'And from what I can work out, although I gave you your file back, someone else has a copy of it. Is this why you're here? Are you being told to do this? Blackmail, even?'

He looked at the window, checking for any kill shots.

'I can get you out of it,' he continued.

Maureen Kyle laughed again. But this time it was a bitter, more brutal one.

'I'm not being blackmailed to do this,' she said. 'This is my opportunity to take down a corrupt, sitting President. This is my opportunity to win the next election. Have you seen his file, the things he's done? The votes he's given to billionaires with their own agenda?'

'I'm guessing your voting record isn't as squeaky clean as you seem to think,' Marlowe snapped. 'Don't forget, I've seen what you've done.'

'Oh, don't get high and mighty on me, spook,' Kyle replied, rising and walking over to the side cabinet. 'I did what I had to do. And I was blackmailed for helping my sister, nothing more, at the start. McKay has done terrible things.'

Marlowe nodded as Senator Kyle poured herself a large glass of water.

'Let me tell you how it's going to go,' he said. 'And trust me when I tell you this, that I know *exactly* what's going to happen, but can't explain how. You're going to be sitting on a moderating table with a CNN anchor Ricky Morgan, Vice President Harrison Caldwell, and facing President Anton McKay, with Senator Ron Tyler next to him. How am I doing so far?'

'Pretty accurate. But everyone knows that, it's been advertised everywhere.'

'It's a closed set,' Marlowe continued. 'No audience. They'll be watching remotely from a separate studio to provide security.'

'That bit isn't as well known,' she admitted.

'The team filming will be cut down, and the rest is mainly security, making sure that everything's okay,' Marlowe continued. 'McKay and Tyler will debate various subjects and you, as a Republican counterbalance, will get to ask questions.'

Kyle slowly nodded.

'Go on.'

'You have a "silver bullet" question that will kill his career,' Marlowe spoke softly now, slowly, making sure every word was digested. 'One you've been given mysteriously by a contact who has the same aims as you.'

'Donziger has his file,' Kyle said. 'He's forcing McKay for a pardon—'

'I know,' Marlowe interrupted. 'Lucien Delacroix had his file as well – but Lucien, as far as everybody's concerned, is dead.'

'As far as everyone's concerned?' Kyle now sat back in her chair.

'Billionaires don't die that easily, I find,' Marlowe sighed, walking over to Kyle. 'Listen, you're there as a sacrifice. Caldwell is Orchid through and through, and is waiting to take over. Tyler's probably still being blackmailed by them in the same way that you were. I have no idea about Ricky Morgan, but I'm guessing they're probably involved as well. If you don't do it, they'll bring in Senator Pearson, and she's definitely Orchid, because I saw her in Versailles.'

'Was this at the special secret meeting you went to?' Kyle raised an eyebrow. 'I wondered when you were gonna get around to that.'

'Maureen, if you do this, you will be killed,' Marlowe said. 'Pure and simple. They will take you out – and McKay, as well. They have a server in Switzerland with a deepfake scenario uploaded already that will make it look like McKay kills you and then himself, but it'll be masked men from the shadows, storming the stage and shooting you.'

He paused, letting this sink in before continuing.

'Have I ever lied?'

Kyle shook her head, no longer mocking.

'So let me ask you one thing,' Marlowe added. 'And be honest. Are you Orchid as well?'

Kyle almost did a double-take at the comment.

'Were you shot as we thought by Ford, or did you fake the injury?' Marlowe pressed on.

'I didn't fake the injury. I was shot by Ford,' she said, but there was a furrowing of the brows as she spoke, a deep secret finally coming out. 'But I always felt that they were holding back on what they could have done.'

She shook her head, still unable to comprehend this.

'Are you saying that they've led me to this moment, just to be a *sacrifice?*'

'I think they have,' Marlowe nodded. 'But here's the problem. You need to carry on.'

At this, Kyle gave a bitter cackle of a laugh.

'You've come here to tell me they're going to kill me for asking a question, and then you tell me to carry on doing it? Explain this, please.'

'We can block what they want to do,' Marlowe said. 'But you need to ask yourself, what happens if you don't take the bait, and you don't ask the question?'

'McKay has a better chance of winning.'

'Does he though?' Marlowe raised an eyebrow as he cocked his head quizzically. 'You'll still have the file. And he'll know this. He'll probably step down due to "health issues" or something.'

'No,' Kyle shook her head. 'It'll be Caldwell.'

'No matter what happens, Caldwell wins,' Marlowe shook his head. 'McKay might be owned by Orchid, but he's just a tattooed millionaire for them. Caldwell's a loyal follower, maybe even High Council, and that's why he needs to be stopped tonight.'

'Taken out by MI5, or rogue bearded agents?'

'Taken out by a CIA agent we can link to you. Thought it might be better for a home soil advantage,' Marlowe shrugged. 'This gives you your chance for the election. But it won't happen unless we remove Caldwell as well, because if their plan works, and the world sees – or at least believes that they see – McKay shoot himself after shooting you, Harrison Caldwell will then become President, saying how terrible this was that these things happened, and asking for unity.'

'Can I at least punch the white-haired bastard?'

Marlowe shrugged.

'Once all hell breaks loose, go wild,' he suggested. 'You have to hold the line and you have to be ready for anything. So, actually, Senator Kyle, I'm not asking you to stand down, or stop, or anything like that. I'm asking you to do exactly what you want to do – but you need to know that if you do this, you could die if we can't get to you in time. Or you can help us, and leave McKay for a later point.'

Senator Kyle shrugged, then walked back to the table.

'You make it sound so enticing,' she said. 'Now if you don't mind, I have some constituency work to deal with, and a debate to prepare for. Will I see you later?'

'Keep an eye out,' Marlowe said. 'You'll see a familiar face.'

'I asked if I'll see you.'

'If you do, you'll know the whole thing's gone to hell,' Marlowe admitted. 'Good luck with the debate, Ma'am.'

With that, Marlowe left.

'HOW ARE WE DOING?' MARLOWE ASKED AS HE RETURNED TO the suite across the road from the Willard. It was now an hour before the debate, and things were starting to heat up.

Trix looked up, chuckling.

'Bridget is having a meltdown,' she said. 'I've been monitoring some dark web forums. She's *really* unhappy that her money seems to have gone, now she's finally managed to check.'

She clicked her fingers, as if remembering something.

'Oh, yes!' she added. 'I also made sure she was sent notifications every time one of the others bitched about her, and I then created accounts in their names and, well, bitched about her, so she got notifications. She's now spreading dissent about Lucien and the others to anyone that'll listen, saying how they've betrayed everyone for money. So that's a good start.'

She glanced behind Marlowe; Ciaran Winston stood at the door.

'How the hell did you get out?' she exclaimed.

'We're working with Sasha again,' Marlowe said. 'Ciaran's here to help you.'

Ciaran walked over to the table, staring at his Frankenstein'd laptop in horror.

'What have you done to it?' he whispered.

'Reverse engineered your software,' Trix said. 'I made it better if you ask me. You're welcome.'

Ciaran sat, looking dejectedly at the software on the screen.

'I've been told the plan,' he said, his humility strangely muted. 'How can I help?'

'Well,' Trix smiled. 'Before I start, you tell me how to break into your vault.'

'You'll need to get there first,' Ciaran nodded as he read through the lines of code. 'Okay, this is good stuff. Workable. There'll be people trying to stop us – they'll know what's going on by now. They'll try to kill you in-game before you get there.'

He grinned.

'Luckily for you, we have the best driver in *Crime City* in this room,' he said. 'Is someone able to sort a last-minute shopping list? I'm going to need to create a second gaming PC in ...'

He looked at his watch.

'About ten minutes,' he sighed.

29

GAME TIME

PRESIDENT ANTON MCKAY TURNED UP JUST AFTER SIX. HIS
security entourage of Secret Service cars took up the whole of
Pennsylvania Avenue as he emerged, but the traffic was long
diverted away, as he was the last to arrive and Vice President
Harrison Caldwell had brought his own entourage shortly
before. Senator Kyle was already there, alongside Senator
Ron Tyler and the CNN anchor, Ricky Morgan, adjusting his
toupée before he was in front of the cameras. They were
shown their positions, and there was a technical run-through
to make sure everything was working. Then, at seven on the
dot, the show started.

The music played, and the lights went on as the cameras
connected to the feed.

'Good evening and welcome to the Democrat Party's pres-
idential primary,' Morgan said, looking directly at one
camera, a red light showing that it was on. 'My name is Ricky
Morgan, and sitting beside me are Republican Senator for
Arizona, Maureen Kyle, and Vice President and Democratic
Senator for Colorado, Harrison Caldwell.'

The cameras now turned to Tyler and McKay on the stage, each behind a podium as Morgan continued. McKay was a tall figure with steel-grey hair and a weathered, yet distinguished face, tanned and lined from years in the public eye. He was impeccably tailored, most likely to present an image of steadfast and conservative authority. Ron Tyler on the other hand, had gone the other way, in his early forties, with a rebellious, slightly messy hairstyle. Favouring semi-casual attire, he'd paired his suit with crisp, yet relaxed white shirt, no tie, and comfortable trainers, something he'd built over the years as his brand.

'The qualification period for the first round is over,' Morgan continued. 'And with only one challenger so far to the President's plans to run for a second term, tonight we will be the moderators of a debate between challenger Ron Tyler, the Senator for Minnesota, and Anton McKay, President of the United States of America.'

He smiled, looked up at the stage at the two podiums facing him.

'Let's begin with opening statements,' he said.

AT A SIDE DOOR TO THE WILLARD INTERCONTINENTAL Washington, a cleaning van arrived. The door opened, and five men climbed out, all in overalls, with the cleaning company's logos on the back. They pulled out large trolleys worth of laundry and cleaning items and started towards the side door.

The guard at the side, a Secret Service agent, hand on his gun secured by a side holder, stared at them, relaxed his grip and then nodded.

'I understand we've got a cleaning issue,' the lead cleaner said.

The guard, counting all of them smiled, nodded and, without even checking their identities, allowed them in. This done, he looked around to make sure no one had seen, and then left his post, following them in.

Marlowe pressed the timer on his watch as they watched the scene from across the street.

'Now it starts,' Brad said, standing beside him. He checked his CIA-standard Glock 19, looking concerned. 'Are you sure you want to go in this way?'

Marlowe grinned, patting Brad on the arm, amused that even now, Brad still looked like Captain America after working as a rock band's roadie for a decade.

'Mate, you're about to become an American hero,' he said. 'Just don't fluff your lines.'

'I've always wanted my own ticker-tape parade,' Brad smiled, and placed a hand on Marlowe's arm. 'I really am sorry for getting that bitch to try to kill you in New York. I was against a wall.'

'Let's not do it again,' Marlowe checked his own weapon, a Sig Sauer P226, as he slipped across the street with Brad and moved to the now-empty, no longer guarded side door. There was other security around, after all the president was in the building, but Marlowe wasn't worried about being stopped.

Sasha seemed to be the ultimate "get out of jail" card.

'You sure you want to look like that?' Brad asked a last time, nodding at the clothes Marlowe wore.

'Oh, I definitely want to look like this,' Marlowe smiled. He knew the moment any Orchid agent saw him, they'd recognise him. So, instead of trying to blend in like everybody else there, he'd gone for a more tactical look of body armour over shirt and jeans, an assault rifle on his back, and a gun in his hand.

If anything, he felt more like he did when he used to go on missions with the Royal Marines.

'Just don't die, yeah?' Brad grinned impishly as he headed off to the left.

Shifting his rifle, Marlowe made for the rear stairs.

CIARAN – OR, TRIX ASSUMED, *PHOENIX ELITE*, NOW THEY WERE in the game server – stared at her as they appeared in the city.

Well, she assumed he stared at her. He kept looking up from his hastily fixed together gaming PC across the hotel suite table at her.

'You're serious?' he asked. 'You're a bloody *angel?*'

'I see nothing wrong with this,' she said. 'Considering you're bloody Jack Sparrow.'

'I'm Blackbeard the Pirate!' On the screen, Ciaran was already running down a side street. 'Come on, I have a car down here. How are your angel wings even getting in?'

On the keyboard, Trix pressed a button and her avatar's wings folded in.

'I think of everything,' she said as Ciaran ran into a garage and returned out a moment later, driving a blood-red truck with what looked to be rockets on the back.

'Get in,' he said. 'One plus note we have is we don't have to talk on the radio, but they'll still know we're here. They'll be on us soon.'

Trix looked up from the screen at Kirk and Tessa, currently putting on Kevlar vests.

'They'll be triangulating us in the real world too,' she said. 'Two PCs online from the same location will be found stupidly fast. You need to stop them getting in before we're done.'

'We need to stop them getting in, full stop,' Kirk replied, checking his Glock. He looked up as there was a knock on the suite's door. Holding a finger to his lips, he moved over, gun ready as he peered through the peephole, then frowned, opening the door as Vic Saeed entered.

'Marlowe sent me to help,' Vic said, hands up. 'Enemy of my enemy and all that. Where do you need me?'

'End of the corridor,' Kirk replied. 'They'll come up the stairs, they won't trust the elevators.'

'On it,' Vic nodded.

'Jackson and Lloyd?'

'Lloyd's at the hotel, and Jackson ... he's in a tough place,' Vic sighed. 'He's at the hotel assisting the CIA, but he said he wouldn't help Marlowe.'

Sighing, Trix returned to the game. On the screen, their car was driving down a city street, Ciaran on the controls.

'How far?'

'We need to get on the freeway and head south,' he said. 'We can – *Christ!*'

The exclamation was because of a police SUV slamming into the back of their car, spinning it around.

'What the hell!' Ciaran shouted down the microphone. 'You don't – oh shit oh shit!'

This second exclamation was because of the in-game police SUV now firing at them.

'Shoot them!' Ciaran shouted at Trix. 'They're trying to kick us out of the game!'

Vic, watching this shook his head, checked his own weapon, and moved back into the corridor.

'I prefer a more traditional approach,' he said as he walked off down the corridor.

MARLOWE HAD SPENT A COUPLE OF HOURS IN THE VIRTUAL hotel, and understood the quickest way to the security room – effectively a closed space with a desk, some chairs and a bank of monitors watching over the hotel. However, there were enough external feed lines to allow them to link to other hotels in the chain; feed lines that could connect to the Swiss server the moment Fractal Destiny slammed through the network.

Marlowe knew there were Orchid operatives online and most likely in the virtual hotel's communication room, but he didn't have time to do anything about that. All he could hope was the other gamers on the server, now armed with the ability to get in, would arrive and cause as much trouble as possible.

He moved up to the corridor that led to the main security office, but stopped as a familiar figure faced him.

'You don't want to do this,' the man, a young Indian with a trendy, close-clipped beard and haircut faced him, an assault rifle in his hand. 'Turn around, piss off and forget this ever happened.'

He spoke in a clear-cut British accent, and Marlowe frowned, rifle raised to face him.

'You were in my house,' he replied. 'Who exactly are you?'

'That's above your pay grade—' the man started, but then collapsed, screaming as the tines of what looked to be a police issue taser slammed into his shoulders, sending him to the ground.

Peter Lloyd, looking like he was about to throw up, stood there, an incredibly reluctant Lawrence Jackson behind him.

'We're here to help,' Peter looked up, setting his jaw. 'What do you need from us?'

'For a start, you can tell me who the bloody hell this is,' Marlowe pointed at the unconscious man.

'Kumar Ahmed,' Peter said. 'He—'

'Was with you in my church. I mean my apartment,' Marlowe nodded. 'You know what I bloody mean. MI5?'

'Christ no, MI6,' Peter shook his head.

'That's good,' Marlowe grinned. 'I can't wait to mention that to McKellan when we get home.'

He looked at Jackson.

'We good? Or do I need to watch my back?'

'Apparently helping you is the only way I avoid a CIA black site,' Jackson sighed. 'So yeah, we're good, you insufferable prick.'

'Just how I like it,' Marlowe grinned.

TRIX MAY HAVE HAD HER ISSUES WITH CIARAN WINSTON, BUT one thing she couldn't complain about was his ability in the game. He knew every inch of the city streets, and as the black SUVs – two now – chased him, he weaved through the crossroads like a man possessed, always heading towards the freeway.

'I know a jump,' he said. 'It's sketchy as hell, but so's being shot.'

'How sketchy?'

'Like, lose our wheels sketchy,' Ciaran grinned, adrenaline coursing through his body as he pulled to the right heading up a rampway onto the freeway. He slammed the accelerator down, the car speeding up as it aimed at the barrier on the other side. Trix couldn't help herself, she gripped the controller tighter—

On the screen, the car burst over the barrier at speed, launching into the air, spinning wildly as it travelled over streets, buildings and parks beneath them before heading downwards, clipping a tree, spinning around as it passed over a wall and down into what looked to be the city's waterways, obviously based on Los Angeles's River Flood Control Channel, the concrete banks along the side that movies like *Terminator 2* had utilised.

Miraculously, the truck landed, rolled a couple of times and then finished upright with all of its wheels, and Ciaran immediately gunned it to the left, heading alongside the river. Behind them, Trix could see one of the SUVs, having tried the same jump, utterly wipe out into the side of a building.

'What happened to them?' she asked.

'Game over,' Ciaran cackled. 'I added god mode to the truck a while back. Takes five times the damage of other vehicles before it shits the bed. Come on, we're almost there. I can jump back onto the freeway here and it's plain sailing to the military camp.'

Trix nodded, but she couldn't help but wonder what was waiting for them there. It was a short thought, however, as a faint sound of a gunshot from down the corridor switched her attention to the suite.

Kirk was already moving to the door.

'Go time,' he said.

On the stage, the debate was continuing. The two candidates had both given their statements, the first question, one about education, had been asked, and now they each had a minute to reply, and then thirty seconds for a rebuttal.

Senator Maureen Kyle wasn't listening, though. She couldn't help it, she kept looking around the darkened room. Was it from behind where her killer would appear? Was it to the side?

She looked over at Caldwell, who sat staring intently at the debate. To anyone watching, he looked invested, but she knew he was simply waiting for his moment to strike.

'Senator Kyle, do you have anything to add?' Morgan asked, looking over at her, and Kyle realised she'd been distracted.

'Um, no,' she said, shaking her head. 'Sorry, I didn't catch the end of the last comment.'

'It doesn't matter, the rebuttal stage is over,' Caldwell replied, watching her. 'This is your moment, if you have something to say, or a question to ask.'

Kyle looked from Caldwell to McKay and licked her lips.

'Actually, I think I do have something to ask,' she said.

Marlowe waited by the security office, listening. There weren't any sounds, and with the actual MI6 guard now unconscious and secured, he looked back at the other two MI5 agents.

He didn't speak; he didn't need to. A look, a raised eyebrow to suggest "shall we," and a nod from the others. A silent count of three, marked by head nods, and then the agents burst into the room, guns aimed and ready for whatever was waiting for them.

There was nobody there.

'This isn't right,' Marlowe said, running to the monitors, looking at the screens. 'They wouldn't leave one guard here.'

'Who said they did?' Jackson said, raising his gun and pointing it at Marlowe's face. 'This is for Versailles, you *wanker*.'

30

SERVER ERROR

IN *CRIME CITY*, THE TRUCK ARRIVED AT THE MILITARY CAMP TO find it in utter chaos. The gamers, now able to get in through the gates thanks to their enhanced API code had arrived in force, and the Orchid-sponsored gamers left facing them were having a bad time as they fought against dinosaurs with ray guns, and flying bikes that fired missiles.

It looked like the mods were already in full force. Trix just hoped it hadn't peaked too soon.

'This way,' Ciaran said, running through the metal door to the building. Following, Trix found herself in the lobby of the Willard InterContinental Washington, and paused in shock as Ciaran continued to the elevator in the corner. The virtual lobby of the Willard InterContinental Washington held a stately elegance, and pristine marble floors reflected them as they ran, surrounded by grand columns and under-stated yet luxurious furnishings within its walls.

Ciaran had excelled himself here.

'It's a mixture of game server design and 3D scans,' he explained as he entered an elevator, pressing the base of the panel, where no button could be seen. 'Special button. Only seen by me. See, you did need my help.'

The doors closed and the screen went black. The next moment, Trix's avatar was in what looked to be a bank vault.

'We need to move fast,' Ciaran said, moving to the vault. 'In the game, you can break gas station and bank safes with these little mini games. I just changed the code a little to make this.'

Trix took the moment to look up from her screen, back into the real world; Tessa had moved outside the suite while Kirk stayed guard. There had been no more gunshots, but that didn't mean everything was okay.

'Shit,' Ciaran hissed, placing the controller down and typing on his keyboard. 'They've changed the bloody password.'

'How did they do that?' Trix replied incredulously. 'I thought you were the coder that created everything?'

'I might ... I might have lied a little about that,' Ciaran replied sheepishly. 'Remember when I said I'd taken code from other apps? I didn't think *they* could lock me out.'

'Christ,' Trix's angelic avatar moved the Pirate-clad Phoenix Elite out of the way in the game. 'Let a bloody professional have a go.'

———

VIC WAS AIMING DOWN THE STAIRWAY AS TESSA REACHED HIM.

'Trouble?'

'Not at the moment,' Vic replied tightly. 'As long as they stay the hell down there, we're golden.'

'How many?' Tessa asked.

Vic looked at her, and his gun rose, pointing straight at her face.

'Well, that depends,' he said calmly. 'On which side you're playing for, little Miss Rubicon.'

'I'm playing for whatever side Marlowe's on,' Tessa replied, equally calm, staring at Vic, ignoring the barrel at eye contact. 'I couldn't give a shit about MI5, the CIA, Rubicon, Orchid all of that. Marlowe saved my life. I'm repaying the debt.'

Vic's finger tightened on the trigger … and then moved away from it as he looked back down the stairs, aiming the gun away from Tessa.

'Then there's one less than I thought,' he replied.

CALDWELL STARED AT KYLE IN SILENT FURY.

'That's your question?' he asked. 'Spending cuts in the military?'

'It's important to me,' Kyle smiled sweetly at him, leaning close, hand over the microphone in front of her. 'And I want to batter him about a bit before I land the killing blow.'

As McKay, grateful for the question, launched into a long and rather repetitive statement on this, Kyle leant back in her chair, feeling the sweat on her brow.

She'd avoided it once.

Next time she needed to *shit or get off the pot*, as her grandma used to say.

Marlowe leant against the desk, his hands up in the air as Jackson covered him, still standing by the door.

'Once a Delacroix bitch, always one, I guess,' he said, keeping an eye on the screens as he spoke. The debate seemed to still be going on; he had time. 'I wondered why there weren't more people here. They knew you were still a team player, so didn't need to. I'm guessing he speaks to you from beyond the grave?'

'He speaks to me in person,' Jackson glanced out of the door, and then stepped aside as one of the cleaners entered, pulling off his black, curly wig and smiling.

'Hello, Lucien,' Marlowe said without the slightest hint of surprise.

'Aw, you ruined everything,' Lucien mocked. 'I was going to be the one to shoot McKay, but now I have to finish you first.'

Marlowe didn't react to this, still sitting on the desk, watching.

'What's your gameplay here?' he asked. 'You're publicly dead. How do you come back? Twin brother? Clone?'

'I don't,' Lucien shrugged. 'I go back and live on my island and take over the world from the shadows.'

'Good luck with that,' Marlowe nodded. 'You might find Rubicon come after you.'

'I have no issues with—'

'Bridget told them how you stole four million dollars of her crypto, while trying to put the blame on Orlovsky,' Marlowe tutted. 'She's coming for you. Good luck with that one. She's a Rottweiler. And as for the Russians ... shit, man. You're screwed. You can't even ask Orchid for help because they all hate you now.'

'But I didn't ...' Lucien went to reply, but then stopped.

'Oh, well played,' he said. 'Turn us all against each other, watch us break apart.'

He walked over, motioning for Marlowe to move aside.

'That won't be happening once McKay's dead and Caldwell takes over.'

Marlowe didn't move.

'You can't kill McKay yet,' he said. 'Kyle hasn't asked her question.'

Lucien frowned.

'Maybe I'll just kill you,' he said. 'Lawrence, please kill Thomas.'

'Wow, killing an active MI5 officer on foreign soil,' Marlowe shook his head. 'How do you think that'll go down with the family and the higher ups?'

'I don't think they'll give a shit,' Jackson smiled, raising his weapon.

'I wasn't talking to you,' Marlowe replied, looking at Peter now. 'How do you think Davey Lloyd would react here? Do you think he'd meekly follow orders? Or would he do what needed to be done?'

'Davey Lloyd was Orchid,' Jackson snapped.

'He was also a rockstar at MI6,' Marlowe replied, still looking at Peter. 'How ashamed were you when you didn't get in there and found yourself stuck in MI5? He never spoke to you again, right? The Orchid membership had been put in before you disappointed him. Do you think he would have nominated you after that?'

'No,' Peter shook his head. 'He wouldn't have done anything until I made good. Became the agent he wanted me to be.'

'Is that one who sits in a room and watches someone get

murdered?' Marlowe continued. 'All so a billionaire can break the world?'

'Shut up!' Jackson hadn't shot Marlowe yet; instead, he was looking at Peter. 'Don't listen to him! He doesn't think you're James Bond! He thinks you're an asset at best!'

'But I *want* to be James Bond,' Peter replied, straightening. 'He's right. If my uncle saw me now, he'd be ashamed. All my life I—'

He stopped speaking as Lucien raised his gun and shot him in the throat. The single act of cold-blooded murder gave Marlowe the moment he needed, ignored by both Jackson and Lucien as Peter fell gurgling to the floor, clutching at his neck, to dive behind the counter, pulling his rifle from his back. It was a Knight's Stoner KS-1, a recent addition to the Royal Marine armoury, and something, worryingly, that Sasha Bordeaux had spare when kitting Marlowe out. It was vicious and felt good in his hand as he started firing, seeing Lucien and Jackson diving for cover out in the corridor.

Even though the rounds were suppressed, they were still bloody loud, though. Marlowe knew others would arrive soon, and the communications room was a bit of a kill zone, as shown by the glassy, dead eyes of Peter Lloyd, his face strangely surprised in death.

But that was fine, Marlowe thought to himself.

All he was doing was waiting out the clock.

THE VAULT DOOR HAD OPENED, AND TRIX HAD STARTED THE download of the connected servers. Unlike the Fractal Destiny theft in Whitehall, this was less of a removal and more of a copying situation, and the file size was far smaller.

'We need to hurry,' Ciaran looked up as more gunshots could be heard down the corridor. 'I think we're about to be taken out real soon!'

Trix muttered under her breath, typing on her laptop as, on the screen, her avatar stood in front of some kind of computer server unit.

'Tell the gamers to send it,' she said. 'We're almost done here.'

Ciaran nodded as, on the screen, he pulled a phone up, sending a message to everyone in the game world right then.

SEND IT

Trix didn't know what that command would entail, but she guessed it would be some stupidly insane things that, if they lived through this, she could relive through YouTube rewatches.

'We just need a minute more,' she said.

Kirk, glancing at the TV screen, now showing the Presidential debate, shook his head.

'I don't think we have a minute,' he said. 'I think Kyle's about to make her move.'

HARRISON CALDWELL SAT BACK, NODDING AT RON TYLER'S answer to his question.

'Do you have anything to add?' Morgan asked, looking back at Kyle. 'This will be your last chance before we move to closing statements.'

Senator Maureen Kyle stared at the two men on the podium, at the white-haired man sitting beside her, and then at the darkness behind the camera, where a kill-squad was likely waiting.

This was the moment history would remember her for.

'Actually, I don't,' she said. 'You'd—'

'What the hell do you mean you *don't have a question?*' Caldwell exploded. 'Of *course* you have a question! Ask the damn question!'

'Fine,' Kyle rose from the chair now and, moving away from the desk she'd shared throughout the debate, she walked onto the stage, making her way over to Ron Tyler.

'Move,' she said, and the tone of her voice meant she wasn't looking for a conversation here. Tyler raised his hands in a "whatever" motion and stepped back, allowing Kyle to take the podium.

'I know this is a little unconventional, but this is an unconventional question,' she said.

McKay, sensing something was up, looked around.

'Okay,' Morgan shrugged, making a smile for the cameras, while unsure what the hell was going on. 'You seem to have the stage, Senator Kyle, and you have a last question to ask. Please, ask away.'

'I want to talk about loyalties,' Kyle said, looking at McKay. 'In particular, loyalties to billionaires and corporations.'

She looked at Caldwell, seeing him smiling slightly at this. She realised what Marlowe had said earlier was more true than she could ever imagine.

He was actively waiting for McKay to be outed.

'Ron Tyler, like me, was one of many Senators, Governors and even members of the White House being blackmailed by Nathan Donziger, who, with the help of a shadowy organisation named Orchid, slithered their tentacles into the very top of the White House,' she said, now looking directly into the camera lens.

There was a silence here; even Tyler, now outed as a blackmailed Senator said nothing, unsure of where Kyle, having outed herself as well, was going with this.

Even Kyle wasn't sure as she looked at McKay.

'So, Mister President, I have to ask you this,' she said, straightening as she now looked back across the stage at Harrison Caldwell. 'Why have you allowed your Vice President to become corrupted and owned by Orchid, under the control of his foreign billionaire paymasters, to the point he wants you killed, right here and now?'

———

THE GUNFIRE WAS GETTING WORSE AND MARLOWE WAS BEING forced into a corner. He could hold out a little longer, but then the earlier comments of this being the suicide mission would come true.

He wasn't unscathed, either; his vest had been struck a couple of times, and hurt like hell, and he knew a few more like that would disable him, anyway. However, he still had one card up his sleeve.

He knew there was a vent at the back, one that led into a crawlspace.

He could get into it, but in doing so he'd be leaving the security room open.

He just hoped he'd done enough, as throwing a grenade out into the corridor, he used the explosion and subsequent confusion to pull the vent away, sliding through and hastening away.

'Now, Sasha,' he said into an earpiece as he turned a corner, moving out of sight.

After a moment, there was silence, followed by Jackson firing once more into the room, before stopping and looking in.

'He's run!' he shouted. 'Get in there! Find him!'

'Screw that! Get the feed up!' Lucien screamed, running into the room, flicking switches. 'She's gone off script! We need to change the narrative! Get in there and stop her!'

He stopped, frowning, his face paling as he looked back at Jackson.

'The server,' he whispered. 'It's not there.'

'What do you mean?' Jackson pushed the billionaire aside now, checking. 'It has to be!'

Lucien laughed.

'They crashed the server,' he said. 'They stopped the feed splitting.'

He leant onto the security counter and sighed.

And then, with a resigned expression on his face, he pulled his Glock back out, rammed it under his chin and pulled the trigger.

THE MOMENT THE ORCHID OPERATIVES MOUNTED AN offensive, Tessa and Vic were in motion, stationed at the top of the unforgiving stairs, Glock 19s gripped and aimed toward the coming threat.

The enemies were breaching; raw power and frantic momentum carried them upwards, faces a blur, weapons drawn. And then time seemed to compress, now nothing more than action-reaction, where everything non-essential fell away.

Vic fired blindly down at them, and a man's shriek perforated the tense air, the sound of a body thudding against cold concrete, before the dead man rolled into view; lifeless, eyes wide in shocked oblivion.

Tessa meanwhile was elemental fury, the training she'd gained as a child taking over, the sharp report of her Glock an echo to Vic's. A spray of red, and the second Orchid attacker staggered back.

She advanced, using gun and fist together, Glock whipping in a brutal arc, using the injured man as a shield as bone cracked, a harsh counterpoint to the stuttering rhythm of gunfire.

Vic was now beside her – each strike a masterstroke of violence, stark against the grey backdrop of the stairwell. The second assailant was on the ground now, Vic's boot finding its home in the hollow of a throat, pressing down with inexorable force until there was a gurgled sigh of release.

Tessa and Vic stood, breath labouring, the metallic tang of blood, rich and overpowering, in the confined space.

Vic nodded, his face emotionless.

'Clear,' he said, and Tessa nodded, her expression a mirror to Vic's own. She leant against the wall, and it was only when another sound echoed behind her did she spin, bringing her gun up as she faced Marshall Kirk.

'Come back,' he said calmly. 'Come back now, princess. It's over.'

It was only then that Tessa realised she was screaming.

Stopping, slumping back into her father's arms, the three of them moved back to the suite, watching the corridor as they did so.

HARRISON CALDWELL ROSE FROM HIS CHAIR IN COLD FURY.

'You bitch!' he screamed. 'That wasn't the question we told you to ask! You were supposed to—'

'I wasn't supposed to do anything!' Kyle shouted back. 'You don't own me! None of you do! He'll get his moment, but right now it's bastards like you that need to be stopped!'

'Kill the feed!' Caldwell shouted out. 'Do it now! Kill her!'

'Yeah, that's not gonna happen,' a new voice spoke as Brad Haynes walked out of the shadows and onto the stage. 'You see, your hired mercenaries, the ones brought in to kill the President and Senator Kyle, while you tried to change the narrative, they're all, well, a little dead right now.'

He waved out into the shadows.

'There's a dozen agencies out there right now, all fighting for the right to execute you for treason, Mister Vice President,' he said. 'Your fake server has been dismantled, your secrets gained. Your political career is over, as is Orchid.'

Brad looked over at Senator Kyle.

'Thank you, Ma'am, for working with us on this sting operation at great risk to your own life,' he said with a wink that the camera didn't pick up. 'The country owes you a debt.'

LAWRENCE JACKSON HAD SEEN HIS CAREER PROSPECTS END THE moment Delacroix's body hit the ground. But it wasn't too late to get the hell out of here. He had a comfortable exit strategy once he got out, and knew where Lucien's plane was. He could get to a non-extradition island, and work out his next steps—

He stopped as, down the other end of the corridor, Marlowe appeared, his Sig in his hand.

'You self-centred, arrogant bastard,' he hissed. 'You should have stayed rotting in the gunroom.'

Marlowe nodded, throwing his rifle to the side.

'You learn a lot in the gunroom,' he said. 'Robbie there, he knows everyone, sees your scores on the range, knows who shoots true, and who pulls to the side when they fire. You know, probably because the Glock's got a dodgy trigger. The pull weight's advertised at five and a half pounds and has connectors to match. However, these connectors actually create a six to eight pound pull. That's pretty hefty for a handgun.'

He smiled.

'And, let's face it, we've proven over and over again that heavy trigger pulls like that ruin your accuracy and speed when it counts. As *you've* shown on your second rate—'

He didn't finish. Screaming, Jackson brought his gun up to fire but his head snapped back as Marlowe, waiting for this and firing first, caught him between the eyes.

Walking over to the dead agent, Marlowe stared down sadly.

'Your second-rate scores, you miss every time,' he finished, before walking away from the body, heading for the exit.

As Kirk, Tessa and Vic entered the suite, they saw Ciaran and Trix downing bottles of vodka and whisky from the minibar, both laughing as they did so. On the TV screen, the news channel showed Brad leading Senator

Kyle out of the hotel, while a news chyron ran along the bottom.

VICE PRESIDENT CALDWELL NAMED AS PART OF TERRORIST ORGANISATION

'I'm guessing things worked out?' Kirk asked, amused.

'We crashed the server,' Trix said. 'We gained everything. Orchid are screwed.'

At this news, though, Vic straightened and reluctantly passed his gun to Tessa.

'I'm Orchid,' he sighed with resignation. 'The list will out me. You might as well get MI5 to take me in.'

Tessa glanced at Trix, technically the only serving member of MI5 there, outside of Vic Saeed, who nodded slightly, silently agreeing with her as she placed the gun back in Vic's hand.

'And I'm a Rubicon sleeper agent,' she said. 'You think I give a shit about secret societies? Besides, I think there will be a lot of Orchid agents revealed to be "undercover operatives" over the next few days for a dozen different intelligence agencies.'

'So, what now?' Ciaran asked. 'Wait for the CIA to turn up?'

'Probably the best plan,' Trix grinned. 'Who wants a relaxing game of Tic Tac Toe?'

EPILOGUE

MARLOWE HADN'T RETURNED TO THE SUITE. INSTEAD, HE'D made his way out of the hotel through the back entrance, again helped by Sasha's agents turning a blind eye, after discarding his operation gear, now in shirt and jeans.

From there, he travelled south three blocks, and eventually met with Sasha herself in a diner, just outside the recently placed police cordon.

'Your people are safe,' she said, passing him a coffee made exactly as he liked it. He'd have expected nothing less from her. 'They're getting drunk at our expense. We'll provide them with a plane back, with yourself included, so you can all find an alibi for not being in this shit show.'

'While the CIA gain all the press,' Marlowe smiled. 'Works for me.'

'Lucien Delacroix is dead, for real this time,' Sasha added. 'They found him in the security room. Peter Lloyd, too. I also saw Jackson's body was found, shot between the eyes. You?'

Marlowe nodded.

'He was Lucien's man from the start,' he said. 'I had a

suspicion ever since Paris, when he was one of the few people allowed to keep his gun.'

'So, why keep him beside you?'

'Because I hoped he'd change, like Peter did,' Marlowe insisted. 'I want you to make sure people know he helped you, Sasha. Peter Lloyd did the right thing at the end.'

'Off the books?'

'Whatever,' Marlowe nodded. 'He died a hero. I want people to know.'

Sasha nodded.

'McKay?' Marlowe now asked.

'He's in the White House and probably knows his days are numbered. Now Caldwell's been outed as Orchid, with all the data your team found, he'll likely retire quietly, agree to not stand again, allow someone else to be the Democratic candidate.'

She smiled.

'Although after Brad's stunt, where he literally claimed she was part of the whole thing, valiantly risking her reputation and life to help everyone, I think there might already be a clear winner of the Republican Primary.'

She looked back at Marlowe.

'I hear Orchid is in freefall right now, with cells fighting against each other and deals being made,' she said. 'Something about millions of dollars of crypto being stolen?'

Marlowe feigned a surprised expression, but it wasn't enough. Sasha shook her head.

'Don't kill everyone in the bloody organisation before we get to turn up,' she said. 'We hate ending your wars for you.'

Marlowe rose, looking around the diner.

'Keep America safe, Sasha,' he said. 'That's another you owe me.'

'We know,' she stood as well, shaking Marlowe's hand. 'And you went above and beyond, even when we tried to stop you.'

Still holding the hand, she leant in, whispering in his ear.

'My first name really is Sasha,' she breathed. 'And that's all you get.'

Before Marlowe could reply, she walked off, whistling.

Two of the diners, now revealed to be CIA operatives watching her back, rose as well, following her out.

Marlowe chuckled, paid the bill for the two coffees with another hundred-dollar bill, and left.

SASHA HAD KEPT HER WORD, AND PROVIDED THE SAME PLANE that took them to Washington back to London, landing at a private airfield north of Northolt. Marlowe knew this was also to make sure nobody could prove any of the people in the plane had been in the US, but although it was a nice journey, and incredibly comfortable, it still felt to Marlowe as if he was politely being told to piss off.

Ciaran had been delighted halfway through the flight when he learnt his server had restarted, already discussing with the server farm in Switzerland on how he could move it from the server plan it currently had, his time with Orchid and Lucien now over. Also, during the flight, he'd also watched countless YouTube videos from his fellow gamers, all talking about how they helped "take down the man," with the explanation of the server finally crashing looking to be a hundred self-spawning fighter jets attacking the military base, while giant cats the size of Godzilla fought them off.

So, basically a Wednesday in *Crime City*.

Marlowe wasn't in a hurry to return.

Ciaran had also decided to stay in London for a few days after they arrived; knowing his Clontarf address was now revealed, and open to "doxxing," apparently, he was on the lookout for a new apartment, and Marlowe actually wondered if this was a ploy simply to stay near Trix.

Trix, meanwhile, had actually offered to help him find a place. Which was surprising.

There'd been cars waiting for them when they arrived; Wintergreen had sent out the welcome wagons. As much as this had been a secret op, Wintergreen saw the fingers of Marlowe and his team all over it, bringing everyone in for debriefing.

Vic's actions had earned him a stay of execution; he was still MI5, the story being, as discussed with the CIA in Dublin, that he'd gone undercover to infiltrate Orchid and MI5 were happy to keep with that, rather than admit the truth.

Peter Lloyd was also classed as undercover, his death being in the line of duty. Marlowe intended to find Davey Lloyd in Vauxhall Cross as soon as he could, and tell him of his son's bravery. And maybe even punch the prick in the face, for disowning his nephew purely for being in the wrong department.

He also intended to point out to McKellan that one of the Orchid agents, now in a CIA black site was an MI6 agent, just to see his face.

THE DEBRIEFING TOOK A WEEK. BUT AFTER THAT, THEY WERE free to go, and MI5 hadn't been able to throw anything at

Marlowe or any of his team. Wintergreen had quietly stated it was connected to national importance, and Joanna Karolides had explained how she too had been involved in this, knowing that somehow this would help her down the line, and also explain why *she'd* been seen at the Paris party of a potential terrorist billionaire.

Trix was reinstated but had asked for a sabbatical, claiming that she had post-traumatic stress from all the action she'd been involved in. Which in Trix terms meant she needed a nice holiday. Marlowe was offered his old spot back, but it was in Section D, and Wintergreen, currently running point while Curtis recovered, was no longer in charge.

If he was being honest though, he wasn't too sure if he wanted it or not. Working for any of the Security Services currently gave him a bad taste in his mouth.

Marshall Kirk was quietly congratulated and thanked, and returned to his East Finchley house where he would carry on gardening, eating prawn cocktail crisps, and waiting for yet another call to action. Wintergreen even kept her promise and offered Tessa Kirk a role in MI5; a position that Tessa Kirk took, claiming she was looking to honour her father.

Marlowe wondered how much Rubicon was still inside her and hoped it wasn't much, yet enough to keep her alive.

Before he left Thames House, he even managed to speak to Tessa. She was sad they were moving apart again, but they promised to catch up in a couple of days once things were organised.

Marlowe knew this wouldn't happen. Finally, he was at the other end of an MI5 agent telling him, "sure, we'll get together next week" without even knowing if they'd be in the country – or even the continent – at that point.

In a way, it felt strange. In another way, it felt quite secure.

Brad, in Washington, was given a handful of medals, and from the interviews he gave looked like he'd saved the Western world single-handed. Which, in a strange, twisted way, he had, officially.

It helped he looked like the All-American Hero, too.

Anton McKay quietly announced he wouldn't attempt a second term, claiming his lack of judgement in picking a Vice President was to blame.

Lawrence Jackson was outed as a traitor to the United Kingdom, and his desk emptied.

And St John Steele was waiting for Marlowe in his home when he arrived.

IT WASN'T A SURPRISE. IF MARLOWE WAS BEING HONEST, HE'D seen Steele arrive through the webcam in his house. Steele hadn't even tried to pretend he was hiding; he'd even given the webcam, one that was supposedly undiscoverable, a little wave as he sat down and waited. So, as Marlowe entered the onetime Nave through the front door, spying the man himself sitting in his favourite chair, drinking a glass of his favourite whisky, Marlowe didn't even flinch as Steele rose and applauded him, an almost mocking slow clap that, for some reason, didn't actually annoy Marlowe more than it probably should have.

'Congratulations,' Steele said. 'You did everything I hoped of you.'

'There are several—'

'Don't worry, I removed the bugs,' Steele smiled. 'It's the

least I can do. I used your fake dictaphone to find them. I hope you don't mind.'

'Is this where you tell me that everything I did was all part of the plan?' Marlowe said, walking over to the sideboard, where he poured himself his own generous measure of whisky. 'Please tell me, I'm dying to hear.'

Steele shrugged.

'What can I say?' he asked. 'I told you I wanted out, and the only way to leave Orchid is to die. Unless, of course, you killed Orchid first.'

Marlowe smiled as he sipped.

'The great St John Steele,' he said coldly. 'Plans within plans within plans, always making sure the idiot MI5 agent knows what to do.'

He sat down, facing Steele.

'I know what you did,' he said. 'You told me to speak to my father so that I'd get into the meeting in Paris, so I'd see Lucien being shot. You wanted a witness, and at the same time, you wanted a backup plan. So, you created a singular key which was given to me at the same event, a key that was designed in such a way that only an expert in Napoleonic and Crimean War weaponry, an American who understood about hundred-dollar bills, and a hacker who understood about APIs and coding – who was in the same group with the hacker in question and recognised their signature – would be able to decipher it together.'

He toasted Steele.

'It's incredibly handy that all of these were on my team, wouldn't you say?'

Steele said nothing, and the moment grew longer. It was almost as if he was judging Marlowe, to see if he was quick to anger, still.

'You needed closure with your father,' he said. 'All kids do. But believe me when I say I needed to be free of Orchid, and of certain people within it. Everything you did allowed me to clear my name from the records.'

'Not exactly,' Marlowe shook his head sadly, the movement mocking in its design. 'You seem to think we got away, but didn't gain any information. The fact of the matter is, Trix gained *everything* that was on that server; the name of every single Orchid agent, all ready for us to line up and pounce on if we so wanted.'

'Great,' Steele replied. 'Sign me up. I'll come with you, because you won't find my name in any of those files. In fact, the only people who can admit that I was even part of Orchid are dead, thanks to you.'

He stared at the whisky in the glass, swirling it around slowly.

'I was an Arbitrator, a role that was always classed as independent of any organisation,' he continued. 'And, let's face it, most of your people are saying it was all part of some undercover Security Service sting operation, or something along those lines. I'm sure I can add my name to that list.'

Marlowe stared at Steele.

'Were you part of the creation of Fractal Destiny?' he eventually asked. 'I know you went to Ciaran Winston and asked him to create a fake world, but—'

'No,' Steele said, and this time his voice was quick, angry. 'I wasn't part of that. In fact, that was what made me decide I needed to get out. That, and McKay, and all the lies finally coming together. I needed somebody who could get me out, and you did that. And for that I owe you, Marlowe. But don't for one second think we're friends. You were, as always, a tool in a toolbox I had access to, that needed to be used.'

He rose now.

'The applause was genuine,' he added. 'You pulled off something I never thought you could. And to be honest, when I first brought you in, I just needed a diversion.'

He chuckled.

'I didn't expect the crypto scam though,' he said. 'Bridget's rather pissed at that.'

'Me?' Marlowe gave an innocent look. 'I don't know what you mean. Although that four million dollars *is* in your account, and *is* linked to you. So good luck with explaining that to Mister HMRC when they get around to you.'

Steele finished his glass, placed it down and then walked to the door.

'You know they won't let you back in,' he said. 'MI5 will find reasons to avoid bringing you back, they'll dump you back in *Section Disavowed,* like the other screwups, and hope you eventually resign. After all, I understand the gopher role in the gun room you once held is now taken by Vic Saeed.'

'I think I'm kind of tired of working right now, especially for the Security Service,' Marlowe shrugged. 'I think I need a break.'

'I know an organisation that has a High Council looking for a few members, and you are still technically a member,' Steele turned fully to face Marlowe now, the door behind him. 'Genuine offer. Your father's no longer part of the organisation and you've been given all of his hereditary titles.'

'You can give them back to Taylor when you speak to him next,' Marlowe replied icily. 'I want nothing of his.'

At this, Steele's face fell slightly.

'You don't know,' he replied.

'Know what?'

'Your father died two days ago,' Steele said. 'Nothing sinister, died in his sleep. Wasn't expecting it, was talking about what he was going to do the following day. The cancer got him in the end. Not spies or rivals. I'm sorry that I had to be the one to tell you.'

Marlowe gave a non-impressed shrug.

'I didn't talk to my father for years,' he said. 'I don't care whether he lives or dies. I just feel sorry for his real family.'

Steele nodded, turned and left, the large oak church door closing behind him.

Marlowe felt numb.

Then he looked up at the stained-glass window he'd kept in his renovated church house.

'If you exist,' he said, 'I know I've said many times my dad needs to rot in Hell, but give him a pass this time? Let him go hang out with my mum for a while. But only on a day trip, yeah? That'd be nice.'

This small prayer finished, Marlowe crossed himself then walked away, down to his underground room, to place his various items in the correct places, and to find new locations for the remnants of Bridget Summers go bag. He intended to pass the gold bars back to her, but only when he could find her, and the chances were she'd try to kill him first. But the remaining wads of notes were being kept, as was the ammo.

This done, he walked over to an armchair he had in the crypt, and slumped down into it.

He was dead tired, and it was the end of a very long day.

Marlowe was ready for something new.

He just didn't know what it was going to be yet.

Tom Marlowe will return in his next thriller

STEALTH STRIKE

Order Now at Amazon:

Mybook.to/stealthstrike

Released 26th February 2024

Gain up-to-the-moment information on the release by
signing up to the Jack Gatland VIP Reader's Club!

Join at www.subscribepage.com/jackgatland

ACKNOWLEDGEMENTS

When you write a series of books, you find that there are a ton of people out there who help you, sometimes without even realising, and so I wanted to say thanks.

There are people I need to thank, and they know who they are, including my brother Chris Lee, who I truly believe could make a fortune as a post-retirement copy editor, if not a solid writing career of his own, Jacqueline Beard MBE, who has copyedited all my books since the very beginning, editor Sian Phillips and weapon specialist Eben Atwater, all of whom have made my books way better than they have every right to be.

Also, I couldn't have done this without my growing army of ARC and beta readers, who not only show me where I falter, but also raise awareness of me in the social media world, ensuring that other people learn of my books.

But mainly, I tip my hat and thank you. *The reader.* Who once took a chance on an unknown author in a pile of Kindle books, thought you'd give them a go, and who has carried on this far with them, as well as the spin off books I now release.

I write these books for you. And with luck, I'll keep on writing them for a very long time.

Jack Gatland / Tony Lee,
London, September 2023

ABOUT THE AUTHOR

Jack Gatland is the pen name of *#1 New York Times Bestselling Author* Tony Lee, who has been writing in all media for thirty-five years, including comics, graphic novels, middle grade books, audio drama, TV and film for *DC Comics, Marvel, BBC, ITV, Random House, Penguin USA, Hachette* and a ton of other publishers and broadcasters.

These have included licenses such as *Doctor Who, Spider Man, X-Men, Star Trek, Battlestar Galactica, MacGyver,* BBC's *Doctors, Wallace and Gromit* and *Shrek,* as well as work created with musicians such as *Ozzy Osbourne, Joe Satriani, Beartooth* and *Megadeth.*

As Tony, he's toured the world talking to reluctant readers with his 'Change The Channel' school tours, and lectures on screenwriting and comic scripting for *Raindance* in London.

As Jack, he's written several book series now - a police procedural featuring *DI Declan Walsh and the officers of the Temple Inn Crime Unit*, a spinoff featuring "cop for criminals" *Ellie Reckless and her team,* and a second espionage spinoff series featuring burnt MI5 agent *Tom Marlowe,* an action adventure series featuring conman-turned-treasure hunter *Damian Lucas*, and a standalone novel set in a New York boardroom.

An introvert West Londoner by heart, he lives with his wife Tracy and dog Fosco, just outside London.

Feel free to follow Jack on all his social media by clicking on the links below. Over time these can be places where we can engage, discuss Declan, Ellie, Tom and others, and put the world to rights.

www.jackgatland.com
www.hoodemanmedia.com

Visit my Reader's Group Page
(Mainly for fans to discuss my books):
https://www.facebook.com/groups/jackgatland

Subscribe to my Readers List:
www.subscribepage.com/jackgatland

www.facebook.com/jackgatlandbooks
www.twitter.com/jackgatlandbook
ww.instagram.com/jackgatland

Want more books by Jack Gatland?

Turn the page...

LETTER
FROM
THE DEAD

"BY THE TIME YOU READ THIS, I WILL BE DEAD..."

A TWENTY YEAR OLD MURDER...
A PRIME MINISTER LEADERSHIP BATTLE...
A PARANOID, HOMELESS EX-MINISTER...
AN EVANGELICAL PREACHER WITH A SECRET...

DI DECLAN WALSH HAS HAD BETTER FIRST DAYS...

AVAILABLE ON AMAZON / KINDLEUNLIMITED

THE THEFT OF A **PRICELESS** PAINTING...
A GANGSTER WITH A **CRIPPLING DEBT**...
A **BODY COUNT** RISING BY THE HOUR...

AND ELLIE RECKLESS IS CAUGHT IN THE MIDDLE.

JACK GATLAND

PAINT
— THE —
DEAD

A 'COP FOR CRIMINALS' ELLIE RECKLESS NOVEL

A NEW PROCEDURAL CRIME SERIES WITH
A TWIST - FROM THE CREATOR OF THE
BESTSELLING 'DI DECLAN WALSH' SERIES

AVAILABLE ON AMAZON / KINDLE UNLIMITED

JACK GATLAND

THE LIONHEART CURSE

HUNT THE GREATEST TREASURES
PAY THE GREATEST PRICE

BOOK 1 IN A NEW SERIES OF ADVENTURES IN THE STYLE OF 'THE DA VINCI CODE' FROM THE CREATOR OF DECLAN WALSH

AVAILABLE ON AMAZON / KINDLEUNLIMITED

EIGHT PEOPLE. EIGHT SECRETS.
ONE SNIPER.

THE
B⊕ARD
ROOM

HOW FAR WOULD YOU GO TO GAIN JUSTICE?

NEW YORK TIMES #1 BESTSELLER TONY LEE WRITING AS

JACK GATLAND

A NEW STANDALONE THRILLER WITH
A TWIST - FROM THE CREATOR OF THE
BESTSELLING 'DI DECLAN WALSH' SERIES

AVAILABLE ON AMAZON / KINDLE UNLIMITED

Printed in Great Britain
by Amazon